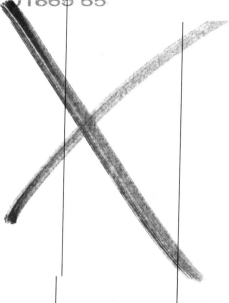

Proudly Published by Snowbooks in 2015

Copyright © 2015 Philip Purser-Hallard

Philip Purser-Hallard asserts the moral right to
be identified as the author of this work.
All rights reserved.

Snowbooks Ltd.
email: info@snowbooks.com
www.snowbooks.com

British Library Cataloguing in Publication Data
A catalogue record for this book is available from the
British Library.

E-book ISBN 9781909679436
Paperback ISBN 9781909679429

Geoffrey Trease – *Bows Against the Barons* (Elliot &
Thompson) used by kind permission of David Higham
Associates.

THE
LOCKSLEY
EXPLOIT

**BOOK TWO OF
THE DEVICES TRILOGY**

To my brother Nick, who tolerated my Arthurian obsession for many years.

Once more his laugh rang out exultantly.

'We'll light the flame in the Midlands, my friends!' he cried. 'But it'll spread, north and south, east and west, till all England's ablaze. The people will rise in a great host, and no strong place will hold out against them. And when the last castle has hauled down its flag, we shall build the new England, the England of equality and freedom – Merrie England at last!'

Geoffrey Trease, *Bows against the Barons*

i
THE SPEAR AND THE CUP

1. STEPHEN MUKHERJEE AND THE OUTLAW

Foreign students teem about the forecourt of the British Museum like bees around a porticoed stone hive, filling the air with buzzing and pheromones. It's a muggy summer's day, and London has the oppressive ache of a thunderstorm about to detonate.

The tourists jostle and throng, colliding sporadically with a man in green, who stands staring up at the neoclassical pediment while he talks on a mobile phone. His head's uncovered, the loose hood of his zipped top draped back across his shoulders. The garment is the green of avocado-skin or pine needles. In his phoneless hand, he holds a long, narrow box which any archery hobbyist would recognise as a bow-case.

'All set?' the man asks his phone.

The man in green is, in the accepted meaning of the word, an outlaw: a terrorist, kidnapper and thief. If the police patrolling Great Russell Street saw and identified him, it would be their duty to arrest him and hold him on charges including robbery, assault, abduction, grievous bodily harm and – most grandly of all, though in reality it's less exceptional than you might imagine – high treason.

This would be even truer if the man were to encounter the servants of certain more publicity-shy authorities, who rank, in their own view at least, above that of Metropolitan Police Commissioner.

The voice on the outlaw's phone says something affirmative, and he replies, 'Good, then. Twenty minutes.'

This man would argue that his offences – most of them at least, the ones he committed out of choice rather than necessity – were basically altruistic: that all his robberies, for instance, were undertaken with the aim of benefiting the vulnerable and needy, by redistributing excess goods from the wealthy and well-insured. It's not an argument which would hold a scintilla of weight with the judicial system, let alone with those more shadowy enforcers I mentioned, but it's one he's come to believe in wholeheartedly.

Around him, foreign visitors stream in and out of out of the august building's vast, pillared frontage. Britain's psyche may be troubled by dark stirrings these days (the man thinks, as he surreptitiously drops the phone into a rowdy, Italian girl's rucksack), its citizens unrestful and its authorities increasingly trigger-happy, but nothing gets in the way of London's tourist industry. The status of tourist, like that of outlaw, confers some welcome exemptions from society's grimmer concerns, at least for as long as that status – and that society – last.

Above him, the sculpted figures loom, censorious representations of the Progress of Civilisation reminding him of times when other buildings just as grand as this were legitimately his for the entering. That's a Rubicon the man in the hoodie crossed some time ago, though. Any regrets he feels on the score are a luxury, and luxuries are in short supply in his new life.

What he's about to do is unforgivable, he knows, according to the code he once lived by. Uptight and pedantic though that protocol now seems to him, he's still disconcerted by the magnitude of the crime he intends. Stealing from his country's national museum is shocking enough (however much he tries to persuade himself that most of its holdings are spoils of empire and should never have been looted from their original owners), but the knowledge of what it is he intends to steal almost overwhelms him, even now.

An outlaw's life, he finds, is one long sequence of miniature Rubicons, a marshland broken by creek after creek, each allowing crossing in only one direction.

The man unzips his hoodie, becoming immediately more respectable as he reveals a sober grey-and-white pinstriped shirt and green tie. He takes a deep breath, hefts his bow-case, and strides towards the steps, up to the glass doors.

* * *

As best the Circle can reconstruct it later, working from eyewitness testimony and the British Museum's CCTV records, the early part of the raid goes as follows.

At 10:41 am, the man in the hooded top and matching tie approaches the reception desk and introduces himself as 'Gavin Locksley'. He claims that he is here to discuss an heirloom from his great-uncle, an antique bow of debatable Tudor vintage, and that he has an appointment with a curator named Jenny Doone. The last part of this is true, so a security guard escorts him to a door to the Museum's restricted area, which he opens with a keycard. Security's been stepped up at the Museum since the Ludgate riots earlier this summer, but a quick search of the bow-case reveals it to contain exactly what it's supposed to. The guard therefore conveys 'Locksley' to Dr Doone's nearby office, returning to duty in the public area of the Museum at 10:45.

Between 10:43 and 10:55, four ostensibly unconnected tourists enter the public lavatories nearest this internal door. A muscular giant in a donkey jacket goes into the gents first, followed four minutes later by an older, leaner, rangier man wearing sawn-off jeans, a pink floral shirt and an incongruous clerical collar. Shortly afterwards, and only a minute or so apart, two women – the older with dyed hair and combat trousers, the younger in jeans and hijab – go into the ladies.

At 10:59, all four of them emerge wearing hooded tops, and walk purposefully towards the security door. Three of them wear conifer-green hoodies to match Locksley's; the older woman's top is the same vivid red as her hair. The huge man wears his under the donkey jacket. It later transpires that the garments were left in ziplock bags in the cisterns the previous evening, by a temporary cleaner who cannot later be traced.

Meanwhile, Locksley has apologised to Dr Doone for taking advantage of her specialism in medieval weaponry; specifically, for seizing the fifteenth-century Damascene longsword lying on her workbench when he arrived and threatening her with it. According to her later testimony, Locksley continues to be 'really apologetic' while gagging her with a roll of duct tape taken from his hoodie pocket, then 'very confused' when he realises her office chair has a central column and there's nowhere to tape her legs. Eventually he settles for taping her ankles tightly together, and her wrists to the arms of her chair, before lifting the notionally Tudor bow from its case and, still apologetically, leaving bow-case and duct tape with her. (They will yield fingerprints later, but by then they'll tell the Circle nothing they don't already know.)

At 11:00, the security guard who escorted Locksley to Dr Doone's office is hurrying towards the four hooded intruders, who are gathering openly around the security door. A moment later it's opened for them, by Locksley using Doone's keycard, and the four of them pile into the Museum's non-public area. Trying to follow them, the guard discovers that they've barricaded the door using Doone's bicycle, which she keeps in her office. After much struggling, the man ends up comedically entangled in the fallen bike frame.

The intruders, meanwhile, are making their way purposefully through corridors and down two flights of stairs. As they go, the small woman takes a lightweight fabric quiver from her hoodie pocket and shakes it open, holding it steady for the modern carbon-fibre arrows that the big man is pulling out of the lining of his donkey jacket. When the quiver is full, she hands it to Locksley, who dons it with a 'Thank you' and passes her Doone's keycard. The longbow is stout and solid, an artificially aged replica made from modern yew-wood rather than the antique he claimed, and as a weapon perfectly sound. Especially given the kevlar bowstring he's been fitting to it as they walk.

Within two minutes they have arrived at a basement floor used primarily for storing items which retain some research value, but are unlikely ever to be displayed. One of these rooms houses a ragbag miscellany of objects called the Nestine-Gull Collection, in which the Circle – and now evidently the intruders – take a particular interest.

The Circle's interest is so particular, in fact, that in light of recent mythopolitical disturbances, the Seneschal of the Circle has seen fit, brusquely overriding the objections of the Museum's own security staff, to post a guard of his own on the Collection during opening hours.

This explains why, when the three men and two women in hoodies turn the corner nearest the plain grey door behind which the Nestine-Gull Collection sits, they find themselves facing two Knights of the Circle in full ceramic-polyamide armour, their carbon-steel swords drawn and their riot-shields emblazoned with, respectively, a chequerboard pattern and a gold-on-purple, double-headed eagle.

Which is where everything starts getting tricky, of course.

* * *

Stephen Mukherjee, the device-bearer of Sir Palamedes, has already been alerted that a break-in is in progress. From the descriptions of the thieves' clothing, he can guess that the intruders are heading this way. As the alert was given over the walkie-talkie which Museum security has reluctantly lent the Knights, he turned to his comrade-in-arms, Julian Blythe, and said, 'Thoughtful of the Green Chapel to pay us a visit. We'd best look sharp, old man.'

Stephen has particular cause to deplore the eco-Marxist anarchist cell. The Knight was badly injured in a Green Chapel attack on a Circle convoy seven months ago, when an explosive projectile lodged between the plates of his armour and left him with severe burns to his chest and hand. The best skin grafts and reconstructive surgery the Circle's fabulously opulent private healthcare plan can fund returned him to active service just a month ago, but others came out of it less lucky. It was – according to the secret history of Britain as seen from the Circle's point of view, at least – the first engagement in a war between the Circle's own venerable mythology and a folkloric upstart barely worthy of the name.

This is why, despite knowing that the intruders carry what must technically be considered devices of their own, Stephen feels no qualms as the Chapel men and women round the corner. He and Blythe have right on their side, after all: right, polymer-coated steel blades, and the devices of two puissant and noble knights.

'You there, stop!' Stephen shouts, raising his sword in challenge with all the authority the Circle vests in him. 'Put down your weapons and surrender!'

The Chapel's lead man has his hood pulled over his face by now, revealing only a firm mouth and stubbly chin. Even so, as he raises his longbow, nocks an arrow and gives it flight, jamming it firmly into the shoulder of Blythe's armour, Stephen knows him.

Stephen turns at once, urgent and keen, pulls out the arrow and throws it in an arc towards the attackers. One of the more absurd details about his recent combat wounds – which he unfailingly though ruefully admits whenever he tells the story – is that the 'explosive projectile' which wounded him was in fact an incendiary arrow. Others who were there lost limbs from the vicious little missiles.

This projectile, however, clatters inertly to the floor, and Stephen realises as he turns to face the charging hooded figures that this was a feint on the hooded archer's part; an attempt to use his battle traumas and his concern for his brother Knight against him. Stephen can hardly approve of the ethics, but he has time to admire the cleverness of the ploy, even as the huge man in the donkey jacket batters into him, his fists connecting scientifically with the weak points of Stephen's armour.

The archer, Stephen sees as he struggles to stay on his feet and bring his sword to bear, is holding back, another arrow ready-nocked, awaiting the need to use it. Next to Stephen, the scrawny man is wrestling Blythe, with the help of the woman in red, trying between them to pull him to the ground: Blythe, too, was thrown by Stephen's involuntary and misguidedly heroic gesture, and is struggling to free his sword-arm from the man's wiry grip. Between them, Stephen realises as the big man grasps his own sword-arm in both hands and twists, the Knights are taking quite a pummelling.

Meanwhile the smaller woman has slipped a keycard into a box-lock, pushed open the battleship-grey door and, lithe as a stoat, slipped inside.

* * *

The hooded man watches as Stephen's combat prowess reasserts itself, rolling with the big man's arm-twist and scything his feet from under him even as his assailant's thrown off-balance by the lack of resistance. Obviously encouraged by this, the other Knight – Julian Blythe he assumes, since he bears the device of Sir Gaheris (it's the wiggly border around the eagle that's the giveaway) – succeeds in shaking off the skinny priest, tossing him against a wall then whirling to address his other antagonist.

Julian is, however, a Knight of the old school, and the moment's hesitation he evinces on finding himself facing a female opponent is ample advantage for the woman in scarlet to press. Again it's the Knight's sword-arm that's his most obvious advantage, so it's his right wrist that she makes the target of a battery of kicks and punches that owe more to East Asian kickboxing than anything authentically British and medieval. It serves the purpose, though, and that's always been the Chapel's primary fighting concern, far above the elegance and chivalry the Knights so prize.

On similar principles, the giant takes advantage of his position on the floor to aim an upward kick at Stephen's groin. The armour's padding absorbs most of the impact, but the thief's thighs are like cloister pillars and the impact lifts Stephen, even fully armoured, a foot into the air. As he begins to descend, his head pulls back, and for a moment the hooded archer has a clear shot at his neck, a notoriously vulnerable point in the Circle men's defences. He takes a breath and lets the arrow fly, only for it to clatter into Stephen's visor as he returns to earth.

Meanwhile, with shockingly little effort, the big man tears a length of piping, part of the heating system perhaps, away from the wall. Oily water first gushes then trickles steadily onto the floor as he launches himself onto his feet and swings the pipe at Stephen like a quarterstaff.

The thin man's returned to the fray now, leaping onto Julian's shoulders and covering his visor with his hands, while the woman in red continues to pummel away at his sword-hand. The Knight looks helpless, and for a moment the hooded man feels an absurd compulsion to go to his aid.

Stephen's assailant, though, has made the mistake of reverting to a form of combat closer to the Knightly style. Stephen is parrying the pipe's swings dexterously and with some panache, barking the man's knuckles on his blade at least once, and swinging ever closer to his unprotected throat. *If only I'd made that shot*, the archer thinks. With his comrade down, Blythe would not have lasted long against the four Chapel fighters. Now there's a serious chance of Stephen getting the better of the big man, and the other two won't be able to stand up for long against two Knights.

The outlaw grasps his longbow like a staff and dives into the fray, getting in a good knock at arm's length before Stephen registers the change of tactics.

Then the younger woman steps out of the room holding

the most precious object in the Nestine-Gull Collection, and everyone stops still.

* * *

Although this is his third turn of guard duty outside the Collection, Stephen has never been inside. Its contents have been known to cause some of the Knights – generally those with the less stable devices – psychological issues, and it's generally accepted these days that access for Circle personnel is on a need-to-know basis. Simply guarding the Collection does not in itself convey a need to see it.

This is, therefore, his first glimpse of the relic, and he responds with all the atavistic fervour of the Saracen Sir Palamedes confronted with the holiest object of his adopted religion: falling to his knees, bowing his head and muttering in prayer. Julian is doing likewise, similarly without giving any heed to their attackers.

Objects can be imbued with devices of their own, and – although this verifiably, demonstrably isn't the vessel used by Christ at the Last Supper – the sight of the Romano-British wooden cup which Sir Lionel Nestine-Gull erroneously identified with it works on the Knights like an old-fashioned dose of religious ecstasy.

Even the Chapel people aren't entirely immune – their own allied devices are mostly Christian ones, which is why the woman with the hijab under her hoodie was the one sent in to grab the drinking-vessel. She holds it with the respect due an ancient artefact, but no more, and is baffled by the looks of awe on her comrades' faces. It is, after all, just a very old wooden cup.

Fundamentally, though, this isn't part of their stories, and for each of them the moment passes. For the hooded archer, who was himself once a Knight of the Circle, the effect is more potent, but unlike Stephen and Julian he has seen the relic before, and was prepared. Gritting his teeth, he falls back along the corridor. His huge comrade glances from the Knights to the cup and back, then shrugs and whacks each of them soundly about the helmet with his length of piping. Julian goes down; Stephen stays kneeling and doesn't appear to notice.

'Reckon that's them out, then,' he says with satisfaction. He follows the scrawny man, the woman in red and the cup-bearer.

'We haven't got long,' the man who called himself Gavin Locksley declares, glancing back at his former comrades-in-arms as he leads his current ones to the nearest emergency exit. Shouts and the drumming of footsteps betray the imminent arrival of the Museum's secular security officers, but it'll take them precious seconds to get past the barrier the Knights present.

It's 11:05. The entire fight has taken less than three minutes. Outside in Montague Street, just the other side of some easily-scaled railings, a battered green van's just drawn up and thrown its doors open.

From here, you can probably join the dots yourselves.

* * *

A couple of hours later the Museum, to the vociferous horror of its Director, is in lockdown. Museum personnel have been placed at the disposal of twenty or so Knights of the Circle, while men-at-arms turn away tourists at the Great Russell Street gates with apologetic talk of a 'terrorist incident'.

'It's a damned bloody outrage, that's what it is,' the Seneschal, Sir Charles Raymond, seethes. He's commandeered the gift shop as his control centre for the operation (generally the Circle prefers the archaic word 'quest', but given what's gone missing today that's not a word anyone has the heart to use), and is absent-mindedly tossing a miniature Rosetta Stone paperweight from hand to hand. Raymond rarely wears his armour these days, except on ceremonial occasions, so he's in a three-piece suit and tie, with a discreet lapel-pin bearing the shield of Sir Kay, his devicial patron.

Museum curators, together with the Circle's secular experts, are combing the Nestine-Gull Collection piece by piece, to determine whether anything other than the obvious is missing or damaged. Given the chaotic eclecticism of the collection and its general state of neglect, this is taking some time, but the thieves' target was surely unambiguous, and nobody really expects to find any further loss. Other Circle employees, and crime scene investigators contracted from a private forensic science facility, are searching for evidence in the corridor outside the Collection, Dr Doone's office and the public loos. The Museum's maintenance people have plugged the leaking pipe in the corridor, but the carpet underfoot is still sodden.

'Bloody is as well, sir. The latest of many.' Raymond's lieutenant, Paul Parsons, who's been doing most of the actual directing from an iPad, is in armour, although given that they're in a locked-down, high-security building he's made the concession of removing his gloves and helmet. His polymer-fibre shield, currently leaning against a display of replica statuettes, bears a design whose simplicity belies its significance: the red-on-white diagonal stripes (three bends gules on an escutcheon argent, if you want to get all heraldic about it) are the device of the greatest Round Table Knight of all, Sir Lancelot.

'No doubt it was Taylor, I suppose?' the Seneschal grunts. There's not the slightest question in his mind, of course, but he's aware that there are proprieties to be observed.

Paul's left hand makes an involuntary fist. His right stays exactly as it was, which is lucky as it's clutching the iPad. It's sensitive as well as strong – a powered aluminium skeleton inside a lifelike silicone glove, controlled by a processor of its own which interprets myoelectric input from his arm-muscles – but not *that* sensitive.

Parsons has even greater reason to revile the Green Chapel than Stephen Mukherjee.

'Hardly, sir,' he says. 'Mukherjee IDed him, and the CCTV footage is clear enough. He couldn't have made it more obvious if he was trying to taunt us, which I suspect he was, actually. Who else outside the Circle even knows about the Nestine-Gull Collection?'

'Almost anyone might, with him and the Wendiman woman at large,' Raymond reminds him sharply. 'We have to consider that any classified information of more than seven months' standing may be compromised. We should have moved the damned thi… the relic, instead of leaving it here.'

Parsons knows his boss well enough not to comment. 'They're going all-out to provoke us now,' he says instead. 'This is a deliberate insult, sir. It's not like the piece has any intrinsic value.'

'No value?' Sir Charles fumbles the Rosetta Stone, catches it awkwardly, then lines it up regimentally with its comrades on the shelf. 'It's a sacred object, Parsons.'

'To us, sir, not to them. It doesn't figure in their corpus at all.' Parsons shakes his head angrily. 'What could Robin Hood's Merry Men possibly want with the Holy Grail?'

2. A GUEST OF BIG JACK BENNETT

Around the same time, having ditched the green van in Islington and bidden a hasty farewell to their female comrades, the huge man, the thin man and the blond man are arriving home from their armed robbery.

Their temporary base of operations is a grotty-looking (and indeed authentically grotty) squat in Hackney. Once a respectable redbrick semi, built in the 50s to house larger working-class families at the council's expense, it was bought up by its tenants in the 80s, sold on and since repurposed as a crack den and ad hoc brothel. In all, it's a bit of a comedown from the morning's neoclassical columns and pediments. The Green Chapel moved in after the last police raid cleared the place, and have been turning away its former habitués politely, sympathetically and only occasionally at knife-point.

It's a risky hideout, if only because of the recent police interest, but they've been needing somewhere within striking distance of Bloomsbury. The hope is that, having gone to the effort of arresting one set of squatters, the police will be grateful that the new lot seem to be largely non-violent and relatively clean, and will give them a few weeks' grace. After today's excursion, though, it won't take long before more specialist elements of the law-enforcement community take an interest, and the Chapel people living here are already making plans to move on.

The three men park a couple of blocks away in the battered Ford Escort they retrieved from a Sainsbury's car park and walk the last few minutes to the house.

'I still say we should have grabbed some of the other stuff while we were there,' the biggest of the men grumbles on the way. 'Some of that Sutton Hoo hoard, say. We could do with the money.'

'Don't be silly,' the man who claimed the name Gavin Locksley says. 'We need the Grail for a specific purpose, you know that. We weren't going to help ourselves to a bunch of national treasures while we were at it.'

The tall archer is in fact, as Raymond and Parsons suspect, none other than Jordan Taylor, BA (Hons) and former Knight of the Circle, known to most of his long-term friends as Jory but to those in his current social orbit as Dan. He's blond, impressively well-muscled if you're keen on that sort of thing (which I understand a certain proportion of the population are), and with the kind of square jaw that fortunately lends itself to the stubbled desperado look as well as that of the clean-cut schoolboy. The latter served him well when he himself served the Circle, his shield and psyche graced by the device of Sir Gawain of Orkney. Since then, as his archetypal persona has evolved in quite unexpected directions, the former look has seemed more appropriate.

'National treasures should belong to us all,' argues the larger man. 'Not sitting behind glass in some draughty museum.'

Jory Taylor's tall, as I say, but he's overshadowed by Big Jack Bennett, a shade under seven foot and built out of tree-trunks, figuratively speaking. Like the third man, Jack's been with the Green Chapel since its most recent inception. Before that he was a shop steward in a Derbyshire car plant, but lost his job after a disagreement with a manager whose idea of improving efficiency was to find pretexts for sacking his less overzealous workers. (Their exchange of opinions involved the guy getting his skull fractured in two places, mind you, so I'm not saying they didn't have a case in Jack's instance.) The Circle have Bennett listed as the Chapel's second-in-command, but that ignores a number of factors, including the group's rejection of leadership on philosophical grounds, the somewhat provisional nature of Jory's position and the behind-the-scenes presence of Malory Wendiman, or Merry as she's known in these parts.

'So you want to liberate them, then sell them to some unscrupulous rich asshole for the cash?' 'Rev' Cantrell interjects. 'You'd make Marx jack it all in and move to Marbella.' He's the smallest of the three – not short, but without a spare ounce on him, a lean and predatory jackal in priest's clothing. Rev is, it so happens, a bona fide man of the cloth: ordained in California some time back in the 80s, still devout in his own way, but long since parted company with any recognisable branch of the church. He claims his move to this country had a lot to do with London's lively gay scene, but unless he'd somehow never heard of San Francisco, we can probably assume there was more to it than that. My guess is that he'd come across rumours of the Green Chapel's allies even then, and came here searching.

Bennett grunts as they turn the corner and see a customised motorbike sitting on its stand outside the squat, gleaming with chrome polish. It's a 1970s Norton Commando, its forks realigned chopper-style, its chassis painted with the lurid, snarling face of a wild boar. The fuel tank bears a stylised 'BB'.

Jory – as I'll call him for simplicity's sake – frowns. 'That isn't ours. Is it?' He knows the bike doesn't belong to anyone from the Green Chapel for two reasons. Firstly, they'd deplore the environmental irresponsibility of running a grossly inefficient petrol engine to transport one person around at high speed, and secondly, the showy, confrontational aesthetic of the motorcycle is all wrong. The Chapel's modus operandi is to blend into the background and to take its enemies by surprise and stealth.

Nonetheless – although this could just be a half-remembered fragment from some long-ago Circle briefing – the boar's face, unsubtly brutal as it is, sets off that itch in Jory's psyche which he associates with the devices and their effects.

'One of the others could have jacked it,' Cantrell suggests calmly.

Jory frowns. 'If they did, I hope the owner doesn't come calling.' Trouble with aggressive motorcyclists is a complication the Chapel people don't need just at the moment. He's very aware of the Nestine-Gull Grail sitting wrapped up in an old jumper in his duffel bag.

'I recognise it,' rumbles Bennett.

Jack's done time in prison, so the fact he knows their visitor does little to assuage Jory's worries. 'Friend of yours?' he asks.

'Must be someone you trust, at least,' Cantrell says pointedly, 'if you told him where to find us.'

Bennett just grunts again.

* * *

Between them, these three and Merry – together with Scar and Zara, the women from the museum, last seen heading for the M40 in a knackered Citroen 2CV – form the core of the Green Chapel. There are others, of course – Ahmed for a start, who drove the van and has vanished into the hinterlands of Islington, and me and Squig and Lee and dozens of others – but those six are what you'd call the heart of the operation.

You shouldn't have too much trouble working out who their devices – or 'allies', as we on the Sherwood team tend to call them – are. Let's face it, there's not a big pool of Merry Men to choose from, so 'outlaw with a bow', 'big guy with a quarterstaff' and 'fighter who wears red' shouldn't present a problem, at least. If I tell you that Merry – Malory – is sort of Jory's girlfriend these days, that should help you place her, too. Some people get confused by Cantrell's skinniness, forgetting that the most important thing about Friar Tuck is he's a worldly cleric, as interested in matters of the flesh as of the spirit. And if you're only familiar with the older, less multicultural versions of the Robin Hood stories, the Muslim warrior who never seems to have the same name twice may have passed you by.

If you're wondering how all these people fit in with the Circle's Camelot-complex, it's… well, complex. Let's come back to that one later.

When they get inside, Jory, Jack and Rev –

What's that? Oh right, yes.

There's one other introduction to make: I'm Dale, and I'll be your storyteller tonight. Or this morning, or whatever time it is right now.

I'm rarely active in the Chapel's direct actions – frankly I'm a bit rubbish at it – but my ally's Alan a'Dale, the minstrel in Robin Hood's band, although a long tradition of bardic impartiality means I've also hung around with the Circle under the name Taliesin.

Not any more, mind you, since they arrested me. I escaped, but it certainly soured the relationship. That was the year before all this happened – 'last year' I should say, given the way I'm telling this story.

Because yes, I'm using what we troubadour types call the historic present, even though we all know the War of the Devices happened decades ago. That may strike you as poncy, but there's a good reason for it.

The thing is, while certain things may be history to you – the Battle of Trafalgar, the Siege of Jerusalem, the Stonehenge Summit – they were once big and immediate and urgent, in a way the past tense just doesn't convey. It's difficult to remember now that decisions and events we think of as fixed certainties were once completely up for grabs. Most of what I'm telling you I've got from those who were there – the ones who were still around to talk to afterwards, at least. (A lot of them I did proper interviews with, with recordings and everything.)

My point is – we think of history as this great big edifice, and so it is, but it's cemented together by tiny grains of trivia. What did this queen or that president have for breakfast that day? What was the weather like when this politician stood for election? When did that front-line commander last get a coffee or a cigarette or a decent night's sleep? Does the person this revolutionary's talking to make them feel angry, or protective, or inferior, or horny? All this is what makes people react to events the way they do, and when those people stand in a particular position relative to history, it ends up determining the lives of *everyone*.

The men and women in this story, more by luck than judgement in most cases, ended up being that kind of people.

In summary… well yes, the other thing you need to know about me is that given half a chance, I pontificate. I'm sorry about that. Shall we carry on now?

* * *

When they get inside, Jory, Jack and Rev find Liss and Laney awkwardly entertaining a hulking stranger in motorcycle leathers. The crustie girls, who've only recently joined the Chapel, are here partly to stand guard while the raiding party are out, but mostly to make this look as much as possible like an ordinary squat.

(No, they don't have allies of their own. There are, what, fifty or so people in the Chapel at any one time? Everyone gets a little bit of generic Merry Man – just enough to blend into the background a bit and be handy in a brawl – but there aren't enough individual personas to go round.)

'About fucking time you turned up,' the biker says to Big Jack as the new trio enter. He's fiftyish, with knotted hair and a grizzled beard, and his leathers are painted, again with that grimacing boar. He smells of leather, sweat, petrol and, currently, weed. He's holding a joint which Liss must have given him, and from the expressions on the girls' faces, he hasn't been showing them how good he is at sharing.

'Torch,' Jack growls, looking about as pleased as the boar. 'What the hell are you doing here?'

'Adze sent me, didn't he,' Torch ripostes. His accent's Mancunian, his voice hoarse from what must be decades of smoking. He's in good shape, though, that's clear from a glance. 'Got some business for you, Jack.'

'Here?' Jack snaps. 'I never said you could bloody come here.'

Torch shrugs and grinds out the spliff. 'Should've answered Adze's texts, then. What, you been too busy?'

'Upstairs, now,' Jack says. Torch scowls, pockets Liss's joint, and follows the huge man out of the room.

'And they say romance is dead,' murmurs Cantrell. He wanders through into the kitchen, where the beer is.

'Wanker,' spits Liss, glaring after the departed biker. She's no more than seventeen, with dreadlocks, an impressive array of facial piercings and a Roedean accent that she makes no effort to disguise, although she spurned everything else her parents paid for when she joined the Green Chapel.

'I didn't like him,' Laney agrees. She's quieter, equally upper-crust, and dressed in imitation of her best friend, who she's devoted to. Whereas Liss left her school, family and comfortable upper-middle-class life out of politics, principle and the desire to enjoy herself with impunity, Laney seems to have left hers so largely because she feels lost without Liss. 'He tried to feel me up while you were in the loo.'

'Did he fuck!' protests Liss crisply. 'I'll cut the bastard.' Her fingers dart expertly as she rolls a new joint.

'Did he say who he was?' asks Jory. 'Big Jack shouldn't be telling anyone where we are right now.'

'He's British Beasts,' says Liss. 'I recognise the paint job. I had a boyfriend who was a biker once. Tosser left me when I told him his Harley was a resource-guzzling murder machine.'

Laney sighs loudly and pulls out a chubby paperback.

Jory allows his attention to wander as Liss begins listing the deficiencies of her former romantic partner. 'I need to talk to Merry,' he says to no-one in particular.

* * *

The derelict house has no phone line, naturally, and (although he'll use them reluctantly for a specific purpose, like today's raid) Jory's always had a bit of a blind spot about managing a mobile. One advantage of this being basically a fake squat, though, is that he can keep a laptop in his room, carefully concealed in a tatty blanket, with only a minor risk of anyone stealing it and selling it for skag. And one of the neighbouring houses, bought by ex-tenants whose children have done rather well for themselves, has slow but basically unprotected wireless broadband.

After he's stowed the Grail carefully in a fireproof strongbox and hidden it under a pile of old CDs in a cardboard box, Jory fires up the computer, piggybacks onto the neighbours' internet connection and logs into Archmail, a secure instant messaging program. He'd never heard of it before Malory installed it for him, but being Jory he has only the haziest of notions even about Facebook. It's written and maintained by geeks and has the reputation of being unhackable, though Malory insists on using various evasions and code phrases even so. Arriving on his user page, he sees the flashing icon which tells him he has a communication from 'Mort', Malory's Archmail ID.

He opens it up.

MORT: How's it going? Sources being frustratingly unspecific. Sure you're fine though.

A quick click on Mort's icon tells him that Malory's online now, and he replies using the username she picked for him.

SABRINA: All fine here thanks, yes. Got you a mug from the gift shop.

Jory, who can be a tad sensitive about his full name, was initially offended that Malory had assigned him the ID of a famously generous-breasted model from the 50s, but Malory explained earnestly that she'd been thinking of rivers to match the name 'Jordan', and that Sabrina was the goddess

27

of the river Severn. It's just enough of a figleaf for Jory to give her the benefit of the doubt, even though it's perfectly obvious that she was thinking of something else entirely.

Malory's obviously been hanging around waiting for him, because she replies straight away.

MORT: Fantastic. Proud of u.

Malory's roughly twenty times the thinker Jory is, but she's sufficiently secure in her intellectual capabilities not to feel the need to spell things out in full in instant messages.

SABRINA: I just hope you get some use out of it.

MORT: Not a prob.

There's a pause which might have been awkward in person, then Jory types:

SABRINA: Any news of you-know-who?

As circumlocutions go, it's not cunning or subtle, but he's tired and Malory will know who he means. The Green Chapel's shed a fair few members over the past months, but there's only one they're actively concerned about.

MORT: Got everyone looking out. Noones heard anything.

This isn't exactly surprising, but it isn't good news either. Jory – who's always found these mediated conversations awkward and trying – considers what else to say. He doesn't quite feel up to discussing Malory's father Edward.

SABRINA: I suppose I'll see you in a few days then. I'll bring your souvenir.

It's pointless to ask where to look for her – they don't discuss that sort of information out in the open any more, not even on this kind of channel.

MORT: Sure. Say hi to Mir&A from me.

'Mir&A' is a persona Malory runs on an online singles service called 'Love-L', and what she means is that he should check the account's latest lovelorn blurtings for clues to Malory's whereabouts. It's a method of contact Jory loathes, although he accepts its usefulness. Malory eschews standard ciphers, preferring to conceal information in the form of cryptic crossword clues, general-knowledge tests and number games, hidden in screeds of unreadably incoherent drivel.

Jory's been told that long-distance relationships can be hard work, but he never expected anything quite like this.

SABRINA: OK.

MORT: Great. CU soon.

SABRINA: Hang on a sec, though.

He considers for a moment, trying to decide whether to encode this somehow, but he can't think of anything that will convey his meaning except saying it.

SABRINA: What do you know about something called British Beasts?

* * *

Twenty minutes later, he closes up the laptop with a sigh. This is going to tax his people skills.

The thing you need to realise about Jory is that he's a disillusioned idealist – or, perhaps, just one who's found himself some new illusions. His career path from youthful Arthurian enthusiast, to student tournament re-enactor, to bona fide Knight in a chivalric order founded – at least according to all its internal documentation – some fifteen hundred years ago by King Arthur himself, was derailed quite violently and unexpectedly last year, when he discovered that two of his oldest friends were founder members of the modern iteration of a group the Circle's long classified as a terrorist cell.

Now, of those university pals, Shafiq Rashid's dead (killed by mistake, assuming you give the Circle the benefit of the doubt), Malory's his girlfriend (though that's a more taxing arrangement than he'd ever imagined), and Jory's somehow found himself the de facto leader of the selfsame gang of violent radicals. These days he more or less shares their communitarian, anti-authoritarian, environmentalist ethics, but – despite the direct action he's just been intimately embroiled in – he's still capable of coming over a tad puritanical about certain things.

29

The difficulty he has to cope with now, though, lies in his claim to that leadership. Jory's life has been entangled with the Robin Hood device's for some time now – he killed its last-but-one bearer, Shaun Hobson, back when he was a Knight, and was trying to rescue Shafiq, the most recent bearer, from the Circle's custody when he too was killed. More than that, though – the Round Table knight whose device Jory used to serve is Sir Gawain, and the Robin device is also known, from an Arthurian perspective, as the Green Knight. Suffice it to say that those two have a history.

It was, in fact, their primal response to one another – expressed through their influence on their respective human representatives – which led to Jory slicing off Shaun Hobson's head and Shafiq very nearly returning the compliment years later. Just as the Circle has its own name for Robin Hood, the Chapel has another for Sir Gawain, and for a couple of weeks last summer, Jory was reconciled to them considering him the villainous henchman Sir Guy of Gisbourne.

The devices are adaptable, however, and the kind of strain Jory went through last year can lead them to alter themselves in strange ways. Malory talks about it as evolution, an organism adapting itself to a changing ecological niche. She has this whole taxonomic system of classification, though it's complicated by some of the Robin Hood devices being flipsides of the Arthurian ones. When they mutate, though – and it rarely happens – it tends to be along lines of affinity, which is why, after he began questioning his loyalty to the Circle last year, Jory began to suspect that he was now playing host to Sir Gawain's substantially less reputable half-brother, the traitor Sir Mordred.

Among the Chapel, on the other hand, it's become pretty much accepted, on the basis of his past entanglements with the Green Knight and his current relationship with Merry, our Maid Marian, that Jory's the next bearer of the Robin Hood device. This, along with his natural charisma and capability at organising and fighting things, have led to his current highly-conditional acceptance by the Sherwood faction as our first among equals.

Human beings need their rites of passage, though, and although the Chapel don't go in for the kind of ceremony the Knights do, with vigils and acclamations and fasting and prayer, it's traditional to acknowledge a new alliance between a Green Chapel member and one of the Merry Men with a bloody good knees-up. So far, Jory hasn't felt ready to take that step.

The manifestations of the devices in their hosts' minds vary greatly, from subliminal promptings which feel rather like artistic inspiration, to full-on auditory and visual hallucinations of the legendary figure in question. During Jory's final months with the Circle, he sometimes heard a very clear internal voice directing – or perhaps reflecting – his own thoughts. It can't have been Robin, because at that point Shaf was still his human ally, but it didn't feel like Sir Gawain either.

Certainly the Circle attributes the Mordred device to Jory (which is one of the reasons they're searching for him quite so aggressively), as well as considering Malory the latest avatar of Mordred's sponsor in villainy, Morgan le Fay. (Interestingly – to me that is, because Jory doesn't give much of a toss about the devices' appearances in popular culture – the actor who played Gisbourne in ITV's seminal *Robin of Sherwood* may have got the part on the strength of his performance as Mordred in the film *Excalibur*. On the other hand, if we go down that road, we end up saying Robin and Arthur are the same person because of Sean Connery.)

Jory's become more cunning during his time with the Chapel, he's sure of that – he largely planned today's heist at the museum, and it went off without a hitch. He's cheerier and less guilt-ridden than he used to be, though some of that could be shrugging off the influence of the Circle. Any of this could be the effect of either Mordred's influence or Robin's.

The clincher, he thinks, will be the archery. He's been practising assiduously to get back to the standard he could boast when he and Shafiq Rashid used to shoot for the university team, before such peasant weapons became beneath his honour as a Knight of the Circle. He's done well, too – against stationary targets. He'll never be Shafiq, but Shaf was an Olympic silver medallist. If his abilities weren't being augmented by *something*, Jory's sure, he could hardly hold his own among a band of outlaws whose personas have been steeped in eight hundred years of folklore.

Recently it seemed as if some esoteric research of Merry's had clinched his place as Robin once and for all, but Jory remains unsure. He had a clear shot at Stephen today and comprehensively cocked it up. That isn't something Robin Hood would have done – or Shaf, for that matter. And it has to be said that archery's not usually noted as one of Sir Mordred's accomplishments.

It's obvious in any case that Jory's still getting help from his device. He just isn't at all clear at the moment who that is.

* * *

Jory, Bennett and Cantrell are distracted inside the house when Liss confronts Torch, detaining the biker in the nettle-infested front garden as he leaves the squat. There's a lot of shouting, several dictionary entries' worth of profanity exchanged, before Liss takes a swing at the man. Torch grabs her fist and squeezes it hard in both hands, until blood trickles down their wrists and Liss shrieks in pain. As the crustie girl's legs give way beneath her, Laney launches herself screaming at the biker's back, but gets a vicious backhander in the face for her pains. By the time the men have realised what's happening and rushed to intervene, Torch is gunning the Norton's engine and departing in a flurry of expletives, having trampled down the front fence on his way.

'Bastard,' mutters Big Jack as he helps Liss to her feet. Two of her fingers are broken, and there are deep bloody weals where her fingernails were driven into her palms. She's swearing with impressive creativity.

Jory is supporting Laney, whose nose is also bloodied and who's whimpering quietly. Rev goes to get the medical kit they've been keeping under a floorboard in the bathroom. They can't risk a London A&E, nor can they stay here long. Torch knows where they live and clearly can't be trusted; the whole Green Chapel party needs to get away from here, and fast.

It's been like this recently. The Green Chapel's always been nomadic, but normally that's meant camping in forests or greenbelt land, setting up a tent village there for a few weeks – sometimes more, sometimes less – before moving on. We've had a rotating, ever-changing roster of sites which have become familiar over the years. Our current existence – fractured, itinerant, forever staying ahead of Circle and police searches, with the occasional cut-and-run which sees our possessions lost, our bodies injured, our comrades thrown in jail – is taking its toll on all the members. Most of the modest reserves the Chapel keeps against times like these – savings accounts held under assumed names, easily-liquidated assets left over from past robberies, handbags of cash left with sympathetic shopkeepers in villages and cities across the country – are gone, as are the proceeds of our last heist of actual money. Without a significant injection of capital, the members' efforts will go towards getting food for ourselves and our families, by legitimate or criminal means, and the Green Chapel will dissipate for lack of human input.

Unlike the Circle, which has stood monolithically for a millennium and a half, the Chapel reinvents itself from generation to generation, disbanding and reforming as circumstances dictate. Jory isn't the only one wondering whether this is what such times look like.

3. A MERRY TALE FOR MALORY WENDIMAN

Although Big Jack doesn't question the need to shift their arses, he tries to minimise the incident. 'Torch won't grass us up,' he insists to Jory. The two of them are gathering up the few indispensible possessions the group have brought here, including Jory's laptop, while Cantrell tends to the wounded.

'No?' Jory doesn't conceal his disbelief.

'Not if he knows what's good for him,' Jack elaborates. 'I've got an arrangement with his boss. All that down there with Liss, that were personal – and Liss started it, too, not that Torch should've gone off how he did. But that don't mean he'll call the Circle on us.'

'And what the hell did you think you were doing, making an "arrangement" with people like that?' Jory demands. 'Do you know what Torch's device is?'

'Aye, it's a bloody great wild boar King Arthur couldn't hunt,' Bennett says calmly. 'And we say "ally" round our way, *Dan*.'

The Circle and the Chapel have different approaches to what we respectively call devices and allies (and what I once heard Malory call 'semi-autonomous culturally-inflected archetypal memeplexes' or 'SCAMs', which is why I usually go with the colloquial version). The Circle see themselves as servants to the original Round Table Knights, doing their bidding in the modern world, which is where – given how fundamentally unsuited those characters are to the current environment – a lot of their troubles stem from. The Chapel take a much more collaborative view of the relationship, hence the egalitarian terminology.

'Don't get pedantic about names when we've got people hurt, Jack!' Jory's surprised by his own anger – always assuming it *is* his own, of course. In fact, he partly blames himself, for deciding to wait until Torch had gone before taking Jack aside for a quiet word... but he's got better at ignoring that kind of guilt recently.

Bennett has the grace to look a little ashamed. 'Aye, I never meant for that to happen to Laney,' he admits. 'Poor lass. Girl's got pluck, mind. Did you see the way she laid into Torch like that? If she'd had an ally...' He shakes his head admiringly.

'But that's what British Beasts *do*,' Jory points out. From what he learned from Malory, the bikers are violent thugs, involved in everything from drug-smuggling to armed robbery. 'Do you remember that warehouse fire in Portsmouth back in April, where that security guard died? She had a two-year-old kid, if you recall? That was them, Jack. Your friend Torch and his mates.'

Jack shrugs. 'Aye, well. You can't be too choosy when the bloody Circle's breathing down your back.'

'What have you been doing for him?' Jory asks. Then, as a new thought occurs to him, 'Is it *just* him?'

'Torch isn't the first one,' Bennett admits placidly. 'When I was inside I knew this bloke called Adze. He were a right piece of work, ex-squaddie turned biker, doing time for throwing a copper through a plate-glass window. He were right angry they'd caught him. *We got to learn to stay a step ahead of the law, Big Jack*, he used to say to me. *Lead them fuckers a proper dance.* He didn't want no more to do with his old bike chapter, though – said they'd left him to rot. He wanted to set up on his own.

35

'Well,' he goes on, 'when he got out back in January, he got in touch. Turns out he had a vision inside, around the time we were dragging you out of that Circle van. This great monster, he said, like a leopard but with hooves and a long neck with a snake's head – much too big to fit inside his cell, but it was there anyway. It made a noise like a hundred dogs barking – hounds baying for blood, he said, deafening him. He thought it wanted him to follow it. Learn how to run and run and never be caught.

'I'd never heard of anything that looked like that, mind,' Big Jack says, 'but I know an ally when someone tells me of one. So I told Adze to read some stories about King Arthur, really read them and pay attention. Well, it weren't like nothing in any Robin Hood story I'd heard, so that only left one option, aye? Then I taught him some of Merry's tricks, the breathing and the centring and all.'

Regardless of what you call it, an ally's a powerful thing, prone to exert a profound influence over its host, often in ways, and parts of their lives, that they'd never have expected. The Circle accept that as the price of their service, but for us Chapel types it takes practice, and a lot of self-discipline, to maintain a bit of parity in the relationship and stop your own identity disappearing into that of the legend. Rev and Merry have come up with various techniques – meditation, awareness exercises, role-playing workshops – to achieve this.

Jory's always assumed that Big Jack isn't terribly good at them, given how little there is to choose between him and Little John, in personality as well as looks. Perhaps, though, that just means he has more need of them than the rest of us.

Jack finishes, 'Next thing I know he's sending me a mate of his to train – bloke who thinks he's some kind of werewolf. Torch were the next. It all took off from there.'

'OK,' says Jory. 'I appreciate you telling me all this.' He clears the CDs from the top of the cardboard box, uncovering the strongbox beneath.

'They've paid for the privilege, mind,' Bennett adds. 'And it's all gone into Chapel funds. You've eaten food paid for by British Beasts' money. Cut it off and we'll lose that.'

Opening the strongbox, Jory says, 'Well, I appreciate that as well. But surely, when you heard about the sorts of things they were doing…'

'Aye,' says Bennett again. 'But by then, the Circle were after us hard, weren't they? And Kinsey's lot. We were rushing round like blue-arsed flies, without a minute to catch our breath. The way I saw it, giving them one more mob with allies to scrap with took some of that heat off of us. It's a good arrangement, Dan. Adze may be a psycho, but he keeps his word. If it comes down to a straight fight, us and the Circle, they'll come and pitch in.'

Jory shudders. 'That won't be necessary.' With his best voice of calm authority he adds, 'This ends now, Jack, do you hear me? I won't have the Chapel associated with *that* kind of criminal activity. We're better than that. If we act like the gangsters the Circle think we are, we're letting them define us.'

Bennett looks sceptical. 'Aye, maybe,' he mutters. 'But maybe that's what we need to be now.'

'Not any more,' Jory tells him, as he pulls out the Nestine-Gull Grail. 'Now we've got a trump card. With this to bargain with, we can get the Circle off our backs permanently.' He wraps it up again in his old jumper, ready to pack it in his rucksack.

Big Jack scoffs. 'How's that supposed to work, then? "You promise to be nice to us, we give your cup back?" And we're supposed to trust their promises?'

Jory shakes his head. 'That's not the deal. The deal is, "The moment you stop being nice to us, we destroy the Grail." We're never going to give it back.'

Bennett looks grudgingly impressed. 'Bugger me with a quarterstaff,' he says. 'You're coming along nicely.'

Jory does his best not to look alarmed at the compliment.

* * *

In fact, despite Jory's confident assertion, using the Grail to blackmail the Circle with is very much Plan B, and he doubts it'll work for long. According to Malory's analysis, there's nothing intrinsic about the Nestine-Gull vessel which makes it the locus of the Holy Grail device, and only the cup's long veneration by the Circle makes it special at all. As she's told Jory on more than one occasion, objects have no power beyond that which people choose to assign them. If the wooden cup were to be destroyed, some other drinking-vessel – perhaps an authentic first-century Judaean goblet, perhaps Sir Charles' Royal Wedding commemorative coffee-mug – would become invested by the bearers of the Round Table devices with the notional presence of the sacred. In time, the Circle are likely to realise this, and will welcome – indeed, they'll try to hurry along – Jory's destruction of the Grail he holds. (That's if they believe he's capable of destroying it at all, which he'd have to admit to certain doubts of his own about.)

In other words, the kind of blackmail Jory just described would be a stopgap at best – although that would be better than nothing, obviously. Malory has a bolder plan.

* * *

'It's already happening,' Malory told Jory a few months ago, when they were able to spend a few days together. 'The schism I warned you about. It's going to tear the country apart, if we let it.'

They were snuggling on a big cream sofa, supported by matching suede cushions and listening to smooth jazz. This surprising comfort was entirely thanks to Malory, who'd used her few remaining academic connections to locate a well-appointed empty house in Oxfordshire whose occupants, Drs Andrew and Christine Gardner and their daughter Lucy, were away in America for a semester, and where there were no pets or curious neighbours to interrupt their surreptitious assignation.

Malory's an academic herself, of course, and one in whom snuggling positively encourages pedagogy. 'Historically,' she told Jory, 'the rivalry between the Chapel and the Circle's been marginal. There's been liminal and ambiguous contact every generation or so between the Robin-Hood-stroke-Green-Knight and Gawain-stroke-Gisbourne devices, but otherwise the Circle's been too busy defending the realm from the manifestations of actively malignant archetypes, while the Chapel's radical programme slips under the radar.'

She turned the jazz down, careless of her fingerprints on the remote. Once this intrusion was discovered and the house examined, alerts would inevitably be tripped, flags raised, messages sent. The Circle would be in no doubt that its prodigal children had been here. A thorough analysis of the grime Malory and Jory had shed in the Gardners' shower might even reveal exactly which parts of the nation's urban hinterland they'd each been staying in over the past week – but no clue as to where they'd moved on to.

'But surely our philosophies are diametrically opposed?' Jory pointed out, sipping some of the excellent merlot they'd found under the stairs. He wore clean pyjamas from the drawer in the master bedroom, whose imperfect fit told him that Dr Andrew Gardner was six inches shorter than him but considerably plumper. 'I mean, I sort of thought that was the basis for me defecting.'

Malory leaned back and put her feet on his lap, wrapping fourteen-year-old Lucy's fluffy bathrobe more tightly about herself. Autumn-red hair hung loose about her shoulders, and metal-framed glasses pincered her nose. She looked like a pre-Raphaelite painting of a librarian.

'Politically, yes,' she said. 'Our two greatest national heroes are a divinely-appointed absolute monarch and a peasant outlaw who demolishes the pretensions of the powerful. But in other ways, Camelot and Sherwood have a lot in common. However we interpret and express our basic ideals, they're rooted in the same Judaeo-Christian conceptions of good and evil. There's rarely been a strong enough reason for us to actually fight, and when it's happened, we've ended up with national disaster. The Civil War, for instance. The motivations on both sides of that are very muddy, and even the Circle's records are incomplete – but on the one side you have Charles I and his supporters, insisting that the monarch represents God and can do no wrong; on the other all those sects of Diggers and Levellers and Quakers and Ranters, trying to build egalitarian utopias in the ruins. It's not difficult to see which sides the Circle and the Chapel would have picked. The rest of the time, though, we're left with this bizarre cognitive dissonance in the British psyche.'

'But we've changed all that,' Jory observed. 'Us and Shafiq.'

'Pretty much,' Malory observed, wriggling her toes in Lucy's slippers. 'Whatever their contact down the ages, I'm fairly sure last year was the first time the Chapel's succeeded in turning a Knight of the Circle. That, and the fallout from that, have begun to polarise the two, which in the long run can only lead to collective psychosis. We're already seeing the signs of that in these recent civil disturbances.'

'Really?' This seemed unlikely to Jory. He had to admit that the world around him had been looking more unstable recently, but he'd put that down to exchanging a secure position of privilege in the upper echelons of an establishment body older than the establishment itself, for a life of scurrying from bolthole to bolthole, forever watching for the boot that would stomp him flat. That would, he thought, affect anybody's perspective on society.

'Afraid so,' said Malory. 'The two camps have become hyper-aware of each other, and we're beginning to react to that. We're defining ourselves in opposition to each other in ways we never have before.'

'Are we, though?' asked Jory, leaning forward to plump up the cushion behind him. 'I mean, the Circle's more authoritarian these days, that's obvious. They've been suppressing devices they'd have left alone before, like that

Gildas chap. As well as coming after us, of course. But I thought that was just because of Sir Charles. Isn't it?'

That Gildas chap was an evangelical pastor from Tyneside named Bill Spink, who'd denounced the Circle publicly as a tool of Satan, had been arrested shortly afterwards for embezzling church funds and had ended up in the Circle's high-security facility, the Benwick Institute. The incident had cast an unfavourable light on the Circle for several weeks, until it was eclipsed by their high-profile prevention of an unrelated bombing campaign. One of Malory's semi-regular hacking forays into the Circle's databases had revealed that Spink was now deemed to bear the device of St Gildas, a cleric who fell out with Arthur after the High King killed the saint's rebellious brother.

Jory topped up his wine and offered Malory the bottle, but she shook her head. 'You're only seeing half the picture,' she told him. 'Listen to our people – they resent the Circle more than ever.'

'Well, that's only reasonable under the circumstances,' Jory argued.

'But it's forcing our ideologies further apart,' she insisted. 'Our lot are getting more bolshie by the day, and they're prepared to be more ruthless against establishment targets. Burn claims to know for a fact that a couple of the younger lads have been in contact with the Sons of Gore – and I mean *since* the bomb plot.'

The Sons of Gore were the bombers the Circle had foiled shortly after taking custody of Bill Spink. A separatist movement for an ancient country which possibly never existed and whose historical heartlands, let alone borders, had never been satisfactorily located, they'd always baffled Jory. If it weren't for their frequent attempted acts of public violence, he would have assumed the Sons were enacting an obscure form of situationist performance art. Perhaps they were, just murderously.

Malory leaned back against the sofa arm and stretched, making young Lucy's bathrobe flex in ways Jory found distracting. 'The more the Circle sees that sort of thing happening,' she went on, 'the more they're going to clamp down on any unsanctioned device. Which means our people become more resentful, and the antagonism grows. It's, and I've been trying to think of a different way of phrasing it because I know you're going to make a stupid pun and this is serious, a vicious circle.' She smiled, but grimly.

Jory considered the stupid puns available. 'So is there anything we can do about it?' he asked instead.

'Don't know yet, sweetheart. I'm working on it, though.' She scissored her legs off his lap and went to fetch the elderly denim holdall she'd brought with her. 'Look, I want to show you something.' She unzipped the holdall and brought out something heavy and rectangular, wrapped in a T-shirt.

She unwrapped it on the smoked-glass coffee table: a book, a very old one, bound between heavy wooden boards and written in a dense medieval script which to Jory looked entirely impenetrable. The pages were unrelieved by the illuminated capitals and marginal illustrations which often punctuate the tedium of that sort of text, for the benefit of the monks who copied them and the students who spend hours these days staring at facsimiles in libraries.

'What is it?' he asked, nose twitching at the smell of ancient must as he tried to force his eyes to render the thick black pen-strokes into some semblance of sense.

'A medieval commonplace book,' said Malory. 'What we'd now call a miscellany. It's a compendium of useful information, compiled by a single scribe from various sources. This is an unusually old one, though. I found it in the Bodleian Library.'

'Found it?' Jory frowned. 'You mean "stole it".'

She sighed. 'Sweetheart, no-one had looked at it since 1907. It wasn't even in the catalogue. I only knew it was there because of some notes a previous advisor to the Circle made. In 1907.'

She was leafing carefully through the pages, turning each with the care she'd use to handle the last specimen of an endangered orchid. 'There's one particular item near the end,' she said, 'sandwiched between a treatise on riverine geography and a recipe for blankmanger. I'd completely forgotten hearing about it, but after that business with the St Gildas device, it started nagging at my memory. It's a joint biography of a pair of British saints I'd never even heard of. Nor has Wikipedia,' she added.

'Well, Wikipedia,' said Jory dismissively.

'Or the *New Catholic Encyclopaedia*, or the Vatican's Congregation for the Causes of Saints, who are supposed to keep the complete list. I phoned them,' Malory said. 'Yes, here we are – *The Lives of St Brelin and St Bellen*. It's in Middle English, but it claims to be a translation from the Latin of a much older oral tradition. Listen to this, Jory, and tell me whether it reminds you of anything.'

* * *

Though they're as pious as you'd expect, Celtic saints' lives can be surprisingly lively, with extended special-effects sequences involving angels, miracles and the odd bit of dragon-taming. There's a lot in the book about the later life of St Bellen especially, but the part that was of interest to Malory and Jory – and so to us now – was the prologue, the story of how Bellen and Brelin came to Christianity. Stripped of most of the sermonising and biblical references, that prologue goes more or less like this.

There was a pagan king in Roman Britain named Boduoc, who ruled at Cirencester. Boduoc's nation was one of those which, when the Romans first came to Britain, fought bravely against their plans for conquest, yet which later, when the invaders' might became too great for it to resist, capitulated and became a Roman vassal state. The tribes who persisted in their rebellion condemned Boduoc's people as cowards, but they thrived under Roman rule.

Boduoc had two sons, half-brothers named Bellen and Brelin. Bellen was the older, but Brelin had been born of

Boduoc's favoured wife, so when he died, the king decreed that both of them should succeed him and rule jointly. The brothers were pleased by this arrangement, for they loved one another greatly, but after Boduoc's death they came to blows over policy. Bellen was loyal to Britain's Roman rulers and proposed to continue the tribe's tribute to the emperor, but Brelin swore that he would never submit to an emperor in a faraway land, no matter how powerful his garrisons in Britain. Bellen entreated his brother to change his mind, fearing Rome's retribution, but Brelin was resolute in his principles. He took two score men and left their lands, to join with a group of rebels in Cornwall.

Bellen knew that, if the Romans learned that his brother had taken up arms against their legions, they would enact a bloody vengeance against his people, so with great sorrow he took two score men of his own and followed Brelin's forces, coming upon them at the River Shippey, where they set to fighting. Their troops were closely matched, and after a day's fighting all but Bellen and Brelin were slain. Brelin fled to the isle of Glastonbury, sacred in former times to the pagan gods, but at that time the site of the first Christian church in Britain.

Bellen continued to pursue his brother, but when he came to the margins of the lake he was met by a monk, who told him that Brelin had taken sanctuary in the grounds of Glastonbury Abbey, and must not be molested for fear of the wrath of the one true God.

Bellen was impressed by the man's humility and holiness, and asked to see the abbot, a venerable old priest who walked with a staff and spoke movingly of the life of our Lord. When Bellen explained that he came with the authority of the Roman emperor to take back his brother, the abbot replied that, while he bore neither Bellen nor Brelin any ill-will, he cared not overmuch for Rome, for it was Romans who had slain the saviour of the world.

Bellen, awed by the old man's sanctity, offered him no violence but meekly asked if he might join his brother at the abbey for a few days. The abbot graciously agreed, and the joint kings were reunited. There they renewed their friendship, and lived with the monks for some time, discussing policy for their kingdom, and how their opposing views might be reconciled.

One day, however, Bellen observed a certain drinking-vessel which the monks treated with great reverence, and concluded that this must be very valuable. At once Satan put greed in his heart, and Bellen began to plot to steal this treasure.

Thinking to enlist his brother as his confederate, he told him of his plans, but Brelin had come to love his venerable hosts, and was appalled at the idea of stealing from them.

As Brelin remonstrated with his brother, they happened to be passing by an old thorn-tree in the abbey grounds, and in his anger Brelin pushed Bellen into the tree, which pierced his hands and side with long sharp thorns, causing him to cry out in pain. Then Satan goaded Brelin into a murderous rage, and he broke the longest thorn from the tree, thinking to stab his brother in the heart with it.

By divine providence, however, the abbot was also walking in the gardens, and when he saw his guests quarrelling so, he prayed quickly for a miracle to stay their hands. At once, the thorn Brelin had plucked turned into a serpent, like Moses's rod before the king of Egypt, and began to writhe in his hands. Brelin dropped the creature, which slithered away into the gardens, and fell to his knees before the abbot, declaring that he was the greatest mage in all of Britain. And the priest replied, 'Not my power, but the Lord's, has done this.'

Brelin and the abbot helped Bellen from the tree, and tended his wounds. Then the abbot revealed to the brothers a great mystery. 'My name,' he said, 'is Joseph of Arimathea, and I am uncle to Mary, the Virgin Mother of our Lord Jesus Christ. It was the tomb I had bought for my own in which my great-nephew was laid after His death, and from which He rose again to glorious resurrected life.

'After our Saviour left this world, I travelled with His disciples, spreading the word of His salvation to the peoples of the world, and fleeing from the ill-treatment of Christians in the Roman lands, until at last I came to Britain, and this isle. I brought with me two things: the cup which you have seen us use in our holy mass, which was formerly used by our Lord at his last supper, and a stout hawthorn staff.

'When I first came to Glastonbury, it was a pagan shrine, dedicated to your island gods. I challenged the heathen priests to a contest of miracles, as Elijah did the prophets of Baal, to prove whose God was the greater. The way in which I won the contest was this: I took the staff which I had brought from the Holy Land and thrust it into the good British earth, whereupon by the power of God's grace it grew branches and leaves and burst into flower, becoming the thorn-tree which you have also seen.

'The pagan priests immediately understood by this that Christianity would flourish in Britain, and they withdrew and left the sanctuary to myself and my followers. Here I have lived for two hundred years, being already over seventy when I first arrived, and here I shall abide until it pleases the Lord to take me to his bosom.'

After hearing Abbot Joseph speak, Brelin and Bellen fell and worshipped the God of the Christians, and both were baptised that day and tonsured, and accepted as monks at the abbey. In the years that followed they became great holy men, though their names are all but forgotten by the church now. Both saints continued to bear the burden of their past discord, however.

Bellen never wholly recovered from his wounds where the thorn-tree had pierced him, but forever after bore scars on his hands and side like those of our Lord at his crucifixion, which he suffered humbly as a reminder that he had offended against the laws of sanctuary and hospitality in plotting to steal the cup of our Lord. When at last the Lord chose to take Abbot Joseph at three hundred years of age, Bellen became abbot in his stead, and remained head of the abbey, and keeper of the holy cup, for many years.

Brelin, by contrast, was mortified by guilt that he had tried to slay his brother, and that in doing so he too had violated the holy ground of the abbey, and before long he left to become a hermit in the woods, where he remained for fifty years, outliving his brother, and his wisdom was much sought after.

...and then we get onto all the other stuff I was telling you about – all the wise decisions Bellen makes as abbot, his pilgrimage to Rome, his mission to evangelise the Irish and so forth. Meanwhile, the serpent Joseph made out of the thorn grows huge and starts hanging around Brelin's hermitage, and eventually he has to get St George in to slay it.

There's also a weird bit where a mermaid tries to seduce St Bellen but he ends up converting her instead. Like I say, they could be a bit wacky, the Celtic Christians.

4. A QUEST FOR STEPHEN MUKHERJEE

'I've no excuse, sir,' Stephen Mukherjee says, shamefaced. He stands to attention in front of a glass cabinet of replica Anglo-Saxon jewellery. 'I failed in my quest, and that's an end of it.'

Shame is ingrained in Stephen's device. As a Saracen – usually meaning a Muslim, although there's no way Islam could have been contemporary with any historical Arthur, and in fact Stephen's family are stolidly Anglo-Catholic – Sir Palamedes is usually held up as one who nobly strives, but regularly fails. Usually what he's unworthy of is the love of Queen Iseult of Cornwall, the wife of King Mark and lover of Sir Tristan, but Stephen's found his device is happy to wallow in unworthiness wherever it finds it.

'That's rarely an end to anything, Mukherjee,' snaps Sir Charles. 'There'll be a reckoning for this, I can assure you.'

'Yes, sir,' Stephen agrees wretchedly. He's always been one of those who experiences his device's influence primarily emotionally, although it's also bestowed on him some marked obsessive tendencies. Fortunately, as a cricket fan, Stephen has ample outlet for these.

From his side, Julian Blythe ventures, 'Fair dos, sir, Taylor tricked Mukherjee with that arrow. The swine knew he'd think it was a bomb. He's obviously lost all his Knightly honour. Taylor I mean, not Mukherjee.'

Parsons looks sardonically at him. 'Goes without saying, what with him stealing the Holy Grail, yeah?'

Blythe winces. 'Well, I suppose so.' He doesn't add 'sir' because technically, unlike the Seneschal, Paul doesn't outrank him. Despite Paul's current privileged position – and Julian's embarrassed one – they're brother Knights and theoretical equals. To Raymond, he adds, 'Mukherjee was trying to help me out, though, sir.'

'His job wasn't to help you,' Sir Charles snaps. 'It was to guard that room. You let Taylor distract you both with his grandstanding, and that thieving little bitch got past you.'

'Yes, sir,' Julian agrees, looking down at his feet.

Conscious that Julian has been trying to help him, and impelled by Sir Palamedes' vigorous desire to make amends, Stephen casts around for anything he can say to defend his brother Knight, other than 'It was all my fault, though.' As things stand, he's said that a number of times already, and Raymond seems to have pretty much taken it on board.

There's a lot more that could be said, of course, if the Knights weren't too proud and stubborn to say it. There's a reason someone deviciously allied to Robin Hood (or Mordred for that matter, although the reason's a slightly different one) is likely to be good at playing tricks on people, and a reason men bearing the devices of Round Table Knights are likely to fall for them. The devices are creatures of story, and allying with them – binding yourself to them, as they say in the Circle – makes you susceptible to the ways of stories. The trickster archetype's a popular one in world mythology, but it's found far more often among underdogs – the oppressed, the dispossessed, the outlawed – than among the upholders of righteous authority. Aside from Merlin, who's unavoidably absent from duties with the Circle at present, the only tricksters in the Arthurian myths are the enemies of the Round Table.

'And now we've lost the Grail,' Sir Charles fumes. 'Say what you like about the cup's history, the Grail is what it is *now* – and it's in the hands of the Mordred and Morgan devices. I dread to think what they could accomplish with it. You thought we were facing some Lincoln-green hippie with a feather in his hat, did you, Mukherjee? A charming outlaw and his jolly chums? This business has Mordred written all over it. The two vilest figures in the whole Matter of Britain now hold its single most precious object. I just hope you're pleased with yourself.'

'It was pretty shabby behaviour of Taylor's, sir,' says Stephen. Somehow, although he's well aware the fault is his and he must be punished for it, he feels as if this hasn't been acknowledged quite enough. 'I'll face the music, though, of course.'

'There's no doubt of that,' Parsons mutters, tapping at his iPad with his good hand.

Though Palamedes would be mortified if Stephen tried to put his discomfort into words, this is generally the point at which it would be acknowledged that the Knights have fallen short of perfection, as Knights so often do, but that the reasons for their failure are explicable and can be forgiven. There might well be disciplinary consequences, but now's pretty much when the Seneschal – the representative of the Circle's ever-absent Head, and dutiful dispenser of his mercy as well as his justice – would let Stephen and Julian know that they were still beloved brothers in the Circle.

Sir Charles has been doing an awful lot less of that, since open war was declared with the Green Chapel.

Indeed, it's almost as if – it's a ridiculous idea, of course, and not at all the thing – but it feels to Stephen almost as if the Seneschal's being unfair about this. In fact, he seems to be enjoying making Stephen the scapegoat for the Circle's collective failure.

Stephen's not an imaginative man – on the whole he prefers cricket to all that sort of nonsense. Imagination in the Knights, beyond the boyhood nostalgia for tales of King

Arthur they all more or less share, is frowned on as a general rule; a popular explanation for Jory Taylor's downfall is that he had altogether too much of it. Although Stephen's aware, like all the Knights now, that the Chapel's people consider themselves the modern avatars of Robin Hood's Merry Men, he's never paused to consider what the Circle looks like from their point of view.

It wouldn't occur to him to speculate, for instance, about who their version of this story might assign the fairly crucial roles of Prince John, or the Sheriff of Nottingham.

* * *

To Stephen's relief, a commotion outside the gift shop distracts the Seneschal's attention. Sir Charles' lips purse as a woman's voice shouts, 'I'm a senior police officer and I'm here to see Sir Charles fucking Raymond, OK? Now bloody let me through!'

A man-at-arms starts remonstrating with the unseen woman, but the Seneschal sighs, squeezes his temples in one hand and calls, 'Let the Chief Inspector through, Weller.'

There's the scuffling sound of a slight but determined woman trying to walk through a burly man who isn't stepping out of the way fast enough for her liking, and a uniformed policewoman bursts into the room.

Chief Inspector Jade Kinsey is five foot two, with a Midlands accent, the ferocity of a crazed polecat and about the same degree of discrimination. She wouldn't be where she is without knowing when to kowtow to authority, though, and once in Raymond's presence she becomes marginally more deferential.

Marginally. 'With respect, sir,' she begins, 'what are your people doing? My officers are entitled to inspect this crime scene, and you're refusing us entry like we were tourists. They only let me in when I threatened to go to the press!'

'You threatened *what?*' Sir Charles's eyes bulge. Like many Knights, he's not at ease with the position of women in

51

the modern world. Treating them as antagonists discomfits him in subtle ways, and he responds with bluster. 'For God's sake, woman, this is the scene of a terrorist outrage!'

'So you say,' Kinsey replies. 'The reports we have from staff here suggest it was a highly targeted art theft in which no-one was injured. So what the hell's the Circle's interest?'

'If it comes to that,' Raymond blusters, 'what's yours? If you'd done your job and – that is, you were supposed to be tracking down –' He stops suddenly.

'Domestic terrorists?' Chief Inspector Kinsey bares her teeth in something Stephen supposes fits the standard description of a smile. 'That's the official remit, sir, yes.'

Jade Kinsey had a number of frustrating experiences last year, as some of the operations she was engaged in got caught in the crossfire between the Chapel and the Circle. Somehow – either through a level of diplomatic skill which those who've met her would hardly credit, or more likely through swearing loudly at selected individuals in the police hierarchy – she's managed to parley this sequence of failures into a promotion, leadership of a team with wide-ranging powers, and a mission that irksomely parallels the Circle's own current quest to bring the Chapel and its adherents to justice.

'Of course,' she sneers, 'we both know I'm cleaning up your mess, running after your rogue agent and his fucking thugs.'

The police as a body may still have no idea what a device is, but an increase in folklore-themed crime – the Adam Bell robberies, the Bronze Bowl Murders, the emergence of violent gangs calling themselves things like the Gormund Boys and the Red Ravagers – isn't a trend that can stay unnoticed for very long. Kinsey was in the right place at the right time, and had more of the right knowledge than anybody else, to head up a unit specialising in such crimes.

As Malory often has to patiently explain, SCAMs enable their bearers to extract the optimum performance from their minds and bodies through psychological and psychosomatic effects, rather than anything supernatural or paranormal. This trifling detail aside, though, Kinsey's effectively appointed herself officer in charge of the British X-Files, and there's one mystery in particular she's determined to get to the bottom of.

'Which leads me to ask,' she says now, 'was it him? Did Jordan bloody Taylor just burgle the British Museum?'

So far, the Circle has reluctantly tolerated this muscling-in on their territory by the undeviced authorities. Given the Knights' signal lack of success in apprehending Jory so far, there's no harm in having a separate team on the job, and if Kinsey gets lucky they can always sweep in and take charge of her whole operation.

From the expression on Raymond's face, he may be on the verge of changing his mind. He visibly restrains himself from giving Kinsey the dressing-down of her life, however, and instead snaps, 'Parsons. Are forensics finished?'.

Paul glances at his iPad. 'Packing up now, sir,' he says.

'Excellent,' growls the Seneschal, making for the door. 'Have everyone out in fifteen minutes, then let the Chief Inspector's people in. Never let it be said that we don't cooperate with the secular authorities, when pressed.'

'I assume we get to see your forensics results?' Kinsey demands, pressing her probably illusory advantage. 'What's been stolen, anyway? None of our informants knew.'

'Some property of the Circle,' Sir Charles says. 'Of minor historical significance, hence its being held here.'

'Why does he want it?'

Sir Charles stalks out wordlessly, leaving Paul Parsons to answer.

'Because he hates the Circle?' he says. 'You see, the two of you have something in common after all.'

He follows his Seneschal, leaving Stephen and Julian unsure as to whether they've been dismissed. Kinsey glares at them until they clatter out, leaving her alone among the postcards and souvenir mugs.

* * *

The Circle's men return to Kelliwick House in a fleet of eight anonymous grey Ford Transit vans. The anonymity doesn't serve any particular purpose, since the Circle have been openly occupying the museum and are heading back to their acknowledged headquarters, but it's an established habit. When every one of an organisation's senior agents has his own emblem, giving it its own brand identity seems excessive. (The Circle does own some vehicles with logos on them, but they're mostly used for undercover observation.)

The building the vans approach is a concrete block of rampantly monstrous 60s vintage, a dreary place where you might imagine office workers toiling away under fluorescent striplights, since the building seems unusually poorly supplied with windows. Indeed, this is the assumption of most of the casual observers wandering the South Bank of the Thames or staring across from the north. While it's no secret that Kelliwick House, known within the Circle as the Fastness, is the Circle's London address, very few people other than the Circle's most trusted employees have ever been inside.

The Transit van carrying Stephen submits to the same checks as the others – swipe-cards, PINs, passwords exchanged over an intercom with a receptionist on the far side of the building – before passing through a portcullis-like grille into the underground car park. It pulls in smoothly beside the van ahead of it, and disgorges its cargo of men as the next slides in. The car park is shaped like a tinned pineapple slice, a ring surrounding a circle of bombproof concrete into which there is no ingress.

While the men-at-arms file ten at a time into a lift, the Knights proceed up a sunlit stairwell, where they pass a second sequence of security checks to be let through a barrier into the secret interior of Kelliwick House.

The outer part of the Fastness is a mere curtain wall, from which the men-at-arms are now emerging, following their own security procedures. Within it, a courtyard surrounds a state-of-the-art military installation rivalling anything operated by the secular armed forces. The keep extends as far below ground as above (hence the Polo-mint car park), and is surmounted by a frosted-glass roof which hides the building's true design from aerial photographers and the tourists riding the London Eye.

Malory and Jory have been here so many times that they could probably brief an architect to build a duplicate. This is one of the many reasons why the Circle's keen to have words with them.

As usual, the inner space is being used as a parade- and training-ground, with men-at-arms marching and presenting arms (in the form of functionally deadly SIG P226 pistols), squires sparring together and pages being trained in fundamentals like helping someone into their armour. Stephen smiles to see Jason, a page he recruited himself quite recently, gently correcting a peer who's quite keen to squeeze a third lad into an upside-down ceramic breastplate.

He calls Jason over, and, at a nod of confirmation from the Knight supervising them, the page comes to talk to him.

'All right, sir,' he says respectfully. He's about seventeen, with all the awkwardness of his age, but neatly turned-out in the pages' training fatigues.

The pages have a slightly anomalous position in the Circle: technically they're the first rung on the ladder to becoming a Knight, so belong to the officer class; in practice, the demands of squiredom, let alone Knighthood, are too much for most, and many end up in clerical, administrative or manual positions, or as sergeants-at-arms. The fact that, since 1982, the most senior among the Circle's few female employees have held honorary page status contributes to this uneasy balance (though the disgraced Malory Wendiman, always technically freelance, held no rank at all).

Stephen, like most Circle officers who become Knights, became a page on leaving university, but it's not a requirement, and the Circle has full discretion to recruit from whatever constituency it wishes – historically, there've been pages as young as seven or eight. Jason is an unusual, but not a special case; headhunted by Stephen from a local youth club cricket team he coaches in his precious spare time, on the basis of his quick intelligence, resourcefulness and wiry physical strength. Three months after meeting him, Stephen had words with the Circle's recruitment officers. From what Jason tells Stephen, he's told his mum and brother he's been accepted into a military training academy, which is as close to the truth as to make no real difference. In the few months he's been at the Fastness – mostly working in the kitchens, but in the meantime training, as all pages do, in the rudiments of the knightly arts – he's shown enormous promise.

'All going well, Jason?' Stephen asks kindly. 'Missing your people much?'

Jason grins. 'Nah, I love it here – we get to learn to fight with swords and that. Between the chopping and cleaning, I mean.' Apparently concerned at his own informality, he adds, 'I'm having a really nice time, thank you, sir.'

Stephen smiles. 'Good show. Keep at it and you'll be a credit to us all. Carry on, page.'

Jason belatedly remembers to salute him, and scurries back to his training exercises.

Stephen heads for the keep, trudging across the moat, over the swing-bridge and through the final layer of biometric scans. Nothing has yet been said about his punishment, for which he's grateful, but it does feel rather as if he's waiting for the other shoe to drop. All he can do for now is enjoy a welcome shower, then watch the test match on TV until he's summoned, whether it be for duty or discipline. Everything else he feels he could do with – a slimline G&T, some shut-eye, a spot of batting practice with the pages – is going to have to wait.

* * *

When Stephen's summoned, it's to the Seneschal's office, on the ninth floor of the keep. His windows look out towards the curtain wall, and down across the parade-ground. It's two storeys below the glass roof and is one of the best-lit rooms in the Fastness.

'Mukherjee,' the Seneschal says. It's about all the greeting Stephen expects from him, at this point.

Sir Charles is flanked at his desk by the ever-present Parsons and by Mr Lister, one of the Circle's secular advisors. Since Malory turned traitor, and with her father Edward Wendiman out of the picture, Mr Lister appears to have taken on most of the functions of senior advisor to the Seneschal. Even Fr Hywel Evans, the Church of Wales priest who's occasionally filled in for them, is too infirm these days to travel down from Monmouthshire.

Mr Lister smiles. 'Sit down, Stephen,' he says, his voice a plausible imitation of friendly warmth.

Lister disconcerts Stephen. He doesn't know how to treat him. It's not just that he's a civilian, apparently in the confidential counsels of the Circle at the highest level – and look at how well *that* turned out last time – it's that the man's devicial status has never been clarified.

All the Circle's other advisors have borne known devices. In Dr Wendiman senior's case that's Merlin, even if it was last seen incarcerated within some forest-prison of his subconscious. His daughter was thought to be the bondswoman of Nimue, the Lady of the Lake, before that proved to be one of the most disastrous mistakes in the Circle's history. And Fr Hywel bound himself a half-century or more ago to St Dubricius, the Archbishop who crowned Arthur High King and served as his chaplain.

Nobody knows who Lister's device is, even assuming he has one (a Knight can normally tell, of course, but Lister plays his personality so close to his chest he gives almost nothing away). There's rampant speculation, much of it blatantly groundless: Lister's the avatar of Merlin's tutor, Blaise; he's King Pelles, the keeper of the Holy Grail, or of Joseph of Arimathea. Stephen's even heard it claimed that Lister bears the device of Brutus, the original Trojan colonist after whom

Britain is named – at least according to the mythic canon, the Matter of Britain, of which the Arthurian myths are merely the most prominent part.

All these speculations assign Lister some degree of legitimate authority, so Stephen supposes it must be something along these lines. It doesn't make him feel any easier in the man's presence, though.

'About this morning, Mukherjee,' the Seneschal says gruffly. 'May have been a bit hard on you. The Mordred device would get the better of most of us, truth be told. Should have brought the Grail here to the Fastness months ago. Too late now. I blame myself. Partly.' He clears his throat. 'Anyway. Punishment's on hold for now. We're giving you a chance to redeem yourself.'

Relieved and grateful, Stephen says, 'Thank you, sir. I'll rise to the occasion, I promise.'

'Let's hope,' Parsons says, but shuts up when the Seneschal glares at him.

Raymond harrumphs. 'We've got a new quest for you. Something more up your street than guard duty, I should think.'

Mr Lister steps in smoothly. 'What do you know about the British Beasts, Stephen?' he asks.

'I say.' But Stephen's used to being put on the spot by now. He assembles his thoughts. 'Well, they're a motorcycle gang, of course, a jolly violent one. We know they enjoy a spot of drug-dealing, as well as all the usual murder, arson, petty violence and probably a lot of traffic offences. Our chaps think they have animal devices, is that right?' As the last sentence passes his lips, he feels a sudden thrill of interest from his own device.

Lister smiles coolly. 'That's correct, yes. They take their identities from creatures in the Arthurian myths, generally the earlier Celtic iterations. They have three chapters: British Boars, British Wildcats and British Wolves. The choice of *predatory* animals is quite deliberate, naturally: there are any number of horses, stags and even domestic dogs named in the sources which they ignore.

'They're a recently-emerging group,' Lister continues, clearly settling in for a long lecture, 'recruited from a number of existing gangs not known for their devicial allegiances. Their leader and founder is one Mark Addis, formerly of the army's Third Mechanised Division and a biker of long standing, with convictions for violent assault and armed robbery. He belongs to none of the chapters, but uses his own emblem, a snake's head. An adder, I believe.' Again Stephen feels that strange quiver in his device, a little like (although it's a comparison he'd be appalled to think of) the first stirrings of an erection.

'The beast devices are minor ones, of course,' Lister says, 'and have little strategic or planning ability. They have considerable *volition*, however, and their strength of will should not be underestimated. In the story of *Culhwch and Olwen* in the *Mabinogion*, the wild boar Twrch Trwyth devastates a fair proportion of the British Isles in the course of King Arthur's hunt, which I might add it ultimately escapes. The manifestations of its device have been rare, according to the Circle's records, but invariably accompanied by violent disruption. Similarly the Cath Palug, the wildcat which kills nine score warriors in the Welsh *Triads*, and the lycanthrope Gwrgi Garwlwyd in the same source, who killed a man a day.' The Welsh names trip as precisely off his tongue as his fussy English. 'These creatures' current bondsmen are the heads of their respective chapters, and we believe that a number of their underlings also carry devices – there are eight boars named in *Culhwch and Olwen* alone, for instance.'

Sir Charles has been visibly fidgeting during this and now groans. 'Oh, do get to the point, man.'

Stephen has every sympathy with him. Though it hardly compensates for her other flaws, Miss Wendiman knew how to make a briefing interesting.

Lister graciously accedes. 'The point, Stephen, is that these creatures have historically appeared in isolation. Most monstrous devices – the dragon of Grève, the giant Retho, the Llyn Barfog afanc – live solitary lives. A group like the

British Beasts, a concerted attempt to unite such a disparate collection of devices under a single agenda, albeit one we're as yet unsure of, is an anomalous departure. It's unprecedented in our archives, and it could be a *terribly dangerous* development.'

Raymond hurries him along. 'Fact of the matter is, it's part and parcel of the current heightened state of alert.'

'Absolutely,' says Mr Lister. 'Either the disruption to the devicial ecosystem is causing these devices to band together spontaneously, or –'

The Seneschal can wait no longer for the punchline. 'Or someone's putting them up to it. Helping them out and encouraging them. Training them to manage and direct these devices of theirs.'

'Someone's domesticating the Beasts,' says Stephen. 'Some blighter who means to use them against us.'

'And I think we can all guess who, yeah?' Paul's back in the conversation again. 'What we need you to do, Mukherjee –'

'It's all right, Parsons, I can guess,' says Stephen, and indeed it's as obvious to him as the light in the room. 'You need me to ferret out the leader, this Mark Addis, and bring him back here to the Fastness.'

The other men exchange glances. 'Well, that's one approach,' Raymond says. 'Your quest is to disband these British Beasts and arrest all members in possession of devices. The others you can leave for the secular authorities – you'd better liaise with Kinsey's people on that. A squadron of men-at-arms will be at your disposal, more available if you need them. You should find all the information you need on the system.'

Stephen smiles. 'It's a bally honour to be asked, sir.'

* * *

The men in the office sit in silence as Stephen strides off to begin his quest. Then Raymond says, 'Well, that seems to have done the trick.'

'It should keep him out of our hair while we hunt Taylor down,' Parsons agrees. 'He's too close to the whole thing.'

The Seneschal looks annoyed. 'It should achieve a damn sight more than that. The Beasts are an irritation we can do without. Mukherjee's a good man. He'll take them down, I'm sure. He may even lead us to the Green Chapel in the process.'

Paul Parson's lazy smile has always resembled a sneer. The similarity's become more marked over the last year. 'I thought the whole point of the Questing Beast was that they never caught it? No-one did? Palamedes only took over the quest after the Beast's last hunter died on the job.'

Sir Charles grunts. 'Lister?'

Mr Lister's been polishing his glasses. 'Usually, that's the case,' he says, replacing them on his nose. 'But there are a few variants where Sir Palamedes succeeds in capturing or killing it. In the Post-Vulgate Cycle, for example, he prevails with the help of Percival and Galahad after his conversion to Christianity. Not that we're *a hundred per cent* certain that Addis is bound to the Questing Beast, of course. The snake's head would suggest it, but –'

'Looks like the Palamedes device thought so, though,' the Seneschal interrupts.

'Well, that's the main thing,' Paul observes. 'Anything else is a bonus.'

5. JORY TAYLOR AND THE VIZIER

'So, what do you think?' Malory asked Jory, those months ago at the Gardners' house. It was later in the evening, and they'd retired to bed. Though he always loved to hear Malory talk, Jory was beginning to hope that they might soon revert to some of the other things couples like doing when they haven't seen each other in a while. They'd taken the guest bedroom tonight, having left Andrew and Christine's bed somewhat dishevelled the night before.

'It rang a few bells,' he admitted cautiously. 'Bellen and Brelin – are they Sir Balin and Sir Balan?'

If he was honest, Jory only vaguely recalled the legend, which he'd read long ago in the *Morte D'Arthur* by Malory's namesake Thomas. Balin and Balan were knightly brothers, who fatally wounded one another when fighting by mistake, some time after one of them – he could never remember which – had struck the Dolorous Stroke which left the Keeper of the Grail perennially wounded. Their ill-fated devices weren't popular among the Circle, and he couldn't remember hearing of anyone bearing either in recent years.

'Clever boy,' Malory beamed. 'Obviously this has echoes – foreshadowings, if I'm right – of that myth. But there are other signs that this story could be genuinely old, as the scribe claims. The way Joseph blames the Romans for the crucifixion suggests a time before Rome became closely associated with the Church – medieval sources usually blame the Jews instead. And there's numismatic evidence of an actual king called Boduoc in the West Country. This hagiography could potentially pre-date not only the legends of King Arthur, but any historical Arthur there may have been.'

Jory said, 'But Joseph of Arimathea coming to Britain – that's not historical, surely? Isn't that a much later legend?' He put an experimental hand on Malory's thigh.

'I'm not denying there are later accretions,' she said, patting it companionably. 'But Christianity *was* established in Britain by the third century AD, and nobody knows who brought it here first. We've no evidence it wasn't a contemporary of Jesus.'

'Well, OK,' said Jory. 'But if that could be an accretion, why not the rest of it? What evidence have you got that any of this is genuine?'

She pursed her lips. 'None, I suppose. Not that I'd be happy to subject to peer review or publish in a journal. But, you know, the devices have a feel for this kind of thing. Mine especially, as it happens. Now shush,' she added, as Jory tried to object again, 'there's something else. I asked whether the story reminded you of anything.'

Jory groaned. 'Not another test, Mal. It's late, and I've drunk half a bottle of wine.'

'Well, don't imagine you're getting any sleep – or anything else, for that matter,' she added, removing his hand, '– until you've grasped this. Have you heard the Green Chapel's standard account of how Robin Hood became an outlaw? You must have, Dale's telling it all the time.'

(She's exaggerates, Merry does. I like the story, and people keep asking me for it. What am I supposed to do?)

'Yes, I think so,' said Jory. 'Prince John comes to stay at the Earl of Huntingdon's castle where Robin of Locksley works as a steward, and he demands a priceless family heirloom as a gift. Robin's loyal to his master, so he tries to trick the prince out of taking it, but eventually the Earl gives in to the blackmail and gives him the silverware. Later Robin shoots John when he's out hunting and ends up an outlaw as a result. The pain from the arrow-wound – which could well be a metaphor for sexual frustration, *now I come to think of it* – is supposed to explain why John's a moody bastard for the rest of his life. Have I missed anything?'

She smiled. 'Only that the family heirloom is supposedly an antique Saxon silver cup. Otherwise, that's an admirable summary. Now, what about that manuscript I had you read in the Circle library? The one which blends the Green Knight and the Grail legends?'

Jory shook his head. 'Your turn this time.'

She shrugged. 'Fair enough. King Arthur's knight Sir Pelles comes to the giant Sir Bertilacus's castle in the forest and discovers that Bertilacus has somehow come into possession of the Holy Grail, although for some reason he's convinced that what he has is the healing cauldron of the goddess Brigantia. Pelles steals the Grail – although he'd say he was taking rightful custody of it on behalf of the High King – and he and Bertilacus get into a fight. Pelles ends up crippled and becomes the new keeper of the Grail. No-one knows what happens to Bertilacus.'

'Yes, I remember,' Jory said. 'So…?'

Malory threw a pillow at his head. 'But don't you see, you chump, they're all three versions of the *same story?* One's Romano-British, one's Arthurian and one's medieval – their settings are, anyway – but they all have the same basic plot. Someone representing authority visits the remote place where the sacred vessel's being kept. He tries to make away with it, but has to contend with someone who wants it to stay where it is. They fight, the authority figure gets permanently maimed but ends up with the vessel anyway, while his opponent disappears into the woods. The End. Except for the arguments with mermaids.'

Jory tried to pick his way through this. 'OK,' he said. 'But surely in the Robin Hood version, Prince John's the bad guy. In the Arthurian version, Sir Pelles is the hero. Oh,' he added, feeling suddenly stupid.

'You're getting it,' said Malory. 'In the hagiography, Brelin and Bellen are both redeemed – the story doesn't privilege either of them. What we're looking at here could be the origin of the schism.'

Jory tried to marshal his thoughts. 'But if Pelles and John are the same – well yes, of course, Bertilacus must be the equivalent of Robin in the other story, although he's bigger and greener. So which of Brelin and Bellen is which?'

Malory started using her fingers. 'Brelin becomes a hermit in the forest, so he's the Green Man – the Wild Man of the Woods, Jack-i'-th'-Green, whatever you want to call the Robin Hood precursor figure. A woodland spirit, standing in opposition to the settled social order. Then there's Bellen, who's given stigmata he never recovers from. He's the Grail Keeper – by the end of the story, anyway – the Fisher King, the divine monarch whose wound causes the entire realm to fester. Ultimately, he's the same archetype as Arthur himself.'

Jory boggled. 'So this is the actual point where the Chapel and the Circle diverged?'

'Well, neither of them would have been called that then,' said Malory, looking dubious suddenly.

'And it all started in a quarrel between tribal chieftains, refereed by a three-hundred-year-old Joseph of Arimathea?' Jory shook his head. 'Mal, that's not... entirely easy to believe.'

Malory stared at him, then sighed. 'No, you're right,' she said, 'I'm jumping the gun. This can't be the origin, not really. There must be earlier versions, pre-Roman, perhaps even pre-Brythonic. Although I think they'd need to be associated with something that persists as an icon in British legend, the way the Glastonbury Thorn does. I don't see how the breach could have become so definitive of Britishness, otherwise.'

'So the story's no good to us?' Jory asked.

Malory shook her head. 'I wouldn't say that. We can still extrapolate trends. In this early account, the Green Man and the Fisher King are brothers. The Arthurian legend has them representing different worldviews, Celtic and Christian – both intrinsic to the Arthurian tradition, though obviously the story gives preference to the latter. By the Robin Hood tale, they've become deadly enemies, and one's definitely the bad guy. We can see them moving apart as the story evolves. What else?'

'I don't know.' Jory tried the hand-on-thigh gambit again. 'Let's think about it tomorrow, hmm? I'm sure there were other things we wanted to be doing tonight.'

'Hold on a moment,' Malory said. 'I just want to get this straight in my mind. There's the Grail, of course... no, stop it, that's distracting... although it's never *just* the Grail. The hagiography doesn't call it that, the Arthurian version gives it alternative identities, and in the Robin Hood one it's just a valuable cup. I didn't mean *actually* stop, obviously,' she added reproachfully.

'Oh, thank God for that,' said Jory. 'I thought I'd need to have a dolorous stroke myself.'

Malory t'sked at his pun. Then, as Jory carried on with what he was doing, she mused, 'We might need to take a closer look at the Nestine-Gull Grail.'

'Fine,' Jory said, kissing her. 'Stop talking and I'll steal it for you sometime.'

* * *

Between that conversation and the day he honoured his promise, Jory would have a number of conversations with Malory on the subject. He'd also have an encounter which – though at the time it felt like just the sort of incident which had been happening all the time recently – would turn out in the long run to have a greater significance.

A couple of weeks after reading about the saintly brothers Brelin and Bellen, Jory was in Gloucestershire, outside the women's commune where his comrades Scar and Zara – who'd later be in on the museum heist, and would be left arguing whether to buy wood-pellet or recycled-paper cat litter at that Sainsbury's in Islington– were hiding out.

The women (and cats) who lived here permanently had no overt connections with the Green Chapel, and such places tend in general to slip beneath the patriarchal notice of the Circle. The pair were paying their way – not that the other occupants would have phrased it so transactionally, but even so – by giving workshops in self-defence and practical eco-activism.

The commune was a large detached Victorian house, with a sign identifying it as the Modron Dobunna Women's Retreat and Healing Centre. Jory wasn't allowed inside, for what he expected were probably good reasons, and was hanging around on the street instead, very much hoping that Scar's rationale for staying here was a correct one and that he wasn't currently under Circle surveillance. He couldn't see anything he'd identify as a sign of that, but under the circumstances, it would have only been sensible for the Circle to vary its methods.

The Retreat and Healing Centre sign had a five-pointed star above the text, silver on a black background. Jory felt an odd nostalgia for the symbol, which in different colours would have been the emblem – the device, in fact – of Sir Gawain. In this context, it was probably identifying this place as being run by neo-pagans. Jory wondered how Zara – who he knew was as devout, if eccentric, in her faith as Rev was in his – felt about this.

(Probably fine, in fact. The Chapel itself attracts a fair number of recruits from wiccan and related persuasions, and the intolerant don't tend to stay with us long. At the Green Chapel encampment last summer, Jory recalls Shafiq, Zara and Ahmed – a young Somali man who carries the ally of Arthur a'Bland – observing the *salat* as best they could early each afternoon, their unrolled mats aligned southeast-by-east towards Mecca. They still joined in – as did the pagans,

67

Quakers, atheists and the solitary Hindu in the camp – with the communal prayer sessions Rev Cantrell led before each direct action.)

After a while, Zara and Scar emerged.

Scar didn't bother with a greeting. 'This Merry's idea, aye?' She sounded robustly sceptical.

Scar's the dyed-haired, camo-trousered martial artist who'd later cause Julian Blythe such difficulties at the museum: foul-mouthed and Scottish, she despises the Circle more than is mandatory even among her peers. She's tight-lipped on the matter of her background, but she's a Glaswegian of Catholic extraction, an atheist and a lesbian, which in combination suggest some ways she could have ended up with such a combative view of the world. Her choice to wear a blood-red hoodie when the rest of the Chapel are in green is partly traditional, as so much is in our line of work, but suits her habitual bloody-minded bravado perfectly.

'She suggested I take Zara along,' Jory confirmed.

'That's fine to me,' said Zara.

Zara speaks English with a pronounced accent: having grown up in Bosnia in the 1990s, she effortlessly trumps her girlfriend in the 'violent sectarian background' stakes. From the Balkans, she was abducted and basically sold into slavery – the usual term would be 'sex-trafficking', except that that somehow contrives to suggest that fucking is being exported in the abstract, without the unwilling involvement of brutalised human beings. Fortunately Zara's kidnappers brought her to Britain, where the Saracen ally adopted her in short order and assisted her in slaughtering the lot of them. All things being equal, Zara would have been much happier fighting Knights during the museum raid than burgling the Nestine-Gull collection, but needs must.

'And we need to talk to this guy why?' Scar asked Jory.

Jory said, 'He's an Iraqi civil servant of some kind. He's coming over to give the Circle information about a rogue Knight, a man we're interested in.' David Stafford, whose squire Jory once was, has been errant for a while now, and

Malory hopes he can be brought round to the Chapel's way of thinking. His last communication had been full of dark and paranoid speculation about the villainy of Sir Charles Raymond– which had proved, in the final analysis, to be entirely justified when the Seneschal had tried to catapult a faction of neo-fascist device-bearers and their followers into government.

'And Merry thinks what?' asked Scar scornfully. 'Only Za can talk to him 'cause he's a Muslim?'

'Well, apparently he speaks English.' Jory shrugged. 'He went to the London School of Economics. I don't even know that he is a Muslim – I mean, it's likely, but you never know.'

'Then why the fuck?' Scar wondered.

'It's fine,' repeated Zara. 'Merry thinks it's good idea, it's fine.'

'Your choice,' Scar said. She turned her attention to Jory. 'But if the Circle kill you both, I'm gonna dig you up and murder you again.'

'That seems fair,' Jory agreed.

As he left with Zara in the Volkswagen Beetle he was currently using, something occurred to Jory – an association from the Arthurian material he used to saturate his reading with, not only while he was with the Circle but as far back as his boyhood. Something about witches and Gloucester. 'How many women live there?' he asked Zara, nodding back at the Modron Dobunna Centre.

'Some come, some go,' Zara said. 'Nine live there all the time, I think. Why you ask?'

* * *

Zara isn't the world's most garrulous conversationalist, which once upon a time used to bother Jory. By now he'd worked out, though, that she just didn't like talking unless there was important stuff to say. It wasn't because of her English, which was improving all the time – after everything she'd experienced, she was just too mindful of the fact that she was still breathing to want to waste her breath. The two-hour drive, mostly along motorways, would have been a lot more difficult if Jory had been constantly making awkward attempts at small talk, so he was happy to let it slide. As they passed between hedge-hatched fields somewhere between Witney and Eynsham, Zara started to hum something under her breath, something foreign and vaguely folky: a moment later she caught herself doing it and glared at him, daring him to make something of it.

To tell the truth, Jory was a little frustrated to be there. He had a temporary solution in mind for the Chapel's increasingly pressing money issues, and this direct action was keeping him from putting it into practice.

Long-standing Chapel tradition dictates that the majority of the proceeds of any given theft of goods be given away charitably, and even if we bend the rules a little when we're feeling like charity cases ourselves (the Chapel has lots of families with children, unallied grownups who can't work for one reason or another, even a few pensioners who can stand the lifestyle, and it would be irresponsible to make them go hungry), the principle's important even so.

This meant Jory needed a way to acquire a pretty large amount of capital from somewhere. Equally important was that the target of the theft be a deserving one – that's the other half of the 'give to the poor' equation. After some complicated research, and a number of phone conversations with a local Chapel sympathiser named Niamh, Jory had his eye on the Cumbrian operations of a particular high-street bank with a record of investment in environmentally terrible enterprises.

Compared with that urgent necessity, his concern about David Stafford felt like background noise. David was his friend, of course, but Jory had had to leave a fair few friends behind in recent months. He felt some guilt about this, of course – the murder of David's boyfriend and his consequent

70

outing had put a lot of strain on the guy, but it had apparently been Jory's capture by the Green Chapel which tipped him over into his breakdown – but if David was back in the Middle East, there was little Jory could do to help him. Unless this Ibrahim Al-Khuzaie was here to tell the Circle that David was dead, he couldn't see why the Iraqi's visit was so momentous as to force the Chapel to put its plans on hold.

Still, Merry had made the decision, and Jory wasn't about to pick a fight with her. He'd arranged the necessary meetup for the next week instead; in the meantime the Chapel would have to go on managing on the meagre contents of its members' pockets.

* * *

They arrived at Heathrow early and sat near the entrance of the short-stay multi-storey. Jory angled the rear-view mirror to the right height to show him the face of anyone driving through the gate in – for instance – a standard Circle-issue Range Rover, and they waited, drinking inky instant coffee from Jory's thermos and listening to Radio 2 on the fluff-muffled stereo. Both were dressed in civvies: the Chapel hoodies would have been altogether too ostentatious here, a fact they were hoping would work to their advantage later.

Stripped of all its extraneous and contingent detail, their task here was a familiar one: to waylay a traveller journeying from one place to another, and to avail themselves of his valuables. That Ibrahim Al-Khuzaie would be in transit through a major international airport terminal, rather than riding the king's highway through the forest, and that his riches consisted entirely of information, were incidental: the task as outlined was simple for a pair of people with their credentials. The only complication was the Circle – Al-Khuzaie would be met by a Knight at least, probably with a squire in attendance. At least the venue made it unlikely that anybody would be toting a weapon.

At five past one, Jory spotted the vehicle he'd been looking for. Careful to avoid eye-contact, he glanced in the mirror at the driver as it passed. It was Ned Ballard in the driving-seat – a squire, which would be suggestive even if Jory hadn't known whose squire he was. Jory guessed that Paul Parsons wasn't driving so well these days.

'Will it work with him?' Zara asked. The doubly individual qualities of the Knights and their allies make it difficult to lay precise plans against them without knowing who you're dealing with, and Jory had been worrying that they'd need to improvise.

'Should do, probably,' said Jory (whose biggest vice was never overconfidence), and grabbed the holdall from the back seat.

They left the car and hurried towards the footbridge.

* * *

The international arrivals concourse was awash with polyglot humanity: people of all ages, sexes, skin tones and other human categories rubbing up against each other, figuratively and literally. This being an airport, nearly all of them were fretful, half-awake, borderline pissed off or a combination of the three. Those lucky enough to have already found their luggage clutched it tightly, for emotional as well as physical security. This sometimes made them careless of their other possessions.

It took less than a minute for Jory to spot the pickpocket. A small man in a cheap but neatly-ironed suit, he was milling around with the others, looking just as lost as them, occasionally squeezing with loud apologies through the narrow gaps between stressed-looking groups of people, and relieving them of a wallet or phone in passing. He made his bad English work for him, distracting his marks with extravagant malapropisms even as they dismissed him from their concerns. Not an artist, exactly, Jory thought, but a man who took some pride in doing his work well. He'd do.

With a glance back up the stairs to the footbridge – it wouldn't do for Ballard or Parsons to arrive and recognise him – Jory walked over to the little man and put a heavy hand on his shoulder. 'I think you'd better come with me, sir,' he said in his most official voice.

The thief began to argue, then registered the size of Jory and the determination on his face. He decided to come quietly.

* * *

At twenty to two, half an hour after Ibrahim Al-Khuzaie's plane touched down but before the passengers had cleared security, Paul Parsons and Ned Ballard were in the arrivals hall, watching for their Iraqi visitor. Jory and Zara watched them surreptitiously, while making desultory conversation with a group of Canadian tourists across the hall. The Knight and squire were out of uniform – smart business suits, with cotton gloves in Paul's case, and no sign of concealed scabbards.

Parsons was glancing occasionally at his watch but gave few outward signs of complaint. He'd never been a patient man when squired to Jory, but Jory supposed the Sir Lancelot device had changed him. The old Paul would have been seething inside. Ballard, uninspired by his boss's forbearance, was allowing himself the occasional sigh or tut at how long it was taking UK Customs to clear a planeful of passengers from the Middle East. It wouldn't be, as Jory knew from long experience, that he thought the security procedures were too stringent, invasive or ethnically targeted; simply that he thought they shouldn't apply to someone the Circle could vouch for. It would be coming as an unwelcome reminder to both that the Circle's authority wasn't absolute.

Ballard had turned to Parsons to make the sort of sarcastic comment Jory had got tired of from Paul, when the pickpocket, Jorge, brushed too obviously against him. Ned glared at the smaller man, and his hand reached for the pocket which Jorge had just emptied. His eyes widened as he registered the baggy green hoodie the pickpocket was wearing, and Jorge (who, once Jory and Zara had persuaded him that they weren't in fact part of the Met's Aviation Security unit, had turned out to be a perfectly nice guy, eager to do them a favour in return for a hundred quid and not turning him over to the authorities, but a much worse fit in Jory's clothes than Jory himself), took to his heels.

Ballard shouted, 'Stop thief!' and pelted after Jorge. Parsons yelled after him, but Ned was too angry to hear. For a moment the Knight was visibly torn between fulfilling his immediate quest and helping his squire chase down an obvious Green Chapel member, then it occurred to him that his subordinate might be running into a Chapel trap, and he decided they could let Al-Khuzaie cool his heels in the arrivals lounge for a few minutes. He hurtled after Ned and Jorge, yelling, 'Stop! In the name of the Circle!'

Silently, Jory wished the thief all the best. He'd assured them he was quick on his feet, and knew the airport far better than Parsons and Ballard. If he was arrested, though, at least he knew very little that the Circle might find useful.

A moment later, as the first passengers emerged from the arrivals gate, Zara unfolded the cardboard sign with 'AL-KHUZAIE' marker-penned on it in Arabic.

* * *

Ibrahim Al-Khuzaie turned out to be a scholarly, bespectacled man, about sixty years old: though tall, he walked with a distinct stoop. He was friendly, personable and charming, and something about him set Jory's teeth on edge. It couldn't be pure xenophobia – Jory had served with David Stafford in Iraq, rooting out the errant Knight Clifford Chalmers from his mountain base near Mosul, and he had never experienced an unreasoning dislike of the local population. (And even if he had, the Chapel would have trampled it out of him since then.)

Jory introduced himself as Paul Parsons, on the grounds that that was probably who Al-Khuzaie was expecting, and Zara as his personal assistant Miss Mahmoud, on the assumption that the Iraqi wouldn't know the Circle's workings in enough detail to realise how unlikely this was.

Dismayingly, their visitor had a minder of his own, a blocky Middle Eastern guy in the traditional black-tie-and-suit combo, but after sizing Jory up the older man turned and spoke to him rapidly in Arabic. The bodyguard protested, but eventually gave a moody nod and stalked off in the direction of Starbucks. Jory felt rather than saw Zara's body tense slightly as the prospect of immediate fighting receded.

'I can talk more freely in his absence,' Al-Khuzaie explained, in excellent English. 'He is an employee of my government, and besides, he's not so familiar as we' – he included Zara, with a charming smile – 'with the matters your Circle wishes to discuss.'

Jory suggested tactfully that a less public place – an exclusive restaurant in nearby Hounslow, for example – might be a more conducive spot for their discussion, and led him uncomplaining to the Tube station. Zara produced three anonymous Oyster cards and beeped them through.

'May I telephone my escort and tell him I might be some while?' Al-Khuzaie asked, as their crowded train chuntered off in the direction of Hatton Cross. 'He might begin to worry about me and create embarrassment.'

'Perhaps I could borrow your phone and make the arrangements?' Jory asked equally politely, although he was growing increasingly irritable. If Paul and Ballard hadn't yet discovered that their guest was missing, it could only be a matter of minutes, and he doubted it would be within the bodyguard's powers to reassure them.

It was probably at this point that Al-Khuzaie realised that he was being kidnapped. He took it calmly enough, though. Perhaps (as Malory had presumably hoped) Zara's presence helped keep him at his ease, or perhaps he'd been menaced so many times in his native region that two rather polite Brits (one admittedly by adoption) couldn't much intimidate him. Possibly he was just very good at poker.

In any case, he showed no outward signs of dismay as Jory pocketed the phone.

If anyone else in the carriage noticed the discrepancy, they showed no curiosity about it. Most likely they had their own concerns.

* * *

On their way out of Hounslow station, they passed a young man doing card tricks on a foldaway table, surrounded by a small but enthusiastic audience. 'Where's that ace?' he was saying, holding up a man's wallet. 'You saw me put the ace of hearts in here, right, but where's that ace now?' Jory made only the most fleeting eye contact with him as he and Zara walked Al-Khuzaie to a coffee-shop across the road.

'If I may ask,' Al-Khuzaie asked when their drinks arrived, 'to whom am I speaking? Evidently you are not Mr Parsons, and I do not believe that your, ah, "device" is as Mr Parsons's was described to me.'

Jory nodded respectfully, trying not to let his annoyance show. There's an etiquette to this kind of encounter, and he owed his abductee the courtesy of following it. 'My name's Dan,' he told Al-Khuzaie. 'This is Zara. We're members of a group called the Green Chapel. Our devices...' he paused. 'We represent an alternative strand of British folklore. I imagine you've heard of Robin Hood?'

Al-Khuzaie nodded. 'Of course. In this case I presume I may rely on your word that I will not be harmed if I give what you need?'

'Naturally,' Jory replied. 'All you have to do is tell us what we need to know.' He was beginning to suspect that he could guess what had been winding him up, and it really wasn't the fault of this placid old man. 'You seem very well-informed about the devices, Mr Al-Khuzaie. Do you have an affiliation of your own?'

Al-Khuzaie nodded proudly. 'I have the privilege to be accompanied by the *qarin* of Ja'far ibn Yahya, grand vizier to the Caliph Harun Al-Rashid. At one time a real man, he is remembered to the world now primarily through the compendium of stories you refer in English to as *The Thousand and One Nights*.'

This meant very little to Jory. He'd heard of the book (which he associated with stories like Aladdin, Ali Baba and Sinbad), and he had an approximate idea of what a vizier did, but that was about it. He was ashamed to reflect that Al-Khuzaie's unprepared knowledge of Robin Hood was evidently more extensive, although admittedly Al-Khuzaie must have spent more time in Britain than Jory had in Iraq.

It did confirm his guess, however. Interaction with the deviceplexes of foreign cultures is notoriously tricky, except in those rare cases where the bodies of myth overlap. Jory's only prior experience of such contact had been some years before, when he was detailed to liaise with a representative of the Paladins de la Republique who was hunting down a French-Algerian criminal in London. His culture-shock then had been fairly mild, since the Paladins' chivalric values and northern European medieval worldview are a close match for those of the Circle. If Sir Gawain and Roland's companion Huon of Bordeaux had ever met, they'd have been able to converse within a largely overlapping frame of reference, and so Jory and the chevalier's *porteuse du blason*, Marie-Odile Laclos, had found each other tolerable company. Indeed, the main thing that had disconcerted Jory was discovering that the Paladins admitted women as bearers of knightly devices.

This felt different. Now Jory was aware of what was happening he could feel his ally trying its hardest to respond to the presence of another device, meshing their stories in the traditional way: with so few narrative assumptions in common, however, there was nothing for it to get traction on. It felt like gears in his head, grinding frantically away against nothing at all. If anything Zara, whose ally was ultimately derived from a medieval Christian crusader's view of the Muslim world, would be feeling even more of a culture-clash with this authentically Arabian device. Jory glanced across at her, and saw that her face was even more blank and expressionless than usual.

He took a deep breath. 'I understand you're here – in the UK I mean – to bring news to the Circle,' he told Al-Khuzaie. 'Confidential news presumably, since it couldn't be entrusted to email. We believe that it relates to an old friend of mine, a Knight named David Stafford. Is that right, sir?'

'It might well be,' Al-Khuzaie replied. 'The person in question certainly claims to be a Knight, and some of my countrymen believe they recognise him from a Circle action in the Mosul area some years ago. Does that sound like your friend Mr Stafford?'

Jory nodded. 'And what were you going to tell Paul Parsons about this man?'

Al-Khuzaie settled himself comfortably back on the black-upholstered bench, sipped his espresso, and stared dreamily into space. 'Six months ago in Baghdad,' he said, 'a family belonging to one of our many minority religions were walking in the street when they drew the attention of a group of young men. The men began to shout abuse at them, calling them devil-worshippers. The confrontation quickly moved beyond mere words, however, and the men shamefully began to throw stones at this family, including their old women and children. At once, and much to the surprise of everyone involved, a newcomer dressed all in black arrived, drew a sword, and with cries of savage anger chased the gang away.

'I do not know how familiar you are with twenty-first-century Iraq, my friends, but I can assure you that that detail – the rescuer's choice of weapon – is far from routine. Equally astonishing was how the man was dressed: in all-black armour, of a modern design, which led some onlookers to believe that he belonged to the one of the insurgent armies from the north. He wore no insignia, however, and the shield he carried was as black as his armour.

'This event occurred, as I say, in the capital. A few days later, this man – or at least a man identically dressed and armed – was seen tinkering with the undercarriage of a van outside a private house in Basra, in the south of the country. The expression on his face and the speed of his gestures betrayed a great urgency, though when passers-by spoke to him he seemed calm enough. From his armour, and because the house belonged to a translator for an American diplomat, they assumed that he was a bomb disposal expert, and when the police arrived they did indeed discover that he had been disarming an explosive mechanism which could have killed many people.

'The police were unable to elicit the man's name, and he told them that he was currently without loyalty to any sovereign. He was evidently a European, however, and one of the officers believed that he sounded British.

'When this report crossed my desk, I realised that this must be the same man who had defended the family in Baghdad – an incident which I already knew I must find out more about. You must understand that I belong to a brotherhood, an alliance of men within our government each of whom is honoured by the presence of the *qarin* of a person from our cultural heritage. We lack the power and prestige of your Circle, but in our humble way we strive to guide the affairs of our ancient nation. One of my brothers was involved in the official liaison with your Circle forces near Mosul during their campaign against the mercenary Al-Wasati – the prodigal Mr Clifford Chalmers – and from his account I recognised this man's description as matching that of a Knight of the Circle.

'I made discreet enquiries of certain contacts of mine in Mosul, which lies in the zone now occupied by Islamist insurgents, and from them I was able to ascertain that there, too, the armoured man had been seen – and that he had been recognised by some as the commander of that very Circle action, though without the offensive Crusader garb which he wore during that campaign.'

Jory was in no doubt now that the Knight was David Stafford. His device was – or had been, perhaps, if he'd really changed his shield – that of Sir Galahad. Their experiences in Iraq had confirmed that the emblem of a red cross on a white background held unrelated, but deeply unfortunate, associations for people in the Middle East.

'I investigated further,' Al-Khuzaie continued, 'and found that this man – this Black Knight, as I naturally came to think of him – had been seen in many places, not merely in Iraq but across our borders. He had assisted many to escape the occupied zone who were being ill-treated there: Christian families, government loyalists, homosexuals. A tiny proportion of those suffering, of course.

'In Saudi Arabia, the Black Knight rescued a young girl from being stoned for adultery after she was assaulted by her stepfather. In Khorramabad in Iran, when the police began shooting protestors who were demonstrating against the government, he rescued many of the wounded from the melee. In Gaza, the man had attacked a group of Israeli soldiers who were shooting at a young Palestinian boy, saving his life. Days later, the same Black Knight decapitated another Palestinian youth, a suicide bomber, before he was able to martyr himself at one of the illegal Israeli settlements.

'You must understand that many of the injuries which this Black Knight sought to prevent through violence of his own were everyday events: deplorable perhaps, but accepted as normal, sanctioned by cultural expectations or even given the blessing of a state. He bore the values of a Westerner with him like a flag, this Knight, and already he was becoming an urban myth. How could he not? Scores of people owed their lives to him. He wandered like a knight across a chessboard, seeking trouble wherever it might be found, and intervening to protect whoever he believed was being victimised.'

It was pretty much the definition of errantry – a deeply unfashionable concept among the Circle, in these days of global travel, instant communication and potentially explosive international relations, but one with a venerable tradition among the Knights of less disciplined past eras.

'Now, this behaviour of his might seem admirable,' Al-Khuzaie said 'to those who prize human life above such qualities as morality, honour, or sovereignty. For our part, my brothers and I, we had already endured the interference of one rogue Knight of the Circle in our territory. We were unwilling to tolerate another such, even before the other nations I have mentioned began accusing us of harbouring a Western terrorist.

'I resolved then that I must meet this man.'

Zara's mobile chimed, and she checked it, tutting. 'Dan, it is Burn,' she interjected. The young street-conjurer was an excellent lookout, though not an inconspicuous one. 'He says there Circle men outside the underground station – six soldiers and a Knight.'

Damn, Jory thought. Paul must have guessed that Al-Khuzaie had taken the Tube and called in reinforcements to search further up the line. They needed to leave, now. They'd already abandoned the Beetle, knowing that a quick getaway would be crucial; their friend Lee, the Chapel member allied to the obscure Merry Man Gilbert Whitehand, should be waiting round the corner in a freshly-stolen car, to extract them via the M4 once they had the information they needed.

The two of them might possibly make it round the corner to the vehicle unrecognised – the Circle wouldn't be looking for Jory and Zara particularly, and if they could avoid their faces being seen, there was a good chance they'd pass unnoticed – but taking Al-Khuzaie with them was clearly out of the question.

'And did you, sir?' Jory asked urgently. 'Did you meet David Stafford?'

Ibrahim Al-Khuzaie smiled, drained his coffee, and signalled for a waiter to bring him another. 'I suggest that you leave, friends. I will allow you ten minutes, then settle the bill here and stroll out to meet Mr Parsons' colleagues.'

Zara had already removed her headscarf and was shaking out her long black hair, something she did only to avoid recognition at times of danger. 'Dan, we go *now*,' she insisted, and Jory knew she was right.

* * *

That evening Jory was back with Malory again, for another council-of-war and lover's tryst. This time they were in the distinctly less lavish surroundings of a backpackers' hostel near Manchester Piccadilly station, into which Malory had checked them using a pair of Australian passports she'd produced from her denim holdall, and a dubious accent which she insisted was authentic Tasmanian. For his part, Jory was doing his best to keep his mouth shut, especially when there were real Aussies around, which was almost constantly.

For now, though, they were squeezed into their cramped room, Jory sitting on the plastic chair with his legs stuck awkwardly beneath the lower bunk-bed, on which Malory was stretching like a cat.

'Burn stayed in position,' he told her. 'He saw Al-Khuzaie come out and meet the Knights, just like he said he would. He seemed very mellow about the whole thing, he said. Then they drove off together in a Range Rover.'

'So we don't know what interaction Al-Khuzaie's had with David, but the Circle do?' she asked.

Jory nodded. 'He was spinning out the story, waiting for them to come and let him off the hook. I should have hurried him along, but… well, it seemed rude. He was in full flow.'

Malory smiled ruefully. 'He found a way for his device to influence yours. Storytelling's a human universal, and *The Thousand and One Nights* is packed to the rafters with nested narratives. Naturally his device would be expert at it. He's obviously as clever and devious as you'd expect from a grand vizier.'

Jory groaned. 'Of course. And now the Circle know whatever he was going to tell us about David. For all we know, Al-Khuzaie's "brotherhood" have killed him.'

Malory considered. 'Not easy. Galahad's one of the strongest devices in the corpus. With a tendency towards

82

self-sacrifice, of course, but they wouldn't know that unless the Circle's actively helping them. I'm guessing that help was what Al-Khuzaie came to the UK to ask for.'

'I'm not even sure David's allied to Galahad any more,' Jory said. 'Al-Khuzaie said he's carrying a black shield. The Black Knight of the Black Lands is still taken, isn't he?' That avatar was one Jory himself had defeated while working with the Circle, in an exhausting swordfight at a bus station in West Bromwich.

'Still in the Benwick Institute, the last I heard,' Malory confirmed. 'Still missing that leg.'

'So what other Black Knights are there?' Jory asked.

'Oh, dozens,' Malory said. 'The Black Knight of the Fountain, the Black Knight of the Mountain, the Black Knight of the Black Forest, Sir Maduk the Black, Sir Baruc the Black... they're all over the place. Sometimes they're other knights in disguise, like Lancelot. Not Galahad, as far as I recall, but... well, it's a common trope, so I wouldn't be surprised. There's no way to guess what David's new allegiance means without more information.'

'Which the Circle has, and we haven't,' Jory grumbled.

'Well yes, but there's no point moping about it,' she said briskly. 'I wish I'd realised Al-Khuzaie had a device – I'd have gone to interview him myself. It would have been interesting research. SCAM studies are terribly insular – I know a bit about the European and North American ones, but nothing about the Middle East. What was the word you said he used?' She pulled an iPad from her bag and booted it up.

'For his device? *Qarin*, I think,' said Jory.

She tapped the onscreen keyboard. 'Probably spelled with a Q if it's Arabic... Yes, here we are. Hmm... looks like a kind of personal djinn, whose job is to tempt the believer to do un-Islamic stuff. Mohammed managed to convert his, apparently.' She read on. 'It means "companion", and the concept predates Islam. Kind of like Socrates' daemon, I guess – that term's acquired negative connotations, too.'

Jory sighed. 'Well, this is fascinating, Mal, but...'

'Sorry – I'll look later,' she said. 'Look, here's something you'll find interesting.'

She passed Jory the tablet, showing him a folder with a sequence of thumbnail images. They seemed to be pages of an ancient manuscript. Jory called one up and peered at it in more detail. The resolution was excellent, enough to show that this was far older than the commonplace book Malory had showed him before. The pages were unbound, the paper curling and crumbling at the edges, which seemed to be resting on a wooden surface. Jory could only speculate about how much the document might be worth.

'Another book,' he observed. 'What is it?'

'I *think*,' said Malory, with just a trace of smugness, 'it's the oldest extant account of the schism between the Green Man and Wounded King devices. It's in Latin, on vellum of about the fifth century CE, which makes it one of the oldest manuscripts in the British Isles. Among many other things, it proves that the legend of Britain being founded by refugees from Troy is centuries older than Nennius. It's never been properly studied. It's been sitting in the Circle's archives for… well, possibly as long as there's been a Circle. If the current archivist hadn't digitised a stack of seventeenth-century catalogue cards without due care to information security, I'd never have found it.'

'The Circle put this on the web?' Jory boggled.

'Ha.' Malory smirked. 'No, but the digital archive's accessible from the top level of the Circle's intranet, and I've still got a backdoor to that. Another kind of trojan, in fact. No, Squig had to get into the archives physically with a high-definition digital camera, and scan these while the custodian was having lunch.'

'Really?' Jory was astonished. Squig's a teenage graffiti artist, the youngest allied member of the Green Chapel, and indeed the youngest device-bearer Jory's met (though Malory apparently acquired hers when she was thirteen). This is because his ally is Much the Miller's Son, a general-purpose Merry Man mostly distinguished by his youth, who's nevertheless there in most versions of the story. Squig's not that handy in a fight, but he's our most adept housebreaker and burglar.

Even with his significant advantages, though, sneaking into the Circle's barely-used and tightly-guarded subterranean repository of ancient texts was nothing short of a masterwork. 'You must have really wanted it,' Jory concluded mildly.

'I thought it was going to be the key to everything,' Malory sighs. 'In fact it's just more of the same. They've made the clash between the Trojan Britons and the pre-Trojan Albionites, and the sacred vessel's become a lake. The weapon's bigger too, but otherwise... it's just the same pattern, over again. Well, nearly. There's a surprise ending, but it's not much help to us.

'We need a new approach to this, I think,' she said. 'And we're definitely going to have to get hold of that cup.'

* * *

The pages Squig scanned (which will later, you'll be pleased to hear, be made available to scholars and the public, and will become known as the Kelliwick Manuscript) are incomplete and damaged: they were kept in a sealed box for centuries, but Squig's inexpert handling wasn't good for them, and in the coming years Malory's scan will, in fact, be a better source for the text than what remains of the document itself. The partial text isn't always easy to make sense of, if you're a historian or a bibliographer.

But... I'm a storyteller. This is what I do. And my best go at retelling what would seem to be the basic story in those pages goes like this.

'When the descendants of the Trojans first appeared in this isle, it was known as Albion (for the name Britain came first from their leader, Brutus), and it was inhabited not by men, but by giants of huge and terrifying aspect. Some of these the invading Trojans fought back to the wild places of the island, where they persisted in caves and forests, in smaller and smaller numbers, until at the present time only a handful are left. Others they took prisoner, such as the twelve-foot monster with whom Corineus of Cornwall wrestled before pitching him into the sea at Totnes.

'A few, though, were peaceably inclined, not warriors but farmers or herdsmen, and some of these were permitted to live companionably alongside Brutus's people, the newly-named Britons. One such was a female, coarse of feature yet of gentle disposition, who became the wife of the Trojan Hellius.

'Hellius was one of Corinaeus' followers, who had been said since his birth, because of his great beauty, to be the son of the sun-god Apollo. Because of his divine ancestry, he had always scorned to marry a mortal woman, but when he met the female giant, whose name was Alba, he declared that at last he had met a mate worthy of him. The two were married, and founded the settlement in Cornwall which is now known as Helston.

'In time, and after a long confinement which she did not survive, Alba bore Hellius twin sons. Half-giant, and, if the stories were true, one-quarter god, the boys grew to be eight feet tall by their sixteenth birthday, with handsome countenances favouring their father, who nonetheless loved them for their dead mother's sake. They lived among the Britons as other men, and it would have been a brave man who questioned their right to do so.

'Despite this, one of the brothers was curious about his mother's people, the giants of Albion, and when he came of age he left his father's lands to seek them out in their wild forest and mountain places, and to learn more of them and their ways. This brother was called Madog. The other brother, Gor, had no mind for such things, declaring that he was a Briton like his father, and like all the children of Troy in this land, and that the origins of a mother he had never known were no concern of his.

'Now, this was at the time when King Brutus, by then an old man, was establishing the city of Troy Novant, the capital of Britain, which would one day become known as London. The site he had chosen, near the mouth of the River Thames, was forested, and contained many lakes and pools. Hellius and Gor travelled with many other Cornishmen to help with the work, of felling the trees and draining the ponds, and Gor's great strength was of much avail in their hard physical labours.

'One day, Gor and his men were told to clear a grove of trees surrounding a pool which stood some little way from the river, the other side of the hill which is now known for King Lud's Gate. This was the site where Brutus had decreed his palace should be built.

'The men would have set to with the same will as ever, had not a few of the native giants appeared, suddenly and silently, at the pool's margin, and with them Madog, son of Hellius. Gor greeted his brother with delight, but Madog reproached him bitterly, telling him that the pool he was about to drain was sacred to their native ancestors, and that it and the grove in which it stood must be allowed to stand.

'Gor laughed heartily, asking whether Brutus' magnificent new palace should be built around a marshy copse of trees, to satisfy the superstition of such savages? This angered Madog, who, casting around for a weapon, laid his hands upon a young tree growing in the well, some ten feet tall and as thick around as a strong man's thigh. This he wielded as a club, striking his brother and crying that the trees he sought to fell would fell him instead.

'The blow was powerful enough to split the skull of any ordinary man, but Gor was only stunned. As he fell, he clutched at his brother, and both men tumbled into the pond. Gor's men tried to pull them free, but the brothers' great weight bore them down into the water. One of the men thought to plead with Madog's giants for their aid, but the savages turned and vanished into the woods, and were never seen again.

'When the pool was drained, the brothers' bodies were recovered, embracing in death. Heartbroken by the deaths of his sons, Hellius ordained that their bodies be burned in accordance with the customs of Troy, but that first their heads should be cut from their shoulders, and buried after the fashion of their mother's people. So great was Hellius' grief that none dared gainsay his odd request.

'So the brothers' bodies were burned, and what became of their ashes no-one knows, but the heads of Gor and Madog are buried beneath what became King Brutus' palace, and it is said that their spirits still watch over and protect the city whose building caused their deaths. But over the centuries their true names have been lost and confused with those of the giant whom Corineus had earlier defeated, and they are now known to the people of London as Gog and Magog.'

6. STEPHEN MUKHERJEE'S PAGE

It's a week now since the theft at the British Museum, and Stephen Mukherjee's pursuit of British Beasts hasn't progressed very far. It has, however, chased out something rather startling along the way.

It's not been glamorous work: mostly it's consisted of tracking paper trails and spying by proxy. The first stage was to read all the existing files – mostly from various police operations, rather than the Circle's own – on the known members of the gang. (The Circle archives hold records of the past bearers of the animal devices back to the 1300s, but they're less immediately relevant.) One thing Stephen learned almost immediately was that Mark 'Adze' Addis was incarcerated in the same nick as 'Big Jack' Bennett, though they weren't cellmates and there's no record of how well they knew each other.

He then bugged the phones of all the members whose numbers he can identify – mostly the junior, undeviced bikers in each of the three beastly chapters. For the time being, the chapter heads – the bearers of the Twrch Trwyth, Cath Palug and Gwrgi Garwlwyd devices – and especially the enigmatic Addis, elude him.

Through the phone-tapping he learned that the Beasts were joining a biker rally planned last Saturday, at a particularly notorious pub off the M6. He considered various options, up to and including compulsorily purchasing the pub and staffing it entirely with men-at-arms, but concluded that the bikers would inevitably be friendly with the current management.

Eventually he settled on placing men-at-arms in leathers among the bikers in attendance, to stroll around taking note of faces and – probably more usefully – the custom paint-jobs on the British Beasts' bikes. Despite the occasional altercation with an overprotective bike-owner, the men successfully avoided blowing their cover, and by Sunday – after the bikers had dispersed, setting light to a nearby barn and causing havoc at various petrol and service stations at receding distances from the pub – Stephen had detailed descriptions of many of the Beasts' motorcycles, including those ridden by the three chapter heads. (Annoyingly, Adze himself seems to have been absent.)

Stephen then detailed men-at-arms of a more clerical bent to search the national police database for incidents involving bikes matching these descriptions. On the basis that the heads of chapters' bikes were emblazoned with a boar, a wolf and a wildcat, he hazarded a guest that Addis's might be painted like a snake, and had them look for that too.

(In this, Stephen is sadly mistaken. Adze does, as Mr Lister said, use an adder's head as his symbol – the bikers' equivalent of the heraldic emblems the Knights wear on their riot-shields – but it's painted on his helmet. He wears leathers painted with scales, too, but the Norton he rides has a leopard-spot pattern, shading into the dun of a lion's haunches at the rear.

If it seems odd that it doesn't occur to Stephen for the moment that he, of all Knights, is pursuing, not a snake, but the Questing Beast itself – well, that's the story-blindness that so often accompanies the holding of a device. Our allies may enhance the workings of the mind in most respects, but in some ways they make us surprisingly dim. Well-read, intelligent men and women, who are well aware of what they signed up for, somehow fail to spot when they reach the crux of their adopted story, ignoring the obvious right up to – and often beyond – the moment it's pointed out to them. It's what got Shafiq killed: when he responded to the Circle drugging him by shooting an arrow out of a hospital window, his death became basically inevitable.

Any other Knight could work out quickly enough what Stephen's missing, but the Circle have no system for examining each other's work for this kind of lapse. That would impugn their honour, or something. This is how Al-Wasati and his predecessors conned them, of course: every generation, the Circle treats the bearer of the Sir Mordred device as loyal until, inevitably – unless he dies first – he betrays them horribly. It wouldn't be sporting otherwise.)

No sign, then, of a snake-painted bike – but in another respect, Stephen was in luck. One of the many reports sent to his desk was an incident where a neighbour had seen a man and two women assaulted, and a fence vandalised, by someone riding a bike painted with Cavan 'Torch' Sturrock's fearsome boar. In itself the account was unexceptional, but the location and timing – a couple of hours after and a few miles away from Stephen's encounter with the Green Chapel at the British Museum – prompted him to investigate further.

Commandeered CCTV tapes from various local businesses yielded images of Sturrock on his bike, moments before he must have arrived at the squat – and, twenty minutes later, of Jordan Taylor and two other known Green Chapel associates strolling through the estate to greet him.

* * *

'This is good work, Mukherjee,' the Seneschal says when Stephen brings him his report. 'Not the job we gave you, of course, but fine work all the same.'

91

'I'm still beavering away at the quest, sir, believe me,' Stephen says. 'But I could hardly let this pass us by.'

'Indeed not.' Sir Charles peers at the static image on the large wall-mounted screen in his office. It shows Taylor, Jack Bennett, Franklin Cantrell and the Chapel members Stephen's identified as Alice Dashwood and Elaine Wardsley bundling into a blue Ford Escort. With two of the passengers being quite large men, it's looking pretty cramped in there.

Parsons is here, inevitably, ever Sir Charles' right-hand man despite his own misfortune in that area. The third person of their trinity, Mr Lister, is away on a visit to the Benwick Institute. Parsons points to the screen, where Dashwood's hand is bandaged, and Wardsley holds a bundled-up rag to her nose and asks, 'Any idea what happened here?'

'I expect it's the assault the witness reported,' Stephen says. 'I suppose Sturrock was to be the courier for the Grail, but there must have been some kind of contretemps. Sturrock clonks Dashwood and Wardsley, then swans off on his motorbike while the others make for the hills. There's no way to know whether he took the Grail with him or not.'

'There wouldn't be,' Raymond grumbles. 'Can we get the number of that car?'

'Of course, sir,' Stephen says, calling up another image with a clearer view of the number-plate. His voice holds not a trace of smugness, and he'd be puzzled if anyone suggested it should. 'I've already traced it: it was found abandoned recently in Bristol. I've got the police there looking for all five of them – and Sturrock, of course, just in case. They know they've to wait for us before taking action.'

'Too much to hope the buggers will still have the Grail, I suppose,' the Seneschal mused. 'Or that they'll still be together, come to that. Still, with luck we can nail a couple of them. Well done again, Mukherjee.'

'I'll head down to Bristol today, then, sir, and take charge of the search?' Parsons said immediately. He's proprietorial about the Green Chapel quest, which Stephen understands, although it's not as if he's the only one with a personal dislike of the Chapel. Stephen's a little disappointed to be sidelined, but he knows his primary quest is for the Beasts.

'I only hope Taylor's still there,' mutters Raymond. 'Him or that Cantrell fellow.' Though Taylor's defection to the Chapel is a source of bitterness for everyone in the Circle, topped only by that of the trusted Malory, the Seneschal's become oddly fixated on Cantrell over the past month. He's a staunchly unimaginative Anglican himself, and he finds the idea of a priest with radical views, and the willingness to back them up with action, a personal affront.

The Tud House incident didn't help, of course.

* * *

Until a couple of months ago Edward Wendiman – retired Knight of the Circle, bearer of the Merlin device, once the Circle's most senior advisor and in his daily life an academic futurologist and father of Malory – was a patient at Tud House, the Circle's medical facility in Norfolk, suffering from advanced senile dementia. The condition came on the octogenarian suddenly last year, and the general belief among the Circle is that the Merlin device had been preventing its onset for some time.

On one level, the device failing in its task, allowing the dementia to advance and occupy Wendiman's brain, is an inevitable part of Merlin's story: the wizard is imprisoned forever in the enchanted forest of Broceliande – sometimes by Nimue, the Lady of the Lake, sometimes by the sorceress Morgan le Fay – at just the point when Arthur needs his counsel the most.

It's a standard storytelling motif, of course – Gandalf, Dumbledore and the prophet Elijah, to pick three similarly wizardly types, are removed from the picture at critical junctures for their protégés – but even so, someone has to be the Darth Vader to their Obi-Wan Kenobi. In this case, the Circle's consensus assumes it was Malory herself – once accepted as the bondswoman of Nimue, now believed to harbour the device of Morgan le Fay, and perhaps the country's leading expert in the workings of the devices – who somehow disabled the Merlin device, opening the way for her father's senility in the process. It's not a pleasant thing to think a fellow human being capable of, and Stephen does his best not to dwell on it.

This became more difficult a month ago, when it became clear that Malory wasn't finished with Edward yet. She'd been denied visiting privileges, of course, since her betrayal of the Circle – if she'd turned up at Tud House, she'd have been arrested like a shot – and the old man had no other living relatives, but when a kindly vicar who claimed to be an old friend of Wendiman's late wife asked to visit, he was allowed in to see the patient.

Truth be told, it's unlikely he'd have been excluded in any case – unlike the Benwick Institute (which is a psychiatric prison in all but name), Tud House isn't a secure facility, and the main obstacle to visiting is finding out where it actually is. The fact that the Reverend Fryer claimed to have been given the address by Malory, who was in sporadic email contact with him, meant that Sir Charles personally ordered the Tud House management to keep on his good side. One Harry Plaice, the device-holder of Sir Geraint who was recuperating at the facility after a run-in with the avatar of the villainous Count Galoain the Brown, was tasked with engaging Fryer in casual conversation during his visit, and probing him about his contact with Malory.

Prior to this point, no-one loyal to the Circle had met Rev Cantrell – or only when Rev was one anonymous hoodie-wearing Merry Man among many. A later background check would reveal that Dr Wendiman's visitor hadn't after all been the Reverend Hubert Fryer, vicar of Wootton-under-the-Water in Somerset, but was in fact one Franklin Joseph Cantrell: a US citizen, born 1958, ordained in the Episcopal church 1982, emigrated to the UK 1987, at which point he ceased to have any formal relationship with the church and instead embarked on a criminal career involving offences such as riot, theft, affray and gross indecency in public lavatories. At the time, though, keen to follow the Seneschal's direction and tread gently, Tud House accepted his credentials, and his reminiscences of friendship with the family, as genuine.

The menial staff at the facility also failed to suspect that anything was amiss when the local laundry which supplied their cleaning needs sent a different van-driver – a woman who, if they'd been paying attention, a couple of them might have found hauntingly familiar from the days when she *had* been allowed to visit her father. In the end, the loss of one of the facility's wheelchairs was the first thing anyone noticed, shortly before Harry Plaice knocked on Dr Wendiman's door to find him, his guest and all his possessions missing.

(The laundry owner and her usual driver were later found tied up in their office, with an envelope containing a large sum of money to compensate them for the inevitable loss of business. Their van was found abandoned on a roadside verge just outside Norwich.)

Sir Charles' fury on this occasion had been epic – and all the bitterer for knowing that his eagerness to find Malory had helped her underhand scheme to succeed. It was Cantrell's flawless performance as a harmless parish priest which convinced everyone involved, however, and the Seneschal's reserved a special animosity for him.

What happened to Edward Wendiman after this is a matter for conjecture as far as the Circle's concerned. Working theories as to why Malory kidnapped her father include that she felt unexpectedly guilty about what she'd done to him, or that she was afraid – either that he might recall some piece of information which could betray the Chapel, or of what the Circle might do to him in its efforts to get back the counsel of the Merlin device.

Wendiman's death would, after all, free up the device to adopt another host, and it's not as if he had much quality of life remaining. Under the circumstances a trip to an exclusive clinic in Switzerland might not have looked so very tragic.

* * *

Stephen's feet are getting itchier by the hour, but he goes dutifully back to his police reports. What he really wants to do is get out in the field and – preferably after a bit of a scrap – bring in some of the British Beasts for questioning, but he knows that isn't the wisest approach. Instead, he goes methodically through the remaining incident reports, searching for anything that seems unusual, or which might be a clue as to where Addis is keeping himself.

The Circle is stretched at present ('It's getting like the Oval around here, eh?', the bearer of the Sir Dagonet device, Desmond Wigsby, put it to Stephen the other day), as devicial crime increasingly proliferates across the ancient bounds of Arthur's realm. The psychic stress of the conflict with the Chapel has been bringing the more dangerous devices out of the woodwork, and taking most of the Knights away on various quests.

Parsons is on his way to Bristol already, with two other Knights, their squires and a squad of men-at-arms. Theo Harte is in Salford, investigating the Bronze Bowl Murders and trying not to bump into Kinsey's police. Julian Blythe's been dispatched to join Harold Lenton's war-party somewhere in the Scottish Borders, trying to work out where the Sons of Gore are actually based so they can attack them. Two delegations, led by William Posnett and Jerry Transom, are across the sea in Dublin and Brittany, collaborating uneasily with the Paladins de la Republique and the Children of Oisín to suppress the Arthurian manifestations in those dominions of Arthur's which have fallen out of British rule.

Even Wigsby is in Newcastle, where a team of Chinese dragon-dancers have supposedly been subverted en masse and are now seeking out another dragon to fight. Stephen isn't sure whether this is an elaborate joke, and if so on whom.

All of which means that, other than the Seneschal himself, Stephen happens to be the most senior Knight in the Fastness when the newcomer comes knocking.

* * *

'He won't go away, sir,' says the receptionist who's phoned through to the keep where Stephen's hotdesking. 'He seems to know a lot about us, too – he keeps insisting on speaking to the Seneschal, and talking about Sir Kay. We've put him out several times, but he just keeps coming in. Some people on the street have started to notice. The thing is, it's a – I mean – he's a black gentleman, Mr Mukherjee. We're worried it might look bad if we're too forceful with him. Will you authorise that, sir, or would you prefer to come down and talk to him?'

If he's honest, Stephen's glad of a bit of variety. He strolls downstairs, across the moat and over the courtyard to the curtain wall, then descends a further set of stairs into the Fastness' street-level lobby. The intruder stands insolently at ease between the two men-at-arms who provide reception with additional security. He's young, with very dark skin and a striking face, and dressed in a baggy, bright-red suit that Stephen guesses is fashionable, expensive and not technically his.

'You aren't the Seneschal,' the young man says.

'No, old son, I'm not,' Stephen replies firmly. 'And you're not going to be seeing him, either. You've had your fun, now toddle off home.' He turns away, but finds something still nagging at him... specifically, at his device. Sir Palamedes, largely quiescent all the while Stephen's been struggling through police paperwork, is taking an interest in the situation.

'Brother knows me better than you do,' the young man says. 'We go way back, Palamedes and me.'

Stephen turns back. 'How did you...' he asks, then trails off. It's not exactly rare for the Fastness to get loonies in off the street, but this one's disconcertingly well-informed.

'Hey, bruv, remember when you first came to Arthur's court?' the lad says, evidently addressing Palamedes directly now. It's the kind of overidentification with the devices which can strike those recently come to bondsmanship, especially outside a support structure like the Circle. 'I knew how it was for you when they said you worshipped the devil. They'd said I was the devil's kid, before. I wanted to get with Kay today, but you're good enough.'

The young man gestures at his jacket, cocking his head at Stephen. Stephen cautiously nods for the men-at-arms to stand back slightly.

From his clothing, the black man slowly withdraws a metal pole that's much too long to have been in there.

The back of Stephen's neck bristles. The devices make the implausible more likely; they can't create impossibilities. Despite the appearances that go with the job, everyone he's spoken to at the Circle has always insisted that actual magic is out of the question.

The men-at-arms look wary, but the interloper's making his movements slow, unthreatening. He strikes the steel rod on the ground, and green flame bursts from the top.

'It's a trick,' says Stephen in disbelief. He steps forward to examine the pole, but the young man replaces it, still burning, inside his jacket, which swallows it whole.

'Course it is,' the youth says sombrely. 'Telescopic pole, pyrotechnic charge, percussion cap. Copper in the charge makes the flame green. You can buy them all online from theatrical suppliers, yeah? *Do I have your attention now?*'

'You're...' *They'd said I was the devil's kid, before.* 'You're Merlin.' As he says it Stephen knows it's ridiculous, but within him Sir Palamedes knows it to be true. 'The bearer of the Merlin device, I mean.'

The black man smiles. It makes him look younger suddenly, barely out of his teens, and oddly girlish. 'Knew you'd get there in the end, man.'

* * *

At seven o'clock the next morning, Paul Parsons is looking at a brightly painted house, the end property in a terrace of reasonably respectable urban dwellings on an arterial road near the centre of Bristol. The squat's known locally as 'Mystic Villas' for the inhabitants' New Age bent, the name immortalised in paint on its walls above a crowd of giant-sized caricatures of establishment icons, all of them wearing suspiciously stoned expressions. Paul has to concede it's competently executed – he recognises Mrs Thatcher, Jeremy Clarkson, George W Bush – even if it is fundamentally an eyesore, and a decadent one at that.

These are the premises where eye-witnesses have placed at least two of the Green Chapel fugitives, Dashwood and Wardsley, and where Paul hopes some of the group's more senior figures may be staying too. Right now, ten men-at-arms are accessing the back garden through an adjoining car park and are preparing to break open the back door while the ten with Paul smash open the front. There can't be more than fifteen people inside, he reckons, probably fewer, and, while they could be armed, it's hardly likely they'll be as disciplined as the Circle's men.

They may, of course, have devices, which is why he has Nick Frith and Doug Felton – and by proxy their sponsors, Lancelot's uncle Sir Bors and cousin Sir Lionel – with him.

I know I've been giving him a rough time in this story, but Paul Parsons wouldn't be a Knight of the Circle if he was a bad man. That's the tragedy of this whole schism that's threatening Britain – everyone involved thinks they're acting for the best, they just have drastically different ideas of how to go about it. (Well, nearly everyone. But we'll get to that later.)

Paul has a strongly-developed, hugely old-fashioned sense of right and wrong, where life and property are sacrosanct, obedience to rules is never optional and constraints like 'duty' and 'service' trump ideals like 'freedom' and 'equality'. His virtues include honesty, courage and unwavering loyalty, which is why he despises Jory so comprehensively for what he sees as his duplicitous, cowardly betrayal. They do not, however, include imagination or empathy.

If Paul had lived in Britain during the Second World War, he'd have fought valiantly for king and country, become a war hero or died trying. In Nazi Germany, he'd have put the same talents just as faithfully at the disposal of his *Führer*. That's just the kind of person he is.

Despite how Paul comes across, this isn't cynicism – it's a respect for civil authority that's practically Roman in its fervour. Paul's superficial, overt cynicism is a protective carapace grown in his schooldays, when his straitlaced uptightness and willingness to report wrongdoing to the authorities caused him to be first teased and then bullied mercilessly.

As a page of the Circle, Paul welcomed a calling whose time-honoured nobility and sanctity, as far as he was concerned, made it morally unassailable. As Jory Taylor's squire, he looked up to his Knight with an awe which Jory did little to earn, and repaid with ill-concealed dislike. And as the bearer of the Sir Lancelot device, he bowed willingly to the authority of a persona for whom honour and public acclaim were guiding lights, and whose private lapses were accompanied by crippling guilt and self-loathing, which was never really going to help matters.

Finally, of course, he found his own sacrosanct person horribly violated by our attack on the Circle convoy, losing a part of himself he'll never recover. Men like Paul always favour 'an eye for an eye' over 'turn the other cheek'.

The Pauls of this world see themselves as better than us ordinary people – and, in some ways, they're right. However much I support the Chapel's ideals, I've never had the physical bravery to fight for them the way Paul does the Circle's, either before or after he was disabled.

Most people are like me, not like him. Make no mistake: the world needs people like Paul.

* * *

Katja Kollwitz, an early riser since her daughter Bella's birth four years ago, is doing a tatty jigsaw with her on the grimy floor of the downstairs front room, sipping the tea she's made on the communal camping-stove, when the front door where she and her friends painted the Duke of Edinburgh with a dopily blissful face bursts into splinters. Four men-at-arms enter rapidly in pairs, shouting and waving guns, and followed immediately by three armoured Knights. Katja and Bella scream and cower, mother doing her best to protect daughter with her arms and torso.

Upstairs, Rev Cantrell, awakened by the shouting after only a couple of hours' sleep, goes immediately into emergency mode. Leaping from his mattress wearing only his boxers, he gathers up his lighter, his Bible and the holdall he keeps packed by the door, before dashing from his room and making for the ladder to the attic. Beneath him, the back door also breaks open, and the second mob of men-at-arms pours in.

The attic sleeps three sets of squatters, curtained off from one another with reclaimed carpet, and Rev stops for long enough to kick one pair awake. He patched up Liss's hand and set Laney's nose when they dropped off Jack and Jory on the M4, and he's got to feel quite fond and protective of the mismatched girls. One storey below, the guy Rev picked up at the club is sitting up and wondering blearily where his shag's gone, when a man with a sword bursts in and begins yelling at him. The other ground- and first-floor rooms, all of them occupied by the ordinary squatters who've been kind enough to extend the Chapel trio their hospitality, get similar treatment.

Meanwhile, Rev, a violently swearing Liss and a tearful Laney are tearing down the cardboard where the skylight used to be and climbing out onto the roof. To an observer in the houses backing onto the terrace, they're standing on a grinning Arnold Schwarzenegger's giant flat-top. This is their agreed escape plan – not a foolproof one, by any means, but they weren't expecting the Circle to find them here. It's sheer luck which handed Stephen the car registration, after all.

All three are in underwear, though Laney's wrapping her hoodie around her shoulders as she goes. These houses are Edwardian, with a flat leaded rim running along next to the gutter where – if you're steady with your footing and don't let the gables slow you down too much – you can run all the way along to the last house in the row. The back garden of that one has a tree in it which the owners really ought to cut back, and gives onto a park. Once there, the Chapel trio can trust to luck and their outlaws' skills at blending into their surroundings.

Well – Laney can at least, and Rev's got a set of clothes in his holdall which will do for Liss. Merry Man or not, he's not sure how inconspicuous he's going to look in his underpants.

* * *

Another thing to say about Paul Parsons – he doesn't expect other people to do his dirty work for him.

While Frith, Felton and most of the men-at-arms check the remaining squatters for familiar faces and begin the fingertip search of the rooms, which will be needed to check the Grail's not here, Paul's out on the roof with two of his men. He treads carefully, aware of the extra weight his armour carries, but he doesn't let it slow him down.

On the ground, four more men-at-arms are working their way along the back gardens, but scaling fences and negotiating obstacles like ponds, washing-lines and trampolines is slowing them down to the point of uselessness. Ahead, the Chapel fugitives scurry like eager ducklings for the end of the roof.

The men-at-arms have guns, of course, the P226s it would shame a Knight to carry – but the escapees are unarmed, and shooting them in the back would be gravely dishonourable, for the Circle and for the Knight in charge in particular. The men-at-arms are trained quite stringently not to do that.

Frustratingly for Paul, this means the Chapel people are getting away. His men can't get to the park in time to intercept them, and even if they did, he knows that hiding and escaping are their particular specialities. Sir Charles will be most disappointed if he learns that they had Cantrell in view and failed to catch him.

'Fire a warning shot,' Paul snaps at the man-at-arms behind him. He steps aside to allow the man a clear view.

'But, sir, what if I hit them?' asks the man, who's been perhaps too stringently trained.

'Don't, obviously!' Paul snaps. The man-at-arms shrugs and fires well over the heads of the escapees, who sensibly drop to the roof. 'Stop there!' Paul yells. 'Next time it won't be a warning!'

The other man-at-arms looks at him askance. This is pushing the boundaries of honourable behaviour, and Paul knows it. Unfortunately, so does Cantrell. He's up at once, with a shrewd glance back at them. He encourages Dashwood to stand and run with him, and they get several steps before they realise that Wardsley is still cowering by the guttering.

'Got you,' says Paul as they turn back to help their friend. At once he's up and pelting towards them, sword flashing in the morning light.

* * *

Laney Wardsley isn't someone like Paul; she's someone like me. She doesn't like conflict – all the less after her run-in with Torch – and she's terrified of guns. (You would be too, if you'd just been woken up and forced to run for your life across a roof, and someone started firing one of them in your direction.)

Rev's the one with the ally here, which should put him in charge, but with Laney cowering and Liss urging her, 'C'mon, Lanes, time to go! We've got to run, bitch, now!', the only thing he can think of is to charge at Paul and give the kids a few seconds more to escape – and code of honour or not, he doesn't care to run right at that sword.

A strategic withdrawal's definitely what's called for here, so he drops to his knees again and murmurs in Laney's ear: 'Come on kid, you can do this! You stay here, Liss and me get taken too, and none of us want that, hey? Come on, get up now.'

Liss glares at Rev, but Laney gets the message and staggers to her feet. Liss puts a protective arm around her friend's shoulders, and they start to run again – but Paul's just yards behind them now, and gaining. Rev turns, sighs and charges at him anyway.

It's an unexpected tactic, and it takes Paul by surprise, especially since impaling an unarmed man wouldn't look good on his CV. They end up wrestling clumsily, with Cantrell – who's troubled by fewer scruples – attempting to pitch Paul off the roof, and Paul trying his hardest to resist him.

It's a one-sided battle, though. Yes, both have allies, but let's be realistic – we're talking about *Sir Lancelot* versus *Friar Tuck*. Tuck was fine in a scrap, but Lancelot was the pre-eminent warrior of his generation – and Tuck's biggest advantage in a clinch, his sumo-wrestler's bulk, is one Cantrell's deliberately decided to forego. It's the work of moments for Paul to toss the scrawny man behind him to his troops, so he can rush off after Liss and Laney.

He's been too occupied to see the hoodie fall from Laney's back; Liss tried to grab it as they went, but had the presence of mind to leave it. Moments later it's under Paul's feet. He trips and topples, the weight of his armour bearing him down, and automatically he puts out both hands to protect himself.

It's his left hand that saves him, the real one, arresting his fall and pushing him away from the roof's edge. His right hand just isn't built for this sort of thing. It snaps open, and the sword it's carrying goes flying forward.

The tip of it just nicks Liss's calf, and she instinctively recoils. Unfortunately it was her right leg – the one nearest the slope – so the reflex unbalances her. She puts a foot down to steady herself, but the sword's under her feet by now, and the polymer coating slips on the leading, sending it flying up into the air.

Unbalanced still, Liss stumbles, fumbles and then tumbles. Laney clutches at her, shrieking, and both girls go wheeling from the roof in a messy double-swastika of limbs, onto the hard paved patio beneath. The sword clatters to the leading and spins to a standstill.

Paul clambers to his feet and stares down. Cantrell tears his arms free of the men's grip, and rushes to join him. They stare down at Liss's smashed corpse in its pool of blood, at Laney rolling dazed from atop her friend's body and kneeling to vomit, before collapsing in a fit of sobs.

The men-at-arms stand back from the scene and watch, as all along the terrace, neighbours come out to stare.

* * *

Stephen's with the Seneschal when Paul returns that afternoon.

'The formal tests will have to wait for Mr Lister, I suppose,' he's saying, 'but I have to say, sir, I'm pretty much convinced. My device responds to this Blaze chap just as it used to with Dr Wendiman. He's a pretty unconventional choice, but the Merlin device has never –' He breaks off as a knock comes at the door.

Paul comes in, head bowed, trembling slightly. These days the Circle don't go in for kneeling or obeisance – they might when faced with an actual monarch, but the Seneschal's only a Knight like Paul – but short of that, his manner couldn't be more apologetic.

Gossip travels fast at the Fastness (except when it's classified), and the Knights in residence know already that Paul's screwed up. No matter how accidental it was, an unarmed, undeviced woman died by his sword while trying to flee: there's no positive way to spin that. Paul's best hope is that the Seneschal sees fit to forgive him. Stephen hopes he does, of course, and imagines he will, while at the same time harbouring just the littlest smidgen of resentment at how Paul's treatment is likely to differ from his own.

'Sir –' Paul begins, but Raymond interrupts him immediately.

'Wait a minute, man, we're busy. No, not outside!' he adds, as Paul retreats. 'You need to hear this as much as anyone. Go on, Mukherjee.'

Stephen's pleased to be briefly in Sir Charles's good books, but isn't under any illusions it'll last. 'Shall I bring Parsons up to speed, sir?' he asks.

Predictably, the Seneschal hasn't the patience. 'New Merlin's arrived, Parsons,' he says. 'New fellow who claims to hold the Merlin device, I should say. Black chap, no education, but as Mukherjee was about to remind me, Merlin's picked fellows off the street before. He likes to keep us on our toes. Have to wait for Lister to administer the proper tests, but Mukherjee's convinced, aren't you, Mukherjee?'

Stephen's not going to stick his neck out too far. 'I'm willing to be proved wrong, sir.'

Parsons voices the question that Stephen's had on his mind, but so far hasn't cared to ask. 'So do we know anything more about Dr Wendiman?'

Raymond harrumphs. 'Well, if Lister's tests come up trumps, we'll know he's not carrying the Merlin device any more. More than one way that can happen, of course, but I know what my guess would be, don't you?'

'That bitch,' Paul says, disgustedly. 'That cold-hearted, vicious…'

'Steady on, Parsons,' Stephen says. 'Wendiman's eighty, and he hasn't been well. Even if he has checked out… well, best not go leaping to conclusions until we've got the facts, what?'

Paul's about to snap at him, then remembers he's in disgrace. 'Suppose you're right, Mukherjee.' He doesn't look ashamed, though, and suddenly Stephen realises that the bowed head and the subdued voice are concealing something. Paul's trembling, all right, but it's not out of contrition or fear

– he's excited. Not sexually, of course – Sir Lancelot may have had trouble keeping it in his hauberk, but his tastes in that direction were entirely vanilla – but almost uncontainably nonetheless. Stephen (who that previous thought would never have occurred to, naturally) recognises his own device's thrill at the chase – the same obsessive thirst for action that's driving him to seek out the British Beasts and give them a damn good pounding.

Parsons may have besmirched his good name and those of Sir Lancelot and the Circle, but something about his ghastly cock-up has made him think it could be an opportunity.

Thick-skinned though he is, Sir Charles seems to have picked up on it too. 'Was there anything else, Mukherjee?' he asks.

'No sir,' says Stephen, 'I think we've covered it. Oh – we're putting Blaze up at the hotel across the road, until we can verify his allegiance. No sense letting him into the keep until we're certain.'

The Seneschal grunts. 'Hmm. Best send over a page, then, to make sure he doesn't drink the minibar dry. Merlin or not.'

'Sir.' Stephen nods to Parsons in a way he hopes looks more sympathetic and supportive than he feels, and leaves.

Down the stairs, across the swingbridge and into the courtyard, he seeks out Jason, who's wide-eyed at the news going round the lower levels of the Fastness.

'They says Mr Parsons killed a Green Chapel woman, sir,' the page insists on telling him. 'She's down in the morgue, Sammy says, and he seen two more brought in and locked in the cells – man and another woman, it were. Have we got them, sir? Dir Mr Parsons get Wendiman and Taylor?'

Wendiman and Taylor. To the pages – especially Jason's intake, who never met either of them – they're legendary, the Circle's very own Bonnie and Clyde. 'I shouldn't suppose so for a moment, Jason,' he said severely. 'Now listen, I've got a job for you.'

* * *

Ten minutes later, Jason knocks on the door of the hotel room, whistling softly to himself. (If challenged, he'd have to admit that what he's whistling is the 'Knights of the Round Table' song out of *Monty Python and the Holy Grail*.) It's a cushy assignment, this one – babysit a guest of the Circle at his plush digs, with an eye open to make sure he doesn't get pissed or nick the light-fittings. Not a prob, especially for someone of Jason's particular talents. Maybe he'll find out whether the minibar has anything to offer a thirsty page while he's at it.

'Yeah?' a voice shouts from inside, and Jason gives the door a little push. It isn't locked, so he steps inside.

'All right, sir,' he says as he steps in. It's a posh room all right, all midnight-blue carpet and wood panelling. It must be setting the Circle back a mint. 'Mr Mukherjee sent me, from Kelliwick House? Just to see if there's anything you need. My name's –' he stops dead, as he sees the man he's supposed to be minding.

'Ah,' Blaze says. 'Thought I might see you, sooner or later. Hey, dude.'

'Well, bugger me,' says Jason.

7. JORY TAYLOR, BIG JACK BENNETT AND JANENE LONG

While all this is going on, Jory's in Cumbria, finally committing that robbery he planned weeks ago.

He's hiked with Big Jack Bennett across the fells from Windermere, having come up by train last night from their respective places of refuge. Since the British Museum robbery Jory's been lying low at a farm in Pembrokeshire, one that supplements its income with tourism. He thinks Jack's been in Peterborough with Lee and Maxx, but on the whole it's better if he doesn't know for sure. All this is business as usual for the Green Chapel, at least according to our recent standards: those of us who haven't gone to ground, like Scar and Zara at the Modron Dobunna Centre, keep on moving from place to place in small, ever-changing groups. We've reached a point, though, where getting our hands on more cash trumps the imperative to keep a low profile.

The Lake District isn't a part of the country Jory's visited as an adult, and the bleak grey-green peaks, scarping treacherously down to sheep-dotted foothills, keep taking him back irresistibly to an early walking holiday with his parents.

(He doesn't often think about his mum and dad these days. He's no idea what, if anything, the Knights have told them about his disappearance, but he daren't contact them in case the Circle tries to use them against him. In the old days that would have been unthinkable, of course, but with the devices of Prince John and the Sheriff of Nottingham in the ascendant, he can't trust his old bosses to resist the temptation such underhand tactics must present.)

Jack and Jory rendezvous with a handful of others at some prearranged GPS co-ordinates, which place them in a meadow full of sheep-dung, uphill from a single-lane B-road and opposite a tranquil lake, reflecting a view which would have (and probably did) give Wordsworth an ecstatic paroxysm. Drystone walls wander across the mountains' lowers lopes like graphite doodled by a giant.

They meet two lads called Rags and Kez on mountain-bikes, each wearing a capacious, empty rucksack; a guy called Twink whose chief talent is being built like a brick wall; and Vicks, a lab technician in the chemistry department at a university with deplorably lax stock-keeping standards. Everyone's come a long way, but it's politic that their current direct action should happen as far as possible from the Circle's usual bases of operations. The Scottish highlands and Welsh mountains are covered by Circle regional headquarters; the Lake District, while conveniently remote, is still reasonably well-off, thanks to the tourist industry. The nearest Circle taskforce is still doing its best to wage Blythe and Lenton's confused and meandering campaign against the Sons of Gore.

Some outstanding work by our local informer Niamh has discovered that the target bank's branches in the tourist towns of the National Park are visited regularly by an armoured security van, and that that same van passes once a week along an isolated stretch of road where convenient mountains block out every mobile phone signal in the spectrum.

After checking everyone's sure of the plan, Jory and Jack, the only members present with allies, send the lads on bikes off a little way to wait their cue. Then they, Twink and Vicks put on their green hoodies, Jory takes a folding bow and arrow-case from his rucksack, and the four of them make their way stealthily down to the roadside and along to the optimum ambush point, where they position themselves behind a drystone wall upslope from the road and await the van's arrival.

It's drizzling gently, which was refreshing when Jory was yomping across the hilly countryside, but is less welcome when hunkering down amongst a spattering of sheep-droppings. The sheep come and huddle around them, and soon the air's full of the smell of damp wool.

After some minutes of nuzzling and bleating, the security van comes into view in the distance, rounding a bend in the road. Using a scrubby tree as his cover, Jory stands and carefully aims his bow, as the sheep amble away in lazy alarm.

The only sensible way to bring an armoured vehicle to a halt without actually blocking the road is to shoot the tyres, and an arrow's just as good for that as a bullet. The two security guards in the driver's cab are something to worry about later.

As the van approached, an arrow flies, embedding itself in one of the front tyres. A moment later the rear tyre on the same side, the downhill one, is punctured by a second shaft, and the van slithers to a halt.

'What the hell's this?' asks Big Jack rhetorically, as Jory stares dumbfounded at the arrow still nocked in his bow.

* * *

Behind a drystone wall on the other side of the road, three people pop up wearing leather trenchcoats and full-face balaclavas. All three carry bows and wear canvas quivers. Their leader – an extremely tall woman rather than a fairly tall man, if Jory's any judge – reloads her bow as they run to the van.

'Are they with us?' Vicks's confusion is understandable. Jory's internal device-alarm's jangling fit to deafen him.

In the van's cab, the guard who isn't driving tries desperately to get a signal on his mobile. The driver puts the van in gear and tries to pull away, but with the tyres out on one side he only manages to grind the van in closer to the edge of the road, partially demolishing the nearest wall.

By now the three interlopers have reached the vehicle. After a brief confab, one of the men aims his bow and arrow at the security guards through the bulletproof glass, and starts shouting at them to get out of the cab. His voice is tinged with slightly hysterical machismo, and the guards very sensibly elect to stay put.

'No,' Jory murmurs. 'No, we're cleverer than that.'

At a word from the woman, the other man picks up a large stone from the collapsed wall and begins to batter it against the glass. It crazes and splinters, but continues to hold as he thumps away doggedly.

'They're going to get someone killed,' Jory observes. The guards won't be carrying guns – at least, if they are they're breaking the law – but they'll be trained to fight off this kind of attack. Sure enough, as the van-batterer raises his chunk of wall for another crunch, the nearer guard kicks the door open, knocking him over backwards. The guard himself follows, kicking the stone from the robber's hands and stomping his thighs.

Taken unawares as they are, it's a second or so later that the other leather-coated man lifts his bow and shoots the security guard in the stomach.

'That's enough,' Jory declares, as the man collapses screaming and his colleague cowers in the footwell. 'Oi!' he shouts, vaulting the wall and starting to run towards the van.

'Oh, for Christ's sake,' Jack complains, but follows loyally. Twink and, more reluctantly, Vicks, do likewise.

As he runs, Jory takes a moment to hope Rags and Kez have spotted what's going on and scarpered. It's less stressful than hoping the leathery outlaws won't put an arrow in his eye. 'There's no need for this!' he yells, hoping to convey that his intentions aren't hostile so much as consultative.

The tall female figure steps round the van and stares at Jory, Big Jack, Twink and Vicks. 'And who the bloody blazes,' she asks through the balaclava in a distinct local accent, 'would *you* lot be?' She sounds honestly curious, but in a way which could turn to homicidal hostility at any moment.

'Never mind us,' Jory says, his device stirring into anger within him. 'Who are *you?*'

She gestures at the scene behind her. 'We're robbers,' she says. 'Next question?' She's staring speculatively at his hoodie, though.

Her comrade who isn't still recovering from a boot to the genitals steps forward, his bow raised, but the woman flaps a hand at him. The security man's still writhing on the ground, an arrow-shaft protruding from his abdomen. 'Twink,' Jory says, 'hike up the road until you've got a signal, then call an ambulance.' The burly man looks sceptical.

'Now wait a minute –' the woman interjects angrily. From her voice and figure, Jory puts her at around his age: late twenties, early thirties. His height, too. He still hasn't seen her face; even her hands are gloved. She seems to be wearing camouflage paint around the eyes and mouth.

Calmly, he says, 'The ambulance will take a good half-hour to get here. We'll be long gone, but it might save this man's life.'

'Right hero you are.' The woman shrugs in grudging permission, and Twink tramps off up the road. 'Reckon we know who you've come as, then. I like your Little John.'

One of her followers sniggers. The other, climbing to his feet now, doesn't seem to get the joke.

'And what about you?' Jory asks again. 'People don't just decide to hold up an armoured car with bows and arrows. I mean,' he adds, realising the weight of current evidence is against him there, 'not without some kind of prompting.'

It's clear enough that the woman has an ally, and however reluctant Jory might be to accept that the narrative entity currently inhabiting his subconscious is the genuine Robin Hood, he's pretty sure this gang's crude tactics aren't inspired by the outlaw's legendary cunning.

All the significant figures in Robin's band are currently accounted for, unless anyone in the Green Chapel's died too recently for him to have heard about it. Given where they are, though, there's another obvious candidate. Jory silently thanks Malory for all the compulsory reading, viewing and even – under extreme protest – computer gaming she's put him through as his education in the various facets of the Robin Hood legend, and says, 'I'm guessing you're a local history buff as well as an armed robber. So when exactly did you decide that the one thing you really needed to make your life complete was to spend it pretending to be the outlaw Adam Bell?'

The woman looks slightly crestfallen. 'Aye, right,' she says. 'And dressing up as Robin Hood's totally normal, like.'

Jory shrugs. 'I'm not judging. Did you never wonder, though, where the *proper* outlaws were?'

Adam Bell's a predecessor of Robin Hood – literally and sometimes, in modern retellings, in the story too. A robber and an expert archer, he lacks Robin's ethics and his refined cunning. When his pal William Cloudsley's captured by the Sheriff of Carlisle, Adam and their other friend Clym of the Clough step up and rescue him – much as Robin would, except that they kill scores of people in the process, including the Sheriff and the mayor. The next stage in their brilliant plan's to go to the King of England and ask him for a pardon, then act all hurt when he doesn't give it to them. Trickster archetypes these lads are not, though Cloudsley at least gets cool points for re-enacting William Tell's apple-on-your-son's-head trick, which is more than any of the Merry Men got to do.

'I'm a Carlisle lass,' says Adam Bell's human ally. 'The local lads are good enough for me.' For a moment it almost sounds as if she's flirting with him. 'Have you got a name, or do they call you Robin?'

'Dan,' says Jory. 'I'm Dan.'

'Janene,' she replies, pulling off the balaclava to reveal herself as a handsome black woman with short frizzy hair.

(*That explains the face-paint,* Jory thinks. Cumbria being one of the least ethnically diverse parts of England, her skin colour alone might give the police enough to work with.)

'Well, Janene,' he says, 'we seem to be working to a timescale here. Tell me, did you come equipped with a plan for actually getting the cash out of this van?'

* * *

Most of Janene Long's story Jory will only learn later, but I'll recap it briefly here. She's Carlisle born and bred, albeit with parents who used to be black Londoners – hospital nurses who moved up here to work without quite twigging what they were letting themselves or their unborn daughter in for. Resigned to standing out because of her height and ethnicity, teenage Janene worked hard on asserting her identity as a local, developing an interest in Cumbrian folktales and traditions which quite surpassed anything her peers could muster. Now, at the age of twenty-nine, she's working as a volunteer guide for the Guildhall Museum.

Everyone's experience of the devices is different, and Janene doesn't talk of any kind of blinding revelation, just a burgeoning enthusiasm for keeping Adam Bell's memory alive. Recently this has grown far beyond a hobby, leading her to carry out robberies of her own and leave notes giving Adam Bell the credit, as well as recruiting local thugs as allies for Adam's henchmen Cloudsley and Clym.

She has another motivation, of course: her boyfriend Larry (who, she'd feel duty-bound to emphasise, isn't a bad man, just an old-fashioned, unimaginative one) holds the purse-strings in their house, and she needs to build up some savings of her own so she can leave him and lead her own life for a change. Now, with three increasingly daring armed robberies under her belt and a nest-egg somewhere in the region of a quarter of a million pounds, she's thinking that after this heist and just a couple more she might feel secure enough to leave Larry, his job as a delivery driver and their heavily-mortgaged £90,000 house.

This kind of cheerfully gaping illogic isn't uncommon among the allied.

Janene's plan for breaking into the security van turns out not to be as daft as Jory feared: they have a tractor parked a little way up the road, and were intending to block the van in place with stones from the walls, then use it to drag the doors off... but it would take too long now. Even without the ambulance Twink's called, the risk of being interrupted by passing cars would be too great.

The Chapel's plan's far quicker, and involves the thermite Vicks has cobbled together from chemicals she's acquired from her employer. They load the injured man back in the driver's cab and push the van off the road to somewhere they'll be less conspicuous, then Vicks sets about burning her way through to the secure interior.

Meanwhile, as Janene's lads tie up and blindfold the intact guard, she and Jory haggle their way to an agreement, acknowledging the Adam Bell crew's prior claim on the van, to split the proceeds fifty-fifty. Jack Bennett is volubly unhappy about this, pointing out that Jory was about to halt the van himself and would have made less of a mess of the follow-up, but the old-fashioned cliché of honour among thieves is still an important concept to Jory.

It's the only kind of honour he has left, after all.

The two plans for getting the loot away are similarly disparate, with Jory's being to stuff Kez and Rags' rucksacks with as many high-denomination notes as they can grab and send them bicycling back to a pickup in Penrith, while Janene's entails burying the lot nearby until the heat dies down. Since she now doesn't trust the Green Chapel not to watch her doing this and dig it up later – not to mention the increasingly urgent question of their getaway – Jory reluctantly allows that Rags will instead wait at Penrith for Keith, Clym of the Clough's ally, to get there by car and pick up half the proceeds.

'We're putting a lot of trust in your laddie, Dan,' Janene points out, while Big Jack fumes in the near distance.

'All our people are trustworthy,' Jory insists. 'It comes with the territory. Listen, Janene...' He isn't sure how to put this. 'I don't know how long you've been doing this, being Adam Bell, but I'm guessing it's not long. I know you're not just re-enacting his life – I expect there are times when it feels like you hear his voice talking to you, aren't there?'

'Are you saying I'm some kind of loony?' Janene asks indignantly. It's a question (a general question, you understand, not one specifically about Janene) which has caused extensive disagreement among those few psychiatrists aware of the devices. She has an evasive look in her eyes, though, which convinces Jory she knows what he's talking about.

'I know how it feels,' he says, 'believe me. I know there are times when it can seem overwhelming. If you ever feel as if your own identity's becoming less real to you than Adam's... well, call this number.' He gives her Rev's mobile number, which the priest has stubbornly hung onto throughout the past year despite the obvious risks involved. It's the only contact point that stands even a small chance of being valid in the long term.

* * *

As the two of them walk back across the fells, Jack Bennett gives Jory a piece of his mind. 'We should've tied up that bunch of hopeless wazzocks and taken the lot,' he insists. 'Instead you roll over like a puppy and let her decide terms? I really hope it's just that you fancy her, lad, 'cause I can't see any other reason to cosy up to that lot. They could've killed that lad, you know, and ended up without the cash even so.'

'I know,' Jory says. They were barely out of sight of the road when the ambulance sirens faded up in the distance, followed shortly afterwards by those of the police. So far they've heard no helicopters, so with luck they can put enough distance between themselves and the crime scene to look like any other mismatched pair of fellwalkers. 'Still, they did get there first.'

117

'Bugger that,' Jack snorts. 'This isn't a bloody playground.'

'What Kez has got will last us a while,' Jory points out. 'Not as long as we hoped, but...'

'So in a few months we need to do all that again, with the Circle breathing down our necks all the time, all because of that daft besom and her mates? Christ.' Bennett shakes his head in disgust, and they walk on in silence.

What bothers Jory more is the coincidence of both groups picking the exact same place to ambush the same target at the same time, especially a place which must be among the most isolated roads in England ever to be traversed by a secure van. To some extent the isolation dictated the choice, of course, but that degree of convergence is the sort of thing you generally only see with two devices acting in affinity with one another.

Of course, it's not in the least surprising that Robin Hood and his analogue Adam Bell should share that kind of connection. But that assumes you're willing to accept that Jory's Robin Hood.

Jack's apparently been thinking along similar lines, but they've taken him in a different direction. 'I reckon this is all your fault anyway, posh boy.'

'It is? How?' Jory asks, surprised.

'All this sitting on the fence about that ally of yours,' Bennett answers. '"Is it, isn't it." Stop buggering about and decide, man. The Chapel needs a Robin Hood, not some prat who can't make up his own mind. The *country* needs a Robin Hood. We all know you're the closest we've had since Shaf died, but you don't come out and say it. I reckon that's why all this happened, because who the bloody hell's heard of Adam Bell, eh? D'you really think he'd be going round recruiting bored housewives to do bank robberies if there was a proper outlaw hero around? The allies know there's sommat missing, and they're looking to fill the gap. Today was a wake-up call, Dan. You've got to shite or get off the pot.'

* * *

To be brutally honest (Jory thinks to himself back at the farm, when the news of Laney and Cantrell's arrest and Liss's death reaches him), he prefers it on the fence. His device has been a constant presence at the back of his mind, but on the whole – having believed himself to be, at different times, the pawn of Sir Mordred and Guy of Gisbourne as well as the convivial Sir Gawain – he feels more comfortable with its identity officially unresolved.

Under their various influences, he killed one bearer of the Robin Hood ally, Shaun Hobson, and was partially responsible for the death of another (because whoever killed Shafiq – and it happens to have been a Circle man-at-arms who pulled the trigger – he wouldn't have been escaping from that hospital in the first place if it hadn't been for Jory). That that same device might respond to his perfidy by adopting him is… galling. Although somehow also exactly the kind of thing he'd expect Robin Hood to do.

It's an honour, though, which Jory feels desperately unworthy of. Like many converts, he's deeply ashamed of his past conduct: in his case, as the tool of the oppressive status quo which made so many of his new friends become outlaws. He used to be the King's man, loyal and zealous, and the fact that the king in question was Arthur rather than John cuts little ice with people who reject even republicanism as too authoritarian a model by far.

Jory blames himself, quite correctly, for Shaun Hobson's death, and with less justice for Shafiq's, but there are also times when he hasn't fought with enough zeal on the Chapel's side. That moment at the museum, when he could have shot Stephen but hesitated for just a moment too long, weighs on his mind. To be sure nobody died as a result, but that was purest luck. The Chapel needs a Robin Hood who'll prosecute its cause without that moment's reservation, with all the vigour, bravery and intelligence at his disposal.

More fundamentally, though, as Jack says, it just needs a Robin Hood. And judging by what Merry found out in Southampton, there won't be another candidate along any time soon.

8. THE DREAM OF JORY TAYLOR

A few days after their unsatisfying encounter at the Manchester youth hostel, Jory had word from Malory that she had the new approach she needed for her research.

'I need fresh eyes,' she told him in the video message left for him by 'Mir&A' at Love-L. 'A fresh brain. Someone who knows as much about this stuff as me, but who hasn't been thinking about it obsessively for months. Someone who can look at this and spot whatever obvious thing I'm missing.'

Staring at her inch-high face on his laptop screen, Jory wondered who on earth she was talking about. Despite the fact that the Circle had other researchers on its payroll – sinister Mr Lister for one, though Malory could scarcely be thinking of asking him – Malory remained the acknowledged authority on the devices, in Britain at least. He supposed she must mean someone overseas.

Love-L boasts a maximum privacy setting intended for personal videos of a titillating or overtly pornographic nature, which delete themselves after a single play. Though Malory used the facility very sparingly indeed, it gave her a freedom to speak openly about the devices which she didn't allow herself on other channels. She said, 'I need my dad. He's the only person who can help. It shouldn't be difficult getting him out of Tud House – I sprung Scar from the Benwick Institute, and the security there's far tighter. Rev's been preparing a cover story. Dad will help, I'm sure. Leave Merlin out of the equation, and he's still one of the cleverest device experts in the world.'

Which made no sense, of course, at any level. The last time Jory saw Edward Wendiman, he'd scarcely been able to remember his own name. He tried the usual channels for contacting Malory, to ask whether she, too, had lost her mind, but received no reply.

Two days later, a private account on an image upload site which was another of their virtual dead-letter drops suddenly displayed a close-up image of a tweed tie sporting the trilithon tie-pin Wendiman used in lieu of a device, and a man's wrinkled hand holding a postcard which read 'GREETINGS FROM THE DALES'.

That evening Jory travelled down to Eastbourne in Sussex, to meet up with his girlfriend and her father – and, as it happened, me.

* * *

My flat in Eastbourne's not the usual sort of Green Chapel haunt, especially in this phase of our existence. It's legitimately mine, for one thing – I inherited it from a great-aunt who retired from teaching in the 1970s, moved here then proceeded to live to 103, outlasting all our other relatives. I hadn't often been there, preferring the nomadic life as I do, but the last lot of tenants had moved out a few months earlier and, given recent developments in our little mythopolitical pond, I'd thought it might be wise to lie low there for a bit. It's in a secluded street in an upmarket part of a town where one of the primary sources of employment is geriatric nursing, and it has a lovely view of the sea.

In many ways it was the ideal place for Merry to bring an elderly relative whose marbles had deserted him, even if he was effectively stolen property, which the Circle would be using all the resources at their disposal to hunt down. (This was before the Grail, of course, which would make the Circle's search for Wendiman look positively half-hearted.) With Jory and Malory, the Circle's most wanted, and Rev Cantrell turning up unannounced into the bargain, Auntie Ginnie's place was suddenly looking a lot like a mobsters' joint.

Not that I objected to harbouring fugitives, of course. Some of my best friends are… well, these particular fugitives were some of my best friends. But a houseful of them? It made me nervous, frankly.

And then there was Wendiman senior himself. I'd met him before, in the days when I'd do occasional storytelling gigs for the Circle, and found him pleasant enough – less standoffish than many in that crowd, though you couldn't call us more than casual acquaintances. I'd been impressed enough by his intelligence then to notice the change in him, but even if you hadn't known what he once was, it would have been pretty obvious that he wasn't it any more.

'I'm sorry, but I don't know who you are,' he informed me for the fifth time in a day, staring at the cup of tea I'd given him as if it was a Chinese puzzle-box. 'I don't know what this plate is, either. Place, I mean. I don't know what this plane is.'

'I'm Dale, Dr Wendiman,' I said. 'This is my flat. You and your daughter have come to visit me. Isn't that nice?'

'I don't know who you are,' he repeated. 'Dane, did you say? Have we met? Are you some kind of doctor? Am I going to be ill now?' He stared at me, bemused.

'Just make yourself comfortable, Dr Wendiman,' I told him, leaving him in the spare bedroom.

'I'm fifteen hundred years old, you know,' I heard him saying plaintively behind me.

In the living room, the others were in conference. Merry was sitting in an armchair, with Jory facing her on the sofa and Rev leaning out of the window to smoke a fag.

'I understand why you did this, honestly,' Jory was saying.

'Your dad's ill – of course you wanted to have him with you. But frankly, Mal, I think he was better off where he was – we're not going to be able to care for him like they did at Tud House. And he certainly can't advise us. I mean, you can see that, can't you?'

Merry looked perfectly composed. 'In his current state, you're right,' she said.

Jory frowned. 'His current state…? But surely he's got Alzheimer's. His state isn't going to improve.'

Merry nodded, slightly too vigorously. 'That's what I thought at first, too. Do you remember when we saw him at Tud House, right after he was first taken ill? I said then that this was part of Merlin's myth, and it is. I thought that meant Dad's Alzheimer's was this generation's prison for the Merlin device. But what if they've both been imprisoned? What if someone's locked Merlin away, and Dad's shackled right there with him?'

Jory remembered the conversation Malory was referring to. 'I asked you at the time,' he said, 'whether someone could have cursed him somehow. You said no.' There was another thing he remembered, too.

Merry gave an annoyed shrug. 'I was upset, remember? But you reminded me of something. I *had* seen some research from overseas, suggesting that some SCAMs, under some circumstances, can impair rather than enhance the functions of the brain.'

'Like Wigsby?' Jory asked, although he wasn't quite sure that that was what Malory had in mind. The buffoonish Knight carried the device of Arthur's jester, Sir Dagonet; who was causing whose idiocy there, though, was something Jory had never been terribly clear on.

'I've sometimes wondered,' Merry agreed neutrally. 'The point is, the idea of a curse isn't as absurd as it sounds. If someone succeeded in afflicting the Merlin device so that it not only failed to function, but imposed limitations on Dad as well… well, it would be theoretically possible to reverse that damage. So I started looking into ways to do it.'

Cantrell had finished his cigarette now. He said, 'Way I see it, we have three options: meditation, hypnosis and drugs. *Lots* of drugs.'

'But who cursed him?' Jory asked quickly. 'I mean... from what you're saying, someone deliberately stopped his brain from working properly – forever, as far as they knew. Who?'

'Lister, presumably,' said Merry at once. 'He'd be the only one with the expertise, unless the psychiatrists at the Benwick Institute have made a huge and highly sinister breakthrough. We never did establish who Lister's device was, but there are other magicians in the Arthurian mythos.'

'OK,' said Jory levelly. 'So how do we proceed?'

'It's an approach they've been experimenting with at Benwick,' Merry said. 'Without success, as far as I'm aware, but I think we know more between us than they do. Like I say, this is a curse on Merlin, not on Dad. It's his device that's making him this way. So all we need to do is separate him from it.'

* * *

It's only much later that I'll learn why that conversation made Jory go so stiff and strange. At the time I put it down to the general oddness of the situation and the strain of being around Edward in his mentally degraded state. We were all feeling it, but there was something else going on with Jory's situation. I'm a storyteller – people-watching goes with the territory.

I put it out of my mind, though, and will come to understand it out only when this particular phase of our story's long since finished.

The fact is, Jory had taken Malory at her word when she first told him that there were no such things as curses. She was the expert, after all, and he was used to trusting her in all things device-related. She'd taught him most of what he knew (in terms of theory at least, the Circle's training tending to concentrate on the practical side) and besides, she was his girlfriend. They may have got together in unusual circumstances (he was effectively her prisoner at the time), but she was still someone he loved and was committed to, and trusted – or wanted to trust – absolutely and implicitly.

The only time his belief in her had wavered had been the previous year, after Shafiq's death. Jory had been arrested and taken for a one-to-one with the Seneschal. It had been a tense affair, full of recrimination even before Jory revealed what he knew about Sir Charles: that the Seneschal had tried to establish a fascist dictatorship in the UK.

The fact that Sir Charles had intended in so doing to hasten the time of Britain's greatest need, and hence provoke the long-promised return of the King Arthur device, hadn't made Jory any more inclined to forgive him. One thing Raymond had said had stuck with him, though: *Miss Wendiman was responsible for bringing on her father's health issues. The doctors are certain now that it's his device that's been affected, and through some form of invasive psychological manipulation.*

Then later: *Whatever you may think of me, I trust you'll take my word as a Knight that neither I nor anyone in my employ had anything to do with Wendiman's illness.*

Whatever his weaknesses, however misguided, pig-headed and arrogant Sir Charles might have been, however much his Knights might use infiltration and deception as tools in their complex armoury… the Seneschal was not, Jory was certain, a liar. Malory, on the other hand, had lived a complex double life for years, working as the Circle's most trusted secular advisor while all the time being loyal to their enemies, the Green Chapel, during which time – when admittedly she'd merely been one of Jory's closest friends, not his lover – she'd been only marginally more honest with him than with anyone else in the Circle.

However he might feel about them both, Jory had less reason to think his ex-boss deceitful than his girlfriend. He couldn't help, then, comparing and contrasting Raymond's denial of responsibility with Malory's rather glib assignation of it to his lackey Lister. Yet the implication if the former had been telling the truth, that Malory herself had forced this degradation on her father, was repellent.

With Edward Wendiman out of sight in Tud House, he'd been able to put it out of his mind – but here, with him present and visible, Jory was finding this old suspicion flooding back. Perhaps, he thought, it was a similarly suppressed guilt which was making Malory so very determined to do the impossible.

Jory spent several days obsessively fretting before the obvious solution presented itself to him. Malory said that Lister had afflicted her father; Sir Charles insisted that nobody in his employ had done so. Therefore, Jory realised with the blissful relief of thunder cracking at the height of summer, Lister must not have been acting for the Seneschal when he cursed Edward Wendiman, but instead was working to his own agenda.

It was a perfect syllogism, and however he prodded it, it held. It also happened, of course, to align entirely with his own prejudices against Lister, and in favour of Malory.

For the time being, he found it satisfied him perfectly.

* * *

Merry and Cantrell worked on Wendiman's restoration for several weeks, all other projects on hold for the time being, while Jory came and went, checking in with Green Chapel cells in various remote parts of the country. My job, it seemed, was to nip out at any hour of day or night for groceries, New Age supplies, prescription drugs and occasionally, at Cantrell's instructions, more exotic pharmaceuticals – not entirely easy to obtain in Eastbourne, but I knew some guys in Brighton, which is far more cosmopolitan. (I hear they have gay people and everything there.)

Wendiman was easily tired and needed frequent rest, as well as help with eating, baths and getting dressed. We all pitched in, though frankly it's not what I'd signed up for. Whenever he felt up to it, Merry and Cantrell would sit down and try and persuade him to concentrate on the sound of their voice, or a spinning crystal, or a meditation soundtrack, or just to sit quietly in a spirit of 'mindfulness'. None of it worked – whatever discipline his mind had once possessed was utterly occluded now, and he answered their attempts with a constant stream of irritable babble.

'You're not my daughter,' I heard him tell Malory one day. 'My daughter's Merrily. Melody. Meredith… She's not as tall as you, you're standing up too much. She's got bland, blind, blonde hair. Hettie, that's her name! Not Mattie. But… but Mattie's dead. So who are you?'

'You're thinking of Mum, Dad,' Merry replied, her voice already husky from talking. 'Mum's name was Hettie, and she was blonde. Hettie's dead, but I'm her daughter Malory.'

'She's dead?' He looked appalled. 'My daughter's dead?' He burst into tears, snivelling like a toddler. 'My little Malory…'

Merry knelt down and held him. 'I'm not dead, Dad. I'm here. I'm right here, look, it's me, do you see?'

He peered at her through his tears, still sobbing. 'Thank you, yes, that's very kind. I'm sorry, I can't remember your name…?'

It was… pretty fucking trying, I have to admit, even without taking into account the smell of incense sticks. And I wasn't the one who was related to the poor bastard.

While they were there, other Chapel people drifted in and out occasionally, in their way along the south coast. At some point Burn turned up, to crash on my floor while he was plying his tricks for the tourists in Brighton. When Jory was there too, the flat – which had probably been on the large side for a 103-year-old woman, admittedly – felt claustrophobically crowded.

Cantrell was varying Wendiman's meds, experimenting with different mixes of psychoactives both legal and illegal. They were certainly having some effect, but it was completely unpredictable. Some days Edward was more lucid than others: once, he remembered not only Malory's name but also Jory's, and even seemed to understand that they were seeing each other. Five minutes later he fell asleep for sixteen hours, and woke up as confused as ever.

Other drugs seemed to bring Merlin nearer the surface, and that was scarier. Well, 'pant-wettingly terrifying' would probably be more accurate. As mythic figures go, Merlin's about as powerful as you get before you start running into actual gods (and as a rule gods don't become devices, I've never been quite sure why). Certainly he was the most intimidating I'd met, and his time in jail was *pissing him off.* Being sworn at furiously in a mixture of Latin, Medieval Welsh and the kind of English you'd hear in a rugby team's locker-room was the least of it. Fortunately these bad spells – actually, I'd feel a lot more comfortable calling them 'episodes' – were rare and always brief in duration, but they always left us shaken.

'This isn't working,' Cantrell said one evening, after a particularly fruitless day in which Dr Wendiman's inner genius had remained firmly locked away. 'I'm sorry to be the one to say it, Merry, but it isn't.'

'It has to.' Merry took her glasses off and pinched the bridge of her nose. 'It isn't about the research any more. I can't stand seeing Dad like this. All the while he was out of sight, I could stop myself thinking about it, but... this is unbearable. We have to find something. We just have to.'

'There may be nothing we can do, Mal,' said Jory gently. 'This may just be Alzheimer's – the real thing, I mean.' (That, of course, was another explanation which fitted the evidence – well, most of it – yet established Malory's innocence.) 'I know that's not what you want to hear, but we've got to consider it.'

'Even if it's not,' I said, 'what you're trying to do may not be possible. All the times I've heard of allies leaving people, it's been the ally who made it happen, not anyone else. And if Merlin could leave your dad any time he wanted, it wouldn't be much of a prison, would it?'

'We can't stay here much longer,' Jory pointed out. 'The Circle will be looking. We can't keep him in one place, and he's too conspicuous to move. We're running out of options. Besides…' He looked nervous bringing the matter up, but soldiered on anyway. 'Some of the others feel it's distracting us. That we should have other priorities. Big Jack was fairly vocal about it, as was Scar. I think we should be doing our best for Dr Wendiman, but we can't let him be our only concern.'

'You can arrange your priorities however you want,' Merry snapped. She was uncharacteristically edgy after the weeks of physical and emotional strain.

There was a long silence, broken only by a clatter from the kitchen, as Burn patiently practised his passes with coins and a mobile phone. After a while, Cantrell started to look thoughtful and wandered over to Merry's laptop.

'Without Dad,' Merry explained impatiently, 'we're stuck at an impasse. I've exhausted my own avenues of investigation into the devicial schism. He's the only person I can bring in who I'd trust.'

Merry had always maintained that her father would see Britain's archetypal crisis the way she did, as something transcending petty factional loyalties, and that he'd throw himself wholeheartedly behind her efforts to diagnose and heal it, if she could only heal him first. Jory was far too tactful to pass on any doubts on that score, but I guessed they were a notable part of whatever reservations Jack and Scar had expressed.

'Well, I don't believe that,' Jory said. 'The first bit, I mean. You're the cleverest person I know, Mal, probably by a factor of ten. You don't need your dad for this – you can work it out without him, I'm sure of it. All this attempted therapy's clever, too, but it's a distraction from what you're really trying to do. You've given it your best shot; now you need to try something else.'

A tiny crinkle appeared in the centre of Merry's brow, as if she was about to say something, but before she could, Cantrell looked up from the laptop. 'I may have something. I mean, about Edward. Maybe we've been going about this whole thing ass-backwards. Merry, do you know of any time an ally's taken two human associates at one time?'

She shook her head. 'Some of them distribute across a group, but only ones which represent a group to start off with. Like the Nine Witches of Caer Lloyw, or the Coraniaid. The individual ones...' She shook it again, more emphatically. 'It's never happened. Nowhere in the Circle's records.'

Rev said, 'Nor the Chapel's either, such as they are.' Nobody really expects hundreds of years of oral history, passed on by keen amateur storytellers and professional liars, to be especially reliable.

Merry was frowning at him, while Jory and I struggled to catch up.

'You're saying –' I said '– instead of trying to force Merlin out of Edward, we should give him someone else to bond with?'

Cantrell nodded. 'It's what you said about Merlin not being able to leave even if he wanted to. I'm guessing there are rules he has to follow. We've been trying to organise a breakout, when we should have been getting him extradited.'

'Can we do that?' Jory asked. 'Bond someone with a specific ally, I mean? At the Circle they always said it was impossible to know who you'd get. And their preparations are pretty rigorous.' Jory's always slightly resented the fact that he had to go through months of training and ritual culminating in a vigil, fasting and prayer before a device accepted him, whereas we in the Chapel just stumble into these things, like Janene Long waking up one morning to find her Adam Bell obsession had become a relationship.

Merry pursed her lips. 'I think we can,' she said. 'Dad allied me to Nimue when I was thirteen, remember. He wanted that device specifically, or at least a closely similar one. The Arthurian devices are old-fashioned about gender, which narrowed the field a lot, but I wouldn't have been much use to him as just some knightly consort, and he definitely didn't want to summon Morgan le Fay. So he tried to channel me into a particular state of mind that Nimue or Vivian or Ninian would find receptive. It's true he had Merlin's cooperation in that, but if Rev's right then so will we.'

'It's got to be worth a try,' I said. 'Can't make things worse, can it?' Cantrell nodded in appreciation.

'Hold on,' said Jory. 'So who do we use as the subject?' He looked around at Rev, Merry and me. 'We've all got allies already. What do we do, pull someone off the street and ask them if they want to play host to an ancient unpredictable wizard?'

Caught up in our discussion, none of us had noticed that the clacking of coins from the kitchen had stopped some time before. 'Hey man,' Burn said now, leaning lankily in the doorway and grinning at us. 'You're saying someone gets to be Merlin? Count me right in.'

* * *

They sent me out for booze, pizza, energy drinks, more joss-sticks and a quite expensive DVD box set. As Jory had said, time was running short, and Burn had never been a big reader. Malory reckoned that forty-eight solid hours spent watching the BBC series *Merlin* should be enough to send anyone into an altered state of consciousness.

That wasn't all she had planned, of course. Jory gave Burn a crash course of Circle training (on the basis that Merlin was an Arthurian device, though one which rarely behaved the way the Knightly ones did), culminating with a buzz-cut, a fortifying pizza, a ceremonial robing in my spare towelling dressing-gown, and strict instructions not to eat during his two-day *Merlin*athon. Cantrell insisted on supplying the prayer component of the vigil ritual, and made us all sit round in a circle for it – as unselfconsciously as he always had with the Green Chapel, and ignoring my agnostic squirming quite as ruthlessly as ever.

Malory produced an antique book full of Latin, which she claimed was a grimoire formerly belonging to Elizabeth I's astrologer Dr John Dee, and stood around reading from it. This was entirely unlike any way of summoning an ally I'd ever heard of, so I guessed it was mainly for the imagery, the idea being that the Merlin ally might have an affinity for books of magic. Presumably, if they'd been trying to summon Sir Dagonet, a joke-book would have been just the thing. (Jory would later confide in me that it was just the commonplace book Malory had stolen from the Bodleian – if 'just' is the word for that – containing the lives of Saints Brelin and Bellen and absolutely no spells whatsoever.)

Whether Burn was regretting volunteering by then I don't know, but the three-quarter-hourly repetition of the theme tune had already put him in a semi-trance state, aided by the bottle of vodka he'd insisted on keeping by him at all times. (Jory had argued at first that this broke the spirit of the fast, but had let the matter drop after Burn explained to him that any spirit that wanted him to do this sober could just fuck the fuck right off.)

For two days Burn endured his shamanic journey into the pop-culture end of the British mythic subconscious, while the rest of us alternated between providing a convincingly ritualistic ambience and attending to Edward Wendiman's bodily needs.

I don't know whether you've ever seen *Merlin*, but it's basically *Buffy the Dragon Slayer*, with Arthur, Guinevere, Lancelot, 'Gwaine' and co as unruly multi-ethnic teens and twentysomethings at the court of Uther Pendragon, acting out generic fantasy plotlines involving computer-generated trolls, pixies and unicorns. Weirdly, Merlin's a young contemporary of theirs (Arthur's manservant and vaguely homoerotic BFF, in fact), who can secretly do magic and has a habit of disguising himself as an aged wizard to dispense sage advice. The last season takes the real Arthurian story in a dash, from Arthur pulling Excalibur from a stone and becoming king to his final battle at Camlann, skipping all the problematic or confusing stuff like Mordred's parentage and the quest for the Holy Grail, and ends with the High King's still-young corpse departing on a barge towards Avalon in the conventional manner.

It's... well, as you may have gathered I have a high tolerance for TV versions of the Robin Hood legend, but, as I've often argued when I'm drunk, it's Robin Hood's nature to be populist. The Arthurian myths demand a bit more gravitas.

I wasn't the target audience for this, though – I was a good twenty years too old – and it was clear that Burn was lapping it up. I'd wondered at the time why Merry hadn't asked for something like the film *Excalibur*, which would have been cheaper, more faithful and (crucially) a hell of a lot shorter; but Burn, born more than a decade after that was made, would probably have found it intolerably mannered and old-fashioned. This was produced for exactly his generation, and it portrayed Merlin as a young guy punching above his weight, who was only ever *pretending* to be an ancient and powerful sorcerer. For our purposes at the time it was ideal, though more than once Jory cringed so hard at some misrepresentation of the source material that he knocked his Red Bull over. I suspect he found it more of an ordeal than his own vigil.

Towards the end, we all noticed that Burn was mouthing Merlin's lines, a moment after young Colin Morgan said them on the TV. He seemed to have retreated entirely from the room, even his vodka forgotten, becoming as utterly contained within that screen as the overly artificial special effects infesting the episodes. Everyone else was silent, awed at his absorption in such a dodgy piece of cultural product: even Edward, when Jory quietly went and fetched him from the bedroom, picked up on the atmosphere and kept his peace.

The final scene, after a dragon with John Hurt's voice prophesied Arthur's return, and a teary-eyed Merlin set his pal floating off towards Avalon – while Guinevere was implausibly acclaimed as his successor – skipped suddenly to the present day, where a lorry passing through the same landscape nearly knocked over a tramp who was visibly an elderly Merlin. Electrified, Burn stood and glanced around him in bemusement, taking in his own modern surroundings. He stared down at his body, as if vaguely surprised to discover he still had one, then, as the episode's closing music played, he told us with total conviction: 'Straight up, man. That TV dragon told it like it is. Arthur Pendragon's coming back, and *soon.*'

'Good Lord,' an elderly voice said weakly. 'That sounds like a spontaneous extrapolatory prophecy based on perceived devicial trends. I haven't heard one of those in years.'

'Daddy!' Merry shrieked, and threw herself into Edward Wendiman's arms.

* * *

We'd all been cooped up for far too long, and the smell of cold pizza and flatulence permeated the flat, so we opened all the windows, took the minor risk of running into a Circle agent on a Wednesday evening in Eastbourne, and went out for a curry.

Edward was on outstanding form, trading intellectual bons mots with Cantrell, his sense of liberation palpable. Even without a device, he had an amazing mind, and now it was unoccluded he remembered the past year perfectly. He was well aware of who we were, our affiliations and relationships, and of what we'd done for him, for which he was modestly but sincerely grateful. Merry, too, was giddy with relief, and downing her Cobra lager with gusto. Jory was quietly pleased, of course, but didn't say much: it was a complicated situation for him personally, in more ways than I appreciated at the time. I did my best to keep the conversational gears oiled, although after the past few days I was about ready to drop.

Burn said little, but what he did come out with suggested someone coming to grips with a whole new perspective on the world. At one point he interrupted Cantrell's well-rehearsed opinions on the qualities of a really good onion bhaji – Rev may not eat much, but that doesn't mean he doesn't appreciate his food – to say, 'Hey, I'm gonna have to learn all that Latin and Greek and Welsh shit, aren't I? Jesus. I couldn't even get French GCSE.'

Another time, while listening intently to one of my anecdotes about some mutual acquaintances in the Green Chapel (though I was being very careful to leave identifying details out of it, given Edward's presence), he absent-mindedly pulled out a pack of cards, shuffled them flawlessly in three different showy ways and drew the top two, at which point he seemed to notice what he was doing. 'Hey – two black kings,' he said, showing us the kings of spades and clubs. 'Did I put those there?'

'It's possible,' Malory said. 'Your fingers are used to that sort of thing. You could have remembered the order of the cards subconsciously, from the last time you used them. Although of course it could be coincidence – ah,' she added, as Burn proceeded to draw the other two kings, followed by a joker. The ones which came after were all numbers.

'You want to be more specific?' Burn asked nobody visible to the rest of us. 'That could mean *anything*.' When we asked him what he meant, he refused to elaborate.

Ten minutes later, apropos of nothing as Jory polished off the last of the naan bread, Burn announced, 'Hey, I can go into a trance whenever I want,' then closed his eyes and immediately started snoring. Jory, Cantrell and I had to carry him back to the flat, much to the curry-house owners' disapproval.

When we deposited him on the sofa where he'd been sleeping since he arrived at the flat, he spoke without opening his eyes. 'Hey Merry,' he said, 'we're talking about fingers doing stuff on their own, yeah? You ever think about automatic writing? Get one of us into this kind of trance, put a pen in their hand, see what they come out with. Might get you closer to the source of that schism, you think? Where'd my fucking Cobra go?' he concluded, before relapsing into unconsciousness.

With Burn asleep on the couch, the rest of us retired to our respective rooms. I considered suggesting to Jory, Merry and Rev that one of us should stay up and keep watch in case Edward, having reacquired his marbles, tried to give us the slip, but it was obvious everyone was too knackered. That said, I heard Merry's giggling from hers and Jory's bedroom for a while before I fell asleep, to spend the night in unpleasant *Alice in Wonderland* dreams about people with allies who were playing-cards.

By the time we clambered out of our various beds the next morning, Burn was long gone.

* * *

We hoped, of course, that the Merlin device had just gone into seclusion, to spend a while adjusting to its new host, but it was all too possible that it was following its traditional loyalties and heading back to the Circle. We left Auntie Ginnie's that day – hurriedly, and in my case cursing prolifically – knowing that Burn knew not only where to find us, but everything we'd been doing for the past weeks.

I may prefer the nomadic lifestyle, but knowing that my pied-a-terre might never again be safe to use had whipped away my safety net. From now on, the Green Chapel's fate was mine as well.

Splitting up to stay inconspicuous during the journey, we relocated along the coast to Portsmouth, where Cantrell had a bolthole set up in a disused warehouse. Always a one for physical comfort, he'd furnished it nicely with stuff reclaimed from skips and the municipal dump, and its reinforced concrete pillars were perfectly spaced for stringing hammocks. Though he milked it for self-sacrifice points, Cantrell gave up the one real bed to Edward, whose ordeal had left him pretty physically frail, and joined the rest of us in dangling between the structural supports.

Merry, Jory and Rev talked between them about cancelling the Grail heist, but since it came as a shock to me that they intended to steal the relic at all, they concluded that they probably hadn't discussed it while Burn was around. Merry contacted the people in the Chapel who knew Burn best, asking them to put out feelers, but she guessed (correctly) that all inquiries would come back empty.

We turned, then, to the suggestion Burn had left us with – that of placing a volunteer into a profound hypnotic state, enabling them to access the deep collective unconscious where the devices had their roots, and getting them to mediate that state through so-called 'automatic writing'. It was a technique for self-revelation which, as Malory explained, had been mostly superseded in conventional psychology. Few things about the study of the devices are conventional, though.

In this case, the hope was that the subject would be able to follow these devicial roots deep enough into the fertile soil of the mind that they could draw out a more ancient version – perhaps, with luck, the very oldest version – of the schism legend which Malory had been tracing through her antique texts. In a sense it would still be a journey of self-discovery, but only in that the devices and their oldest structures formed a deeply submerged part of everybody's self.

'Though how it can be that deep in the past, yet still be shaping the British psyche, I'm not sure,' she said. 'We've traced the archetypes as far back as Brutus, and he's our foundation myth. We could follow them to Troy, I suppose, back into Homer. But without some permanent iconography that's specifically British I can't see how it's still so relevant.'

'Could be that's the wrong strand to follow,' Rev suggested. 'Could be it's the Joseph of Arimathea connection. Go into any Anglican church and you'll see British versions of imagery from first-century Judaea.'

'Wouldn't that be interesting?' was Malory's only response.

As for the hypnotic subject, there was only one real candidate. Wendiman senior didn't have a device any more, and Friar Tuck and Alan a'Dale are lightweights on the mythic scene. Merry herself was plugged into a more primal archetype, but whether as Nimue or Maid Marian she was still peripheral to the story she was becoming increasingly convinced formed the skeleton-key to the British psyche.

Jory, on the other hand, might be carrying the Robin Hood ally – and if he wasn't, had at least borne that of Sir Gawain, the Green Knight's counterpart. The device that went by the names of Robin and the Green Knight, and who'd been represented in those other tales as St Brelin and Madog son of Hellius, was, at root, one of the two whom this fundamental breach had sundered. Since the other – present in the stories as Gor, St Bellen, Sir Pelles and John Lackland – was the Fisher King, ultimately an identity of the ever-absent Arthur himself… well, we really weren't likely to find a better candidate than Jory.

It wasn't anything like as elaborate as the ceremony to free Merlin had been. There was a certain amount of scene-setting with candles and the like, but the only actual requirement was to put Jory into a particularly deep trance, while leaving his hand free for writing. He lay down on a sofa Rev had liberated from a skip in very decent condition, rested his hand on a luggage trunk where an A4 notepad had been placed, and held a black Bic biro. I stood by ready to turn the pages, while Malory talked him though the usual routine of concentrating on a rhythmic, repetitive sensory input at a carefully calculated frequency – in this case a metronome app on her phone, which she kept fine-tuning as the session progressed.

When he was under, she asked him, 'Who are you?'

His hand skittered across the page, and everyone leaned in to see what it had written. Disappointingly, it just said 'Jordan Taylor' – although for Cantrell and me, who still knew Jory as 'Dan', it was the first time we'd actually seen his full name.

Merry said, 'I'm not speaking to Jordan Taylor now. I'm talking to the device who Jordan Taylor has allied himself with. Please tell me who you are.'

Again Jory's hand spasmed across the paper, and a new name appeared there: 'Robin of Locksley.' Merry gave a long, satisfied sigh.

'Thank you, Robin of Locksley,' Malory said. 'We're glad you're here. We're interested in the other names you've had. Tell us, please – do you remember your name before you were Robin of Locksley?'

More twitching, further names: 'Robyn Hodd. Robyne Godefellwe. Wodewose.'

'We know that, Robin Hood,' Merry said. 'We know those names. The ones we need are older. You had another name before you were Robin Hood. What was it?'

The hand wrote, 'Þe Grene Knyȝte', using the Middle English letters *thorn* and *yogh*, and once again Malory let out a breath.

'Thank you, Green Knight,' said Malory. 'And what name were you known by before that?'

'FRATER BRELINVS,' wrote the hand. Jory himself by now was quite immobile, breathing deeply, completely relaxed, his hand moving apparently without any dependency upon the rest of him.

'Is that right?' Cantrell asked in a whisper. 'We found that name in one old text, that's all. There's no sign it was ever cultural currency.'

'This is Dan's mind, remember,' Merry murmured. 'It's the name he calls that iteration of the archetype. And before then, Brother Brelin?' she asked more loudly. 'What were you called then?'

The hand hesitated.

From his chair, Edward Wendiman whispered, 'There's a good chance that any version prior to that will have been illiterate. It's only Brelin's monastic training that would mean he wasn't.'

'Robin Hood would have been illiterate too,' I muttered, but nobody paid any attention.

'Write out the name as Jordan Taylor would,' Malory suggested.

Jory wrote, 'Madog of Britain.'

'Excellent, Madog,' Malory said. 'Now, we need you to think back further still. You have a brother, Gor. You and Gor were once closer than you later became. Do you remember?'

The hand leapt again. 'Twins. In Alba's womb.'

Personally, I shivered. Scientific all this might be, but talking directly to the devices underlying the devices was giving me the willies. I flipped to the next page in the notepad.

'I mean before that,' Merry said again. 'I think Madog and Gor were closer once even than that. I think that once you were the same person.'

'Malory, that's a leading question,' Edward chided.

The hand wrote, 'No names then. None that remain.'

'That's all right, friend,' Merry said, 'we don't need names. We just need to know the story.'

'The story,' Jory wrote.

'The story,' Merry said, 'of how your two halves came to be sundered. It's very important that we know.'

'I failed,' said Jory, his deep voice breaking the silence. 'The old women chose badly,' he continued, his face still perfectly serene as Malory scrabbled for the voice recorder on her phone. 'I couldn't kill him.'

* * *

The story that Jory told – or rather that that primal ur-device, the oldest that survives in this island's realm of ideas, told through him – went like this.

'He tracked me through the forest, loping like the wolf as it runs down the deer. Just as I had taught him. Just as I myself had done before him.

'He was my son, our people's best huntsman, bettering me, although it was I who had trained him in the hunter's ways. The skills he had learned from my lips and at my hand would serve him well now, as well as they had served me nine winters before, when I had chased my mother's brother, the king before me, through these woods.

'The forest is where the sun dwells. This we know, all of us who graze our sheep on the plain, learning it in childhood on our grandmother's laps. Each day, the sun leaves his woodland home and climbs high into the sky, blessing us with his warmth. Each evening he returns to his forest, tired from his journey, to sleep and recover before the next day's exertions. Like all the beasts of the forest, the sun is his own creature, wild and untameable. As with all forest beasts, one may come to know him, to learn his ways, to seek him out in his domain and then perhaps, after a worthy struggle, to bring him home to the people.

'The greatest hunter of all is he who hunts the sun.

'My mother's brother, an eighteen-year king, had forgotten his hunting skills by the end, bringing the sun home at winter's depth in strange and meagre forms: a young deer, a badger, once even a rabbit, for which the old women had soundly derided him. I, though, was still the man they had chosen to succeed him nine years before.

'I had been a good king: a brave warrior, a skilled hunter, a prolific fatherer of children – one of whom, now a grown man of thirteen years, the women had chosen to hunt me. Throughout my reign I had striven to be fearless and selfless, to protect our homes and enclosures from the wolves and the raiders, while our crops flourished with the sun's blessings.

'For nine midsummers I had celebrated the sun's bounty, burning food on our village altar when he was at his height, sending its smoke up to sustain him on that longest of his journeys. For eight midwinters I had hunted the sun through the forest, at that time each year when he would try to flee from us, leaving us alone forever in the chill and dark. Eight times I had brought the sun home, gashed and dripping his warmth, in the shape of boar or stag or, once, a bear. Eight times we had fed on the sun, tasting his light, and so had been sustained until the spring.

'Now I had reached the ninth midwinter of my kingship, and it was my turn to be the quarry. Wrapped tightly in a sheep's fleece, leaning upon my ash-wood spear, I trod the flint-hard earth, my bark soles sliding on the slick ice. I did what I could to conceal my passing, but I knew I would be leaving spoor: broken twigs, flattened leaves, bark-shod footprints in the shallow snow. My hunter had been my student, and I had taught him well.

'Tomorrow he would take the sun home in my body, my side torn open by his spear. From me to him would pass the name of hunter of the sun, and thus of king – the title, yet also the hunter-king's inner essence, the story-shape which gives the people of the plain their nature, gifted at the holy place from one king to the next.

'I imagined him prowling after me, hard on my scent, his beard icy, the wolf who would devour the sun. His breath would make clouds before his face, like those which forever threaten the sun. Perhaps they are a wolf's breath, too.

'He would not press too hard behind me, I knew. He could not risk confronting me before we reached the sacred place. If that happened, how would he know where to go when his time came, nine years hence? (So the women said, yet I suspected that some of them, at least, knew where the sanctuary was. A king might fall in combat, or die at the tusks or antlers of an angry beast, and who would tell the new king where to lead his hunter then?)

'A long time we played that game of wolf and stag, until at last I came to the holy place. I stood beside the spring, the pool of clear water bubbling from the ground, and leaned on the ash tree whose roots fingered the water, the tree in the well, from which I had cut my own spear nine years before. My son knew the place already, I had no doubt – playing with his brothers, hunting the ordinary beasts of the wood, perhaps even sharing intimacies with the village girls – but it had not been sacred then. Only now, at midwinter of every ninth year, was it the holy well where the holy tree stood.

'I drank from the well, thirsty after my trek. Knowing that by now he was nearby, would be watching me, I gathered branches to build a shelter beneath the ash-tree, chewed some of the dried mutton and herbs I had brought with me.

'At last – imagining the agonies my son must be feeling, crouching cramped in the frozen woods, breathing as little as he could so no clouds of vapour would betray him – I lay myself down to sleep.

'His duty now would be, without awakening me, to cut a branch from the tree above me and to shape it into a spear, the emblem of his own kingship. Then – again if he could manage it without arousing me – he would gore me with it in my sleep, as I had thrust my own spear through my mother's brother's chest nine years before. He would build a sled of branches and drag my carcass home to the feast, the embodiment of the sun which he, the new young king, had vanquished.

'If he awoke me, I would defend myself. That was my right. My son was younger than me, yes, perhaps stronger, but I was still the wilier, more experienced warrior. Instead of being killed, I might kill him, and then the sun would return to the village in *his* body, and *I* would reign for another nine years. My mother's brother had done this, killing his own son in his ninth midwinter, and the legends of the village said that one king had managed it twice, and ruled for twenty-seven years. He must have died a haggard, withered old man of forty or more.

'I have never found sleep to come so hard as then. But come it did, and was filled with cold dreams of stories long forgotten, of loves and killings in a land of eternal ice, abandoned by the sun.

'I awoke to a cracking sound, the breaking of a frozen twig beneath a bark sole. In an instant I was outside my shelter, clutching my spear and facing the young man who would have killed me with his own.

'Dismay was etched onto his face at his mistake, but he rallied quickly. He called to me to make my peace with this world that I would soon be leaving – which I had done long before – then came in for the kill.

'I cursed him, then. I had done my part, performed the tasks which merciless convention had set out for me. If he had carried out his own duties, I would already be dead, and there would be no need for this terrible struggle. Why had the women not chosen a better hunter than he?

'He bellowed and ran at me. I sidestepped his spear-point, but could land no clear blow of my own. Instead, I struck the back of his head with the spear's shaft as he passed. He barely seemed to notice.

'We shifted warily, moving back and forth at the pool's edge, thrusting at one another but never connecting, grappling but never gaining the advantage. Once, he had me pressed against the holy tree awaiting the killing blow, but in desperation I kicked my branch shelter, scattering the wood at him and forcing him to stumble back. Once I nearly forced him into the pool itself, but he recovered his balance in the shallows, stabbing fiercely to force me back.

'Again, then, we were at one – no longer hunter and quarry, but two warriors engaged in the eternal dance of combat. Once, I had danced in his place: one day, if he were successful, he would dance in mine. He was my son, and I had loved him as I loved myself. At times I almost forgot that we were two men, not one.

'Our contest seemed to last forever, though when I stole a glance at the moon, she'd barely moved.

'I soon came to realise that I had the advantage. I had refreshed myself in sleep while he had been enduring a cramped, painful watch. I might be old, but he was exhausted. Eventually one of my thrusts met its mark, and my spear-point pierced his furs to sink into his groin, pinning his member to his thigh. He cried out and sank to his knees, forgetting everything except the burning pain of it, and there awaited my death-blow.

'I stared at down at that familiar face, rent with agony now, and remembered his birth. The midwife had handed him to me, a tiny thing wrapped in furs, crying softly, and I had held him, spoke soothingly to him and stroked his brow until he fell asleep.

'I remembered the joy he had given me as he grew – his endless curiosity at the world, his awed respect for my adult's knowledge of its ways, his pride at being the son of the king.

'I recalled the times we had hunted together in this wood, his quickness to learn and the skill with which he put my lessons into practice.

'He stared at me, the agony on his face excruciating. It was I who had done this to him.

'I lowered my spear. It seemed the women had chosen badly not just once, but twice.

'We were alike, then. So similar that we should indeed have become one, as custom demanded. Indeed, I sometimes feel that it was I who returned the next day to the village, hobbling with pain, to claim a kingship which all knew that I had never earned, while he stepped away into the forest, never to walk among the people of the plain again.

'It was not so. I bound his wounds and left him, later leaving the carcase of a wild pony next to his sleeping form. Using the sled I had made, he dragged it back with him to the village, and told them all that I was a coward, that I had fled the forest instead of sleeping at the sacred well. The pony, he insisted, was the body of the sun, and he had conquered it.

'The women accepted it – what alternative was there? They were reluctant, but my son had the support of the young men, and with me gone into the woods he was the only king they had.

'For my part, I became a hermit, a wild man, an outcast – living a solitary life at first, a figure glimpsed among the trees, an object of awe and ridicule. In time, though, others came to me – those who disagreed with my son's rule, but were afraid to challenge him. In time, we became a tribe of our own, the hunters in the dwindling woods.

'Because the new king was making changes. At his first midsummer he led a party of young men into the woods with stone axes, and they cut down the ash-tree in the well, and stopped the spring with stones and clay. The tree they dragged to the village, and used it to make flint-tipped spears for every man of hunting age.

'I broke the dam and released the spring, but it was too late. The power of the holy place was broken. In the autumn there was a small rebellion against my son, but he fought it off, impaling the leader on his ashen spear, and after that few raised their voices against him.

'From now on, he decreed, no man must kill another to become king. He himself was to reign until he died, and then the people would choose another to rule in his place, who might perhaps train a son to follow him as I had trained mine.

'For his part, though, the new king's manhood had been ruined by the blow I had struck him in the forest, and though he took a consort he fathered me no grandsons or granddaughters.

'To placate those who did speak, telling him that the sun would desert the people if he were not hunted in a king's body every ninth midwinter, my son announced a plan to build him a midsummer altar greater than any he had ever seen, and one that would suffice for midwinter too. It would be devised with the help of the wisest women and men of our own and other villages – a holy place there on the plain, where the stones themselves would herald the sun's coming, and where the heights of summer and winter would be marked by special ceremonies, signalled by his rising over particular stones.

'Within my lifetime the first stones had been brought to our plain, many trees cut from the forest to make logs to roll them on. My new followers and I killed some of those who came to take the trees, but the scheme was a vast one, and soon the king had forced or cajoled help from many of the other villages of the plain. In time they too came to accept him as their ruler, and he became the greatest king of any in the stories. Though many left the plains for the diminishing forests, to join me in attempting to protect their heritage, I could see that our old way of life was ending.

'My son's plan would succeed. It would take many generations, but in the end there his stone edifice would be built, a fastness for the sun upon that ever-growing plain, a place which would persist in people's minds for as long as the land itself.

'And that,' said Jory, 'in the snap of a twig, is how the unbroken succession of the hunter of the sun came to be sundered, how the tree was torn from the well, and how the wounded king and the outlaw in the woods came to be.'

* * *

Jory fell silent then, and after a moment or two Merry told her phone to stop recording.

The rest of us were silent too, trying to absorb the import of what we'd just heard.

Malory shrugged. 'That's it,' she said. 'We've got it all.'

'Stonehenge,' said Edward, fingering his pinless tie.

'Stonehenge,' she agreed. 'Pretty much the oldest, biggest and most famous cultural artefact this island's ever produced. Yes, I should think that would just about do it.

'We've got it,' she said again. 'We know how the schism began. We know where, and even approximately when. Now all we need to do is fix it.'

9. A FEAST FOR BERNARD MADDOX

Merlin's new bondsman wears a chunky silver signet-ring in the shape of a dragon's head. Though it's not his place to find fault, Stephen feels it's rather tasteless.

Not being a knight, the Merlin device has no associated arms, so traditionally Merlin's representatives are allowed to adopt their own symbols – like the Stonehenge tie-pin which Edward Wendiman no longer wears. The device-bearers in question have been a mixed bag, ranging from earls and bishops to beggars and vagrants, and the emblems they've chosen have been wide-ranging, including on one occasion a live bird of prey worn on the arm. Seen from that angle, Blaze's ring is hardly an outlier, but to a Knight whose emblem consists of monochrome squares, it looks gaudy.

Still, he knows that other people – specifically, though he wouldn't dream of saying so, working-class people – can have different ideas about such things.

It has to be said that Blaze's flamboyant manner is different altogether from the quiet, courteous eccentricity of Edward Wendiman. The man's a showman, forever doing minor magic tricks to entertain the men-at-arms and pages; it's crossed Stephen's mind that he might even be a conman, but so far their every test has confirmed the presence and affiliation of Blaze's device. If he's a hustler, which still seems entirely possible, then he's a hustler for King Arthur.

Though the newcomer insists on being called 'Blaze' – either a stage name or a street name, though given that he generally performs on the street the difference seems academic to Stephen – he's happily surrendered a birth name, Bernard Maddox, and enough personal details to allow a background check. He's nineteen, born in Peckham, with a conviction for arson at the age of eleven and a couple for drug possession in his early teens. Given that start in life – as Stephen, who's done a lot of work with adolescent boys, knows – Blaze's accomplishment in becoming a self-taught conjurer deserves congratulation, but some in the Circle are experiencing moral panic about their new advisor's criminal past.

It's irrelevant in any case – there's only one Merlin device, and the contribution it can make to the Circle's functioning now is as great as it was in Arthur's time. There's no possibility of the Circle doing anything other than embracing its new avatar.

Because Merlin's bondsmen arrive so unpredictably, there's no fixed equivalent for them of the Knights' investitures, with their feasts and vigils and ceremonial dubbings by the Circle's tame peer of the realm, the perpetually baffled Lord Northwood. Mindful of his new colleague's youth, Raymond suggested that some modified form of vigil ceremony might be an appropriate way to induct him into the solemnity of the Circle, but Blaze rejected the idea with some vehemence, declaring, 'Seneschal, you have no idea what I went through to get this gig.' Since he refuses to elaborate, everybody else remains in the dark on the matter.

In the event, the Seneschal has opted for a modest welcoming ceremony in the Fastness boardroom, with a few informal speeches, drinks and nibbles, and all the Knights who can reasonably be assembled to greet their new comrade at this busy time. It's the sort of thing a lot of people would only go to for the free food, frankly, but the Knights are mostly friendly, clubbable types who'll happily stand around talking shop and chuckling at jokes a five-year-old could have thought of.

There are exceptions, of course – like Paul Parsons, hovering moodily by the canapés like a cyborg Mr Darcy, while the perpetually gloomy Harold Lenton, making a flying visit from the Borders, complains to all and sundry about the Sons of Gore and their unsporting habit of hiding from the paramilitary forces sent to arrest them. Mr Lister's out of his element too, holding his glass of wine and plate defensively in front of him and keeping to the edges of the room – although since the venue's dominated by a large circular boardroom table, the accessible bits of it are mostly edge.

Still, for the most part – and as long as Blaze can be dissuaded from spontaneously bursting into card-tricks and rounds of the shell game with three tea-cups and an olive – everybody seems to be having a good time. Stephen sees Jason among the handful of pages pouring the drinks and handing round the finger food, and gives him an encouraging smile.

* * *

Laney Wardsley was released this morning, into her parents' custody. Legally she's still a minor, the Circle has nothing specific to tie her to any crimes except trespass and possession, and the last thing the Seneschal wants is to alienate the armed forces. Laney's mother, an RAF Group Captain, was tight-lipped but grateful as she stood with her husband in the Fastness's reception; the latter, a doctor, was visibly emotional at having their errant daughter returned to them. He started when he saw her still-puffy nose, but a moment's examination told him the break was older than her arrest, and he just shook his head wearily.

Laney's co-arrestee, Franklin Cantrell, has been less fortunate. The Circle's tightened its intake procedures considerably since the days when Jack Bennett's and

Marianne 'Scar' Millar's devices eluded detection, and the tests it now applies to prisoners are capable of picking up any stray manifestation of the Robin Hood mythos. Rev's on his way to the Benwick Institute, from which he stands little chance of emerging any time soon. Again, Scar's escape from Benwick last year, and Jory's violent rescue on the way to the facility, have closed off any security loopholes that might have remained.

Alice Dashwood's body's been handed over to her own grieving parents, both City lawyers, who arrived with the undertaker's van this morning. It seems they gave up on their daughter some time ago, and blame her lifestyle rather than the Circle for her untimely death – though they've accepted a handsome compensation package in return for not speaking about it publicly. Paul Parsons spoke to them this morning – briefly, but as charmingly as he can be when necessary.

He also talked to the Wardsleys about the tragic death of their daughter's unsuitable friend, and assured them that Laney was entirely blameless, in this and anything else. Without Liss's unsuitable influence leading her astray, he reassured them, the chances were she'd settled down again like a dutiful daughter.

I wasn't there to see the look Laney gave him, but I can't imagine it was pretty.

* * *

At the reception for Blaze, everything goes swimmingly through the arrival of the various guests and their easy small talk, Desmond Wigsby's introduction to the proceedings (during which, as the uncontacted tribes in the Andaman Islands could have predicted, he does indeed utter the phrase, 'I'm told he's a bit of a wizard!') and Sir Charles's stupefyingly dull and conventional welcoming speech, right up to the point when Blaze himself takes his turn to speak.

'Hey there,' he tells the assembled Knights. Despite his youth, his obvious lack of public-school education and his almost solitary blackness, he seems to Stephen entirely at ease. 'Thanks for the welcome, all of you. I really feel like I've come home, you know what I'm saying? I feel I belong here.'

Stephen, who's very slightly more attuned to ethnic irony than most of the other Knights in the room, thinks he may detect it here. On the other hand, Blaze might be sincere. He catches the eye of Freddie Obote, the bondsman of Sir Ywain the Bastard and the only other non-white Knight present, who gives the tiniest of shrugs.

The newcomer proceeds with his speech. 'The bloke who had this job before me, Edward Wendiman... well, I never really knew him, but it sounds like he was a fine man. I know you must be thinking to yourselves, "Who is this new guy? Who's he think he is, this new dude, coming over here and taking over from our good pal Eddie?"

'Well, I'm not Eddie, and I'm not gonna be replacing him. I know I'm young, I ain't no university professor like Edward, and I'm kind of *urban*. Some of you may not like me, and that's cool. Not everybody likes everybody, and we're all pros here, yeah?

'But you ask who am I to take over his job here?' Blaze asks rhetorically. 'Well then, I'll tell you.

'I'm fucking *Merlin*, man, that's who. Merlin the wizard, Merlin the bard, Merlin the druid. I was the advisor to Arthur the High King, and to his dad Uther Pendragon, and to King Vortigern before them. The Romans call me Merlinus Ambrosius, the Welsh Myrddin Wyllt, and I've had a bunch of other names. My mum was a virgin, my dad was a spirit, and the Lady of the Lake was my girlfriend. I prophesised the coming of the Saxons, and how they'd come to rule this country. I've faced down witches, emperors and dragons. I introduced the High King's parents, yeah? I was right there in the next room when he was conceived, and when he was born it was me took him away to his foster-mum and foster-dad. I was there when he pulled that sword out of that stone, too, and I've been around him and his people ever since. I'm

Merlin who doesn't die, who gets locked up in a wood but comes back every time, to serve that High King's Circle and to await his coming.

'I'm Merlin, for real, and *I don't take kindly to rivals.*'

The whole room jumps as one. Nearly every man there has a device (naturally there aren't any women there), and each of them can call on his own impressive reserves of charisma and rhetorical prowess – but there's a hypnotic rhythm in Blaze's delivery that's drawn them into his account of his device, an effect he's deliberately shattered with his sudden vehemence.

'When Merlin was a tiny boy,' he says, his voice quiet now, 'they brought him to this place of King Vortigern's. He was trying to build a tower, a fastness just like this one of yours, but every time he built it, it fell down. There was two dragons fighting underneath it, yeah, in a pool under the ground, and every time the king's people laid their foundations, those dragons fought and shook the ground, and sent it crashing down again.

'See, Merlin knew that. But no-one else did. Must have been his blood, I suppose.

'I'll tell you who *truly* didn't know, and that was the king's magician. *He* said the ground needed a sacrifice. *He* said the mortar of that tower, the concrete, had to be mixed with a young boy's blood. But not just any boy, no. He said it had to be a boy without a father. One born of the spirit, yeah?

'That's why they took him there, Merlin – to be killed. But he set them right. He told them about those dragons, and he showed them how to dig down to the pool and drain it, set those flying lizards free.

'Vortigern built his tower, all right. But first he set my man Merlin up in place of that magician of his. That ignorant, cowardly, murderous magician who'd have seen a kid killed rather than fess up that he didn't know his job – Vortigern fired his arse. *Isn't that right, Maugantius?*' he snaps, and everybody starts again.

Then everybody turns in silence to follow Blaze's gaze, which has settled on Mr Lister. Lister, who's been edging ever closer to the stairwell during this harangue, stops in his tracks. 'Are you, erm...' he begins. 'I'm not quite sure what you're implying.'

'Don't give me that *shit*, Maugantius,' Blaze thunders. 'I knew you soon as I saw you. You've been taking advantage while I've been away, poisoning these good people's minds with your bad advice, just like you did King Vortigern. Well, it's over now, you hear me? You are *out* of here. Aren't I right, Sir Charles?' he adds, so smoothly that to his own dismay the Seneschal finds himself nodding along.

'Well,' Raymond vacillates, but he's been seen to agree now, and being the man he is, he can't bear the prospect of losing face in front of his subordinates. 'Of course you are,' he barks. 'The Merlin device was out of the picture, so the Maugantius device was the best we could do. But now... you're right, it's untrustworthy. The man too, I shouldn't wonder. Felton, Frith, escort him out of here. We'll send your personal effects to your home address,' he adds, bathetically.

'This is...' blusters Lister, even as a burly Knight grips him by each arm. 'Sir Charles, this is outrageous. I'm an employee! I have rights!'

'Talk to HR,' says Raymond. 'They'll arrange your severance pay. Damn it, I'll write you a reference if that's what it takes. Now get out of my sight!'

And Frith and Felton drag the Circle's formerly highest-ranking secular advisor away, leaving a stunned silence in his wake.

The Seneschal looks thunderous, but he still can't be seen to acknowledge that any of that might have been a mistake. 'Come on,' he booms in a sickly imitation of good humour. 'Can't let good food and drink go to waste! We're entertaining our new arrival!'

After a moment, some sycophant volunteers, 'I never much liked Lister anyway,' and there's a general chorus of agreement. However abrupt and disconcerting his departure, the advisor wasn't a popular man. New conversations start up, more wine's poured, and in a few minutes, the party's back in the fullest swing it was ever realistically going to achieve.

Blaze drains his glass of wine and beckons Jason over to take it back to the kitchens with him. Then, with a cheery greeting to a visiting liaison Fiann from the Children of Oisín, he starts juggling lighted cigarettes in blatant contravention of the Fastness' strict no-smoking rule.

* * *

There's something I probably need to clarify at this point. Burn doesn't actually remember all that stuff with Vortigern and Maugantius and the dragons, or the later stuff about Uther and Arthur either. It's not like regressing Jory, where he was describing (admittedly in the first person) his device's deepest structures, far down in the collective unconscious – these are specifics of a man's life that Blaze is claiming to remember consciously. Either he's lying to impress the Knights (which is possible, but a hell of a risk) or they're false memories based on his own reading of the legend.

That he's been reading up on his new identity is obvious, of course. He wouldn't have got any of that stuff from the TV. And sure, he's overidentifying – like I said earlier, that's normal enough while an ally's bedding in. The fact remains, though, that a device-enhanced brain doesn't have magical access to memories that exist outside itself. Anything that looks that way is a fabrication based on our knowledge and expectations.

Not being Malory, I don't have a clue about the psychological mechanisms which can create false memories, but I know they turn up all the time – from the people under hypnosis who suddenly recall an alien abduction or bout of satanic abuse which previously slipped their mind, to the rest of us often being absolutely certain we put our keys down somewhere we blatantly didn't. Given all the other abnormal functions a device can produce in the human mind, it's not surprising this is part of their repertoire. It's not universal – I've never 'remembered' being Alan a'Dale, apart from a couple of times in dreams – but it happens.

I'm sure Burn's memories of being threatened by Maugantius as a boy are as vivid, detailed and real to him as his memories of doing magic tricks for coins on Peckham High Street, but they no more reflect the actual events of the seventh century AD than the average *Merlin* episode. Any resemblance to external objective reality – which of course is impossible to confirm in any case – will be down to whatever factual basis there is for the accounts he's read.

You want proof? Fair enough.

Each device – each one that represents a person, at least – has had a succession of holders. Sometimes dozens, sometimes hundreds – some allies are older than others, some crop up more or less frequently, and a lot of them grant their bearers the gift of a quite short life expectancy. (Older survivors, like Sir Charles or Edward, who bore the device of Sir Menw son of Teirwaedd before he acquired Merlin's, tend to be the exception.) Merlin, though, has been in almost constant play, and rarely near the front lines. Assuming the stories about him date back to 600 CE or so – which is debatable – and that his device-bearers have an average lifespan of forty years once allied – which is generous, but it makes the maths work out – that means there've been about thirty-five past Merlins. Thirty-five minds the device has passed through on its way from the original wizard – if there was one – down to Burn himself. Thirty-five past lives.

But he's not talking about thirty-four of those, is he? He's not even claiming to remember being Edward, who he's actually met. If the devices brought all that baggage with them, Burn wouldn't just be struggling to incorporate new memories of a past life as Arthur's magician and prophet – he'd be assimilating fourteen centuries as an advisor to the Circle, not to mention all the in-fighting over research grants and space in the common-room fridge that used to come with Edward's day job. I'm not sure any human mind could stand the tedium.

But then, if the allies could give us access to the real past lives of other human beings, they'd be doing magic, and we're always told that's impossible. It's not just that it would prove the existence of Jung's collective subconscious and Dawkins' memes – which Merry says pretty much have to apply for any of this to work – it would mean that there was such a thing as life after death, at least for our memories if not our consciousness. Even that kind of afterlife would be a pretty damn revolutionary discovery, but it could only possibly happen by those memories travelling between separate human brains.

The devices change us in all sorts of ways, but they don't turn us telepathic. That, Malory says, would be scientifically ridiculous.

And she's the expert, after all.

* * *

The men-at-arms' and pages' dormitories at the Fastness are in the curtain wall. One room sleeps two, in bunk beds. They're comfortable enough, with chairs and a desk and a window to the central courtyard – pretty similar to the youth hostel where Malory and Jory stayed in Manchester, in fact. The pages are free to roam the curtain wall's interior – they've got their own TV room, games room (ping-pong and Cluedo, not PlayStation and Wii) and a modest library, as well as kitchens and communal showers – but the doors to the outside, and to the courtyard, are kept locked at night, with access for Knights only through the underground car park.

Theoretically, a page who fancied a nocturnal excursion could set off a fire alarm, triggering a staged evacuation of the building – but there'd be little chance of getting back in again with nobody's suspicions aroused, and very little of staying on the Circle's payroll afterwards. The Circle may operate on a general principle of trust, but the pages' loyalties are relatively untried, and the higher-ups are always alert to the dangers of one of them being suborned.

Also in the curtain wall, there are armouries, concealed gun emplacements and observation posts, as well as storerooms, offices, and a mainframe server which acts (unless you're Malory) as a firewall for the secure servers inside the keep. In theory, somebody hoping to sneak out of the building at night might be able to open one of the gun embrasures and abseil down, but they'd be discovered quickly afterwards, possibly from the street outside but certainly from inside the building. At night there's a constant rotation of men-at-arms on patrol, making sure the weapons are secure, checking the exterior for suspicious activity and so forth.

It's a bit of a cosmetic exercise, since to take the Fastness would require, at a minimum, a large and well-equipped army with advanced air support. The UK only has one of those, and it's supposed to be on the same side as the Circle. Still, improbable though a twenty-first century castle siege is, the Circle likes to be prepared for any eventuality short of a direct nuclear strike. It's not unthinkable (if you widen your definition of 'thinkable' sufficiently) that London might end up occupied by a hostile, device-driven foreign power. More realistically, riots aren't exactly uncommon in the capital, and it's conceivable that one might be used by a major anarchist organisation – such as the one the Circle's currently at war with – to mask an assault on the fabric of Kelliwick House itself.

This is why the Fastness has a sally port.

It's a vertical design, which in a traditional castle would be a chimney-like tube leading from one of the upper guardrooms to a concealed hole at ground level, through which a scout could be sent to spy on a besieging force. The hope would be that the spy's exit wouldn't be observed, but if it was it would do the attackers little good, as the sally-port would be effectively unscalable without a rope lowered from the top. Even an agile climber who made the attempt could be effectively discouraged with showers of sewage, boiling water, burning coals or whatever else took the garrison's fancy.

The Fastness is a state-of-the-art military installation, and its arrangements are more advanced. Its sally-port's located in the northern guard post on the seventh floor, under a steel manhole cover which usually has a heavy crate on top of it. Beneath the cover's a small chamber containing a huge winching-drum which spools out a wire ladder, and a bench on which a guard can sit and await the scout's return. Below this, a sheer-sided forty metres of aluminium piping, less than a metre across and set firmly in concrete, drops directly to a closet-sized space on the ground floor. A metre-high metal door marked 'DRY RISER INLET' separates this from street.

The manhole and the door are locked, of course, and the guard post patrolled regularly. But the page known as Jason is a natural with a lockpick, and has a genius for obfuscation.

As soon as he's certain from his snores that his roommate – a fellow kitchen-page called Ben, a dense lad who'll never make squire, let alone Knight – is fast asleep, Jason pulls out the piece of paper Burn palmed to him along with his empty glass. He still doesn't know exactly what the conjurer's doing at the Fastness, but it's obviously some kind of scam about pretending to be Merlin, and it has all the Knights fooled. Dan and Merry will have told him that Jason, carefully placed in a position where Stephen would spot his potential and recruit him, is the Chapel's man on the inside, which will be why he trusts him to get this message to them. It's a less challenging mission than his last one, that's for sure.

After collecting a few items from his locker, Jason goes to the toilet, where he adds a few words to the note in his own handwriting, then seals it in a plastic ziplock bag. Then quietly and cautiously, avoiding the patrols whose routes and times he's carefully memorised, he scurries to the seventh floor and its northern guard post.

This room boasts one of Kelliwick House's rare exterior windows, but Jason has no time to admire the view over the Thames and across to Tower Bridge. He has six minutes before the next patrol arrives. Six minutes to empty the crate and distribute its contents artfully among the rest of the room's clutter, then to superglue the empty box to the manhole cover. He picks the lock while it dries, then opens the cover and slips through, returning the lid and crate to their normal rest position with seconds to spare before the men-at-arms' next inspection.

He pauses on the bench while one of the men checks the room above and gives his partner the all-clear. He worries for a moment that he's forgotten the canister of acetone he'll need to dissolve the superglue on his return, but feels it in a side-pocket of his rucksack.

He hears the guards leave and, working as quietly as he can, he unwinds the wire ladder. It creaks and clangs, but the walls of the guard-post are solid, and he knows when to pause for further visits up above. Once it's at its fullest extent, he climbs on and scampers down, as lithely as a squirrel.

At ground level, his lockpick makes short work of the inlet door, and (leaving the ladder in place, of course) he eases himself out as unobtrusively as he can. A fish-eye lens in the door gives a view of the street, so he picks a moment when no passing police-cars, Knights returning from evening quests or random citizens might see what he's doing and recognise it as definitely illicit.

Once outside, fleetly, and merging with the shadows in the way that only someone allied to an outlaw of Sherwood can, he crosses the road and jogs up a sidestreet until he reaches the railway line. He easily scales the wall protecting ordinary people from the mainline trains which run to and fro between London Bridge station and the south coast, then creeps along until he reaches the spot where, at the same time every weekday night, one particular train stops to wait for a green signal before moving on to the platform.

Thirty seconds later – because Jason believes in cutting things fine – the engine hauls itself to a stop, a foot from his nose. Crouching down just in case any of the late-night passengers are bored enough to glance outside, he scuttles along to the foremost carriage door. He needs to work more quickly than ever now: these trains are rarely stationary for more than a minute. With a roll of duct tape from his rucksack, he attaches the ziplock bag to the underside of the carriage, then steps back as far as he can and, with a spray-can of quick-drying paint and a flourish, he tags the train door with a triumphant green 'SQUIQ'.

A second or two later, he ducks down once more as the train pulls away towards the station.

Tomorrow morning, it will head out of London again. When it reaches Haywards Heath, an elderly trainspotter called Malcolm, whose wife Hazel had the Green Chapel to thank for the cost of her care for several years prior her death, will be waiting on the platform as he does every weekday.

* * *

Since meeting Janene and the Adam Bell gang, Jory's been back in hiding at the tourist farm in Pembrokeshire – feeding the animals, giving the kiddies tractor rides and helping out at the working smithy. The day after these events at the Fastness, he comes back sweaty from the forge to find Merry waiting in the tiny, ill-appointed Victorian labourers' cottage he's been borrowing, ready to bring him up to speed.

Through the other squatters at Mystic Villas, the Chapel have heard about Laney and Rev's arrests, and about Liss's death, all pieces of news which have horrified Jory. A rescue mission for Cantrell's sadly out of the question – which hasn't stopped Big Jack, for one, arguing passionately for the attempt to be made – so the Chapel's reaction has tended to focus on organising a wake for Liss. Her background may have been privileged, but she gave all that up for us. Despite the ardour with which the Circle have been hunting us, Liss is the first Chapel man or woman to die at their hands since Shaf Rashid, and she deserves the appropriate send-off, even if her body can't be there for the occasion. Most of us liked her, abrasive though she could be at times, and we're determined to remember her personal conviction and courage.

A few among the Chapel – Merry, Jack himself, Scar and Zara, and me – know that this isn't only a celebration of a young woman's life. Assaulting a house full of non-combatants isn't atypical, sadly, of the Circle's behaviour since the start of hostilities with the Chapel – but killing an unallied Green Chapel member undeniably escalates the conflict, and we need to consider our response. For the six of us, and those others in the Chapel whose strategic advice is valued (rather more than mine, I expect), this is to be a council of war.

This makes it all the more vital, of course, that we meet up somewhere our presence won't raise any questions, and which is unlikely to be under the Circle's surveillance. Malory has a venue in mind, for which the timing's worked out perfectly: it involves a certain expenditure from the Chapel's hard-stolen funds, but no-one begrudges Liss that.

This is all complicated by the messages from Laney and Squig, which arrive at pretty much the same time.

Laney's comment on one of Malory's auto-generated fake blogs is disguised as spam, but it informs Merry that she's at a Chapel safe house in the Midlands and will be joining the rest of us at Liss's do. (We'll later learn that she bailed on her parents within ten minutes the first time they left her alone in her old room, playing Enter Shikari at top volume and shutting the dog in there to provide authentic teenage crashing-around noises, while she shinned down the creeper festooning the Wardsleys' seventeenth-century Hereforshire vicarage, lit out for the nearest road and hitched a lift with a passing HGV driver. Much later, we'll learn that said lorry-driver is actually an undercover man-at-arms, which will tie in with certain themes in the second message.)

Meanwhile, Malcolm has retrieved Squig's package and faxed the note from his local library to a print shop in – as it happens – Arbroath, where a Chapel sympathiser named Amy has digitised it and posted it as an image file to a private Archmail account, to be picked up by 'Mort'.

The note, as scrawled in haste by Burn and annotated with less than perfect accuracy by Squig, reads as follows:

ATTEN BONNIE & CLYDE (i think he means mery & dan)

HEY – YR FRIEND LANCE INTERESTED IN RECENTLY BEREAVED LADY. PLANS FOLLOWING HER TO CHAPEL, CRASHING FUNERAL. CLD DISRUPT SERVICE. SUGGEST CLOSE CHAPEL / TELL HER CHAPEL CLOSED.

that bits burn, thisis me (squig). burns here bein merlin, mr litster out on ear. wahey! x s

This is the first anyone in the Green Chapel has heard of Burn joining the Circle.

'I suppose we should have predicted that,' says Jory, though he's always known it was a possibility. 'Why hasn't he exposed Squig, though? And what's he doing warning us about Paul's plan?'

'Well,' muses Merry. 'The obvious explanation's that his loyalties are still conflicted. That now he's allied to Merlin he's happy to work for the Circle in general – which is fine in itself, of course – but still doesn't want to see any of us hurt. The more cynical theory would be that that's what he wants us to think.'

'But it's not as if he's trying to lure us into a trap,' Jory points out. 'He's warning us about one. At least if all that stuff about Paul and Laney means what I think it means. And he's got Mr Lister sacked, which has to be an improvement.'

Malory shakes her head. 'We can't assume that's altruistic. Merlin's not keen on competition, although to be fair his competitors invariably turn out to be evil. And he's *devious*. Maybe avoiding the trap *is* the trap, somehow. They could be trying to turn Laney against us, perhaps – our cancelling Liss's wake might be their proof that we don't care about our unallied members like her and Laney.'

'Difficult for them to persuade her the Circle's better,' Jory says mildly. 'Especially given what actually happened to Liss.'

164

'People's loyalties can be odd things, sweetheart,' Merry says, adding with a smile: 'I remember someone else who swapped sides after being captured and locked up.'

Jory scowls. 'That was different. You and Shaf persuaded me that the Circle was in the wrong. And you hadn't just killed my best friend.'

'Even so,' says Malory. 'We can't assume Burn's working for our benefit here. And even if he sent the note in secret, there's another consideration. If Paul's watching Laney, then when he sees the wake's off, he's going to start wondering whether we were warned. He'll start looking for a leak – and he'll suspect the pages a lot earlier than the senior device-bearers, even a newcomer like Burn. If Burn is working to his own agenda, this might be his way of neutralising Squig without answering awkward questions like how he knew he was a spy.'

'For heaven's sake.' Jory shakes his head. 'Sometimes I think you could find a double meaning in a Christmas card.'

Merry whistles. 'Don't get me started.'

'So what do we do, then?' Jory asks. 'Go ahead with the wake next week, and the meeting, knowing that the Circle will follow Laney there and attack us? Or change our plans and risk playing into Burn's hands, if he isn't on our side?'

'It's a poser,' Malory agrees. 'Or would be, if honouring Liss's memory wasn't obviously the right thing to do – and if I didn't already have a plan. That's what I was going to talk about at the meeting, in fact. We'll just have to work a little bit faster than I expected.'

10. A WAKE FOR LISS DASHWOOD

The Nutwood Festival is one of the biggest events in the UK cultural calendar, although you have to be below a certain age to appreciate the fact. (These days, I think it's about fifty.) Founded in the late 60s as a hippie festival, it's grown to mainstream levels of popularity without – according to the organisers, at least – compromising its essential countercultural principles. These days you can go there to watch and listen to some of the biggest bands in the world, not to mention (as the media generally don't) theatre, dance and circus troupes, comedians, magicians, puppeteers and a dozen more obscure forms of performance art.

For many people of a certain bent, for less than a week each year, this handful of fields in the Cheshire countryside is the nearest this earth comes to heaven – although admittedly they tend to be people who, possibly thanks to the mellowing influence of large amounts of drugs, are perfectly relaxed about spending that time living in a tent, surrounded by and eventually covered in mud, shitting in a chemical loo and never getting any sleep because of their neighbours playing Billy Bragg songs badly on the guitar at three in the morning.

I'm being cynical, of course. Though I'm hardly a regular, I've been at Nutwood a few times over the years, and even done a couple of unpaid storytelling gigs there. It was there I first met Merry, Rev Cantrell and Shaun Hobson, in fact, back in the days when they were setting up the twenty-first-century iteration of the Green Chapel.

It's *our* sort of place, in other words, while still being popular enough to feel innocuous, and unlikely to be of much interest to our friends of the Knightly tendency. With attendance most years close on a hundred thousand people, many of whom dress, act and talk an awful lot like us, the Chapel meeting here to hold Liss's wake is the perfect application of Edgar Allan Poe's purloined letter principle.

Plus Merry knows a bloke who gets cheap tickets because his sister's on the organising committee.

After some discussion, we rejected the idea of the Chapel posse all camping in one place, and getting together to mourn Liss in the middle of it. That would make us too conspicuous and vulnerable for too long. Instead we've opted for what you might call the flashmob approach. The festival provides a number of licensed watering-holes as part of the festivities, and it's at one of these, a marquee self-consciously called the Village Tavern, that we assemble on the Saturday evening, arriving at the festival gates in cars or buses or on foot, or simply strolling over from the tents we've set up in different parts of the campsite, to get riotously pissed together and mark our friend's passing. Here we'll be indistinguishable from the rest of the crowd pressing eagerly towards the bar.

It's a sunny August evening, warm enough for the fifty or so of us to congregate in the marquee's outside area. It's fenced off in a nod to the licensing laws, but the licensees are laid-back enough to tolerate the kids and adolescents among us provided they don't make too much noise and confine themselves to discreet sips of an adult's booze. From here there's a fine view across the festival village – where banners fly from a forest of flagpoles, revellers queue for exotic food stalls and booths offer everything from candle-powered steamboat toys to 'Tibetan gong massage' – down to the third-largest music venue, Just a Stage, where a South

London hip-hop band are rapping out swearily political lyrics to compete with the acoustic guitar stuff being piped from the temporary pub.

We're far enough away from Just a Stage that the overall effect is very floaty and peaceful, especially after a couple of pints of the lovely walnut-tasting Nutwood Brown Ale a local brewery puts together for the festival. Nearby, a stiltwalker painted like a harlequin's taking a break from fire-eating to chat cheerily on a mobile.

It's the first time since Shafiq's wake that the lot of us have been together in one place – though there are faces missing of course, Rev's and Squig's prominent among them. Despite the occasion, it's good to see them all again. While no-one's being open about it, there's quite a strong smell of covert marijuana among the drinkers here, which is by no means limited to the Chapel contingent. The atmosphere's tender and supportive, and Laney's getting a lot of hugs.

('I'd have done anything for her,' she told me when I said how great it was she could come. 'Just like she would've for me. When she told me she was running off to join the Chapel, we both knew I'd be coming too. There just wasn't any question about it.')

Big Jack Bennett's downing pints in one, without noticeable effect, and joking in various bloodcurdling ways about what he'd like to do with the Knights and men-at-arms who raided Mystic Villas and killed Liss. Curled up against his side, a kid called Finn is quietly rereading *Harry Potter*. Scar and Zara, never quite at their ease in social situations, are doing their best to unbend (sometimes literally, as they demonstrate self-defence moves on one another for the benefit of an admiring crowd of young women). Twink is very drunk already, and rocking his own idiosyncratic groove to the weird musical genre mashup that we're hearing. Kez is stealing sips of his vodka while Rags tries with epic ineptitude to get off with a girl called Bonnie.

Lee, the human ally of Gilbert Whitehand, is involved in some kind of arm-wrestling tournament with Arthur a'Bland's avatar Ahmed and a young goth called Maxx, who's allied to David of Doncaster. Brian, the elderly ally of Will Stuteley and the only remnant of the Chapel's previous incarnation in the 60s, reminisces about the arms he wrestled back in the day. The minor Merry Men take their moments of glory where they find them.

Me, I'm regaling anyone who'll listen with an account of the heroic exploits of the departed. There's some poetic licence required – Liss joined in with the Chapel's direct actions with the best of them (a lot more than certain people I could name if, say, I looked at the front of my driving licence), but she didn't really distinguish herself. 'She always mucked in and did her bit' isn't the sort of material great eulogies are made of, though, so I'm expected to exaggerate a bit. The fight with Torch becomes a lot more even-handed, for instance, and the rooftop confrontation with Paul is positively epic. (Poor Laney has to go to the loo for a bit of a weep after that bit, accompanied by Vicks.)

Jory and Merry are sitting quietly together at a table, arms around one another's waists, Merry's bulky holdall beneath the bench: joking and smiling and drinking along with everyone else, but maintaining a watchful air.

This is the Green Chapel. Not the wider network of sympathisers and informants – trainspotter Malcolm isn't here, nor Niamh from Cumbria, nor Amy from the Arbroath copy-shop – but the Chapel proper, patchwork and raggedy-edged though that grouping may be. In the old days, before the Knights started properly gunning for us, these are the people who travelled together from place to place, setting up our camps in forests or tolerant farms or Britain's few remaining bits of common land, a gang of nomads just like the persecuted medieval outlaws we emulate. Some leave, some join, our social clusters forever changing, but the Chapel stays the same.

As far as the Green Chapel has a geographical location, it's here and now: this place, this time, where we're all gathered together. For these few hours, these temporary licensed premises in a field at an overpriced and muddy music festival are the sacred place where Sir Gawain, one of the foremost of King Arthur's knights, faced down and was humbled by the ancient spirit of the woods.

It's only natural they'd want to get us back for that, I suppose.

* * *

By the time I've finished my short oral biography of the late Alice Dashwood – not my most compelling narrative, I'll admit, although it's better than the time I got pissed and ill-advisedly put a zombie army into 'Robin Hood and the Newly Revived' – the others are beginning to shuffle with impatience. Some of the kids are still listening raptly, but most of the adults have picked up on something else.

Merry's about to sing. She's standing, her russet hair hanging about her shoulders like a copper-beech's crown. She squeezes Jory's hand and he slips away quietly somewhere, but everyone's eyes are on Merry herself. Her poise admits no nervousness, no embarrassment at bursting into a song in a packed pub where many of the drinkers are complete strangers, as she begins:

> *'The outlaws' flag is Lincoln green,*
> *the emerald of a forest scene.*
> *Beneath it rests a martyr true,*
> *enfolded in its fir-tree hue.'*

Her voice is good: not professionally perfect, but strong and clear, capable of real feeling while still hitting the notes every time. Which, having played in a folk band, I can tell you isn't to be sneezed at.

> *'So raise the verdant banner high,*
> *forever green against the sky!*
> *Through winter's chill and summer's cheer,*
> *we'll keep the green flag flying here!'*

It's not one of the Chapel's oldest songs, of course – 'The Red Flag', which it's obviously riffing on, wasn't written till 1889, and even 'O Tannenbaum' is only a couple of hundred years old – but it's one of our most guaranteed crowd-pleasers.

'It waved above the wooded glade
where friar, soldier, miller, maid,
all victimised by unjust laws,
were joined together in its cause.'

She launches into the chorus again. It's not a difficult one to learn, and there's something irresistible about the combination of beer and singing that appeals to even the non-drinkers present. By now the Chapel people are standing and joining in, while the Village Tavern's other punters look intrigued, tolerant or embarrassed depending on temperament.

'The standard raised up by that band
proclaimed the goodness of the land,
the right to work it, living free –
the overthrow of tyranny.'

Another chorus. By now, some of the other clientele are joining in – although, yes, a handful are pointedly leaving. It's a pretty clear message, after all, and most of the people here probably feel they can get behind it. The rest probably think we're selling breakdown cover.

'Behind it stood united then
the Christian and the Saracen.
Now, black or refugee or gay,
the leafy pennant marks our way.'

The singing's becoming more rousing, and more rowdy. There'd be beating of beer-mugs against the table, if we weren't all drinking out of biodegradable plastic glasses.

Then, like the trees in Kirklees wood,
one outlaw fell, another stood.
And so our sister, perishing,
will be reborn in legend's spring.'

Now we're onto the last verse. To the outsider I have to concede it might look a little disconcerting, perhaps just the tiniest bit 'Tomorrow Belongs to Me', as we go into the final chorus.

'Our emblem bright, our ensign green,
too many martyrs has it seen,
but like the fir-tree's sturdy bough,
it will not change its colour now!'

'So raise the verdant banner high,
forever green against the sky!
Through winter's chill and summer's cheer,
we'll keep the green flag flying here!'

While we've been singing so enthusiastically, the stiltwalking fire-eater has loped away, distracted by something in the distance. The shouts over at the Mainstage have been too distant to hear above the song's chorus, and the first influx of people hurrying into the festival village simply suggests that some band's set has finished somewhere. It takes the panicked, yelling state of those who stampede in their wake to bring us out of our slightly pissed choral reverie.

Overall, we're not as well prepared as we could be when a phalanx of forty mounted Knights of the Circle burst through from the path to the Mainstage, men and horses in full armour followed by two all-terrain vehicles full of men-at-arms, toppling booths and flagpoles and innocent festivalgoers as they advance, and wheel around in tight formation before charging directly for the tables where we're sitting.

* * *

Anyone else would have met up in the car park, but the Knights, like us, were concerned about not being conspicuous. Word would have got out of a cavalry unit forming up between the five-door family saloons, even a modest-sized one with minimal infantry support and no heavy artillery.

Instead they struck a deal with a neighbouring farmer (who was probably none too well-disposed towards his hippie-loving neighbours even before the Circle started waving money at his bank account), and assembled in his barn. A gently sloping field where cows would normally have grazed undulated down to a tall chain-link fence delimiting the edge of the festival site. Almost immediately beyond it stood the rear of the Mainstage, currently playing host to a Celtic metal band who are momentarily and inexplicably in vogue.

Forty Knights of the Circle have been called back from service across the country and beyond, to assemble here under Paul Parsons' command. As Stephen arrived in the barn twenty minutes ago, he saw the golden double-headed eagle of Sir Gaheris (borne by Blythe, back from the Borders with a good many others, leaving the despondent Lenton a token force to track down the elusive Sons of Gore with), the red cockscomb of Sir Dagonet (Wigsby, with nothing to show for his Newcastle dragon quest apart from some queasy jokes about Chinese takeaways), Sir Ector's gold sun (young Harte, his Salford quest fulfilled with some distinction, as the bondsman of the murderous Sir Turquine goes to his arraignment and eventual imprisonment in the Benwick Institute), the three green-tongued red serpents of Sir Geraint (Harry Plaice, fully recovered now after his time at Tud House), the purple-sailed gold ship of Sir Lavaine and the blue-and-white quarters of Sir Galagars (Transom and Posnett, recalled from overseas liaison and replaced with less experienced Knights for the duration), the vertical gold band on blue of Sir Ywain the Bastard (Freddie Obote, looking glad of a break from paperwork), the stars-and-stripes and stripes-and-ermine of Sir Bors and Sir Lionel (Felton and Frith, Parsons' loyal aides-de-camp still) and a score of others – lions and dragons, flags and castles, trees and dogs, crosses and battlements and fleurs-de-lis – before Lancelot's red-on-white stripes presented themselves.

Stephen presented himself in turn to their bearer. 'Reporting for duty,' he told Parsons. He was pleased he'd be in at the arrest, even if the Green Chapel weren't his primary quest right now. They'd been a thorn in the Circle's side for some time, an annoyance everyone would feel better for being rid of – and Taylor, in particular, was owed a good thrashing for causing them all this hoo-hah.

'Suit up sharpish then,' Parsons replied, 'we've got a positive ID and location.' Next to him, his squire Ned Ballard was on the phone, occasionally giving Parsons updates. In front of them was a Nutwood Festival programme whose schematic site plan Ned was cross-referencing with an Ordnance Survey Explorer map of the immediate area. 'Get a move on, yeah?' Parsons repeated. 'Or you'll miss the main event.'

Dressed and armoured by his own squire, Stephen was presented with Sir Palamedes' chessboard-patterned shield, and led to his horse.

Though Stephen's fond of horses, the Knights use them rarely. When they are deployed on the battlefield the animal a Knight's sitting on is one of his greatest assets, so the Circle's stables train their charges exactingly, to follow orders, placidly put up with wearing armour, and remain calm in the face of carnage. In practice though, the situation's so uncommon that it simply isn't worth the investment of a Knight's time to establish a perfect rapport with a particular mount. Only a few enthusiasts insist on it, the rest generally trusting to their device-enhanced equestrian skills.

In any event, Stephen was a stranger to the young grey mare he was assigned today, so he spent a few minutes introducing himself and reassuring her, before mounting and coaxing her into line with the others.

The riders formed up on the far side of the barn, concealed from the festival by the corrugated-steel structure and the Mainstage itself. Nearby, a platoon of men-at-arms was piling onto a pair of Supacat all-terrain mobility platforms, ten to each six-wheeled vehicle. Other men-at-arms lay close by the boundary fence – beneath camouflage webbing, in case of implausibly sharp eyes among the crowd – to step up with wire-cutters at the crucial moment. They must have been deployed there hours ago, Stephen thought, before the day's music programme started. He took a moment to appreciate their dedication.

At a crisp command from Parsons, relayed by Ballard over a field radio, those men stood up and set to work, while simultaneously the Knights stepped out, took a turn round the field, then cantered past the barn and went into a gallop as they descended the slope towards the festival site, the Supacats grinding after them at a surprising speed for such functional machines.

The men-at-arms pulled aside the fence seconds before their arrival, and the charge thundered through between the Mainstage itself and one of the giant speaker stacks, gaining pace as it hurtled into the dense and terrified crowd.

There are, of course, important health and safety considerations involved in such an action.

The Circle's reputation is inevitably tarnished by any harm to undeviced civilians resulting from its quests, although injuries from standing too close to a cavalry charge are traditionally considered accidental rather than deliberate damage. Honour would demand that any member of the public suffering such an injury be amply compensated, however, and despite its enormous wealth the Circle has to justify this kind of extravagance to its accountants. Under other circumstances, Parsons would certainly have evacuated the Mainstage area, but any such action would certainly have come to the attention of the Chapel.

In most instances, a sense of self-preservation is enough to get a member of the public out of the way of a charging horse with some dispatch – and if not, a rider can usually veer to avoid them – but of course such expectations are problematic in a closely-compacted concert crowd.

Stephen aimed for the least packed parts of the ground and trusted to luck and Sir Palamedes. Festivalgoers in colourful clothes and a variety of statement-making hats skittered and scampered as he approached, often clearing his way only by a hairsbreadth. Behind them, he heard the Celtic metallists' instruments thud and twang and hoot to a startled silence, the lead singer's heartfelt 'What the *fuck*?' amplified a thousandfold.

As his mount, pressed on one side by Sir Galagars' – that was to say, of course, Bill Posnett's – horse, and on the other by a Knight whose shield was out of view, approached a cowering family huddled in terror on a picnic-rug, Stephen experienced a twinge of misgiving about the adequacy of their precautions… but as his mare gracefully leaped the obstacle, clearing their heads by ample inches, he dismissed it from his mind as being hardly helpful in a combat situation.

The idea that all forty of them were behaving with recklessly insane irresponsibility due to a collective psychosis caused by the fragmentation of the archetypal infrastructure of the British psyche simply didn't occur to Stephen. That sort of malarkey wasn't his department, really.

They were approaching a stream spanned by a wide bridge, across which the main path to and from the Mainstage was funnelled, and which was crammed with frantic audience-members who'd made the mistake of dashing for the obvious exit. Most of the riders simply jumped the stream, but a few of the least good horsemen, Wigsby among them, charged across the bridge regardless, scattering concertgoers into the brook as they went. The men-at-arms followed, the Supacats slowing down to walking pace to ensure they didn't crush anyone under their treads as they dipped down into the ditch then climbed effortlessly out again.

The unit reasserted its formation in the approach to the festival village, delicious smells eddying dizzyingly past the Knights as they crashed along a parade of food vendors selling Arabic-style pizza, churros with hot chocolate, and authentic Tibetan momos. A site-vibing sculpture of a dancing couple was trampled in pieces under the outliers' hooves; one horse burst without hesitating through a canvas graffiti wall. Stephen himself drew his sword and, with a whoop, hacked down a jolly-rogered flagpole as he passed. This was the most fun he'd had since that time he'd got to lob some practice balls at Sachin Tendulkar.

And now the horses are in the open again, in a field fringed with booths and marquees, at one end of which a sign announces 'The Village Tavern'. Joyfully, Stephen directs his steed in a wide arc, keeping formation with his brother Knights, and turns her head towards the whitest, widest of the giant tents – where even now a motley assemblage of men and women in hoodies of various colours, but with green predominating, are gaping in alarm, and scrambling clumsily to their feet to face the charge.

* * *

'So, what do we do next?' Jory asked Malory, last week at the cottage in Pembrokeshire.

'Well,' she smiled, 'thanks to you we have the information we need. We know now that before Sherwood and Camelot, long before the Chapel and the Circle, the British psyche had already begun to polarise. Establishment and outsider, authority and outlaw, settlement and greenwood – even monotheist and pagan, if you allow the sun as a single god – it all goes back to that Neolithic divergence, when the young and old kings of the Salisbury Plain tribe failed to kill each other. Instead of the kingship surviving in one man, their whole tradition was split in two. That was our Dolorous

177

Stroke, if you like, and the injury it dealt our whole nation hasn't healed in five thousand years. You've rediscovered the prehistoric ur-myth of British politics, Jory.'

'Yes, but,' said Jory, who'd been trying to get a word in edgeways. 'Who's to say that's any more historical than the other versions? I mean, I don't know how tribes in Stone Age Wiltshire governed themselves, do you? Does anyone? Stonehenge has kept mystics and hack authors in mystery for centuries – do you really think a cheap stage trick is all it takes to discover who started building it and why?'

She clicked her tongue, disappointed at the slowness of a student. 'Historicity's not the point. It never is when it comes to the devices.'

'Yes, but –' he said again. 'For Heaven's sake, Malory, you're a scientist. Why should we believe *any* of this stuff when you heard it just come out of my head?'

Jory's memory of that time – a few weeks earlier, before he stole the Grail – presented him with a perfect blank between the time when he lay on Rev's couch listening to the metronome on Malory's phone, and his hearing her count to five, perhaps half-an-hour later, in a noticeably smug tone of voice. He'd looked at the pages of scrawled-upon notepaper and listened to the recording of his voice, and recognised absolutely nothing he'd written or said.

Malory nodded, accepting the point. 'Because this iteration presents as true. By which I mean authentic, not factual. The other versions all have accretions, period detail. They philosophise and draw morals. The cup and weapon are arbitrary symbols, with nothing to connect them. In your version, they're parts of a cohesive whole – the ash-tree in the spring – which becomes separated. It feels like the myth from which the others grew and evolved. And no,' she added, 'in conventional science our feelings wouldn't count as evidence, but since the phenomena we're studying only exist in people's heads, the contents of mine and yours are as admissible as anyone else's.'

Jory tried to swallow his scepticism with the same enthusiasm Malory was swallowing this nonsense. To him the drivel he'd spouted under hypnosis didn't sound a lot like an archetypal story which had determined the fate of his country for millennia, but what did he know? Malory was the expert, she always had been.

'So, what do you suggest?' he asked again. 'I mean, I assume you're still talking about healing this schism? What do we do, reinstate a nine-year cycle of sacrificial kingship? Leaving aside the fact that we're meant to be anarchists, I can't see the Royal Family taking to that too well.'

'It would make a marvellous reality TV show,' said Malory impishly. 'But no. We know now that the breach was a symbolic one, so we need to mend it symbolically. Ideally with as many devices as possible witnessing the event.'

* * *

Now Jory's lying on the roof of the Village Tavern, his belt looped round the tallest support pole where it protrudes through the marquee's canvas, the quiver he retrieved from Malory's holdall slung over his arm, and a bow in his hands.

He's wondering what the hell he's doing here, mostly. Malory's plan sounded merely audacious when she outlined it at the cottage, but here, in the face of the immediate and epic violence about to be visited on the Chapel by their enemies, it's looking flimsy. It relies on Jory's archery skills, which is, in his view, never a good idea. And even if it works, he's far from convinced the end result will be what Malory says. As ever, he does his best to have faith in her, but faith in himself comes much less readily, and he's afraid that this time she may have exceeded her reach.

Beneath him, in the festival village, the mounted Knights gallop towards their quarry. Jory draws his bowstring, takes careful aim at the rider carrying the shield of Sir Bors – not that he really has the leisure to choose – and shoots. It strikes Nick Frith in his breastplate with a blinding flash and hiss, which makes his horse rear in alarm while he flails and flaps. Before he comes unseated Jory's eyes are elsewhere, as he fires another arrow into the breastplate of another Knight, with the same brilliantly white result. And then does it again, and again, and again.

It feels good, suddenly, and right. He did a lot of archery at uni with Shaf Rashid, and while he could never even have tried out for the Olympic team, he did end up reasonably good at it. This is the first time since he joined the Chapel that he's felt as if he might be recapturing those skills at last – although there's a much bigger test of them about to follow.

If he could look directly down now, which is something he definitely doesn't have time to do, Jory would see Jack Bennett uprooting one of the palings from the fence and charging with it towards the Knights, with Scar and Twink and Maxx and Ahmed following suit. He'd see Lee quickly handing out a frightening variety and quantity of weapons from Scar's rucksack. He'd see Zara taking aim – not with a bow and arrow, but an actual gun – at Paul Parsons, before Malory places a hand on her arm to dissuade her. He'd see a stream of non-combat-ready Chapel people and ordinary drinkers leaving through the back of the marquee, and being detained by the men-at-arms from one of the Supacats, which drove straight to the rear of the premises when it arrived. He'd see Brian gaping in amazement at the spectacle as he zips himself up on the way back from the gents.

Another arrow loosed, another flash. They have simple magnesium flares woven into the fletching, activated by a percussion trigger. They're harmless – at least, that's the plan – but highly disorientating. Entirely against his usual habit, Jory finds himself laughing – joyfully, liltingly, merrily even – at the confusion sown by the prank.

It's the kind of trick Burn would also appreciate if he were here; and indeed the harlequin's still in sight, off in the middle distance, watching from the lofty vantage of his stilts while the professionals take on the combat part of the quest. Malory spotted him the moment he spindled past them on their way to the Tavern. It's a typical rookie mistake to think that having a device means you can outwit other people every time, even when they have allies of their own.

The men-at-arms in the second Supacat have realised what's going on by now, and are trying to fire on Jory's position – but every time one of them raises his gun, he's hit by an arrow from another direction entirely. Jory's grateful to know that if he looked – which, as previously mentioned, he can't – he'd see Janene Long and her friends Geordie and Keith, putting Adam Bell's violent streak to good use from carefully-chosen positions of cover around the field.

As more and more of the flare-arrows find their targets, the Knights' charge becomes ragged, many of them becoming separated from their mounts. Jory sees Jerry Transom go down clutching at his chest, and Doug Felton, and Frazer Daughtery, who carries the red-barred eagle of Sir Gareth, kin to Sir Gaheris' border-engrailed one. Others are being felled by Big Jack or the others, though Ahmed's down too, a sword wound in his arm, and Twink, rolling from side to side to avoid being trampled by a riderless horse.

Another arrow. Stephen Mukherjee, cannier than most, manages to raise his shield in front of his eyes in time, and the bright actinic flash illuminates his chequerboard sable and silver, spooking his mount but not unseating him.

Jory doesn't have time for maths, except for the insanely complex and chaotic yet wholly unconscious calculations of ballistics which are informing his every shot. If he was doing the same sums as Merry, he'd count forty Knights (assuming they're all still conscious), ten individual Merry Men (now Brian's back from the loo), one Merlin and the three members of the Adam Bell gang. It isn't quite the critical mass that she was hoping for, but soon…

Ah, yes. Even if the car park was no use to them as an assembly point, the Circle really should have put someone on watch there. They might, in that case, have had warning of the twenty-five customised motorbikes which two minutes ago loped up to the gates and, without stopping, roared past the frantically gesticulating stewards into the festival grounds, before arriving, barking and howling, in the festival village field. Big Jack's called in his favour with British Beasts at last.

One of the bikes, its chassis painted with a boar's bristles, runs over the fallen Frazer Daughtery with an audible crunch, continuing on its way without a pause, and Jory's laughter dies away at once. Field medics run to help Frazer, but even from here Jory can tell that the man's a goner. He feels a sharp and unexpected grief: like Julian Blythe, Daughtery's an old drinking-companion from the days when Jory bore the device of Gawain, brother to Gareth and Gaheris. Almost without thinking, he reaches for his last arrow to bring down the motorcyclist, but catches himself in time: he remembers, fingering its different fletching, that the time for that one isn't just yet – and only then recalls that the bikers are notionally on his side.

In disarray, the remaining horsemen regroup, some of them still with blackened stumps of arrows protruding from their armour, and face the bikes.

The motorcyclists' heads are blank, encased in crash-helmets. Their only faces are the Beasts' muzzles painted on the noses of their vehicles, whose engines grunt and snort their defiance. The boar Twrch Trwyth is there, and the grim-faced grey wolf Gwrgi Garwlwyd, and the striped and snarling wildcat Cath Palug, each with the others of their kind in tow.

Only one of the machines lacks a face. It's painted with the markings of a great cat, and straddled by a rider in snake-scale leathers, a gaping adder's head gracing his helmet. After all Stephen's searching, Adze has come to him.

Not all the members of British Beasts have named devices, but it's enough. Malory calculates that the assembled company represents roughly a quarter of all the currently-active SCAMs in the island of Britain.

'Stop!' Merry cries, jumping up onto a trestle table. Nobody pays any attention, obviously, so she reaches into her denim holdall, untangles the Nestine-Gull Grail from her spare bra and holds it up, yelling 'Stop!' again.

She leaps down and marches forward bearing the Grail aloft. 'Knights of the Circle, peasants of the Green Chapel!' she cries, raising her voice above the quietening melee as the combatants begin to spot what she's holding. 'You British Beasts and you, the Adam Bell gang,' she continues, as the realisation spreads. 'You too, Merlin!' she adds, as Blaze tries to slink away. 'You stay there. And all of you, stop fighting! This is sacred ground!'

Above her, Jory nocks his final arrow and holds it ready.

The Knights are falling to their knees now, having in some cases got up laboriously first. The Beasts' engines growl nervously and whimper. The Chapel, understanding this symbol's power though they don't share its imagery, fall silent.

Only Janene, who wasn't briefed about this bit, shouts, 'What the hell's that supposed to be?'

'It's for healing,' declares Merry. She lifts the Grail higher, and with Jory, with all the flair and grace of the Robin Hood ally alive in him, sends his last arrow glinting through the air towards the tiny cup.

* * *

'It's simple,' Malory told Jory, back at the cottage. 'We need to restore the tree-in-the-spring archetype. It'll be a symbolic gesture, but from a living symbol's point of view there's nothing more powerful. If enough of the devices see what we've done, it'll set off a chain reaction which will create a seismic shift in the British devicescape.'

'That makes sense,' agreed Jory, thinking that it made very little sense. 'So how do we rebuild something that doesn't exist any more?'

'It exists,' Merry replied. 'The symbol was split in two, not destroyed. The Circle have been keeping one component safe for centuries – since 1766, anyway. The spring became the Grail, and – thanks to you again – we have what the Circle believe to be the Grail. In this case, of course, belief is everything. As I say, historicity isn't the point.'

'But – and I hate to point out the obvious here, Mal – we haven't got the other half,' Jory said.

'We haven't got it yet,' she told him, taking out some kind of jewellery presentation-case from the depths of her holdall. It was large and flat and square, of a size to hold perhaps an elaborate necklace. 'As I say, the vessel changes relatively little in the stories – first it's a well, then it's a cup, but that's it. The weapon takes all sorts of forms – an ash spear, a tree-club, the Glastonbury thorn, Bertilacus' sword, one of Robin's arrows.'

'So what form do we need?' Jory asked. 'What would be the counterpart of the Grail? Excalibur?' As far as he knew, in the absence of the Pendragon itself Arthur's sword had never manifested as a device – although if it was going to, it would be the Lady of the Lake who'd possess it, if anyone. The box Malory held, though, was too small to contain any conventional weapon.

She smiled, shaking her head. 'No, sweetheart. The Grail is the Circle's symbol. For balance, the weapon should come from the Chapel.'

Jory frowned. 'So, an arrow, then?' But the Chapel used arrows all the time, and discarded them too – although they tried to gather them up when possible, to avoid environmental wastage. An arrow wouldn't be a symbol of anything.

Malory was smiling encouragingly. He considered harder. There was a special sword in *Robin of Sherwood*, but that was surely far too recent. This would need to be something that had been associated with the legend for centuries – something everyone who knew the legend would associate with Robin Hood. Did Robin have a special bow? Not that Jory had ever heard of.

But… 'There's the silver arrow,' he said. 'The one he wins, at the archery contest in Nottingham.'

Malory grinned. 'Is the right answer.'

'A silver arrow couldn't work as a weapon, surely,' Jory pointed out. 'It would be too soft. Also, we haven't got one of those either.'

'It doesn't have to work as a weapon,' Malory reminded him. 'It has to work as a *symbol*. And the Chapel has always made its own symbols.'

She passed him the case. He took it, and was surprised to see the logo that was embossed on it.

Then he opened it and suddenly he wasn't surprised at all.

* * *

As chance would have it, Robin's previous ally, the late Shafiq Rashid, was, before he gave up his day-job to devote his time to the Chapel, a crystallographer in a large university chemistry department. (It was Shaf who introduced Vicks to the Chapel, in fact.) As part of his research he once made an artificial diamond, relatively worthless but as hard as any natural crystal, which he gave to Malory.

Jory – who's always been a little jealous of Shaf's relationship with his Maid Marian, platonic though Merry insists it was – doesn't quite know how he feels about this gift. As he fires that last, heavier arrow, though, and understands with quiet finality that only Robin Hood's avatar could have shot such an unconventional projectile with such a perfectly unerring aim, the idea of resenting an earlier Robin's love for his Marian seems suddenly absurd.

It's also spectacularly beside the point at this precise moment, as the arrow they smelted from Shafiq's Olympic silver medal flies straight and fast, directly into the hand-lathed wooden cup held high in Merry's hands.

Silver, as Jory says, is quite a soft metal, whereas two-thousand-year-old wych-elm is bloody hard. The diamond at the arrow's tip, though, splits the ancient grain with ease. It passes through both sides of the vessel's bowl before sticking fast, its feathering pointing up towards Jory's position on the marquee roof while its tip sparkles down at the kneeling Knights.

Malory hasn't flinched for a moment during the impact, trusting her lover – or the legend within him – utterly. She brandishes the Grail still as the device-bearers present gasp a collective gasp, the symbolism of the moment electrifying them all.

The long silence that follows is broken by the sudden baying of Adze's bike, as he revs it up and pulls away, leaving the festival site the way the Knights came. A moment later, Torch and the rest of the Beasts follow him, roaring and bellowing. The Adam Bell gang, and the warily watchful Blaze, stick around to see what happens next.

Paul Parsons is standing — whether he's dismounted voluntarily, or whether he was one of the Knights unhorsed by Jory's pyrotechnics, nobody's quite sure. He marches forward angrily, and tries to snatch the pierced cup from Malory, shouting, 'What have you done? That's Circle property!'

Smiling, she hands it to him. Behind her, Jory's making the undignified clamber down the canvas of the Village Tavern, but no-one's interested in watching that. Instead, they stare as Paul tugs roughly at the arrow, trying to loosen it. He pulls and frowns and twists and wrenches, but it stays in place.

'Damn it to hell,' he snaps eventually. 'It's this bloody hand.' He passes it to Stephen, who's dismounted and is standing beside him. 'Here Mukherjee, give it a try, for God's sake.'

Stephen pulls harder on the gleaming shaft, to no avail. He struggles to get a better grip, but there's nothing doing. It's as if the two objects have become one.

'It's not your hand, Parsons,' he concludes at last, as Jory steps up to stand beside Malory. 'It's stuck fast.'

Nobody could shift this, he's sure about that. Not without some kind of special equipment, at least. It reminds him irresistibly of something. Not the same image, exactly, but the same idea: a weapon, buried in a chunk of nature. Embedded fast, beyond anybody's ability to remove it, but waiting... for the time when someone...

Stephen holds it up again, this combined cup-and-arrow object, and gazes rapt at the sunlight playing on the silver, the dull grey of the old elm. The arrow in the wood.

Oh, for heaven's sake.

Blaze is stilting towards them now, his face urgent. But Stephen knows exactly what he's going to tell them.

'Dear me, Taylor,' Stephen finds himself saying. 'The Seneschal's not going to be happy about this.'

Sir Kay couldn't pull it out that last time, after all.

II
THE WOUNDED LAND

11. SWORDS AGAINST THE SAXONS

A year after stealing the Holy Grail, Jory Taylor is in Canterbury, being shown round the headquarters of the ultra-nationalist pressure group known as the Saxon Shield. He's part of a depressed-looking Green Chapel delegation which includes Scar, Maxx and a simmering Jack Bennett, all wearing their hoodies and distinctly out of place in this clean and trendy office space.

They're being greeted by a smartly-dressed woman named Bretwalda Ward, the leader of the SS since its recent reformation took the Chapel and the Circle alike by surprise. 'We understand we have an image problem,' she's telling them. 'Mostly because of the smear campaign run by the Circle's spin machine, although admittedly our previous management didn't do us many favours there.' Trim in a burgundy business suit and kitten-heel shoes, she's thirty-one and used to work in PR. 'Even so, with the immigrant agenda dominating politics and the public discourse, someone needs to stand up for the rights of the indigenous Anglo-Saxon minority in this country.

'Luckily,' she adds interminably, 'when the Circle shut down our earlier operation, they didn't think to outlaw the actual organisation. They haven't yet made it a crime for us to speak our minds, although I'm sure the PC brigade are working on it.' She laughs, gaily indifferent to the fact that she's the only person in the country who'd equate the Circle with 'the PC brigade'.

Jory realises his teeth are grinding together and separates them with some effort.

Bretwalda ('but call me Bret') Ward bears the device of Rowena, daughter of the Saxon warlord Hengist and wife of Vortigern, one of King Arthur's predecessors. As far as Malory can determine, the devices of Hengist and his brother Horsa have remained dormant since the deaths at the Circle's hands of those not-entirely-helpful former SS leaders, Colin Hill and Alfred Noake. Ms Ward's reinvention of the disbanded organisation is only one of the unexpected devicial developments of the past year.

'Aye,' Scar agrees blandly, 'we're dead impressed with how you've turned this outfit round. Seeing a place like this'll soon make folk forget them stockpiled guns and grenades and shite like that. Soon they'll forget about your old boss trying to suicide-bomb that train station, and all.' She's still pissed off that Jory wouldn't let her bring her Muslim same-sex partner with them to meet the fascists.

'That's our goal.' Bretwalda Ward's smile doesn't waver. 'Although the Norman-dominated media don't help with that, of course.'

Politically speaking, the Saxon Shield inhabit a weird parallel universe where the ethnic divisions of the eleventh century remain as relevant as those of the twenty-first. They're upset that they're not allowed to treat the Gaels and Celts the way they used to any more, because it might offend the delicate sensibilities of the incoming French and Norse.

Which isn't to say they don't hate blacks, Jews and Asians as much as the next far-right nutcase, of course – just that they have surprising additional layers of hate available beneath that.

Ward asks the Chapel contingent about their coffee preferences, then goes on: 'Of course we've nothing against immigrants, despite what they all say about us. We've nothing against them, as long as they stay in their own country. England's full enough as it is, without foreigners coming over here with their different languages and customs and imposing them on us. Sally, *fecce dryncas for* ūre *féðegestum*,' she adds sharply to a passing assistant, forestalling Jory's immediate objection to part of that at least.

(He notices she hands the drinks order over on a notepad, though. He's pretty sure there isn't an Anglo-Saxon word for 'coffee'.)

In contrast with the last Saxon Shield headquarters that Jory stood in, these offices are open and airy, with an abundance of soft seating and remarkably few racks of weaponry. Noake and Hill's SS was a blue-collar brotherhood of exclusively male neo-Nazi skinheads, who'd brought the Circle's wrath down on their heads by torturing one of its Knights – specifically David Stafford's lover Trevor Macnamara, who did not survive the experience. By the time Jory arrived in their survivalist-themed mead-hall, David had daringly modified their decor with splashes of blood and piles of dead or maimed bodies.

Here, by contrast, there are big picture windows entirely free of gun emplacements, and everyone seems to prefer skinny lattes to mead. An enormous photo of the White Horse of Uffington hangs, fashionably unframed, on the far wall. Half-height room dividers fence off the islands of comfortable seating (upholstered in the same tasteful corporate red as Ward's suit) from the desks and workstations. Fascist logos are discreetly confined to tasteful lapel-pins.

Cosmetically, Ward's SS is very different from the one which Jory was instrumental in demolishing. Appearances be buggered, though: the very ambience of the place is are giving him some horrendous flashbacks. To some, Bretwalda might look like evidence of the 'second time as farce' theory of history, but Jory knows how dangerous she actually is.

As if to confirm this, she continues: 'The public still remembers the incident at St Pancras, but Mr Noake was under a great deal of pressure at the time due to being victimised by the Circle, and I for one don't believe for a moment he'd have gone through with it. I think everyone's beginning to realise that that was a long time ago, and it's high time we all moved on.' Behind her, portraits of the ancient kings of Wessex cycle on a PC screensaver.

Behind Jory, Jack Bennett makes a noise like Brian Blessed dreaming of slaughter.

'Well, quite,' says Jory. 'And this is just what we wanted to talk to you about, Bret,' he adds hurriedly. 'The Green Chapel has an image problem, too, and it's also thanks to the Circle. Too many people in the, er, Plantagenet-Hanoverian establishment elite associate us with thefts and kidnappings and terrorist incidents, when really we're just wanting to peacefully celebrate our ancient Saxon heritage just like yourselves. We wanted to discuss with you some ways of, ah, sharing good practice between our two organisations.'

Ward looks wary. 'Are you talking about harnessing our resource in a consultancy capacity?' she asks. 'Or did you have something more...' – she selects the word carefully – '...proactive in mind?'

Jory's not sure what to say next and is weighing up the relative merits of 'We're interested in accessing some of the legacy skills and systems from your previous corporate structure, starting with the guns and bombs my colleague mentioned,' and 'Shut up you ghastly woman, shut up *now*,' when all the windows blow in and the Knights of the Circle come crashing in on abseiling ropes.

Jory's rarely been so pleased to see them.

* * *

It's impressive in a way, how quickly the SS people react to discovering that at least some of their paranoid fantasies of persecution are true. At once they're producing handguns from their desk-drawer units, or from holsters concealed under their suit jackets, or in some cases both. Ward's assistant

Sally, on her way back from the machine with two lattes, an Americano, a double espresso and an iced caramel mocha, flings them all at the nearest Knight's helmet and dives for cover, pulling out a Walther PPQ en route.

Someone else presses an alarm bell, and within moments the building's security staff are thundering up the stairs, carrying Heckler & Koch submachine-guns which Jory recognises from his last encounter with Shield forces. Meanwhile, the clerical workers have taken up defensive positions behind the room dividers and are laying down covering fire. Bretwalda Ward's crouched behind the divider nearest Jory – which he imagines would hold up suspiciously well to gunfire, if there was any coming from the Knights' side – blazing away with a Glock automatic pistol.

The Knights, of course, have brought only their polymer-steel swords, though there'll be men-at-arms waiting on the roof to provide firearms backup if things get out of hand. The Shieldspersons have retreated to the more immediately defensible centre of the office, so for the moment the intruders are using their blades for show, shattering the overhead striplights and slashing at the furnishings. The stuttered bellow of the guns is deafening – as is the shrieking of the building alarm – but the Knights' shields and armour hold firm as they march like inexorable sci-fi robots across the open-plan office space. Through the choking cordite smoke, Jory can see Paul's red bars, Stephen's checks, Transom's elaborate sailing-ship, juddering with the multiple impacts. The burgundy upholstery's taking a shredding from the swords, not to mention the gunfire, and there's a computer exploding every few seconds.

Maxx, Jack and Scar have been itching for a fight since the moment they walked in here. They were frisked for weapons at the door by those same security staff, naturally, but somewhat inexpertly. Within a second of the windows breaking, Maxx and Scar are holding flick-knives pulled from out-of-the-way folds of clothing, while Jack, whose best weapons are ones he can't be easily deprived of, is laying

194

about him with fists and feet. Jory contents himself with grabbing a nearby Shieldsman as he brings his gun to bear on the intruding Knights, smacking his head hard into his PC monitor (which being made of plastic entirely fails to provide the satisfying shattering noise he'd hoped for) and relieving him of his Walther. He finds himself laughing again – the good-natured merriment at a jape well executed which he now knows comes, at the most inappropriate times, from Robin Hood – and does his best to shut it up.

The SS may not have entirely trusted their Chapel visitors, but faced with the tangible threat of hostile armoured men flying in through the windows, their defensive instincts naturally turned outwards. This was, of course, exactly the reaction everyone involved in this joint quest was hoping for.

Reversing the gun into his left hand, Jory smacks the butt into the underside of Bretwalda Ward's wrist, which has been concentrating her fire on a Knight whose riot-shield bears a blue-clawed gold fox on a red background. As her gun flies upwards into Jory's waiting right hand, he wonders idly how long Sir Melian's device has been back in circulation, and who's wielding it these days.

Ward turns yelling and claws at Jory's face, forcing him to bat her hands aside with the Glock as he fires the Walther over her shoulder at a Shieldsman who has turned on Maxx with murderous intent. The man goes down, and with the report Ward appears to register that the assailant she's facing unarmed is now holding a gun in each hand. Her hesitation gives Jory time to grab her, spin her round and grip her arms and lower torso in the classic gunman-with-hostage pose. This does mean that the Glock's now pointing into his own midriff, so he hastily thumbs the safety-catch.

Meanwhile, he lifts the Walther to Ward's temple and shouts 'Stop shooting and surrender, or Bretwalda goes down!'

* * *

The bluff wouldn't work with some devicial groups, of course. The more ethically elevated, or just less ignorant, would be well aware that Robin Hood, outlaw and thief though he may be, would never execute an unarmed enemy. (Well, not according to your standard modern consensus. There are some incidents in the early ballads that don't do him much credit on that score – you might want to check out 'Robin Hood and the Monk' in particular – but they're not often remembered these days.) Walking into the enemy's den and getting the better of them through deception and trickery is right up his alley, though.

The recruits who the SS attracts don't tend to be the brightest and best, and most of those present don't even have a device – indeed, unless Malory's intelligence is unprecedentedly poor, Bretwalda Ward's Rowena is the only one. Despite being inducted by Ward into the murderous folkloric pageant that's Britain's secret inner life, her acolytes probably have only the haziest idea of the Shield's own part in that drama, let alone the starring roles played by the Circle and the Chapel. It's hardly surprising that the news of the unexpected détente between the two hadn't reached them – nor that they accept Jory's spoken threat at face value, and grudgingly lay down their weapons.

They don't exactly surrender immediately – the pair Jack's busy beating the shit out of don't stop fighting back for a couple of minutes – but it's close enough.

'Fuck you, you bleeding Norman lapdog!' Bretwalda Ward yells, her voice significantly shriller and more Estuary than before as Jory propels her into Stephen's waiting arms. 'We're a non-violent pressure group! This is against our human rights! What's the charge, you *elpéodiglican* wankers? What have we done?'

'It's the Circle's job to worry about process, "Bret",' says Jory. 'We're just glad to have fewer fascists about, giving quotes to the *Daily Mail* and generally bringing down the tone of the place. But since you ask – and taking the multiple firearms charges as read – supporters of yours have been involved in assaults against a number of Bulgarian and Romanian immigrant families, including Raina Dimitrov and her children, who were under the Green Chapel's protection. Apparently you also started a fire at the Dover Immigrant Removal Centre, which I only mention because it's astoundingly stupid even by your logic. What did you think was keeping the asylum seekers inside?'

She spits at him as Stephen drags her off, all her fashionable polish scoured away, at least until she has time to compose herself and reapply it.

In practice, all the unallied Shieldsmen and -women arrested today will get a normal trial, if not (as some in the Chapel would likely argue) necessarily a fair one. Ward herself will get a rigged one which will result in her being interned at the Benwick Institute, but after a modicum of discussion the Chapel's central cell have agreed they don't have much of a problem with that. On such flimsy accords temporary alliances are made, and this one's worked out nicely for Circle and Chapel alike.

'Good work, Taylor!' Paul Parsons beams through his open visor as he comes over to shake Jory's hand. He's disturbingly affable these days. 'We were listening in on the whole thing, of course. You were very convincing. Almost believed you were going to double-cross us, actually!' He guffaws and punches Jory's shoulder with his prosthetic hand. With his gauntlet on, the impact's quite heavy. 'Well done, you others, too – Bennett, Millar, erm...' He can't remember Maxx's surname, which is fair enough because Jory doesn't think the goth has ever given it. Maxx nods coolly back even so.

'Well, we weren't the ones being shot at,' Jory concedes. The Circle's armour's bloody good, but it isn't perfect. There was always the chance of a bullet finding one of those less-protected gaps.

'Wasn't exactly safe for you fellows, though,' Paul observes. 'Damn good showing all round, I'd say. Let's get these prisoners processed and head back to the temporary HQ for a celebratory glass of something.'

'I say, old boy,' adds Stephen to Jory, back from handing Ward over to the men-at-arms, 'it's a good thing you didn't have to drink that coffee.'

'Why's that?' Scar asks in a tone that, though confrontational, is so much less so than normal as to count as conciliatory. Stephen's the second Knight of the Circle she's discovered she slightly likes, and the first who hasn't left the Circle to become her not-in-any-sense-boss. 'Could have done with a caffeine hit before the scrap. When did offices go all non-smoking, eh?'

'Forgotten your Geoffrey of Monmouth, Taylor?' Paul's terribly amused. 'Watching *Maid Marian and Her Merry Men* and *Robin Hood: Men in Tights* left no room in your head for the real Matter of Britain?'

When Paul was Jory's squire, Jory always used to tick him off for not reading enough Arthurian literature. He tries to cast his mind back. 'Rowena...' The recollection comes to him. 'She killed her stepson, Vortigern's son Vortimer – shit. She got a servant to poison him.' It hadn't occurred to him to look for danger in that form.

'You might have been all right,' Paul adds judiciously. 'Could be she took you at your word. Maybe not, though. Not a risk I'd have liked to take, personally.' He laughs again, and claps Jory heartily on the back.

Jory's finding some aspects of the new order rather difficult to adjust to.

* * *

This time, the Circle's temporary HQ, graciously shared with the Green Chapel's support team, is at a nearby primary school. The place has been closed for the day on the pretext of asbestos being discovered in the ceilings, and five hundred grumpy parents have had to make last-minute childcare arrangements. Compared with the scale of inconvenience experienced by, say, the Nutwood Festival organisers, it's a minor irritation.

Rev Cantrell's pushed together twelve tiny chairs in the school's reception lobby, and piled up cushions on top of them before taking a nap. He looks precarious but serene. As Jory enters with Stephen, he opens an eye and grins.

'Hey, big fellows,' he says, leaping to his feet with an agility that shouldn't be possible at the age of fifty-four and on thirty cigarettes a day. 'I take it the country has one batch less of racist fruitcakes to worry about this fine afternoon?' Like Zara, Rev wanted to accompany them to the SS headquarters, but Jory felt a strict no-foreigners rule would be their best approach under the circumstances. He was dubious enough about how Scar's Glaswegian accent would go down.

'All in custody,' Jory confirms. 'Everyone who was in the office, anyway. They probably have more supporters out there, but with their device-bearer out of the picture, they can't do much harm. Unless Hengist or Horsa re-manifests, of course, in which case –'

'Come here, both of you,' Cantrell interrupts, and hugs Jory and Stephen with one arm each. Jory's used to this sort of thing; Stephen looks a bit nonplussed. Scar and Jack join them – in the lobby, that is, not the clinch – and Rev shepherds them all through to the school gym, while the rest of the task force, minus Paul and his cleanup team, begin to file in behind them.

'These squires are all dicks,' opines Zara, emerging from the office as they pass. 'Wrestling and jumping off things. "My Knight is stronger than your Knight." The gym was not the best place to house them, I reckon. So much macho in one room can't be good for their health.' She holds Scar back for a momentary kiss hello, letting Jory, Rev and Stephen go first into the room full of alleged dicks. They cluster around Stephen, clamouring to know how the quest went.

The Knight holds his hands up for silence. 'Mr Parsons will give a proper debrief later, chaps, but in a nutshell – we got the buggers.' The squires send up a cheer. 'We fulfilled our quest, and everyone's fine. That's all that matters for now.'

Jason comes over to start stripping off Stephen's sweaty armour, carefully not meeting Rev's or Jory's eye as he does so. 'Glad to hear it went well, sir,' he says in a quieter tone. 'Worth you being here, d'you think?'

'Oh, I expect so,' Stephen sighs, as the other Knights file in and start being disarmed. 'The other quest can wait a day or so, I suppose.'

Jory doesn't inquire – the rapprochement between the Chapel and the Circle is too delicate for casual information-sharing, especially regarding a group the Chapel has had connections with in the past – but he knows from Squig's occasional reports that Stephen's still assigned to the quest for British Beasts. Frustrated at having had them in his sight last summer, yet having them slip through his hands as the Grail took up the Circle's attention, he's taken to spending all his free time as well as his duty hours in schemes to track down and incarcerate the Beasts, and the elusive Mark Addis in particular. He's had considerable success, culminating in a massive raid on a biker rally three weeks ago which ended in the arrests of the Twrch Trwyth, Cath Palug and Gwrgi Garwlwyd devices, together with most of their chapters. Adze, though, continues to evade his grasp.

This narrow focus means that since Squig – Jason, that is – was promoted to Stephen's squire, his ability to pass on useful intelligence has become rather more limited. Still, he claims to be enjoying himself, and it's always useful to have a man on the inside, so the Chapel have left him in place despite the occasional awkwardness it causes. The Miller's Son is a more evanescent ally than most, and it's likely to transfer itself to some younger host before too long. Squig may not be Much much longer, and the Circle's as good a career path as any for when that fails him.

'Miss Wendiman not joining us today?' Stephen asks Jory, obviously making an effort with his social niceties.

'She's with her dad,' Jory replies. 'I'm joining them later on.' The Chapel proving that Edward Wendiman was not dead, just retired, was one of the many necessary adjustments following the symbolic healing at Nutwood last summer, like their promising to forego any further contact with British Beasts (an agreement which caused even Jack Bennett only a half-hearted rumble or two of annoyance). For their part, the Circle released Rev from Benwick as a grudging demonstration of goodwill, while Paul Parsons made a personal, and by all accounts a heartfelt, apology to Laney for the Mystic Villas incident.

Some of those gestures turned out better than others, it has to be said.

'Great scrap, Dan,' Jack says appreciatively, while a Circle field medic patches up his cuts and bruises. 'Give me Nazis to beat up any day. I love it when they realise they're not the bloody supermen, after all.'

Maxx gives an enthusiastic 'Yeah!', despite having broken a couple of fingers on an unusually tough Shieldsman's jaw. The medic moves on to splinting those.

Jory circulates among the Knights, saying hellos to Transom, Blythe, Obote and others who he knows well. The lad who's discarded Sir Melian's fox shield was a page last time Jory noticed him, although he clearly must have been through squirehood since. *I'm getting old*, thinks Jory, only half-facetiously. *Old and out of touch.*

A stirring at the door alerts him to what he assumes is Paul's return: as Knight in charge of the quest, he's guaranteed a hero's welcome when he arrives. Instead, to Jory's discomfiture, the figure wears a loose-fitting, powder-blue suit.

Merlin's always a figure of awe among the Circle, as you'd expect, but this avatar's habit of putting on impromptu magic shows at the drop of a hat has endeared him more than usual to the lower ranks. Today Blaze seems relatively sombre, pausing only to produce a dove from one end of the metal pole he carries as his staff, before crossing to talk to the Chapel party.

The bird perches on the upper rungs of the climbing equipment. 'Caretaker won't thank him for that,' Jack points out sourly, as it defecates on the parquet floor.

The device-bearer formerly known as Burn isn't a popular figure among the Green Chapel, although so far nobody's risked Squig's cover by revealing the magician's background to anyone in the Circle. It's a moot point whether they'd even care any more: Blaze has been a loyal servant of the Circle nearly a year now without his undisclosed history being an issue. Although his defection was clearly a response to his forced and sudden alliance to the Merlin device, many in the Chapel still see him as a traitor for abandoning their cause so easily. Thus far, though, he seems to have kept their secrets – most obviously Squig's identity, although it might be that he's keeping that in reserve just to maintain a hold over them all. The Merlin device is so damn devious it's pointless trying to second-guess it.

'Hey Jory,' says Blaze. 'I hoped your girl would be here. She busy?'

Blaze hasn't been involved in the quest against the SS, and he can talk to the Knights any time he wants. Of course he's here to see the Chapel people. Given that he's been formally introduced to Jory and Malory in his capacity as Merlin, no-one's likely to think anything of this, as long as he doesn't slip and call them 'Dan' or 'Merry'. And the Merlin device is too wily to let him do that.

'She's at her dad's,' says Jory shortly. As a turncoat himself he knows he should have more sympathy for Blaze, but the man's never yet apologised for all the stress and unpleasantness he put them through last summer. (And then there's the stuff that happened *after* the sixty-five episodes of *Merlin.*) 'Is there something you wanted to see her about?'

'Yeah,' Blaze tells him quietly. 'Few days now I've been getting one of those extrapolatory prophecy things. Serious disturbance-in-the-force shit. Dreams, voices in my head, you name it, man. Feels like some new device is on the way, one none of us have seen coming. It's not the Pendragon – not yet, anyway. This is something else. Gonna mix things up like we've not seen in centuries, according to my boy Merlin. I'm hoping Malory might have some ideas about it.'

'Well, that's reassuring,' Jory replies, although he knows the accuracy of these 'prophecies' is down to individual insight and judgement, as well as the essential randomness involved in extrapolating trends. Certainly there's been no sign yet of the Pendragon's return, as prophesied by Blaze on his accession to Merlinhood, at Nutwood a year ago and at every opportunity since.

He says, 'I'll pass it on to her,' before thinking to add, 'Hasn't she given you her mobile number?'

'She's not taking my calls,' Blaze replies. 'Tell her to get back to me, yeah? This thing could be serious.'

'Wanker,' mutters Zara as he stalks off, clonking his pole and scratching the parquet, to talk to the Knights. Her English swearing's come on a lot during the past year.

Paul returns shortly afterwards, to the cheers and general approbation of his men. He acknowledges it, delivers a rousing speech about how well they've all done – taking special care to acknowledge their friends from the Green Chapel, whose co-operation represents a new dawn in British mythopolitical history or something equally inspiring – then turns to Ned Ballard for his own disrobing. As he does so, the guest he's brought along with him slips into the hall, and the two of them talk quietly while Ned lifts off the various components of Paul's armour.

'Oh fuck,' growls Scar. 'What's *she* doing here?' The newcomer is the one person who's even more unpopular with the Chapel these days than Blaze.

'What's it look like she's doing?' Big Jack growls. 'She's shacking up with her best friend's murderer.'

'Hey, how about we show a little forgiveness?' Rev suggests sharply. 'It's none of our damn business anyway. So she's found a little happiness with someone. God knows she's entitled.'

'She's entitled to happiness with someone good,' Zara agrees. 'Not that bumhole.' (OK, perhaps the swearing still needs a little work.)

'Paul's mellowed a lot recently,' Jory protests, feebly. The whole affair seems very odd to him as well, and not because of the age difference. Paul's only twenty-four or so, after all. Some of Liss's boyfriends were twice her age.

Laney's oblivious to it all, though. She trots cheerfully over to them a minute later, and asks them all how they're doing. Her nose-, ear- and eyebrow-rings are gone, giving way to a pair of modest silver studs in the conventional position, and her dreadlocks have been cut away to be replaced with a year's growth of straight blonde hair. She's wearing a rather pretty floral print dress in blue and purple, and generally looks completely unlike the woman who broke her nose fighting a biker outside a squat this time last year.

Rev gives Laney a hug and tells her how good it is to see her doing so well. Jory makes small-talk awkwardly but politely, while Scar and Zara at least acknowledge her. Jack acts as if she wasn't there, while Maxx stands up and pointedly leaves.

'After Paul came to apologise about – you know –' she tells Jory a few minutes later, when inevitably he feels compelled to ask, 'we stayed in touch. I didn't expect to, but I realised I kind of liked him. I know he… well, he kind of killed Liss… but it was an accident, after all; he was only there to arrest us. And he was so sorry about it all, even though it wasn't really his fault. And it turns out he's funny and sweet and knows loads of interesting stuff. Mummy and Daddy thought he was excellent boyfriend material, obviously, but it took me a while to come round to it. But he was always so kind and thoughtful, and… I think after going off the rails like that last year I needed someone very straight, very firm about doing the right thing, you know? So, well, yeah. One thing led to another, really.'

By now, the Circle have cracked out the wine – a quite expensive Sauterne, which nicely complements the pâté and biscuits. Jack Bennett's started making booming noises about everyone going to the pub later, which are gaining some traction among the men-at-arms. Laney's still acting as if she wants to catch up with her old friends and is surprised and a little hurt at how they're treating her, which suggests she's mildly delusional.

After she wanders off to chat to some of the Knights, Jory gets another chance to talk to Paul. Whatever he or anyone else might think of Laney's behaviour, it's certainly true that Paul's a different man these days. A mystic might attribute it to the healing of the schism; a cynic would say it's probably the regular sex. In any case, these days you'd be forgiven for finding Paul pleasant company, even a worthy bearer of the Lancelot device, as Laney evidently does.

For the moment, though, Paul's all business. 'Thing that's still troubling me, Taylor,' he says. 'Bretwalda Ward's not especially well off, there's been no hint of any wealthy donor to the SS. But office space like that, with furniture and computers and so forth, doesn't come cheap. Guns neither, of course. And her employees weren't all interns and volunteers.'

'What are you getting at?' Jory asks.

'We know where the last lot of Saxon Shield got their money from, because it was mostly us,' Paul says. The Seneschal's dirty secret is accepted now as a historical, though distasteful, operational necessity. 'But we weren't bankrolling them this time. Don't worry, we don't suspect your lot either – we know you don't have that kind of cash to spare, yeah? But *someone's* been financing their operation. At some point we're going to have to work out who.'

With Laney's arrival, the Chapel people have been getting itchy feet, and before long Jack leads that pubward exodus. Given permission to celebrate, some of the squires and many of the men-at-arms join him, but only a couple of the Knights. Rev, Scar and Zara follow, but Jory makes his excuses and leaves.

He has an appointment with the guardian of the Grail.

12. A TRUE TALE OF TREVOR MACNAMARA

That evening, as the summer heat cools and sunset stains the distant blue sky of the Somerset levels like the juice of a blood-orange, Jory is parking in a side street in the small town of Glastonbury.

The green Mini he's driving is legitimately registered to him, with a valid tax disc and everything, and when he walks the few minutes to the High Street it isn't an attempt at misdirection or concealment, but simply because the parking in the small town's a nightmare.

He strolls past vegan cafes, New Age bookshops, crystal healing centres and suppliers of paraphernalia for what the shopfronts variously describe as 'WITCHCRAFT,' 'SPELLCRAFT' and 'MAGICK'. Incense and tarot cards, runestones and dreamcatchers all fail to capture his attention, as do the books of Goddess Scriptures dictated by passing spirit entities to people with names like 'Moonraven Shadowfox'. Although he does stop to stroke a small black cat.

Glastonbury – an ancient site associated with legend and religious ritual for millennia, as Malory's manuscript researches confirm – was thoroughly invaded by hippies in the 1960s and 70s and hasn't declared independence since.

To be fair, the locals seem to like it that way – for one thing, it gives the town a reliable summer tourist trade. The street's not bustling, nor is it deserted – most of the shops are shut, but the restaurants and pubs are still open. A shabby couple sitting in a shop doorway with a dog look like vagrants, at first, but turn out to be waiting for a taxi.

The shop Jory's heading for is called The Tree in the Well, and its store-front is much like the others. In the window, tie-died linen cloths are spread beneath a display of dowsing rods and pendulums, clay goblets engraved with runes, wood-carvings of the Goddess and the Green Man, vials of earth from various sacred sites, books about the Glastonbury Thorn and the Chalice Well, and the ever-present crystals. A bonsai thorn-tree and a miniature landscaped indoor fountain, complete with fairy ring, are obviously there for display only.

In a sense, though, that's true of the entire shop.

The opening hours advertised on the door are well past, and the shop's lights are off, but the door's unlocked. Jory pushes it open with a jangling noise and steps inside. More of the same expensive New Age tat sits on knotty wooden shelves around the room: behind the counter, lit by the evening sunlight, hangs a gigantic, garishly-painted cloth showing an anthropomorphised tree bursting from a suspiciously-shaped pool in an explosive imitation of childbirth.

Locked under the glass of the counter-top, among standing-stone paperweights and runic jewellery, sits the Nestine-Gull Grail, still pierced inextricably by the home-made silver arrow forged from the relic left by Shafiq Rashid. A discreet tag next to it reads 'NOT FOR SALE'. In this place, nobody – without a device, at least – is likely to give it a second glance.

'Hello?' shouts Jory. 'I'm here!' He goes behind the counter and pushes aside the painted curtain to reveal an ordinary suburban living-room, with a sofa and plasma-screen TV, a computer corner and a bay window looking over a modest but well-kept garden. Malory sits at the PC, working on a spreadsheet of accounts. Edward's on the sofa with a newspaper, half-watching *EastEnders*.

'Evening, Jory,' he says. 'I won't get up.'

'Hello, love,' Malory adds.

'Shouldn't you lock that door?' Jory asks.

'We will now you're here, obviously,' Malory replies patiently.

He says, 'But anyone could walk in here and –'

'And what?' asks Malory. 'Ask us which chunk of semi-translucent rock works best for curing a broken heart? This is Glastonbury, Jory, not inner-city Glasgow. Nobody's going to break in and steal a rather unimpressive sculpture. Besides,' she adds sensibly, 'we'd hear the bell tinkle.'

'You didn't get up just now,' he feebly protests.

'We were expecting you, silly,' she says. 'Now take your shoes off and sit down. I'll get us all a cup of tea.'

He really misses her when they're apart.

* * *

Everyone insisted on having a go, that day the schism was healed. The thirty-nine surviving Knights, all the Merry Men present, Janene Long's gang – in the end, everyone with an ally at the Village Tavern had attempted to free the arrow from its moorings, except for Blaze, who stilted around explaining to everyone who'd listen that only the Pendragon, the elusive Head of the Circle, would be able to separate them now, and Merry and Jory, who stood to one side looking justifiably smug.

Nobody without a device was allowed a go, of course; the Knights would never have stood for it. This was lucky, probably, because as Jory understood it the difficulty of the task was more by way of a mental block, one of those psychosomatic limitations the allies impose on those of us who've made deals with them. It was entirely possible that someone unaffected by a device would have been able to remove the arrow with only moderate difficulty, and risk being hailed by the Knights as their returning Head.

The sense of awe, a strong appreciation of the numinous strongly tending towards worship, was everywhere in that field, which the Knights simply commandeered for the rest of the afternoon, detailing the men-at-arms to create a perimeter so that they and the Chapel contingent could stand inside and boggle at the new symbol Jory and Malory had created.

Everyone seemed to understand its import – everyone with a device, anyway. The ordinary Chapelgoers, those not allied to a specific Merry Man, participate in what Merry calls the 'Sherwood distributed devicial emanation', which was enough to stop them taking the piss at least. There's nothing comparable for the men-at-arms – presumably because of the Chapel being egalitarian while the Circle's hierarchical – but they're used to their bosses behaving in deranged ways, so they just humoured them, firmly turning away festival security, the ordinary Nutwood punters and, when they finally arrived, the local police, while looking forward fervently to their next pay cheque.

Paul, after his initial angry and frustrated outburst, became oddly calm, and after a few minutes' contemplation of the arrow-in-the-Grail, started displaying a serenity so Zenlike that Jory wondered whether he was having some kind of breakdown. 'This puts everything in perspective,' he said. 'The Pendragon's coming. This is the proof we need, and you fellows gave it to us. There's no sense in our fighting you now, you know.'

The other Knights agreed. Ned Ballard handed a phone to Paul, who went off with Blaze to have what must have been – to say the least – a challenging conversation with Sir Charles. At one point Blaze came back to video the interlinked objects for a couple of minutes, and messaged him the footage. Eventually Paul reappeared, and said, largely redundantly by now, 'Orders from the Seneschal, boys. It's time to stand down.'

It was agreed that the pierced Grail should be kept by a neutral party, at some out-of-the-way place known only to a select few in the Circle and the Chapel. Edward Wendiman, with his complex ties of long service to the Circle, but of family and gratitude to the Chapel, was an acceptable candidate, and other than Malory and Jory only four people – Rev, Paul, Blaze and the Seneschal – know that this shop is where he now guards it. (If 'guards' is really the word for 'sits behind a counter nearby, mostly reading back-issues of *Fortean Times*'.)

Despite today's joint action, however, the new accord between the two devicial orders has mostly consisted of them not bothering each other. What contact there is has been friendly, and there've been times when particular Knights have offered the Chapel informal support and vice versa. A few times they've even socialised together. The unified assault on the Saxon Shield, though, has been the first time they've actually fought alongside each other. Jory wonders whether maybe Paul's right, and this is indeed the beginning of a beautiful friendship.

* * *

The odds are against it, of course. If you're thinking that this whole rapprochement thing seems a bit cheap, a bit glib – implausibly easy, in fact, given the bad blood that's present on both sides – well, you're not the only one.

Interpretations of exactly what it was that Jory and Malory achieved, that day at Nutwood, have differed. When she's at her most optimistic, Merry hopes that they have in fact closed the schism for good; that uniting the symbols of the divergent devicial groups has begun a process which will, in time, see them completely unified.

Others are less sanguine about this. Rev Cantrell, for one, believes that they've merely delayed the inevitable – because, while the hierarchical Circle are marvelling at the omen presaging the return of a divinely-appointed monarch to take up his rightful place as ruler of the ancient lands of the Britons, the egalitarian Chapel would naturally prefer for this to happen over their dead bodies. 'The great thing is,' he said after his release, when Jory and Merry had brought him up to speed, 'for now it doesn't matter. Whatever you think about some ancient British warlord coming back from the grave to subjugate us, we have a sign it hasn't happened *yet*. For now, it's all academic and we can get on with our lives.'

Sir Charles takes a dimmer view: he's apparently convinced himself that the Head was about to return anyway, this latest manifestation of the schism being the fabled 'time of Britain's greatest need' which Raymond's been obsessed with for a while now – and that the Chapel's actions at Nutwood have actually delayed his coming. A few at the other extreme, mostly Big Jack, see the whole thing as the Chapel buying into Arthurian propaganda (though the promise of a scrap with neo-Nazis was more than enough for him to abandon his misgivings for camaraderie today).

But then, Jory considers, tension is inevitable. The Chapel and the Circle have millennia of disagreement and conflict – as many as five of them, apparently – behind them. That's hardly likely to dissipate overnight. As Rev says, for the moment they're not actively trying to kill each other, and that's surely triumph enough to be getting on with.

* * *

Merry comes back with a teapot and three cups, saves her spreadsheet, then curls up on the sofa with her feet on Jory's lap. Jory sips his cuppa and appreciates her feet in his lap, recounting highlights of the day's proceedings while the muted inhabitants of Albert Square go about the four-times-weekly melodramas of their lives.

He feels insanely lucky to be here – in a home, with a woman who loves him, accepted by her family (even if that only means her dad) and not in any imminent danger of discovery, assault or capture. He hasn't felt so settled since before his abduction by the Chapel, two years ago – and what he lost then was a routine bachelor existence, with nothing of the domestic contentment of times like this with Malory. Given that he started his pagehood with the Circle directly after his student days, Jory's really had nothing like this since leaving home.

He's even introduced Malory to his own parents – once they'd been reassured that he was in fact alive, and that his temporary disappearance had been a matter of the national security they've always vaguely trusted that he's involved with – and they've pronounced themselves satisfied with their son's choice of life-partner.

He only gets to do this part-time, of course. He's got his flat in Knightsbridge back, no longer (he's been promised) under Circle surveillance, while Malory's back at the university, having somehow convinced her Head of Department that she was merely on an unexpected and unannounced sabbatical. And of course they both spend time at the Green Chapel's semi-permanent encampment in Thetford Forest. They see a lot of each other, in various locations, but it's only here that he really begins to understand what it could be like for them in the long run, if they made a home together.

Within him, even the Robin Hood ally is happy. Isn't this what Robin wanted, after all, for most of the time – a quiet life with Marian, with no Sheriff persecuting them, and no injustices demanding his attention? (Well, maybe it was and maybe it wasn't. The process whereby the devices shape their host minds isn't exclusively one-way.)

He's about to wonder aloud about the possibility of getting some kind of pet, when Malory's phone rings. She unpockets it, then makes a face. 'Oh,' she says, 'it's Burn. I can't stand hearing him bang on about the Pendragon any longer. I thought he'd got the message.'

Edward frowns. 'If Merlin's phoning you, isn't it a little unwise to block his calls?'

'Oh,' Jory says guiltily, 'I remember. He's got another thing he wants to talk to you about. Some kind of crisis he thinks is coming, with the devices. Other than the usual, he says.'

'Well, I'm not talking shop now,' says Malory, and rejects the call. She rests her head on Jory's shoulder, which given her feet are still in his lap demonstrates impressive suppleness. 'It's your turn to make dinner, by the way. Anything particular in mind?'

Before he can splutter at having that foisted on him without warning, her phone goes again. This time it's a text message. 'For God's sake,' she grumbles, opening it.

It's from Blaze, of course. Malory stares at it for a moment, then says sharply, 'Dad, switch over to Channel 4.'

Edward does as he's told, unmuting the sound for good measure. A male journalist's voice says, '– merely an effective law-enforcement organisation, whose taste for pageantry is as harmless as the Trooping of the Colour or the state opening of Parliament. But there are persistent rumours that the Circle has a more significant, hidden role, and a more sinister hidden agenda.'

Photos of recent Circle actions, most of them apparently taken by members of the public with mobile phones, are appearing in a montage across the screen. Jory recognises Nutwood, Mystic Villas, St Pancras and a dozen other places.

The images freeze then, on an image of the Thankaster shopping centre cavalry charge, and the camera zooms into the photograph, concentrating on one armoured figure. His face is invisible behind his visor, of course, but Jory knows the blazon on his shield. A circle appears around him on the static photo.

The journalist continues, 'Someone who knows more about this than most is this man, who served with the Circle for eighteen years, both in the UK and the Middle East. He parted company with the Circle two years ago, since when he has been involved in humanitarian work abroad. Today he returns to Britain, to tell the public about some of the more disturbing aspects of his former employers' work.'

The grainy photo disappears, replaced with a shot of the man, less impressive now in black slacks and polo-neck, sitting in an office chair against a neutral background and listening politely as an Ulster-accented woman begins to interview him.

He's aged a bit – his hair's going grey in places – but nobody in the back room has any difficulty in recognising David Stafford.

* * *

As it happens, I'm watching Channel 4 as well, back at the flat in Eastbourne. I try to keep up with politics, and it's something to have on in the background when you're mending a hole in your spare trousers. (It's a glamorous life we storytellers lead.) I'm not really paying much attention, on the basis that the report sounds pretty much like your typical exposé of an establishment institution which turns out to be predictably corrupt, until I suddenly realise that it's actually an exposé of *the Circle* turning out to be predictably corrupt, and that for a programme like that to be made and broadcast they must have dropped the ball in a pretty major way.

In one sense, of course, you can't do the stuff the Circle does and expect to keep it secret. The British Museum closing down at the height of the tourist season, a shootout with abseiling armoured men in a small city business district – this sort of thing generates publicity. The Knights try to keep the detail under wraps, though. Things like the extent of their operations, the limits of their power, and most especially the rationale by which they choose their targets can't be allowed to become common knowledge. The British people have been kept ignorant of the devices for at least twelve centuries, according to all the records (what most people were aware of before that is anyone's guess, really), and the last thing the Circle wants is for that to change.

They try to enforce that through wielding a hefty influence in high places, applying information-control techniques learned from the espionage services, and buying witnesses and editors off with truckloads of cash. They also employ a PR firm with a long-standing strategy of distracting the public from the bland substance of its announcements by having them delivered by out-of-work actresses in short chainmail skirts.

So, unless you were on the spot at Mystic Villas or the Nutwood Mainstage, all you'd know about those quests would be the vague press releases saying 'Two of the terrorists involved in the incident at the British Museum were apprehended today at a house in Bristol; a third unfortunately died resisting arrest', or 'The activities of a dangerous paramilitary cell have been halted following an operation by Circle personnel at a music festival.' And if you were there at Nutwood, with the Circle paying out hard cash in compensation for psychological as well as physical trauma, while clamping down on any reportage in the interests of protecting the Grail, your motivation for going ahead and denouncing their methods would be significantly reduced.

(If you were at Mystic Villas, of course, like Katja Kollwitz or four-year-old Bella, you're probably a filthy junkie squatter whose word no-one's going to pay any attention to anyway. Keep Bella Kollwitz's name in mind, incidentally – it might turn out to be important one day.)

There are the conspiracy theories, naturally. The Circle is an arm of the Templars, or the Rosicrucians, or the Knights of Malta; their name refers to the moon, or a fairy ring, or a hydrogen atom, with the various scholia of hidden wisdom each of those implies; the Knights' armour is impregnable, robotic and was designed by Roger Bacon. My favourite rumour (and one that's arguably within a missile strike of the truth) is that the Circle exists to guard and conceal the actual occupant of the British throne, the House of Windsor being just a family of frontmen for the inbred, deformed and possibly part-amphibious *true* royal lineage.

All this is perfectly normal. In a world where people routinely assert that the RAF have evidence of UFOs, the Civil Service is run by the Illuminati and Lord Lucan killed Princess Diana on behalf of Oftsed, it would look suspicious if the Circle was missing out on this kind of wackiness.

What they really don't want, though, is for any of those theories – let alone, perish the thought, the truth – to go mainstream. By, for instance, being broadcast on a major terrestrial TV channel at primetime.

* * *

It starts innocuously enough, with a discussion of modern policing methods and how they sometimes cross the line, and how reports of brutality or misconduct are usually handled. 'There's one law-enforcement agency, though,' the narrator says, 'that's almost never challenged in this way. It's one of the oldest such bodies in the UK – so old, in fact, that its historical origins are shrouded in mystery. Right up to recent times its record of arrests has been exemplary, including organised crime bosses, terrorists and serial killers – and yet its remit is confusingly vague, and its powers have never been clearly defined in law. What's more, some reports of its techniques are frankly disturbing.

'It's such an established part of British public life that we never question it: so old that it doesn't have a descriptive name like "Counter-Terrorism Command" or "Military Intelligence", but instead is referred to with a symbol – a simple geometrical shape whose circumference seems to be everywhere. Tonight we ask: what lies at the centre of the Circle?'

That's the first advert break, so obviously I go and make myself some popcorn.

* * *

After the break, the journo reports on some of the eye-witness accounts of Circle actions that have got through – stuff gleaned from blogs and social media and some of the less laughable anti-establishment websites. So far nobody's accusing the Circle of being reptilian alien shapeshifters, but it's obvious that any broadcastable version of the actual

216

truth – that the Circle reckon they're haunted by the ghosts of King Arthur's knights, basically – is going to sound just as ridiculous to the audience. This programme won't be going there without a totally trustworthy source.

And that's when they wheel out David Stafford.

I know who he is, of course: even met him a couple of times when I was doing my regular gigs with the Circle. Nice guy – a bit standoffish, like a lot of them, but I know people well enough to see that in his case it was shyness, not snobbery. I'm aware from talk after the direct action to kidnap Al-Khuzaie that the guy's defected from the Circle, that he's been in the Middle East, and that he's of interest to Jory and Merry. It doesn't really prepare me for what he says.

He starts off by praising what the Circle does, talking about some of the people and things they've put a deserved end to. He talks about his own experiences in Iraq, the first time round – tracking down Clifford 'Al-Wasati' Chalmers, the Old Etonian warlord who was terrorising Mosul in the wake of the last war there. He describes some of the things Chalmers did, like the Mosul Dam massacre and the Feddon beheading video, and he emphasises how necessary it was for the Circle to stop this kind of behaviour.

Then, at the interviewer's probing, he talks about times when the Circle's gone too far. About the Thankaster shopping centre raid which he led, where the public were recklessly endangered, although he acknowledges that Nutwood was a more recent and more serious example.

'I saw some terrible things while I was a Knight,' David says. 'I was responsible for some of them. But that's something of a pattern with the Circle, I'm afraid.' He's eloquent, persuasive, his once-crippling stammer emerging rarely and lending an air of sincerity to his manner when it does.

He talks about times when individual Knights have gone off the rails – by executing criminal suspects without trial, for instance – and how the Circle covered it up. Clifford Chalmers wasn't the only one who beheaded his enemies,

David points out. He doesn't name the Knights responsible, but the cases he lists include the would-be-art-thief Shaun Hobson and the serial killer James Ribbens. Jory's not the only repeat decapitator on the Circle's had on its books, but Ribbens the Beard Collector was one of his, and he's the best-known victim on the list.

'The main problem the Circle has,' David claims, 'is that it's too similar to its enemies. It likes to claim it practices the virtues of chivalry, as the medieval knights did. In fact, though, most medieval knights were brutal thugs. Ironically, the Circle's enemies recognise that, but the Circle itself is in denial.

'And then, of course, sometimes the Kn-Knights themselves become the enemy.'

Then he mentions that Clifford Chalmers was himself an ex-Knight of the Circle.

* * *

Another ad break comes in then. It's followed by a brief profile of Chalmers, culminating in his bloody suicide during the Knights' final advance on his mountain HQ. There are photos of that, too, which there shouldn't be – some man-at-arms is going to be in serious trouble. Then they cut back to David.

'The Circle cleans up its messes in the end,' he tells the interviewer. 'But not before they've caused untold mischief. Do you remember the incident at the British Museum last year, which the Circle moved so quickly to contain? The ringleader on that occasion was another former Knight.' Again, he doesn't mention Jory's name.

Instead, again apparently prompted by the interviewer – though there's no doubt now about who's in the driving-seat here – he mentions that the targets in the Thankaster quest, the Saxon Shield – men who carried out racially-motivated attacks against British citizens, who were assembling caches of guns for an armed insurrection, and whose leader survived that raid to attempt a devastating suicide attack in the heart of London – were bankrolled by the Circle itself.

'They hoped to use them to get closer to other far-right groups, I b-believe,' David explained. 'If so, it b-backfired dreadfully.'

'Tell us about Trevor Macnamara,' suggests the interviewer, apropos of nothing.

David nods. 'Trevor was the Circle's intermediary with the SS. They tortured him to death as we prepared our attack on them. They stripped him and beat him and cut his throat, because they found out the Circle had used him to get to them. We arrived too late to save him.'

He takes a deep breath. 'Trevor was my p-p-p-partner. I mean that he was my lover. There isn't a day that passes without my mourning him and cursing the men who caused his death – both the SS and the corrupt Knights who funded them.'

There's a respectful pause, and then the interviewer's voice asks, quietly, gravely, 'Did the Circle know that you and Trevor were romantically involved?'

David looks tired suddenly. He says, 'No. They only found that out after Trevor died.'

'And were they sympathetic about your loss?' she asks.

'No,' David says. 'They froze me out. They made my position intolerable. The Circle caused my boyfriend's death, and then they left me to deal with it on my own. They didn't care whether I lived or died, just like they hadn't with Trevor.'

* * *

Another break then, but it's clear that that was the money shot. The documentary's done its worst now, and the final segment will just be a recap. They haven't time to get into the whole devices issue at this stage, which suggests David's kept that under his hat at least.

They let him sum up at the end.

'If the Circle hadn't trained Clifford Chalmers to be a killer,' David says, 'I doubt he'd have ever become such a force for chaos and destruction in post-war Iraq. If they didn't teach their Kn-Knights that might and right were interchangeable, I don't think they'd kill or injure nearly so many people. And if they'd kept themselves from meddling in politics, the Saxon Shield would have remained a laughable fringe group with no real force at their disposal. And my p-partner, Trevor Macnamara, would still be alive.'

It looks like that PR firm's going to have its work cut out for a while.

13. JASON SMITH, PRINCE OF THIEVES

'How the hell did this happen?' Sir Charles demands the next morning. He's as angry as you'd expect, which – in case you haven't been paying attention – is absolutely bloody livid. 'Stafford's going to answer for this, I can tell you that!'

'It's… difficult to say, sir,' Paul replies. This isn't a formal briefing, just an opportunity for Raymond to yell at everyone within a certain radius. Those Knights who were present in the Fastness when he blew his top are assembled, along with Blaze, round the giant wooden table in the boardroom. Stephen's there, annoyed to have been dragged away from his pet project once more. He looks like he hasn't slept since the Saxon Shield raid yesterday.

Parsons continues, 'Obviously the editors didn't approach us for a comment, or we'd have shut the whole thing down sharpish. Which is why they didn't, presumably. Bad journalistic form, though. We've put in a complaint.'

'Fat lot of use that is!' Raymond rages. 'Damage is done now. The public knows about Chalmers and Taylor and Macnamara and our arrangement with the bloody SS. Too late to issue a DA notice. Slap them with a libel writ, more people will hear of it. Just compounding the problem.' He runs out of steam on that train of thought, but quickly jumps aboard another one. 'How the blazes did Stafford get back into the country without Khuzaie's people warning us? I thought they had him under constant surveillance.'

'Actually, we can't be totally sure he *is* back in the country, sir,' Parsons continues. 'Other than what the programme said, we've got no proof of it.'

'No, he's here all right,' Blaze mutters declaratively. 'He's causing all kinds of disruptions with the devices. Like I say, this is some new thing. It's different from all that stuff in the records. Thing like that, it couldn't do its business from far away. Gotta get here with us.'

'Oh, hang on. I thought Stafford was bound to Sir Galahad?' Julian Blythe points out.

Blaze gives his head an emphatic shake. 'Not any more.'

'As I recall Sir Galahad caused a fair bit of trouble at the High King's court when he first showed up,' Blythe insists.

'Disruption,' the Seneschal says. 'Not this kind of trouble. Inclined to agree with Blaze on this one.' It's not exactly common knowledge among the Knights that a person can change their device, but it's not a secret either – it's the basis on which Blaze's predecessor got his job, after all. It's unusual, exceptional even, but then we live in exceptional times.

'Are you sure, sir?' Blythe's never known when to keep his mouth shut. He starts regurgitating Malory (Sir Thomas, that is) at them. 'Galahad turned up and sat in the Siege Perilous, which proved he was the knight who'd one day find the Holy Grail, blah blah blah... Then he pulled the *other* sword from the *other* stone, the one that proved he was the best knight in the world, and then – oh, sir, my goodness. Sir, you don't think – ?'

It's at this moment he realises it might be a good idea to put a sock in it. Sir Charles glares at him for several ominous moments, then says, 'Well, I suppose you've got a point. We'll place a discreet guard on the Grail, just in case Stafford has an interest in it. Congratulations, Blythe, you've volunteered. I'll brief you later.'

'Yes, sir.' Julian doesn't dare say anything else. The other Knights in the room are looking uneasy.

'If he isn't Galahad, Blaze, what is he?' Raymond demands. 'Has he picked up some filthy foreign device out there?'

'Al-K didn't recognise his *qarin*,' Blaze recalls. He never met Al-Khuzaie, of course (unless you count seeing him walk past outside the Hounslow Tube) but he's read the transcripts of the Circle's meeting with him. 'Called him the Black Knight, though. We probably want to start looking there.'

'I suggest you attend to that immediately, then,' Sir Charles says icily.

Blaze gives him a long, cool look, then saunters out of the boardroom. (Because it takes up an entire floor of the keep, this involves sauntering down the stairs, which is less easy to do nonchalantly than sauntering through a door, but he manages it.)

'Sir, we might have a problem,' Theo Harte puts in. He's one of the younger Knights, but he bears the device of Sir Kay's father Sir Ector, so is marginally less likely to be shouted at by Sir Charles than some of the other men. Having thought of what he's about to say, his Knightly honour compels him to say it in case one of them does, and gets into bigger trouble than he will.

'Thank you for that dazzling insight, Harte,' the Seneschal snaps.

Theo tries again. 'I mean, sir, there's a specific thing which this might cause us a problem with. However we deal with Stafford, with all this going on I presume that we'll be under increased scrutiny. All our quests will need to be by the book for a while.'

'Yes, yes,' agrees the Seneschal testily. 'What's your point?'

'Well, sir,' says Harte, 'it's Bretwalda Ward. She'll be up for trial shortly on the conspiracy charges. It sounds like it might be a bad idea for us to do the usual and get her sent to Benwick on the nod.' (Needless to say, Theo's Knightly honour has no problem with the Circle's normal practice here – it's only right and proper, he'd reckon, that criminals with devices should end up in the Circle's custody – but he's aware of how it looks to the outside world. This isn't hypocrisy or doublethink, just an inevitable consequence of working for an organisation which ascribes itself ultimate authority, even in only one sphere.) 'If there's even a hint that we're fixing trials as well as everything else, things could get iffy,' Theo concludes.

Sir Charles groans, but he doesn't savage Harte. 'All right,' he says. 'Another good point. I'll have a word with our legal team. Parsons, you stay. The rest of you, dismissed. Get back to whatever you were doing. Leave us to sort this lot out.'

The Knights file out and down the stairs, leaving the Seneschal and his aide alone. Parsons gets to his feet as Raymond stands, but then is forced to stay still and attentive while Sir Charles paces out a complete circle of the boardroom. Outside, the courtyard floodlights are off but the morning sun hasn't yet topped the curtain wall, and the concrete ring around the keep is stuck in twilight gloom.

Eventually Raymond returns to his starting-point, and sinks back into his chair. 'Can't decide,' he sighs. 'Is this the Green Chapel or is it something else? Is Stafford working with them, or alone?'

Paul's as startled by his boss's rare moment of somewhat reduced self-assurance as by the question itself. 'The Chapel, sir? Why would they be involved? They benefit far more than we do from the truce. Surely they're hardly likely to start trying to undermine it?'

Raymond snorts. 'Your girlfriend tell you that, did she?' Paul knows better than to reply. 'I don't know whether you noticed, Parsons, but Stafford contrived to blame half the things Taylor's done on the Circle without mentioning his name once.'

Paul had noticed that. 'They're old friends, though, sir. Taylor was Stafford's squire. He might want to protect him whether or not they're in contact now. Surely if they were, though, Taylor wouldn't have pulled that stunt with Al-Khuzaie at Heathrow?'

Sir Charles dismisses that. 'Ages ago. Plenty of time to act on Khuzaie's information and put out feelers.' He stands again and paces around the room again, anti-clockwise this time. At the other end he halts and gazes out towards the murky courtyard. 'Bring him in,' he tells Parsons.

Paul gives him a guarded look. 'Stafford, sir?'

The Seneschal turns. 'Of course bloody Stafford!' he barks. 'If Blaze is right, he's in the country somewhere. Find him, bring him in. Simple as that.'

'Of course,' Paul says. 'What charge, though, sir, if anyone asks? As Harte says, we need to do things by the book at the moment.' Appearing on TV to denounce the Circle may be a colossal violation of the Knightly code of honour, but it isn't actually illegal.

'I don't care,' Raymond says. 'Just think of something. Get Khuzaie to issue a warrant for his extradition if you must – he's bound to have done something illegal there. Just being a poof, probably.' (He's wrong there, as it happens – and the UK government wouldn't extradite David for homosexual activity in any case – but Sir Charles is furious, and his finger's hardly on the pulse of international law at the best of times.) 'Iraqi gaol sounds just the ticket for the filthy traitor, just so long as you bring him here first. I want to talk to our Mr Stafford myself.'

* * *

Downstairs in the Knights' communal office space, Stephen finds Blaze waiting for him. 'Hey, Steve,' the younger man says, 'can we talk?'

'It's *Stephen*, Blaze,' Stephen reminds him, wishing he could politely insist that Blaze just use his surname. 'And I'm rather busy just at present. Didn't the Seneschal give you a job to do?' He's close to a breakthrough in the quest for

Adze, having finally enticed some information out of one of the junior undeviced British Beasts, a Wildcat, captured in the recent raid. He'd be closing in for an arrest on Addis himself if it weren't for these constant interruptions. Deep in his hindbrain, something growls.

Then he remembers that annoying though he may be, Blaze is Merlin's bondsman, and he's just been incredibly rude to him. Hastily he adds, 'What's it about?' A couple of other Knights in the hotdesking area are staring with great intentness at their screens so as not to look like they're earwigging.

'Your squire,' Blaze replies. 'Jackson.'

'Jason,' Stephen reminds him again. 'Jason Smith.'

'Jason, right,' Blaze agrees. 'Some of the other Knights have been talking about him.'

'Oh, dear Lord,' Stephen sighs. 'What's he done?'

'Listen,' Blaze says, lowering his voice, though not enough for the other Knights not to be able to hear. 'You ever think he might already have a device?'

'What?' Stephen's startled. 'How could –'

Blaze says, 'He's quick, good with his hands, stronger than you expect for a skinny kid. He aces all the combat training. He's up and down that climbing wall like a spider. And you've seen him playing cricket. That kid can *run*.'

All of this is true: it's what convinced Stephen that Jason would make a good recruit in the first place, and what bumped him so quickly from page to squire. 'But how could he have a device already, Blaze? He hasn't been through any of the usual rigmarole.'

'I've been reading up,' Blaze tells him. 'There's a thing that happens sometimes. Not often – last time was 1957. In the books there's a bunch of different knights who show up at Arthur's court incognito. Usually 'cause they're some famous dude's son and want to prove themselves, shit like that. Sir Gingalain, Sir Brewnor, Sir Carduino – even big guns like Lancelot and Percival do it in some stories. They start off as a servant or a squire or whatever till they get to do whatever's needful to show off their valiancy, then they get knighted.'

Stephen recognises the legendary trope, of course – they call it 'The Fair Unknown' – but he's never heard of it applying to real life. 'Sir Gingalain?' he recalls. 'Isn't he Gawain's son?'

'Whatever,' says Blaze. 'My point is, sometimes – like 1957 – a page or squire turns up here at the Circle, and they've already got one of those devices hitching a lift.'

'Really?' Despite his impatience, and the constant call of his pursuit, Stephen's intrigued. 'I never heard of that.'

'No,' says Blaze. 'They don't tell you lot except when it actually happens. Bad for morale when you guys have to go through all that discipline and hardship and shit, to see some other bloke just wander in and get recognised.' Blaze grins, doubtless remembering his own arrival at Kelliwick House.

'And –' Stephen glances across at his brother Knights, who immediately bury themselves in their screenwork – 'you think it's happened now?'

'Too early to say, man,' Blaze says. 'So, can you set me up a meeting with Jackson?'

'Jason,' Stephen repeats. 'Feel free to buttonhole him whenever you like.' Then he remembers something. 'Hang on a sec, though – you've talked to him before, haven't you? I thought you had a feel for these things. Isn't that part of what your device does?'

'I'm getting conflicting signals,' Blaze admits. 'Not sure how it all adds up, yet. I'll tell you one thing, though – if he gets upped to Knight just like that, your Jason's one lucky teenage white boy.'

He turns to leave. With a sigh of relief, Stephen calls up the British Beasts files, and starts to go through the transcript of Tom the Wildcat's testimony.

There's something nagging at him, though. He resolutely ignores it.

* * *

'So,' Blaze asks Jason later, in one of the small meeting-rooms in the curtain-wall that generally get used for this kind of mentoring, 'you been thinking about what we talked about, bruv?'

'Yeah,' Jason says, 'yeah. You're right, I should go for Knight. I reckon they'd totally let me. It's easy, this stuff, when you've got an ally already. I keep having to pretend I'm really clumsy, like. "Whoops, I dropped me sword when I could've been stabbing you in the chest with it." They're dead gullible, these Knights. Well, you'd know all about that.'

Squig's not a big talker, generally, but there isn't anyone else he can say this sort of thing to these days.

The room's small, but it's at courtyard level, and with a window looking inward towards the keep, it doesn't feel too enclosed. (The window's bulletproof, of course, and it doesn't open, just in case someone drops poison-gas shells through the glass roof of the courtyard, but still, it gives the required illusion.) Somebody well-intentioned in HR has made an effort to decorate the room with a framed print of John Pettie's sentimental *A Knight's Vigil* on one wall and a moody black-and-white photo of Tintagel Castle on the other. Squig's sprawled on a chair, with Blaze perched restlessly on a corner of the meeting-table.

'You're up for higher-level infiltration then, yeah?' Blaze says. 'That's my boy. See, these Knights may be all upper-class and oppressing the people and shit, but what I've learnt since I've been here is that they all mean well. They want the best for everyone – they're just too rich, too male, too straight, too bloody *white* to know what that means, you know? Fuck, even your Indian guy's too white.'

'That's right, mate,' agrees Squig affably. (His name really is Jason Smith, incidentally, just as Blaze's is actually Bernard Maddox. It's not easy, constructing a false identity that's rigorous enough to fool the Circle's background checks, and why would you bother when there's no record of you belonging to the Chapel? Admittedly Jason, like Burn, came to the Circle with a known criminal record, but among their many quite genuine virtues, the Knights have a touching belief in the power of redemption.)

'See,' Blaze goes on, 'Merlin's supposed to have the Seneschal's ear, right, but the Seneschal's an old guy, set in his ways and all, you know? He don't listen to me much. He can't last forever, though – like I say, he's old. And the next Seneschal won't be Sir Kay either, because an ally takes a while to find itself a new host, and the Circle needs a new Seneschal right away, yeah? When he goes, someone else with some other ally's gonna have to step up, for a time at least.'

'And that one'll listen to you?' Jason suggests.

The message has filtered back to him, of course, that Burn's not working for the Chapel any more. Still, the way he sees it, Burn warned Jory and Merry about Laney's surveillance, and after a year he still hasn't mentioned to anyone in the Circle that Jason's a spy, so whatever, he's basically sound. Besides, these days, from what Squig gathers, the Chapel and the Circle are all friends anyway. Squig enjoys his undercover work (though someone a touch more introspective might perhaps wonder whether what they were actually enjoying was working for the Circle), and he's made a number of friends among the squires and pages... but Burn's his oldest friend here, and he's happy to trust him.

'I'm hoping he'll listen to both of us,' says Blaze. 'Together, you and I could turn this Circle into something more like the Chapel. Make use of all these old white dudes. They got to be good for something, yeah? Get them to stop charging round on horses arresting our brothers and sisters, send them after the real criminals for a change. The rich, powerful people like them. The Man. How's that sound to you, Squig?'

'Sounds bloody brilliant,' Jason agrees. 'But to do all that, you reckon I've got to be made Knight? Yeah, I'd be up for that.'

'I think you might do better than that, bruv,' Blaze says.

* * *

For a while as he works, a terrible distraction nags at Stephen, the way, in certain texts, the Questing Beast's offspring gnaw away at its inside. There's something about Blaze's parting words that's working away inside him somehow. The conjurer's enunciation is terrible – from him that final phrase sounded like 'one lucky tee'age white boy'. For some reason since he said it, Stephen's been thinking of the childhood of King Arthur. He ignores it, sifting through Tom's accounts of the movements of the chapter leaders and his sightings (rare, even for the Wildcat chapter member) of the ever-evasive Mark 'Adze' Addis… then, after half an hour the pieces fall together in his head, demanding his attention in a way he can't ignore.

What he's been thinking of is *The Once and Future King* by TH White, a four-book cycle about the life of Arthur – in which, as it happens, the Questing Beast plays a minor part – but specifically of its first book, *The Sword in the Stone*. It's a modern text (because 1938 counts as modern for the Knights) which also uses the Fair Unknown motif.

In White's whimsical fantasy, though, the character of Wart – the incognito son of a king who works as a kitchen-boy and then a squire before eventually proving himself, in his case not merely as a knight – is the young Arthur himself.

'Bally hell,' Stephen mutters involuntarily, then looks up, embarrassed, to see whether anyone heard. While he's been concentrating on work, though, the two Knights who were sharing the office space have gone elsewhere.

The baying of the Beast is calling to him, though. In just a few moments, Stephen will have forgotten all about this momentary revelation in the urgency of the hunt.

Not so the other two Knights, or those they talk to today.

* * *

Coming to a tacit understanding with the Circle hasn't meant an end to the Green Chapel's problems with the authorities. Fundamentally, we're an organisation devoted to benefitting the general populace through crime – hacking banks, sabotaging polluters, robbing and ransoming millionaires so the proceeds can be donated to the more deserving – and just because the Circle's turning a blind eye these days doesn't mean the police aren't interested.

Chief Inspector Kinsey's unit, in particular, have become more dogged and tenacious since their (always grudging) cooperation from the Circle dried up. Originally, after the Nutwood incident, some of us suggested relocating to our ancient stamping-ground in Sherwood Forest, but Jory vetoed that, on the grounds that even someone as stubbornly unattuned to any kind of imaginative endeavour as Jade Kinsey would be able to make that particular connection.

Thetford Forest, which straddles the Norfolk-Suffolk border, is a better bet: not remote exactly, but not on any of the main routes up and down the country either, and one of the largest wooded areas in England. Us Chapel people camped here are justifiably cautious, then, but not actually paranoid. Which is why that afternoon, when a lone figure in black-painted Circle-issue armour, carrying a black riot-shield and a sheathed sword, steps out from the trees like a bipedal beetle, lifts his visor and tells the lookout, 'I'm looking for the Green Chapel,' the lookout in question is a scrawny thirteen-year-old girl called Finn, who's sitting with her back to a large rock and a laptop on her knees.

Finn peers up without losing the beat of her fingers on the keyboard, and squints through a thick pair of glasses at the newcomer. 'You're that bloke,' she says. 'The one on YouTube.'

'Probably,' admits David Stafford. 'I haven't looked.'

'You'd better leave that sword here,' says Finn, still tapping away. 'And the shield. You can cave someone's skull in with one of those, my ma says.'

'I've never tried,' says David, but he follows the girl's instructions.

Finn deigns to stop her typing, stands, and leads him into in the clearing behind her, where among the tangle of tents stands the giant three-lobed family affair that's Rev Cantrell's domain. I come out of my own tent – because I came straight up after watching the *Squaring the Circle* documentary last night – in time to see Cantrell himself appearing through the flap, still buckling his belt. 'Hey Finn,' he says, 'this better not be one of your practical jokes, kid. Because –' he stops when he sees David. 'Never mind,' he says, staring at the newcomer. 'Keep up the good work, sis.'

'I was looking for Jordan Taylor and Malory Wendiman,' David tells Rev. 'I understood I might find them here.'

'Not today,' says Cantrell. He runs his eyes appreciatively over David's armour. 'Hey, anyone ever told you black's really your colour?'

David blushes under his visor. 'I'm D-David Stafford,' he says. 'I used to be –'

'Yeah,' says Rev, 'we watch the TV here. Young Finn there messaged me soon as she saw you. My name's Cantrell: these good people call me Rev. These here are Scar and Zara, and that's Dale.' He nods at me as I cross over to join him and the women. 'That was some impressive rhetoric you used about the Circle in that show last night. You mean it all?'

David looks into his eyes. 'Every word.'

'See,' I say, 'we've got a bit of a dilemma here. On the one hand, you're dressed kind of like a King's man, if you don't mind my saying so, and historically speaking we don't much like King's men round here. On the other, we're supposed to be friends with the Circle nowadays.'

Scar snorts.

Cantrell says, 'Yeah – you could say some of our best friends are King's men. Although you'd be missing a couple of important 'ex'es if you did. And you've just embarrassed those pals of ours mighty badly, and on national television as well.'

Scar says, 'What these soft pricks are dancing around is this could go either way. You may've left your weapons at the door, but coming here dressed like that, no-one here'll give a toss if we beat the shite out of you.'

'Why *have* you come here, Mr Stafford?' Zara asks. 'I think you should think very carefully before you answer this.'

'No need for that.' David smiles. 'I'm done with the Circle. If this is a chapel, I'm asking for sanctuary. I'm here to defect.'

Scar asks, 'You're sure about that, aye? We aren't exactly living in luxury here, your Knightship.'

'Ex-Knightship,' says David. 'As far as the Circle's concerned, at least. And I've spent the last two years living in a contested post-war reconstruction zone, with occasional excursions to deserts, minefields and occupied territories. Camping in a Br-British wood is my idea of heaven right now.'

'Well then,' Cantrell says, 'I'd say you're welcome to it. Three cheers for our new recruit, friends!'

And the Green Chapel raises up a heartfelt huzzah for the Black Knight.

* * *

Sir Charles's orders to take Stafford into custody are easier to give than to obey, but Paul's an old hand at this sort of thing. First, he sends men-at-arms to the offices of the production company who made *Squaring the Circle*, to inquire forcibly as to his whereabouts and contact details. This is predictably fruitless – according to the producers, Stafford met with them at times he prearranged using a pay-as-you-go mobile, and asked for any fees from his appearance to be donated to charity – but it eliminates the obvious.

Next, Paul fires off a bunch of parallel enquiries – to Al-Khuzaie, asking when Stafford was last seen in Iraq; to the air- and sea-ports, circulating Stafford's picture; to Chief Inspector Jade Kinsey, instructing her to devote some manpower to flagging up any reports of armoured men submitted to the police that don't correlate with known Circle activities.

Then, needing to be seen to do something active, he visits Stafford's house in Richmond. It's been under light surveillance since the Knight's disappearance two years ago and was thoroughly checked then for evidence that Stafford might have taken any Circle materials with him, or been influenced by any villainous device. The searches turned up nothing then, and Parsons finds little to interest him now.

After a few hours, he sits on David's sofa, puts his feet up his feet on the coffee table (barely dusty at all, as the Circle's been paying a cleaner to call in once a week in Stafford's absence) and checks in with the office via his iPad. Immediately he finds replies to all three of his queries. At first he's impressed by the efficiency of this, but then he reads them.

The first is Kinsey's, and is a precise anatomical description of what he can do with his request for help.

Tutting, he turns to Al-Khuzaie's response and discovers that the Black Knight is still under surveillance in Baghdad. For the past few weeks, though, he's been seen doing little more than wandering around the market in full armour, spending extravagant amounts of dinar and exchanging pleasantries with stallholders in fluent Arabic. Paul groans and resists the temptation to fire back an angry screed denouncing Al-Khuzaie and his agents as cretinous incompetents. The Iraqi civil servant's nothing if not cunning, and probably acquiesced to the deception just to be blamelessly rid of the hassle David Stafford represents.

The third response is more helpful: it's from the chief security officer at Edinburgh Airport, noting that a man closely matching Stafford's description disembarked off a flight from Queen Alia International Airport in Jordan some weeks previously. Paul immediately emails the forensic accountant who the Circle's employed to look into the source of the Saxon Shield's unexpected wealth, asking her to move tracking the payment for Stafford's ticket to the top of her to-do list.

Paul ponders, practicing finger-movements with his prosthetic. Whatever Stafford's new device might be, it's clearly induced him to adopt the 'Black Knight' look, which means it must be smarting at having to leave it behind. That decision was inevitable, of course – David appears to have made his original journey to the Middle East overland, but borders have tightened recently, and certainly no airline in that part of the world is going to fly weaponry and armour as part of a passenger's luggage manifest.

Unless Stafford's returned to Britain to retire, Paul suspects that reassembling his Black Knight outfit is going to be a high priority for him. He checks the flat's wardrobe, but Stafford's two spare sets of armour, sword and shield are still where they were logged after his departure.

Parsons taps out an email instructing men-at-arms on various regional deployments to inventory the armouries at the Circle safe-houses in all the major cities in the country, kept there for times when a Knight might find himself weaponless and unable to contact the Fastness for backup. Stafford would know their locations, of course, and they're usually unmanned. Although the codes and protocols have changed, it's not impossible that a security-savvy ex-Knight could have found his way in.

Then he goes home, to the Islington flat he shares these days with Laney Wardsley.

* * *

Jory takes Cantrell's call on Edward's business line. He's spent the day helping out in the shop, which is always a pleasant diversion. He's no use at telling the customers anything about the wares – Jory can't replicate whatever it is that enables Edward and Malory to navigate conversations about chakras, ley lines and creative visualisation, be that expertise, bullshit or a masterful combination of the two –

so he's confined himself to taking their cash, stacking shelves and accepting the occasional delivery, calling on whichever of the others is out the back for the more complex requests.

He's found it quite relaxing, actually. Compared with life-or-death struggles with psychotic Arthurian literature geeks – whether they're wearing ceramic-polyamide armour or cloaks made from the stitched-together beards of their victims – running a shop is a restful way to spend one's time. And it gets him brownie points with Malory and Edward, who've brought him so many cups of tea he's started worrying about kidney stones.

It's late afternoon when he picks up the phone and says 'Good afternoon, The Tree in the Well, how can I help you?' and Cantrell replies, 'Hey, Dan. Can you get out of that ridiculous shop and go somewhere we can talk?'

Jory calls Edward to come and take over at the counter and steps out of the back door into the well-tended herb garden. Edward remains, after all this time – and despite his long service to the Circle – a bit of an old hippy, and Jory's half-convinced that some of the 'herbs' here might be of interest to the police. Although if the police in Glastonbury worried about that sort of thing, they'd be too busy to go to the loo.

'What is it, Rev?' he asks.

'Your pal Dave's here,' Rev tells him. 'Came looking for you and Merry, but now he says he wants to defect. I've made him welcome, but we could still ransom him to the Circle if you think it'd be worth it.'

'God, no!' says Jory, alarmed. 'If the Circle want him, it won't be to give him a welcome-home party. We can't hand him over to them. No, if he wants to join up with us, he's welcome to, I'd say. I wouldn't have thought it was his sort of thing, but we've been out of touch for a while.'

'That's what I hoped you'd say,' said Cantrell. 'God, the ass on that guy. And I just know he's up for it.'

'TMI, Rev,' says Jory patiently, not for the first time. 'Did David say anything about his ally?'

'Nah,' says Rev. 'Didn't seem tactful to ask. If he's defecting, he's either lost it or he's somehow got one of Arthur's men to abandon the Round Table. Rude to bring it up either way.'

'Merry seems to think it might have mutated into something different. We're going to have to ask.' Jory sighs. It looks like the holiday's over. 'OK, Rev, I'll come up during the day tomorrow. It's what, a four-hour drive? I'll be there for lunch.'

'OK, big guy,' Cantrell's saying. 'See you then.'

'Hold on,' Jory adds quickly. 'How does he seem to you? I mean… he's been out of circulation a while. On TV last night he sounded pretty bitter. Does he seem… well, nice? He always used to be nice.'

'His ass is nice,' Cantrell says. 'Dan, I don't know what he was like before. Only you can judge how much he's changed. Which you can do tomorrow, right?'

'OK,' says Jory doubtfully, and hangs up.

Inside, Malory's at the computer again. She's spent most of the day either here or on the phone, trying to learn more about David's return to the UK and find some indication of whose device he might be channelling these days. She's convinced there's more going on here than is obvious, but it's not clear yet what exactly she suspects.

'David's turned up at Thetford,' he tells her. 'Any progress identifying which Black Knight he's turned into?'

She stops and stares at him. 'Not so far,' she says. 'But I think you've just narrowed it down.'

* * *

Like Merry said earlier, Black Knights are ten-a-penny in Arthurian lore. Leaving ethnicity out of the equation (you might think it wasn't much of an issue at the time, but Palamedes shows it's not as simple as that), black has plenty of connotations, the most prominent of which are 'evil' and 'cool'. There are plenty of knights in the mythos who want to look one or both of those: buying a black horse, decking it out with black trappings and strapping a blazon sable onto your shield-arm was the Arthurian equivalent of putting on mascara, dyeing your hair black and listening to The Cure.

A few of the Round Table knights seem to have gone through a goth phase – Lancelot and Tristan for two. Of the obscurer ones, Sir Acanor was known permanently as the Black Knight, but in his case it does seem to have been a racial epithet (he was also known, charmingly, as the Ugly Hero). Sir Crinides the Black is mentioned too, but only by name and he seems to have never surfaced on the Circle's roster.

As for the plentiful Black Knights who fight against Arthur's men, there's no real pattern to their behaviour – they argue with the Round Table knights over women, territory, magical relics or just their right to sit on a horse in the middle of the road and kill everyone who comes past. Since these are the main causes of disagreement in the legends, this doesn't really tell us much.

So far, the Black Knight who's looking like the closest match for David's story is Sir Maduc the Black, a knight of Arthur's in some obscure French texts who rebelled against the High King after the latter fought a successful war against his brother, Sir Raolais the Red. Reading Trevor Macnamara as the 'brother', that could just about fit if Merry squints, but she's not happy with it – especially since the rest of Maduc's story would seem to suggest that David's going to fall in love with an old flame of Sir Gawain's. This strikes her as unlikely, since – barring a new bearer of the Gawain device – the only obvious candidate for the position would seem to be Merry herself, and David's inclinations don't run that way.

Still, Maduc's the best fit for David's current blazon and behaviour Merry's been able to find – in the Arthurian mythos. Up to the moment when Jory said 'David's turned up at Thetford,' it hadn't occurred to her to look in the Robin Hood stories.

'Good grief,' she says now. 'That puts a completely different spin on the whole thing.'

You may think of Robin Hood – certainly if you've been paying attention to the stuff I've told you about the Green Chapel – as fundamentally an anti-establishment figure. If so – well, you're closer to the original and authentic tradition than a lot of people. If you'd made a study of it (which I'm not actually expecting you to do, though it might sound like it sometimes), you'd certainly have noticed the number of stories where Robin is a loyal subject of the crown, forced into the outlaw life against his will by corrupt agents of the king's authority – and where the king himself sorts things out in the end, punishing the cruel officials and restoring the outlaws to their rightful positions. Often Robin's some kind of nobleman, not a yeoman at all – you can hardly expect a mere peasant to be any good at leading other peasants, after all.

The most common variant of this establishment-propaganda Robin Hood story is that Robin's outlawry is a product of the corrupt regency of Prince John, during the period when John's brother King Richard I, aka Richard the Lionheart, is away at the Crusades. In this tradition, when Richard returns, Robin and the Merry Men aid him in retaking the throne and abolishing John's manifold excesses, and are rewarded with pardons for their trouble. The natural order's restored, all's well with the world, and everybody goes home happy without bothering themselves about what might happen when John succeeds to the throne a few years later.

As you might guess, I don't have a lot of patience with this version of the narrative. Possibly my favourite thing about the 1980s TV series *Robin of Sherwood* (and there's plenty to love, from Clannad's haunting incidental music to the early-career work of Ray Winstone as a particularly murderous Will Scarlet) is that, when Richard returns and pardons Robin and the Merry Men rally to his cause, he turns out to be just as big a bastard as his brother, and they all bugger off back to Sherwood in disgust.

Anyway, a lot of this can be traced back to the novel *Ivanhoe*, by the notorious Hanoverian running-dog, Sir Walter Scott. Earlier stories had Robin meeting the king – or *a* king – in disguise, but Scott is the first to make Robin and Richard comrades-in-arms against Prince John.

Scott's Richard comes back to England in disguise to avoid assassination by John's agents. Not just any old disguise, though – he feels he deserves the respect of rank, at least. Which is why the attention-seeking prat enters a tournament kitted out as an anonymous coloured knight straight out of the Arthurian myths and is known accordingly until he reveals his true identity four chapters from the end.

So: guess what colour Richard's armour, horse and shield were – according to Walter Scott, who presumably thought it signified the height of cool, and not evil at all.

Go on, guess. I bet you'll never get it.

* * *

The phone call comes while Paul's having supper – tagliatelle carbonara lovingly cooked by Laney, with a bottle of Rioja she picked out for them at Waitrose.

'Sergeant-at-Arms Thackett here, Mr Parsons,' says Bob Thackett, who as it happens is the bloke who arrested me two years ago. He's been promoted since then, and is on permanent deployment at the Circle's garrison in the Midlands. 'I'm at the Peterborough armoury. You were right, sir – there's two suits of armour gone, plus three swords and two unblazoned shields. No sign of a break-in, sir. We'd never have noticed without a full inventory.'

'Good work, sergeant,' says Paul, already wiping his lips with his napkin. 'Send whoever's with you out to get CCTV logs from any local retail outlet that might sell black paint. DIY stores, decorators' suppliers, car and motorbike accessory shops – run up a list, yeah? Meanwhile, you sit tight and watch the place. I'll be with you in a couple of hours.'

'Where are you going, hon?' Laney asks, looking perturbed at her beloved's sudden restlessness.

'Peterborough, babes,' Paul replies. 'Circle business, I'm afraid.'

'But do you have to go tonight?' she pouts.

'I'm chasing a lead,' he tells her. 'Can't wait.' He kisses her head, picks up the permanently-packed, heavy valise containing his own armour and weaponry, bids her goodbye and leaves. Laney sits silently for several minutes, staring at her half-eaten carbonara, before getting up and tipping it into the bin.

14. KNAVES IN THE WOOD

The Circle respects its Knights' autonomy, to some extent at least. Without being overly prescriptive, though, there exists a sensible convention that any Knight out on a quest – unless he's in deep cover – should check in with the Fastness at least twice a day. For a Knight assigned a particularly dangerous task – like Trevor Macnamara's liaison with the Saxon Shield – one failure to report is enough to raise the alarm, but generally any Knight who goes for more than two days without making contact is deemed to have either been captured or gone errant.

Paul Parsons' field reports are made directly to the Seneschal. Sir Charles is a troubled man these days, and some of the junior Knights suspect privately, as Blaze does, that his never overly impressive mind isn't quite what it used to be. He wouldn't necessarily notice the absence of a formality he's generally taken for granted.

Perhaps it's lucky, then, that Sergeant-at-Arms Bob Thackett phones the Fastness early the next morning, asking politely why Mr Parsons didn't arrive in Peterborough last night, and whether he, Thackett, might be allowed to stand down and go home now. Otherwise, it might have been a couple of days before the Seneschal realised that his lieutenant had gone missing.

* * *

For twelve months now, Stephen Mukherjee has heard the Beasts in his head. Other noises can drown them out – he's listening to more music than ever before – but when there's silence he can hear them still: the purr of their engines, the thrumming of their hooves, the squealing of their brakes, the howling. Above them all, the voice of the lead bike's motor, the baying of a hundred hounds. They've made the pregnant silences of cricket almost intolerable for him.

He still hasn't seen Adze's human face; the helmet's visor covered it completely. But on that day at Nutwood, he stared into the painted eyes of the snake, with their black vertical pupils, and knew that that was the true gaze of his quarry. Hooves of a hart it may have, the haunches of a lion and the flanks of a leopard, but the face of the Questing Beast is that of the serpent.

Stephen's never been as close to Mark Addis as in that moment, but he's been relentless in his pursuit. He's followed the Beast's spoor through trashed pubs and dodgy chatrooms, service-station forecourts and the records of court proceedings. He's laid traps, and seen the wily creature spring them harmlessly. He's thought his quarry cornered, only to find his sights full of lesser prey. He's used other creatures as bait.

In desperate moments, Stephen's essayed wilder schemes, like trying to interest the leader of an evangelical Christian biker gang in the sparse stories about Arthur's hunting-dog Cabal, in the hope that the hound's device might stick to him. He's struggled to invent a ritual for invoking the devices of the Wild Hunt, which the Celts called the Cŵn Annwn and the Anglo-Saxons the Herlathing: a ghostly pack of dogs and company of men said to ride through the sky at moments of great import for Britain (and surely hunting down the Questing Beast would be just such a moment), whose only tenuous connection with the Matter of Britain is that their leader – variously thought to be Odin, Herne the Hunter or Satan himself – is also sometimes identified as King Arthur.

243

Stephen understands, in a distant, theoretical sort of way, that this obsessive mania of his is a function of the Sir Palamedes device, but the knowledge doesn't really touch him. His urge to act out Palamedes's story is so strong it occludes that part of his cognitive processes – just as it never occurs to, say, Desmond Wigsby that some of the quests he's sent on might be practical jokes, while Paul Parsons persistently fails to consider the relevance of the fact that two of Sir Lancelot's lovers were called Elaine.

...And now Parsons is missing, apparently. His car seems to have left the main road somewhere around St Neots, and no-one in the Circle has been able to locate him since. All the Knights at the Fastness, including Stephen, have been ordered to make the quest for his safe return their first priority.

Which is infuriating, because Stephen needs their manpower for his final strike against the Beasts.

With Tom the Wildcat's information, he's confident he's identified a time and place where the unpredictable Mark Addis will be. The biker leader has a young son by an ex-girlfriend, it seems, and while he doesn't live with them, he never misses the boy's birthday – which, as malicious chance would have it, is today. Stephen isn't so naive as to assume that Adze's arrest will be automatic – the man's as fleet as a deer and as lithe as a big cat, and he writhes and twists like a snake – but the chances of his capture are greater than they've been at any other time.

At least they would be, given proper resources. Ideally, Stephen would like a phalanx of armed Knights backed up by men-at-arms with artillery, like Parsons deployed at Nutwood, but he acknowledges that might be seen as excessive for one arrestee. Stephen's joy as just such a force descended on the Beasts three weeks ago was fierce and exultant, turning rapidly to bitter frustration as it became clear that Adze wasn't with them. He's been hoping that he'd be able to bring at least half-a-dozen brother Knights along with him today, to assure the final completion of his quest.

Instead, even he himself is asked – impossibly – to stay away. In his current state of mind, oath of fealty or no, Stephen is no more capable of such restraint than, dying of thirst, he could resist an offer of poisoned water.

Stephen checks carefully that the office space is empty. It is, of course – most Knights in residence are preparing for the journey to Cambridgeshire, with only Stephen pleading a need to finish up some urgent paperwork before he scoots off.

Instead, he lifts a phone, and dials a number he has on a business card. He waits for the person he's calling to pick up, for her peremptory bark of a name. Her yap makes him think once again of a loyal hunting-dog.

'Hello, Chief Inspector,' Stephen says. The hunt has made him cunning. 'What would you say to an opportunity to bring in the leader of a major criminal gang, and poke the Knights of the Circle in the eye at the same time?'

* * *

Jory and David are walking the perimeter of the Thetford encampment together, two middle-class Englishmen awkwardly renewing a dormant friendship. They've already covered how long it's been since they last saw each other, their broad general health and recent meteorological trends, so now they're at a bit of a loss.

The sunny day, the cooking smells, the tents (their guy-ropes brightly strung with pennants and drying laundry), the shrieks of children playing, and the music systems playing at what for the Chapel counts as a civilised volume, all remind Jory of his first sojourn in the Green Chapel encampment, the one he spent as a 'guest' of Shafiq Rashid. He remembers the strange peace which began to infiltrate his consciousness during those earliest days – the peace which, at the time, he ascribed to simply being resigned to his situation, but which in memory now feels like a recognition that this place (or rather, the gathering of people temporarily located in this place) would in the future become his home.

Is that how David feels now, Jory wonders?

Feeling the need to break the silence, he says: 'I should thank you, you know, for warning us about the Seneschal. Malory and I owe you a lot.'

Without the message David sent two years ago, Jory might well have approached Sir Charles with his concerns about the Saxon Shield and found himself volunteering for some quest which would have proved just as dangerous as Trevor Macnamara's. Raymond isn't by nature a ruthless man, but in his position it's seductively easy to think of the Circle's human resources as being the devices, who never really disappear even when their hosts are killed, rather than its actual humans.

'It was my p-pleasure,' David says grimly. 'If I helped save you from what happened to Trevor, it was the least I could do.'

'I couldn't believe it at first,' Jory remembers, 'when you told me he sold Trevor out to the SS.' He'd thought that, whatever his faults, the Seneschal was at least loyal to his men. What he'd failed to take into account was how far the old goat might be willing to go for what he considered the greater good.

'I could,' David replies immediately. 'I've known him longer, and I've never trusted him. It's difficult to put your life the hands of someone who hates the sort of man you are. His influence has held the Circle back, made it a hostile place for much longer than it should have been. I'm still angry that Trevor and I could never be honest about our lives.'

Jory makes a vague, sympathetic noise. The scale of the hurt that David's experienced at the Circle's hands still upsets him to think about.

'It wasn't just the homophobia, though,' David goes on. 'Raymond's not at all clever, he's totally inflexible, and I've always felt he's weak. He covers it up with bluster and machismo, but I think he's scared a lot of the time. That's not a commanding officer you can trust.'

'I think you're right,' says Jory. 'I feel sorry for him, in a way.'

It's the wrong thing to have said, Jory realises. David purses his lips and says, 'I suppose you have that luxury. I've had a lot of time to think about it, and I understand him better now – but that's not the same thing as forgiving him, not at all. Stupidity and weakness are dangerous in a leader, but ideal in an enemy. If I can bring that bigoted old b-bastard down, and his Circle crashing after him, I will. *Squaring the Circle* was just the start.'

'I see,' says Jory. In the car on the way over, the Radio 4 magazine programmes were full of the discussions about the Circle that the TV documentary threw up. A whole phalanx of establishment figures, from retired cabinet ministers to senior police officers, have been mobilised to argue that the Circle does a damn fine job and that David's a lone crank with a grudge, but there's a strong undercurrent of dissenting voices – journalists, human rights charities, even rank-and-file police – who feel it's long past time the Circle's record was subjected to scrutiny.

'I'll tell the country about the devices, if I have to,' David claims. 'I kept that back this time, but I think the threat was pretty clear.' A black-eared mongrel runs across their path, barking excitedly, chased by a gaggle of small boys and girls. A larger dog follows them watchfully, in loco parentis.

Jory finds this conversation's direction concerning. Even accounting for the change in loyalties, this isn't the David he knew. David was indignant in the face of cruelty and injustice, yes, but he was a kind man, never vengeful or vindictive. Forgiveness wouldn't have been so alien to him. Still, Jory doesn't feel entitled to judge him after what he's been through.

That doesn't mean he has to give him his help. 'So, is that why you're here? So you can use the Chapel against the Circle?'

David frowns. 'N-not *use*. The people here have real grievances, as do others elsewhere. It's an alliance we'll all benefit from.'

'Others?' asks Jory.

'Well, we both know there are other groups opposed to the Circle,' David elaborates. 'They're all coming out of the woodwork these days. The Caer Lloyw Witches. The Adam Bell gang. The Children of the May.'

Jory wonders where David would draw the line. This side of the Saxon Shield, presumably, since they're the ones who actually killed Trevor (not that David seems to be keeping that very clearly in mind), but who else would he deal with? The Red Ravagers? British Beasts? The Sons of Gore?

He says, 'They might be able to help you, but the Chapel can't. In case you haven't heard, there's a truce on.'

'For the moment,' David says. 'Do you believe it will last? I'm not sure I do.'

'Malory does,' Jory asserts, remembering that privately even she has doubts.

(...'Are we being arrogant, Jory?' she asked him once last winter, one night in the early hours when their tent was freezing and neither of them could sleep. 'To think our generation can reverse five thousand years of worsening relations between two demigods, in one grand gesture? Can you and I really be the ones to change British mythopolitics forever?'

He did his best to reassure her, but there are times when he, too, fears that this is just a temporary respite, that all their good intentions have been for nothing. *Between the idea and the reality*, as his favourite poet put it, *falls the shadow*.)

'Well,' says David. 'If so, there are others who'll be willing to do what's n-necessary. For the moment, the Chapel are welcoming and friendly, and most importantly for me you have a strong track record of hiding from the Circle. I'm very happy to throw in my lot with you for now, if you'll allow it. I can see how the others see you and Malory as leaders, though I'm sure they'd deny it for form's sake. You've come a long way since the Circle, Jory.'

'So have we all,' says Jory.

David smiles. 'You needn't worry that I'll exploit them, you know. I may have changed, but not that much.'

Jory reserves judgement. Instead he asks, 'What does Sir Galahad think about all of this?'

For the first time, David looks annoyed. He says, 'That's between him and me, Jory, you know that. I don't have to give an account of my device to you or anybody else. Now if you'll excuse me, I think I ought to help with lunch.'

And there, for now, the matter rests.

* * *

'You going up north with the others, then?' Blaze asks Jason.

Squig, who's originally from Sheffield, snorts at the Londoner's impression that Cambridgeshire counts as 'up north'. Then, seeing from Blaze's raised eyebrow that the question hasn't evaporated, he says, 'Dunno. Mr Mukherjee hasn't told me yet.'

The two of them are in the meeting-room again, the advisor notionally mentoring the young squire but in fact doing what my generation would have called 'hanging out'. This time, though, Jason's standing, jiggling about restlessly. After a nomadic adolescence, he's found the settled life of the Fastness a comfort, and not knowing where he'll be in a few hour's time is an odd sensation for him. Blaze is leaning back in a chair, filling the cramped space on his side of the room, shoulders against the wall, legs intertwined on the table. He's wearing one of his usual baggy suits, this one in bottle-green, and his tubular metal staff leans up against the door-jamb.

'Good luck finding Paul Parsons if he doesn't want to be found,' Blaze observes. 'If he's gone errant, like that David Stafford guy, or our man Dan...'

Jason's surprised. 'Why d'you think he'd do that? He doesn't seem the type.'

'Nor did they, until they did,' Blaze guesses. He doesn't actually have a clue; he's just making conversation. He'll have to head for Peterborough himself at some point, to show willing, but he's not relishing the prospect. 'Now they're both with the Chapel.'

Jason stops jigging for a minute. 'Who are?'

'Jordan Taylor,' says Blaze, 'and that David Stafford dude.' When Jason doesn't answer he elaborates, 'Off the telly, remember?'

'That bloke's with the Chapel? At the camp?' Jason doesn't get it. 'I thought the Chapel and the Circle were working together now. Why'd they take him in, then?'

'You know what they're like,' says Blaze. He reaches out for his metal pole and idly telescopes it in and out a couple of times. It always amazes Jason to see how small it goes. 'Bit of a soft touch, sometimes. And they probably thought that stuff he said on the TV was kind of funny.'

'Yeah.' Jason grins. 'It was bloody funny, too, weren't it?'

Blaze smiles gravely. 'Yeah. The Seneschal went completely postal about it.'

They chuckle together for a moment. Outside in the parade-ground, a troupe of men-at-arms files past, probably on their way to the car park. Probably bound for Peterborough.

'Hang on,' says Jason. 'How do you know this? I thought that lot weren't taking your calls no more.'

'I've got a source,' Blaze says. 'She's with this lot called the Nine Witches of Caer Lloyw.' Still not entirely comfortable with Medieval Welsh, he over-enunciates the name in deliberate self-parody. 'That's an old name for Gloucester. She talks to Scar and Zara sometimes.'

'Ah.' Jason smirks. 'A woman.' He's not getting a lot of female contact these days.

'Not like that,' Blaze says. 'I ain't ever met her, she just emails me about... well, witchy stuff.' He looks embarrassed for a moment, as if he's admitting something sordid. 'This Stafford bloke, though...,' he adds hurriedly. 'He's not someone the Chapel would want round if they knew.'

'What, that he used to be a Knight?' Jason asks. 'No, they must know that. It was on that telly thing.'

'Not that,' says Blaze. Idly, he makes a coin appear between each pair of his fingers in turn, before vanishing it into one ear and manifesting it from the other. His silver dragon-ring flashes in the diffuse light from the courtyard. Jason finds it faintly hypnotic.

'There's this consultant does work for the Circle sometimes,' Blaze says. 'A forensic accountant. She finds out where money comes from and where it ends up. Money-laundering, Swiss bank accounts, shit like that. That twat Parsons thought the Saxon Shield had cash they shouldn't've, so he set her off looking for where they got it. Then, just before he disappeared, he told her to find out who paid for David Stafford's plane ride from Jordan. And guess what?'

Jason's started jiggling again during that, but he stops and thinks for a moment. 'Roman Abramovich?' he says. 'No, not a clue, mate, sorry.'

Blaze puts his hands behind his head. 'Same place,' he says.

Jason recaps the conversation in his head. 'Hold up,' he says. 'So those SS arseholes paid for Stafford to fly here?'

'Not quite,' says Blaze. 'Their biggest donor did, though. The accountant doesn't know who it was yet, but both lots of cash came out the same offshore bank account.'

'Christ.' Jason's sincerely disgusted. The SS are the one group the Circle and the Chapel despise pretty much equally. 'You're right, he shouldn't stay there with our lot. D'you want me to get a message out?'

'Nah,' Blaze says. 'Gonna send them a text.'

To punctuate the point, he plucks his mobile out of thin air and glances at it. 'Ah,' he says. 'I wondered what that tickling was.' Seeing Jason's confusion, he adds, 'Elasticated pouch in my armpit. Twangs it out into my hand. It's a conjuror thing.'

He frowns and prods a few buttons on the phone, then says: 'You know what? Fuck Steve Mukherjee. That guy's off in his own little world these days, hunting for God knows what. You come north with me. Anyone asks, tell them I requisitioned – no, what's the word? – seconded you. We're gonna join in the hunt for Mr Parsons.'

* * *

'So, David,' Rev Cantrell says at lunch. 'Dan tells us you've been in Iraq.'

We're eating homemade houmous with spicy falafel cooked over a portable hotplate, stuffed into pittas which Jory (vaguely inspired by his friend's Middle Eastern sojourn) picked up fresh from a bakery this morning on his way through Cambridge. It's a nice day, so everyone who's around at the encampment has dragged their deckchairs, beanbags, garden furniture and a few big logs into the big central area between the tents.

David feigns reticence. 'Ah well, there are a lot of stories there.' The Chapel people, sensing entertainment in the offing, cock an ear each in his direction.

'I'll bet.' Cantrell waggles his eyebrows. 'So pick us out a juicy one.'

Rev's being genial and friendly, with only an undercurrent of flirting which David's ignoring gracefully. Given that David met Trevor through work, Jory wonders how much of his life he's actually spent socialising with other gay men. The ex-Knight isn't letting it throw him, though: in general, David's being as charming as he knows how.

'Well,' David says, and considers. 'One thing you might all be pleased to hear is that the fellow the Circle thought was keeping an eye on them for me – an Iraqi government official called Ibrahim Al-Khuzaie – was actually covering up for me a lot of the time.'

Really? Jory thinks, slightly aggrieved. He keeps his silence, though.

'You see, while I was out there I was… well, I was on a bit of a crusade,' says David, and Jory takes care to suppress his jolt of recognition at the word. 'I'd been in the country before, shortly after the war finished, as a Knight of the Circle with a very specific mission to bring in an embarrassing renegade of ours – but while I was there I saw a great deal of injustice and suffering which, as a Knight, I wasn't supposed to notice.

252

'You see,' he says, 'the Circle only cares about the trouble the devices cause – the entities I believe you call "allies" – and even that's supposed to be limited to British devices or foreign devices active in Britain. Clifford Chalmers was the bondsman of Sir Mordred, so even in Iraq he counted as our problem. Iraq's sectarian in-fighting, though, the oppression of minorities, domestic violence – none of those were caused by anything connected to the Matter of Britain, so none of them were things we were allowed to intervene in.

'When I decided to part company with the Circle, my first thought was to rectify that. I had my armour and weapons shipped to a family I could trust in Baghdad, who I'd met during the Circle campaign, and travelled overland from Dieppe to Turkey – hitchhiking, mostly. I crossed the mountains into Iraq, skirted around the territories occupied by the Islamist insurgents and eventually made it to Baghdad. I set myself up with a house there, and set about... well, fighting crime, I suppose, in Iraq and its neighbouring countries. After a while I started getting a bit of a reputation for myself.

'I wasn't entirely p-popular with the Iraqi authorities, as you might imagine. They feel they've had enough of Westerners coming in and trying to fix their problems, thank you very much. I was probably lucky that the first official to approach me was Ibrahim – he's a bit of an Anglophile, but more importantly a pragmatist, and a particularly wily one. He'd been watching my vigilante activities for a while and had worked out how I could be useful and acceptable to his administration.

'They were experiencing certain issues, you see,' said David, 'involving foreigners with diplomatic immunity, which the government couldn't be seen to rectify for obvious reasons. Ibrahim promised me that the police would "devote insufficient resources" to stopping my crusade, provided I agreed to undertake, at his instruction, certain quests which he promised would be of particular interest to me.

'I was dubious at first, but then he told me what these problems were. A minor Saudi royal was channelling enormous funds to the jihadist militants in the north; a Chinese embassy official was running a profitable sideline selling smuggled heroin to teenagers; a US army officer on secondment to the government itself had a penchant for violent sex games involving underaged local girls.

'So, suddenly it wasn't too difficult for him to convince me.

'I won't go into detail about how I approached these assignments, but... well, one morning at the souk the Saudi prince became convinced that an armoured figure was stalking him. He became so frightened he broke away from his bodyguards and ran; when they found him again, he was so terrified he'd soiled himself. He wouldn't tell anybody what had happened, and he left the country in his private jet that evening.

'The Chinese official swerved and crashed his car into a wall in a deserted street in a Baghdad suburb. The wall wasn't too well built, and it collapsed on top of him. When the emergency services cut him free he was paralysed from the waist down, and after a short stay in an international hospital he, too, returned home. He later claimed he'd swerved to avoid a warrior in armour who appeared out of nowhere in the road ahead of him, then vanished without trace.

'And speaking of which... the American disappeared from his house one night and was never found. Afterwards, though, the families of the girls he'd abused were noticeably calmer and more measured in their demands for reparation from the government.'

Jory shivers at this. The Circle metes out justice according to its intricate code, and the Chapel according to its own, more streamlined ethics, but all of them have boundaries. Vigilantism is one thing, but kidnapping a man and killing him in secret – by God only knows what methods – is quite different. Even if you believe such a man's actions put him beyond any kind of humane consideration, what about his family? Even if he terrifies and abuses them as well, they deserve to be sure he's never coming back.

'Meanwhile,' David continues blithely, 'I carried on doing my best to help the locals, using the abilities I'd inherited from the Circle. Ibrahim had explained that he would need to report my whereabouts to them – he couldn't risk the consequences if it were thought that the Iraqi regime had been deliberately harbouring me – but he could reassure them he had the situation under observation and control.

'Even as a deniable asset, though, I had a fairly limited shelf life. There are only so many times influential foreign diplomats can be terrorised, maimed or abducted before it starts reflecting b-badly on a nation's authorities. Two months ago Ibrahim came to me at my house in Baghdad and told me it was time for me to leave. He said he'd been contacted by an anonymous sympathiser back in the UK, who was paying my passage home. He gave me the contact details of a production company in Edinburgh who were interested in doing an exposé of the Circle, and he said he'd cover for me with his contacts here until they noticed I was back.'

'Did you ever find out who the sympathiser was?' I ask curiously.

David spreads his hands. 'Still no idea. Someone he'd met while visiting England, Ibrahim said. He wouldn't go into any more detail than that.' He addresses himself to his pitta, signalling that the story's over.

It's gone down well enough: the Green Chapel love tales of villains getting their just deserts, and they assume a certain level of embellishment. Everyone bigs up their accomplishments here, and probably nobody apart from Jory, who knows David's no liar, has taken the details seriously.

He reflects that David's doing a pretty good job of fitting in, and indeed of winning these people over. Whatever his device may be these days (and he continues to deflect all questions on that score, though more gently when it's someone other than Jory asking), his gift for coaxing out people's loyalty hasn't diminished since he left the Circle.

If he keeps this up, Jory thinks worriedly, it's appallingly possible that the Chapel could end up replacing its Green Knight with a Black one.

Rev's phone has started singing to him, and he faces away towards the tents and surrounding treeline to answer it. A moment later he turns back to Jory. 'It's Merry,' he says as he hands it over, adding patiently, 'Handy little gadgets, these. You might want to get yourself one someday, Dan.'

'Someday,' Jory agrees. He's never been able to get organised about phones. He's always losing the leads, so that the power runs down. *No charger have I*, he thinks vaguely as he takes the handset from Cantrell, *and no sword by my side.*

He says to the phone, 'Hello?'

'Beloved,' says Merry very briskly. 'I've just had another text from our friend Burn. Tell me, is David acting out of character at all?'

* * *

Stephen Mukherjee stands in the ruins of a small child's birthday party, surrounded by police officers, angry parents and crying children. A birthday cake lies in bits on the floor, a wreckage of racing-car-printed icing and uncomfortably few candles. The door to the council flat hangs from its hinges, splintered into two distinct sections. The sirens of the cars Kinsey's people arrived in still sound from the street below.

Somewhere beneath the unbelievable cacophony, an MP3 player plugged into tinny speakers is still working its way through a compilation of children's songs. If he strains his ears, Stephen can just hear the melody of 'Puff the Magic Dragon', only slightly louder than the ever-present growling of the Beasts in his mind's margins.

Chief Inspector Kinsey is trying to placate the mother of the birthday boy and is evidently hampered by her inability in this context to return the woman's prolific swearing in kind. Whenever she gets an instant's grace, she devotes it to sending a filthy glance across the room in Stephen's direction, promising all kinds of retribution as soon as she's at leisure to pursue it. Her officers are mostly ensuring that she and Stephen aren't mobbed by the murderous-looking parents of the other party guests, or the neighbours from the block of flats who are amassing menacingly outside.

Needless to say, Adze isn't here.

When Kinsey's police could see no sign of his distinctive bike anywhere on the estate, Stephen assumed he was just being characteristically cautious. In fact, it looks very much as if he's nowhere in the vicinity. Stephen may never have seen Mark Addis's face for himself, but he's studied the army records and the prison mugshots, and he knows his features as well as he knows his own. If he's one of the furious dads in attendance here, he's had a face transplant.

The birthday boy, Addis's natural son, has stopped wailing now, his sobs subsiding to snivels. Cautiously, Stephen crouches down to talk to him.

'Boston,' he asks the four-year-old, 'where's your daddy? Is he here?'

Mutely, Boston Addis indicates the fuming, burly man being held back by two officers and shouting imprecations on the entire law enforcement profession, domestic and international. Assuming Stephen's information's up to date, this is Bruce Foddern, Adze's successor as the boyfriend of Boston's mother, Kylie Hall.

'I meant your real daddy, Boston,' Stephen says awkwardly. 'Isn't he here? Doesn't he come to all your birthdays?'

'Mum doesn't let him,' Boston replies shyly, between shuddering breaths. A naughty smile crosses his face as he recalls, 'She said he was a fucking wanker.'

'Righto,' says Stephen, standing up. When he sees Tom again, he's going to... to... to give him a jolly good piece of his mind. He wonders whether this was the Wildcat's own initiative, or whether Adze set up the misdirection in advance. Probably the latter, Stephen thinks. He should have realised it was suspicious that a junior chapter-member would know so much about his secretive leader's private life.

Somewhere among the racket, he feels the vibration of his phone ringing. Fearing the worst, he checks the caller ID, but it's only Freddie Obote. Either the Seneschal hasn't noticed his absence, or he's ordered Obote to do his dirty work, possibly because he thinks they're friends. (In fact Stephen's always got on well with Freddie, but not, as Sir Charles would doubtless assume, on the grounds that his grandparents came originally from Calcutta while Obote was born in Uganda.)

Taking a deep breath, Stephen answers.

'Mukherjee, where in God's name are you?' Freddie asks.

'Obote,' says Stephen. 'I'm... otherwise occupied, old fellow. I've been following up a lead in my other quest. Urgent business. Couldn't wait, I'm afraid.' He winces from the glare Kinsey gives him as she hears him say that.

'For pity's sake!' Obote exclaims. 'The Seneschal's going to have your guts for garters, man. How quickly can you get to Peterborough? He might not have noticed yet that you're not here, but when he does...'

Stephen looks down. He's in full armour, naturally, having expected Adze to be here. His sword's back in its scabbard now, but he was brandishing it when he followed Kinsey's battering-ram though the door. Sir Palamedes's chessboard riot-shield lies at his feet.

He doesn't think these facts will have escaped the attention of the civilians here. And the expression on Kinsey's face promises him she's going to raise hell about this. 'I think he's going to find out,' he says wretchedly.

Through a momentary lull in the shouting, he hears the MP3 player promising him that, should he happen to go down to the woods today, he's guaranteed a big surprise.

* * *

'Which way now?' asks Squig, peering through the tree-trunks some hours later. It's late enough, in fact, that the summer evening's beginning to arrive, and the forest's getting visibly darker. Off in the distance, occasional shouts can be heard as the small detachment of Knights and men-at-arms detailed to search this wood near Huntingdon blunder about their business.

Other details are have been sent to the other bodies of woodland lying along Parsons's presumed route. Quite why the Seneschal thinks his lieutenant might be found in a forest isn't clear, but Jason shrewdly suspects it's somehow connected to the Green Chapel, at least in the old git's mind.

'What can you see?' Blaze asks him over the phone. For some annoying reason, the magician insisted on dropping Jason here and scarpering, heading for the main Circle assembly-point on the outskirts of Peterborough. He commandeered a bog-standard Circle-issue Ford for the journey up, too, depriving Jason of a ride in his flashy BMW.

Jason himself is kitted out in his squire's armour, which always feels loose on him despite being the smallest size, and is carrying his plain grey shield. His sword is in its scabbard, which ought to be more comforting than it is. These woods are getting gloomier by the minute, and the shouts of the main Circle detachment are too distant to be much comfort. Despite all the time he spent at the Green Chapel encampment, Squig's a city boy by heart, and he's watched a lot of horror films. Alone in a wood like this, he feels old fears coming back to him. He knows – he's not bloody stupid – that he stands much more chance of getting run over or mugged in central London than of being attacked by wild animals or families of inbred rural cannibals here, but the alienness of it all still bothers him.

'A bunch of trees, mate,' he says. Trying for bravado he adds, 'Trees straight ahead of me, trees left and right of me. Tell you what, I'll have a squizz behind me and see what's there, shall I? Oh, look at that, it's trees.'

'Keep going east,' says Blaze. 'You're nearly there. East is away from the sun,' he adds patiently.

'Can't bloody see the sun, can I?' Squig points out. 'I might not have said, there's trees in the way?' All the light in the forest's coming from one direction, though, so he starts walking away from it. As the twilight closes in, he can't help feeling this is exactly the wrong thing to be doing, although even if he started running the other way right now, he could hardly keep up with the rotation of the Earth.

'I've found a load of mud,' he reports a little later. 'That on your map, is it?'

'Right before you get to the bears and man-traps, yeah,' Blaze replies. 'Just keep going, bruv. Not far now.'

'Why're you so sure Mr Parsons is here anyway?' Jason asks petulantly, as he squelches on. ''Cause even if he's in a wood, which I don't see why he would be, I can't see how you'd know what wood he's in, or where.'

'Fuck's sake, Squig, I'm bloody Merlin,' Burn replies.

'Yeah?' Jason's robustly sceptical. ''Cause I thought it might be something to do with that that text you got. Plus on the way here, you kept on checking the satnav.'

'Yeah, so what?' Blaze sounds annoyed. 'No use knowing where something is if you don't know how to get there, is it?'

Jason 'Mmm's sagely. 'Right,' he says, 'you got a mystical vision of some map co-ordinates. On your phone. So what's Gandalf's GPS reckon now, then?'

'You're nearly on top of it,' Burn says. 'I'd shut the fuck up if I was you.'

'It'd take more than that to shut you up,' Jason mutters.

'Keep going right ahead,' Blaze instructs him. 'There'll be like a… a bit with no trees. You'll know it when you see it.'

Jason sighs. 'Thanks, Davy Crockett.'

'Call me when you've found him,' Blaze says. 'Got to say hi to the Seneschal now.' And peremptorily, he hangs up, leaving Jason alone in the darkling woodland.

'Fuck,' Jason says. Nearby, a lone bird trills a half-hearted dusk chorus, then falls silent as if embarrassed.

It's getting quite dark now. The trees make shapes against the sky that really don't look very much like hideous tangle-haired witches and ogres, but Squig didn't end up allied to a device of the Green Chapel by having an underactive imagination.

He tramps forward in the direction Blaze pointed him in. As the light goes, the patches of mud become obscurer, and he often has to grab onto branches to steady himself. Trunks, limbs and clumps of leaves conspire to whack him unexpectedly in the face. At one point he shouts 'Christ!' as something the size and shape of a dog dashes from the undergrowth one side of the meagre rabbit-path and vanishes the other, leaving Jason with an instant's impression of russet fur and teeth glinting in a sardonic-looking mouth.

Ahead, though, he can see that clearing Blaze was talking about. There's something there that's probably red in daylight, its colour drained to a muddy purple in the half-dark. As he draws closer, Jason can see that it's a one-man tent.

An owl hoots, which really feels to Jason as if nature's laying it on a bit thick. 'Mr Parsons, sir?' he calls, and a one-armed naked man bursts shrieking from between the trees to his right and starts beating him about the head with a hefty tree-branch.

For a confused thirty seconds Jason's attention is divided between swearing at his assailant without any great attempt at coherence, ducking the thudding blows, struggling to get his sword out of its scabbard and trying not to accidentally look at his assailant's crotch by mistake. Somewhere among this medley, though, he gets a good enough glance at his face to confirm that his attacker is indeed Paul Parsons.

Fortunately, Jason's helmet is sturdy enough to deflect the worst of the blows. They are in fact no heavier than one would expect from someone with Paul's disability who was suffering from exhaustion and exposure, and Parsons is visibly tiring. Eventually giving up on the sword, Squig opts for the more familiar mode of fighting he learned with the Green Chapel, grabbing the Knight by the shoulders and diving in for a headbutt.

There's an unpleasant thump of ceramic against cranium, and Paul drops like a stone. Quickly Jason whips off a gauntlet and checks his pulse and breathing, which are steady. He pauses for a moment to get his breath back.

'Yeah, thanks a fucking million mate,' he mutters to the absent Burn. Then, remembering the last thing the conjurer said to him, he fumbles his mobile from his hip-pouch and dials his number.

The phone rings for a while before Blaze answers. 'You total bastard,' Jason says to him.

'You found him, then?' says Blaze. 'Fucking A. Now listen, this is how we're gonna play this...'

15. MALORY WENDIMAN AND THE HACKER OF THETFORD

'She's challenging our what?' Sir Charles thunders the next morning.

'Not challenging, sir,' Theo Harte tells him nervously. 'Challenged, successfully. It's all over, bar the shouting.'

They're at a hotel in Peterborough, where the Seneschal's holding court over breakfast in a private function room. Most of the Knights and men-at-arms were stood down yesterday evening, following the successful conclusion of the quest to find Paul Parsons. Remaining at the hotel are the Seneschal himself; Harte, who's acting as his aide while Paul convalesces, and finding the task an exacting one; William Posnett, whose squire Parsons was for a time and who still takes a fatherly interest in him; Frith and Felton, whose devices' familial connection to Sir Lancelot gives them similar hanger-on rights; and Desmond Wigsby, who's stayed behind for no reason anyone's been able to fathom and who now chirps, 'She's certainly challenged!'

Raymond, Harte, Felton, Frith and Posnett ignore him. Most of them have already finished breakfast, but the Seneschal appreciates a hearty full English and is refusing to be hurried. Theo dabs crumbs of croissant off his mouth with a napkin as he elaborates, 'She claims that her arrest was irregular, sir. Given that we carried it out in concert with a known criminal organisation.'

'I thought we were keeping that quiet?' asks Felton.

'You know, mentally,' Wigsby explains to nobody at all. 'Mentally challenged.'

'The proceedings are in camera, yes,' Harte agrees, 'but we can't stop Ward's lawyer raising it. And since we're not exerting our usual pressure over the judge this time...' he tails off.

The Seneschal stabs at the air with his fork. 'Your idea, Harte, as I recall,' he grumbles. He spears a sautéed potato and eats it fiercely.

'I stand by it, sir,' Theo says awkwardly. 'The timing was unfortunate, but under the circumstances, further media scrutiny was the last thing we needed. Unfortunately...'

'*Mentally* challenged,' repeats Wigsby. 'It's means doolally. It's what they say nowadays. It's madness gone politically correct!' he japes.

Nick Frith sees the expression on his boss's face. 'I say, Wigsby, I need a bit of help totting up the charges on my minibar. Are you any good with that sort of thing?'

Wigsby accedes with alacrity and is hurriedly ushered out of the room.

Raymond chews his bacon ruminatively for a while, then says 'I didn't like the sound of that "unfortunately," Harte.'

'No, sir. The fact is, there's been a leak overnight, to an online news source.' Harte raises a placating hand. 'Not from our end, of course, and Ward's lawyers agreed with us to keep that aspect of the case away from the public. It's not in their interests, either, for everything we know about the SS to come out. Regardless, the judge isn't pleased. She contacted us in the night for confirmation that the Green Chapel were in on the arrest. I told her the truth, sir, naturally.'

Sir Charles sighs, but says nothing.

'And... well, she's planning on throwing the case out first thing this morning,' Harte admits. 'We could start applying some of that pressure now, I suppose, but that would look even worse. It's not a complete dead loss, mind you. If we keep Ward under surveillance from now on...'

'Yes, yes,' snaps Raymond. 'Anything that gives us any chance of salvaging this. So who do we have to thank for this leak? The Chapel? Bloody Stafford again?'

Theo says, 'We're still looking into that, sir, but I have a suspicion. Chief Inspector Kinsey's no friend of the SS, but at the moment she might overlook that if it meant she could embarrass us. She really is *very* cross, sir.'

'H'm. Well, just this once I agree with her.' Seething fury is Sir Charles's rest state, though, and it doesn't stop him mopping up the remainder of his fried egg with his last piece of sausage. 'Mukherjee still at the Fastness, I take it?'

Harte nods. 'Being kept under guard for now. They say he seems depressed, sir; I don't think he's going to make a break for it.'

Raymond snorts. 'Depressed? I should bloody hope so, after a stunt like that.'

Theo knows better than to say anything in Stephen's defence. Besides, while Mukherjee may be guilty – clearly is, in fact – of defying orders, poisoning relations with the secular police and bringing the Circle into disrepute, he's worth too much to the Circle for anything really harsh to happen to him. Even if Sir Charles sacked him (and the Circle just doesn't work that way), he's already lost his Gawain and his Galahad. With his Lancelot indisposed, and no sign of a new Percival since Trevor Macnamara died, the last thing he needs to be dealing with is a third rogue Knight, even bearing a device of second-tier calibre.

Still, Mukherjee will be up before a disciplinary debriefing the moment the Seneschal returns, and he won't just be looking at a penitential pilgrimage to Tintagel. Some serious restrictions of privilege are likely.

Sir Charles has evidently been thinking along different but parallel lines, because as he butters a piece of toast he says, 'That lad who found Parsons. Mukherjee's squire, isn't he?'

265

Theo agrees that he is.

'We'd better get him assigned to someone more responsible, then,' Raymond says. 'How much d'you know about him?'

'Jason Smith, sir?' Harte exchanges looks with Felton and Posnett. 'Um, he's supposed to be very able. Strong Knight material, I'm told.'

'But?' Sir Charles hasn't been the head of an esoteric military order for twenty-five years without being able to spot when someone isn't telling him something. Sometimes, anyway. At least when it's someone as guileless as the average Knight.

'It's more *and* than *but*, sir.' Harte clears his throat. 'Some of the Knights feel that there's something a bit... special about him, sir. They wonder whether he might have a device already.'

Sir Charles' brows rise. 'Do they, now?'

Harte shrugs. 'Well sir, I'm only telling you what they say.'

'Hmm,' muses Sir Charles. 'Had a bit of an odd conversation with Blaze about him last night, as it happens. Said the lad insisted on joining the quest when Mukherjee wouldn't order him here. Went straight to that wood place. Found Parsons almost immediately. Blaze seemed impressed. One thing I've learned in this job, anyone that impresses your Merlin bears watching. Still here, is he?' he asks suddenly.

'Smith?' Harte's taken by surprise, but Felton nods. 'I believe so, sir,' Theo says smoothly.

'Send him in, will you? Like to meet him properly. Hero of the hour and all that.' The Seneschal finally pushes away his breakfast plate and pours himself a coffee.

* * *

In the back room of the Tree in the Well in Glastonbury, Merry is hard at work. She has her laptop set up next to her dad's desktop PC and is streaming a third strand of data through her smartphone.

Malory's a mid-level hacker at best — good enough to leave herself a window into the Circle's servers, but hardly capable of breaching the security of a major international banking conglomerate. There are only so many areas of human knowledge a woman can specialise in, after all.

She has access to some expert advice, though.

'OK, Finn,' she says into the landline, 'I've breached the security of the major international banking conglomerate. What do I do next?'

...OK, so that probably isn't what she says.

I've been doing my best to give you the whole story here, to be an omniscient narrator as well as a reliable one, but this is somewhere we run up against the limits of my understanding. I can bandy about words like 'trojan' and 'firewall' with the best of them, but when it comes to the actual mechanics of extracting encrypted information from the systems of one of the most secure repositories of financial information on the planet, I'm as much in the dark as you are — possibly more so, since I'm also pretty hopeless with financial stuff.

As with all the other events we're talking about, the people involved will talk to me much later — as far as availability allows, at least — and give me a vague handle on what's going on here, but it's probably best we draw a veil over the actual details.

What Merry's doing is following the same trail as the Circle's forensic accountant, but unhampered by the same considerations of legality and jurisdiction. (The Circle's authority to act internationally is shaky at best, which limits their penetration in cyberspace, and their trust issues with civilian personnel mean the accountant can't even wield all the authority they do have, giving Malory a double advantage.)

Blaze's text gave her the name of the offshore bank holding the account which paid David's travel costs and funded the Saxon Shield. With the assistance of thirteen-year-old Finn, Merry has... done some magic of some kind... and ended up with the details of the account involved. She's now following back the traces of the payments made into that account, through various shell accounts and… stuff…, until she's finally able to identify where all this money came from in the first place.

The answer comes as quite a surprise to Malory. It's an account she's familiar with – she used to have access to it, though she almost never used it. It's a discretionary account made available by the Circle to Knights and a select few secular advisors for the payment of extraordinary expenses. Like much of the Circle's affairs, it's administered according to an archaic honour system and rarely audited. When it is, its near-bottomless reserves mean that sums of a little under a thousand pounds – which are what's been going into this other account every few days for about a year now – are unlikely to make much of a dent.

Merry can't access the identities of the individuals making the payments, but she can see them cycling regularly through a dozen or so unique IDs. This strongly suggests to her that none of the individuals owning those IDs are at all aware that their account access is being hijacked by a third party. It's not, she would hazard a guess, something they'd be pleased about if they knew.

The question is – who's doing it? It surely has to be someone who's had legitimate access, past or present, to the account. Malory knows it's not her, and she has to trust her father and Jory. David himself is certainly a prime candidate; Blaze too. Then there's the possibility that a serving Knight – Paul Parsons, perhaps, or the Seneschal himself – is once again clandestinely funnelling Circle resources into a black-quests account.

Why any of those people would have wanted *both* to bring David back to the UK *and* to subsidise the Saxon Shield, though, is opaque to her. For David to fund the SS – the organisation that actually killed Trevor – would suggest a level of vindictiveness against the Circle bordering on the psychotic. Besides, it would be a bit dim for him to disguise his embezzlement so thoroughly, then use the money to buy himself a traceable air ticket.

She can't see how any of it serves the Circle's purposes at all, though.

Still, *somebody* obviously has a use for this money – and it looks as if they're engaged in a sinister social engineering project, with the devices as their tools. It's not the first time Merry's seen something similar.

'Merry, you there?' the phone squeaks, and Malory realises she's been mulling this over with Finn still on the line.

'Yes, sorry Finn, of course,' says Merry. 'Just a bit distracted, that's all. I have to say, though, that was stellar work just now. You've been on fire today, girl.'

'I know,' the girl's voice says, with the unflappable self-confidence young teenagers work so terribly hard to project. 'Yeah, can we talk about that, Merry? Thing is, I've been getting better at this stuff recently. A *lot* better.'

'Well, that's great, Finn,' Merry smiles. And then the import of the girl's words sinks in. 'Hold on, hon,' she adds. 'What are you trying to tell me?'

'It's like something's prompting me,' says Finn. 'Like a messenger window in my mind. Not telling me factual stuff, yeah, but coming up with clever hacks and workarounds. Things I could've thought of myself, but wouldn't've so quick before, you know? It's like… well, it feels like what it sounds like.'

'I see,' says Merry.

'Thing is,' Finn says, 'I didn't think there was any of our allies free at the moment. Are there?'

* * *

'So, young Smith,' the Seneschal says genially. 'They tell me you found my lieutenant. Good work, that man.'

'Yes, sir,' says Jason, trying not to jiggle from foot to foot in panic. 'Thank you, sir.'

'Tell me,' he beams, 'how did you do it?'

Jason has agreed with Blaze that the latter's name should be kept out of this. Unfortunately his friend hasn't provided a good alternative explanation of where his information came from. ('Just wing it,' he said when they spoke on the phone last night. 'Let him think you're not quite sure yourself. Long as you don't act all shifty it'll be fine.')

'Just lucky, sir, I reckon,' he says with a reasonable facsimile of a carefree smile. 'I knew you'd said to look in the woods and that, then once I got there I just went to where it felt like he'd be.'

This sounds lame even to him, but familiarity with the allies can make people believe unlikely things. Some devices are natural hunters and trackers; others bring freakishly – though not, of course, supernaturally – good hearing, or profound insight into the motives and behaviour of others. Any of those could plausibly have sniffed Paul out in that wood. The idea of it happening through luck alone isn't actually impossible, of course, but the improbability of that is supposed to steer Sir Charles towards the conclusion that Jason has a device.

Which he has, of course, just not one that was giving him much help yesterday evening.

Much help, he thinks, *that's a good one.*

'Well, young man, the Circle's in your debt.' The Seneschal's affability is beginning to freak out even Theo Harte, who now stands beside his chair in the otherwise abandoned breakfast room. 'Tell me, how did Mr Parsons seem to you?'

'Well, sir,' says Jason, 'it's tricky to say. He obviously wasn't quite his usual self, sir, with having no clothes on and hitting me head with a great big stick and that. Sorry I had to hurt him a bit to get him to stop, sir. Seems to me hospital's the best place for him now, till he feels better, like.'

'Quite right, quite right,' Raymond agrees. 'And of course you had to protect yourself; nobody will blame you for that. Not even Mr Parsons, once he's up and about.'

'No, sir.' Jason isn't at all certain of this, but feels it wouldn't be wise to say so.

'The fact that you left Mr Mukherjee without permission is another matter, of course,' Sir Charles proceeds, a little more sternly.

'Yes, sir,' says Jason, gazing at him with all the earnestness he can muster. 'I'm sorry about that, sir. He'd said he didn't need me, though, and I knew you wanted us all there to look for Mr Parsons, and I was sure I could help. Mr Mukherjee was too busy, but I thought I could represent him. Sort of thing. Sir. Sorry that that was wrong, sir.'

'Well, a little,' the Seneschal says gravely. 'But very understandable, I'm sure. Tell me Smith, how have you found working for Mr Mukherjee?'

'Oh, great, sir, thank you,' Jason says eagerly. ('You got to sound loyal,' Blaze told him. 'Be the bloke's biggest fan even when you're stabbing him in the back.') 'Mr Mukherjee's been a great inspiration to me, sir. Of course he's been very busy recently with this British Beasts quest of his.'

'Indeed he has,' the Seneschal agrees. 'You may have heard he's in a little bit of trouble because of that.'

'Oh really, sir?' Jason does his best to look shocked. 'But he's been working at it so hard. It's the only thing he thinks about these days, sir.'

Raymond looks stern. 'Yes, well, I'm afraid he's been thinking about it a little *too* hard, Smith. And not nearly hard enough about some other things, like his duty or the reputation of the Circle.'

'Oh but, sir, Mr Mukherjee's all about duty,' Jason protests, laying it on a bit thick now. Then, as Sir Charles' affable expression begins to slip, he adds a well-timed: 'That is – I'm sorry, sir. I spoke out of turn, sir. I'm sure you're right, sir.'

The Seneschal nods approvingly. 'Well said, lad. Loyalty does you credit. In this case though, I'm afraid Mr Mukherjee was in the wrong.'

'Yes, sir.' Jason's home and dry now.

'And, well, I wouldn't want to pre-empt the disciplinary hearing,' Sir Charles says blithely, 'but the services of a squire are a privilege which can sometimes be revoked. Now, if that were to happen, young Smith… well, my own squire's very nearly ready for his vigil and acclamation.'

Behind him, Theo Harte gives a little gasp which turns quickly into a cough.

The Seneschal ignores him. 'Mr Mukherjee's mistakes are no fault of yours, lad. You shouldn't suffer for them. You've shown yourself able and loyal, though perhaps not as disciplined as you could be. I think we know whose door to lay that at, though. So, if the tribunal takes the view I think it will… how would you feel about coming and working for me?'

* * *

Jory leaves the encampment that morning, on his way back to Glastonbury to consult properly with Merry. He's mildly uneasy about leaving David there with the others, but he dismisses the feeling as irrational. Whatever his agenda is – and Jory hasn't reached any conclusions on that score – he certainly doesn't believe his old friend's going to harm any of them.

Once again, the radio is full of what it's calling 'fresh controversies surrounding the Circle, the UK's oldest law-enforcement body'. Bretwalda Ward's release, and the violent disruption of a child's birthday party, have contrived to keep the *Squaring the Circle* story alive for another news cycle. An off-message MP calls for Sir Charles' resignation and a comprehensive public investigation. Chief Inspector Kinsey apologises to the family of Boston Addis, then spoils it by blaming the entire thing on the Knights.

Jory stops off at Bury St Edmunds to phone Janene Long. As usual, his issues with mobile phones oblige him to spend a while finding a payphone that works and doesn't smell too badly of piss, as well as carrying around a pocketful of change.

On this occasion he only needs the 50p he shoves in first, because Janene's at work. Although her successful criminal career's allowed her, after a great deal of vacillating, to leave her boyfriend Larry, she still lives in Carlisle, and volunteers at the museum two afternoons a week, taking every opportunity to tell visitors about the legend of Adam Bell.

'I'll call you back,' she tells him, and Jory has to loiter near the phone booth, pretending implausibly to browse in a bakery window, until Janene takes a cigarette break and the payphone rings.

'What's all this about, Dan?' she asks him. 'You still owe us a favour after that festival last year. Whatever the bloody hell *that* was.'

'It's good to hear your voice again, Janene,' says Jory. He's not being funny, either: he's fond of the brash thief, and not just because of the affinity between their allies. He admires her bravery, her bloody-mindedness and her willingness to step outside an ordinary life and into the strange world of the devices without the help of the conventional support networks. He also, as Big Jack once suggested, fancies her slightly, though nowhere near enough to make him feel he's being unfair to Malory.

'Not a favour this time,' he says, 'just a question.'

'Ask on, then,' she tells him.

Jory asks, 'Has a man called David Stafford been in touch with you at all?'

David's comments about others with good reason for resenting the Circle have been bothering Jory, and the Adam Bell gang was one of the names David – perhaps without knowing Jory's connection to them, though it's always possible someone at the camp's been talking – mentioned.

'Is he a posh white southern twat like you?' Janene asks cheerfully. 'Doesn't like these Circle lads we keep hearing about on the news?'

'That sounds like him,' Jory agrees.

'Aye,' says Janene, 'he's made himself known.'

Jory asks, 'What did he say?'

'He'd heard we had a spat with the Circle at Nutwood,' Janene replies. 'I told him it were nothing personal, like. We were just doing your lot a favour, and no hard feelings on our side. He asked, would we do you another favour. I'd spotted his angle though, so I asked, did that mean more fighting with the Circle? He said yes, so I said that was up to you to ask. *Him* I didn't know from Adam, excuse the expression. I take it he wasn't speaking for you, then?'

'No,' says Jory. 'No, he certainly wasn't.'

'Thought he sounded like a twat,' Janene concludes.

'He's a good chap, usually,' Jory says awkwardly. 'I just don't know what he's up to.'

'Well, that's between you and him,' says Janene. 'I'm gonna love you and leave you, 'cause I want an actual fag in my fag break. Listen though, Dan – if you do ever want some more fighting done, give me a call, right? We could take care of this Stafford fellow for you, for a start.'

'I'll certainly bear it in mind,' says Jory, smiling.

* * *

Paul is being looked after at the most expensive private hospital in Cambridgeshire. Sir Charles saw him brought in unconscious last night, waited until the doctors were certain that his life was in no danger and that it was just a matter of waiting until he woke up, then went back to his hotel.

He returns this morning, with Harte and Posnett in tow in the first instance – and also Jason, on the grounds that Parsons should damn well thank the man who found him. Raymond still has no idea what his lieutenant has been doing, whether this whole thing's something he brought on himself or something inflicted on him. If the person in question hadn't been a Knight, he'd have suspected drug abuse. It's possible Parsons *was* drugged by another party. In any case, Sir Charles' view is it can't do the man harm to know the trouble he's put them all to.

The news of Jason's sudden, as yet unofficial adoption by the Seneschal is spreading through the Circle's grapevine like an inkdrop in clear water. The Knights and squires have been wondering about Jason's possible device since Blaze began dropping his subliminal hints about TH White: now, Sir Charles has made it known that he intends to take Jason as his squire, just as the young Arthur was Sir Kay's.

In all likelihood, the Seneschal hasn't give a moment's consideration to this implication. Perhaps that's a result of his own story-blindness. Most likely he's just got other things on his mind.

It hasn't occurred to anyone to invite Laney Wardsley up to the hospital either, though Theo did phone her late last night to let her know that Paul was OK and being kept safe until he was ready to travel. Not wanting to exceed his authority, he didn't give her the address of the hospital.

The four of them are driven to the clinic in the Seneschal's Rolls-Royce Phantom by Hutchings, the man-at-arms on permanent assignment as his chauffeur. They're signed in by a white-uniformed senior nurse and walked though olive-and-cream corridors hung with tasteful photography and abstract art, to Paul's single room.

It's bright and airy, its white paint somehow giving the sense of a stucco villa in Umbria rather than a hospital room in the Midlands. There's a bunch of sweet-smelling hothouse gardenias on the dressing table.

Paul's up when they arrive, sitting on his bed in a towelling dressing gown. A nurse is holding a basin while he cleans his teeth awkwardly with his left hand. At a signal from her superior, she makes herself scarce.

'Here he is!' the senior nurse says brightly. 'I'm afraid he's still a little confused about some things, aren't you Paul?'

Paul gives her a boyish grin. 'I've brushed my teeth, yeah?' he says nervously. His prosthetic hand wasn't found at the woods: the Fastness are supposed to be sending up his spare. Without it, he looks vulnerable and unbalanced.

'Good show, old boy,' the Seneschal says with grating bonhomie. 'Soon have you out of here, I'm sure.' He's never been at his best with ill people: like many naturally active men who've always enjoyed rude health, he privately suspects them of malingering and itches to shout at them to buck their ideas up.

The nurse discreetly withdraws to hover near the doorway, but she doesn't leave.

Paul smiles at the Seneschal. 'Hello?' he says. 'It's nice of you to come?' There's an edge of panic in his voice.

'Least we could do, old man. Least we could do, after... well, whatever it was that happened. Plenty of time for you to tell us about it later, of course.' Sir Charles leaves the implied question hanging in the air.

'And the rest of you, too!' Paul gasps. 'How nice to see so many friends!'

Theo Harte frowns slightly and glances at Jason. This conversation's definitely off-kilter somehow.

'So... how are you feeling today?' William Posnett ventures.

Paul shrugs. 'Oh, you know? Felt better, felt worse?' He smiles again, but this one comes out as a rictus.

'Good, good,' Sir Charles booms, sticking to his script. 'Treating you well, are they?'

'They're fucking bitches,' Paul snarls with a savagery that takes everyone's breath away.

Raymond is taken aback. 'Oh, surely not. They all seem perfectly charming.'

'Well, you're a fucking arsehole too. Would someone mind passing me a glass of water?' Paul asks politely.

Jason slips forward with a half-full glass from the table behind them. 'Mr Parsons, sir, do you remember me?' he asks.

Paul turns terrified eyes towards him. 'Of course, mate! How are you doing?'

'"Mate"?' repeats Posnett. 'You're his superior officer, Paul.'

'I'm the one found you last night, sir,' Jason says. Paul looks at him in alarm. 'Sir, 'scuse me asking, but d'you recognise anyone in this room?'

For a second or two, it looks as if Paul is going to laugh in self-deprecating embarrassment and admit that no, he doesn't have a flipping clue who any of them are, sorry about that, mate. Then he screeches with sheer terror and starts flailing around and breaking things.

The nurse already had her hand by the panic button and slaps it immediately. Two hefty orderlies run in at once and elbow everyone else out of the way. The nurse ushers the Circle party out as tactfully as she can.

Theo commandeers a visitors' waiting room for them to regroup in.

'He's gone bonkers!' Sir Charles barks. 'Completely doolally.' He winces at the verbal reminder of Wigsby's idiocy that morning.

Harte, who's been consulting with one of the nurses, and who's finding his current function more exacting by the minute, says, 'Some kind of temporary psychosis, the doctors are saying. At least they hope it's temporary. Plus amnesia brought on by a psychotic break, whatever that means.'

'Bloody trick-cyclists,' mutters Sir Charles. 'What it boils down to is, he's off his rocker, and they don't know how long he'll stay that way, am I right?'

'In a nutshell, sir,' says Harte. 'They're doing a toxicology analysis in case he's, er, been given something pharmaceutical. Or it could be all in his mind.'

'His mind, my arse!' barks the Seneschal. Fortunately he's not looking at Jason at the time, so he doesn't see the silent facial struggle this wording brings on. 'I know exactly what's happened to him. Seen it before. Poor bloody Wendiman went the same way, when his damned daughter put that hex on him.'

Uh-oh, thinks Jason, suddenly less amused.

Harte says, 'Sir, you don't think…'

'Think? I damn well know, Harte. Something like that happens to one of your chaps, you don't forget about it in a hurry. This is that witch Wendiman's work. In fact... that little bitch Parsons is shacked up with – Wardsley, is it? She used to be with the Green Chapel, didn't she? My God, she'll pay for this!'

Theo tries to soothe him but immediately sidetracks himself. 'Sir, I honestly don't think Miss Wardsley – oh my God, her first name's Laney, isn't it? It's the Elaine of Corbenic story, sir!'

Raymond groans. 'Of course! Of all the stupid, story-blind... But she's Chapel all the same. We never did sort out whose device Miss Wendiman was carrying, did we? That leak this morning, whoever's bribing our enemies to make trouble for us, now this... I can feel her hand in this, Harte.'

Jason's thinking fast, but he can't come up with a single thing to say that won't end up with him being shouted at and possibly thrown out of the Circle. This is out of his hands now.

'I'll tell you this for nothing,' the Seneschal's thundering. 'After this, the Green Chapel can damn well kiss their so-called truce goodbye.'

* * *

A footnote or two may be in order here.

As I said earlier, Sir Lancelot had at least two girlfriends named Elaine. I say 'at least' because Elaine's the most common women's name in all the Arthurian myths, closely followed by Iseult. In fact it was Lancelot's mum's name as well, so he may have had a bit of a thing for it.

Of Lancelot's Elaines, Elaine of Astolat's the one we know best as the Lady of Shalott. Her story comes in several variants, but essentially she fell in love with Lancelot, who accidentally encouraged her despite being faithful to his true love (if you can really call it 'faithful', given that his true love was Arthur's wife Guinevere), with hilarious results.

This Elaine's an exemplar of unrequited love and its fatal effects. The Victorians adored her because unlike Guinevere she was also a model of chastity (although if she'd just shrugged it off and shagged the next vaguely good-looking bloke she met a-maying she probably wouldn't have ended up in any myths). She either pined away or killed herself: she died, anyway, on a pile of flowers on a barge floating down the river to Camelot, and ended up as a pretty corpse in about sixteen hundred pre-Raphaelite paintings.

According to Tennyson, Lancelot's best shot at a eulogy to this woman who'd died for love of him was to say she had 'a lovely face', which gives you some idea of his depth of character.

Elaine of Corbenic, the mother of Lancelot's son Sir Galahad, is a lot more interesting. She was a beautiful young woman who, for not terribly well-founded reasons, had been imprisoned by Morgan le Fay in a bath of scalding water for five years. When Lancelot happened along and rescued her – casually killing a dragon for an encore, the showy git – Elaine understandably fell in love with him as well.

This Elaine had a bit more gumption though, and after Lancelot explained that he hoped they could be friends but he just didn't think of her in that way, rather than moping about it till she died she enlisted an enchantress called Dame Brisen to help her win him over. They opted for the popular impersonation spell used previously by Arthur's father Uther Pendragon and his half-sister Morgause, meaning that Galahad shares Arthur and Mordred's distinction of having been conceived by someone who thought they were getting it on with their true love but in fact weren't.

In most versions of the story, Brisen and Elaine pull the trick twice – once when Lancelot's lying exhausted from his dragon-fight at Elaine's father's castle at Corbenic, and later at Camelot, after Elaine's shown up to present the ensuing infant to his father. The first time, Lancelot's too out of it to realise that Guinevere's nowhere near, whereas on the second occasion she actually is. Which is unfortunate, because she walks in on them.

At this point Lancelot realises how spectacularly he's fucked up and goes howling batshit barmy. He runs off naked into the wilderness and stays there for years, living off roots and berries and barking at the moon. Eventually he... well, as always, it's complicated, but he gets cured, marries Elaine for Galahad's sake but eventually leaves her for Camelot and Guinevere, whereupon Elaine also ups and dies, though in a less attention-seeking manner than her namesake.

This may sound extreme – though it's far less catastrophic than what ensued when Lancelot and Guinevere were finally caught in bed together – but the point is that through entering into a relationship with a woman called Elaine, Lancelot ends up wandering and mad. When they realised Paul Parsons had gone missing, the Circle might have thought to expect this.

Overall, if you're bearing the Lancelot device, I'm afraid it's probably best to just avoid shagging anyone.

* * *

Finn spends the morning with Rev, trying to establish how much her mental acuity's increased.

Unfortunately there's no baseline. Finn's performance is impressive, but she's always been the Chapel's resident whizzkid, and no one, even the Chapel people who've been home-tutoring her, has really troubled themselves about measuring precisely how good she is. At logic puzzles, lateral thinking exercises and the more cerebral kinds of computer game, she's the biz, but then she always has been. Standard IQ tests don't measure much except the ability to pass standard IQ tests, but even so, you don't score above 150 points without some impressive stuff going on upstairs.

Finn's testimony remains that she wasn't this good until a couple of weeks ago, but there's no real way to back this up with hard facts. It's the physical stuff that's the clincher.

After lunch, Cantrell watches as Scar and Zara put her through her paces. The girl's always been a bit awkward and uncoordinated, and so far the gangliness brought on by the onset of adolescence hasn't been helping with that, but there's no doubt she's showing a lot more promise suddenly.

Despite her interests, she's not an inactive kid – the Chapel doesn't really produce those – but she's never been the kind to track her personal best in running or jumping. Her results, though, are respectable for an untrained athlete of her age, which Scar profoundly doubts would have been the case a month or so ago. ('No fucking way does that lassie get these scores from sitting in front of some computer screen,' is how she puts it.) Finn's aim with a bow and arrow has improved markedly, and attacking Zara with a quarterstaff she actually causes the hijabi woman to look as if she's concentrating while effortlessly fighting her off.

Eventually Rev Skypes Merry, and the two of them spend some time huddled over their respective laptops, occasionally consulting paperback versions or YouTube clips of the Robin Hood stories.

Two hours later, Cantrell emerges from his tent and calls Finn over. The two of them talk intently for a while. Then Rev summons the whole camp together.

I've spent a lot of the day watching David, who's obviously intrigued to see how the Chapel do this sort of thing. Bad guys aside, I'm guessing his only point of reference for this stuff is the Circle, who have their own rituals to summon the devices. The idea that someone might just acquire one organically, through a kind of mythopolitical osmosis, will be new to him.

And sure enough, he's been following the whole thing with an intensity I find slightly disturbing. If Jory hadn't filled me in on his predilections, I might be a bit concerned for Finn, the way he's been looking at her.

Now Rev calls for silence and makes his announcement.

'Hey guys. You all know Marlene's daughter Finn, AKA Fiona Quinn.' (Finn's ma is standing off to one side, looking on with troubled pride. Anyone from the Chapel would want their kid to have an ally, of course, but as I've mentioned it doesn't exactly enhance life expectancy.) 'She grew up right here among us, and she'll always be one of us. She's a quick, clever kid, with her feet and her fingers and her brain. She's no slouch in her own right, our Finn, but today we found out she's doing even better than we thought. Finn has an ally, people.'

There's a great cheer from the assembled company, although those of us who keep close track of these things have already started counting on our fingers.

'That's right,' says Cantrell when the hubbub dies down again. 'We thought they were all accounted for, but it seems we thought wrong. This would be a lot easier if we could contact Squig, but as you guys know he's in deep cover with the Circle.' (From his expression I'm guessing that David didn't, in fact, know this, but he seems interested.) 'Merry and I are pretty sure, though. Whether Squig's on his own now or whether he's got himself a new ally, his Merry Man's come back to us.' He holds Finn's arm aloft as he calls out, 'Friends, welcome back to our encampment Much the Miller's Son!'

We give another cheer, though a distracted one this time. There's an unrelated murmur on the edges of the crowd, a reaction to something I can't see yet but which is taking people's attention away from Rev's improvised acclamation.

And then I see it. There's someone else returning to the Green Chapel.

'Hey, look at that,' Cantrell says, not wanting to be upstaged – or, more charitably perhaps, not wanting Finn to be. 'Two pieces of good news in one day!'

But Laney doesn't look as if she's bringing good news.

16. FIONA QUINN AND THE VALIANT KNIGHT

'I was just sitting there, waiting for them to phone me,' Laney tells us later, desperately upset. 'I was waiting for them to tell me when I could see Paul. They hadn't even told me where he was, had they? They don't give a toss about anyone who's not in their precious boys' club.'

Zara swears sympathetically.

We're sitting in the clearing between the tents. Laney's flanked by Scar and Rev, both ready to offer emotional support. They and the rest of us with allies here sit in a circle: Zara, Maxx, Ahmed, me, and – looking awed and a little scared at her own importance – Finn.

Everyone else who wants to listen and be sympathetic is standing close by. David's among them, but so are many others. The Chapel may not approve of Laney's recent romantic choices, but when one of us is in trouble we don't hold a grudge. (Also, we love a good drama and can't pass up an opportunity to say 'I told you so.')

Laney stops to take a swig of water, which Rev has kindly put gin in for her. 'And when the phone finally went, it was Squig. I said, "Oh, so does the Seneschal's lieutenant's girlfriend not even warrant a Knight now?" and he said, "Well, I'm the Seneschal's squire now, so yeah. Listen Lanes, they told me to tell you to wait and a car'll bring you here. But that's bollocks. You got to get out of there first. Run to the Chapel or something, just don't be there when they get there.'"

She takes a deep, shuddering drink. 'Obviously I was all over the place – I hadn't a clue what he was talking about. Then he told me Paul had gone mental, like Merry's dad that time, and that those... *bastards* thought I did it to him. He said they were wittering on about Elaine of Carbonate, but he didn't even know what that meant. Apparently there's some story that says Sir Lancelot shags a woman called Elaine then goes mad, and apparently that means it's all my fault when Paul has some kind of breakdown. So now not only can't I see him, but the Circle are actually hunting me. They think I'm a... bloody *sorceress* or something.'

'You're under our protection, kid,' Cantrell says. 'The Circle are our allies now. They won't go to war just to get at you.' He does his best to sound authoritative and reassuring, but those of us who know him best can hear the doubt in his voice.

Laney shakes her head. 'I don't know about that. Squig couldn't talk for long, but he said the Seneschal blamed Merry too. He's really peed off with all of us.'

Maxx and Ahmed exchange a worried look. Finn hugs herself, though it's a warm afternoon.

'Elaine of Corbenic,' a voice says. I look up, with only a little surprise, to see it's David. 'They think you're Elaine of Corbenic. But she wasn't a sorceress, she just hired one. Sorry, chaps,' he adds as he sees all of us looking at him. 'But with Jory and Malory elsewhere, I'm guessing I'm your expert on Arthurian mythology.'

'Well, I wouldn't exactly –' I begin, a little aggrieved, but Scar cuts me off.

'What the hell makes you think we need one?' she demands.

David chooses his words carefully. 'There's... a ramification.'

'I'll ramify you in a minute, pal,' Scar promises, but Rev shushes her.

'Dave, I don't think this is the time,' he says.

David grimaces. 'I think this may be urgent, though. Laney, do you *feel* as if you have a device? An ally?'

Laney shakes her head.

'That doesn't mean anything,' I say. 'This stuff only has to be in Paul Parsons' head, not hers.'

David nods. 'I think you're right,' he says. 'I think it is. Listen, from what you've told me, Malory and Edward have the Nestine-Gull Grail in a safe place, yes? Somewhere neutral, that you, Rev, and a couple of people in the Circle know about, is that right?'

'Only Blaze and Raymond now, with Paul out of the picture,' Rev says.

'Well, someone needs to go and g-get it,' David says. 'When Lancelot goes mad in the *Morte D'Arthur*, the thing that heals him is the Holy Grail. The Circle will be wanting it, rather urgently, I should think.'

Cantrell shrugs. 'Let them have it. The Grail's their symbol, not ours.'

'It's a joint symbol now,' says David, who's obviously been catching up on this stuff. 'If I've understood the situation correctly, it's the thing that's been holding this truce together. If you retrieve it now, you can use it as a bargaining chip.'

'That didn't work so great before,' growls Zara.

'They didn't want it so badly before,' David insists. 'Trust me, if Raymond thinks it's the only thing that can cure Paul – and he will, once he's sat down and thought about it for a few minutes – he'll move heaven and earth to make it happen. If you have it instead, you can –'

'We can what?' protests Laney. 'Have the Knights hunt us down for it, like they did last time? Are we all forgetting here what happened to Liss?'

'You can still mend the truce,' David insists. 'Get hold of the Grail, then offer to meet Paul in a neutral location – a church, say, they'd respect the ancient sanctuary laws. Take the Grail to him there.'

285

'He won't be able to drink out of it,' Finn points out archly. 'It's got holes in.'

'He doesn't need to,' David says. 'Paul knows the legends as well as any other Knight. Just show him the Grail and it will cure him, I guarantee it. You'll have shown your goodwill, and Raymond will stop blaming you. Nobody wants the Chapel and Circle at war again.'

Nobody except you, Jory would say if he was here. But he's on the A303 between Andover and Wincanton – passing, as it happens, within a stone's throw of Stonehenge.

* * *

Julian Blythe has been in Glastonbury for some days now, notionally guarding the Nestine-Gull Grail from theft by David, and he's still trying to work out how to blend in. He has a particular problem in that the building containing the treasure in question, the Tree in the Well, is staffed by people who know him by sight and would find his presence in Glastonbury distinctly suspicious, so he's been doing a lot of covert lurking.

After checking in at his B&B – carefully selected for quick access to the High Street – he spent most of the first day out and about, scoping out the town centre, taking tactical notes of approach and escape routes, potential choke-points and bottlenecks. This gained him a number of suspicious looks from passers-by, and after a while it belatedly dawned on him that he probably looked like exactly the kind of criminal he was here to thwart.

Realising that he might need to become more unobtrusive, he also took careful note of what the locals were wearing. This varied widely, of course, as in any town, but with certain sartorial tendencies amplified, and others – such as open-necked white shirts with dove-grey slacks, brown loafers and Blythe's old school blazer – dialled back considerably. The second day here Julian spent buying tie-dyed T-shirts, bead bracelets and pre-washed jeans, and – in a finishing touch he's particularly proud of, however much it amused the woman at the hairdressers' – hair extensions with beads threaded onto them.

It's an odd sensation for Blythe, who's used to the Circle's regulation short back and sides, to be carrying that much extra weight on his head, but he's willing to go along with it if it'll get the job done. With a pair of mirror sunglasses completing the ensemble, he's now confident enough to hang around near the Wendiman's shop, often directly in their line of view, without fear of being rumbled. For about half an hour he tried affecting a Welsh accent, but gave up after a shopkeeper asked him if he'd spent a long time living in India.

Julian is aware that he could be in Glastonbury for a long haul. The Seneschal isn't a forgiving man. Furthermore, these days he's quite a forgetting one. The chances are Blythe will be here until the next time Raymond thinks to ask, 'Remind me Parsons, who's bearing the Gaheris device these days?' Longer, indeed, if the answer to that question annoys him.

The Circle's coffers will support him here indefinitely, of course, but in the interests of fitting in, Blythe's been wondering whether he should get some kind of part-time job. There's a vegan wholefood café with a decent view of the shop which has seemed when he's had lunch there to be chronically understaffed. How difficult can waiting on tables be, he wonders? It's just a question of writing things down then taking them to the right people when they appear. Compared with duelling the avatar of the giant Aupatris on the set of one of his black-market porn films, it'll be a doddle. Certainly there'll be less to distract him.

Blythe is loitering outside the café considering his options when his mobile goes off with a text message. He looks around shiftily, then walks twenty metres up the road to read it.

'QUEST OBJECTIVE UPDATE,' it reads, and gives the Seneschal's personal authorisation code. 'RETRIEVE HG. UNINVOLVE EW/MW. RETURN ASAP.' Sir Charles isn't a man for unnecessary words, or lower-case lettering.

Julian stares at this for a bit. As mission creep goes, the transition from 'make sure nobody steals this priceless artefact' to 'steal this priceless artefact' is quite a radical one. Eventually, he shakes his head and taps out 'Please confirm order. Steal Grail Y/N? PS How?' He thinks about this for a while, deletes the last seven characters, and sends it to the Circle's covert command number.

A moment later, the response comes back. The authorisation code again, then: 'YES CONFIRM NEW QUEST OBJECTIVE ARE YOU BLITHERING IMBECILE Y/N'. Which clears things up a bit, at least.

Blythe goes back to the café and considers this over a fair trade coffee. So far, he hasn't been able to check out the security arrangements in the shop, but he assumes there'll be a hi-tech system of some kind, alarms and sensors and the works. Somehow he'll need to get past that without waking the whole of Somerset, extract the Grail and make it back to the B&B, where his car's parked. Once he's away from Glastonbury he should be clear – the Wendimans are unlikely to contact the police, and even if they did, that's the sort of problem the Circle can make go away.

That's underplaying the difficulty of the earlier steps, though. To stand any chance at all of retrieving the Grail from the shop, he's going to have to go inside and scout out the security system – and that means testing his disguise more severely than he'd anticipated.

Julian waits for quite a while, until he's sure there are at least two other customers in there. Then, nervously, he steps out across the road towards The Tree in the Well. He spends some time peering into the shop window, feigning an interest in the earth mandalas while checking out the interior. Edward Wendiman is serving a shopper while the other browses the figurines. The old man should be sufficiently distracted for Blythe to enter and inspect the alarm system under the pretence of examining the wares.

The bell jangles as he pushes his way into the shop, and the Grail sings to the Gaheris device in his mind, disorienting him momentarily. While he's adjusting, Wendiman looks up and greets him heartily.

'Blythe! What brings you here?' he says, and Julian groans. Even without a device, the old man's far too sharp to be fooled by someone as inexperienced in spycraft as him.

Wendiman's smile falters, though, as he takes in his attire and hairstyle. 'Good heavens, man,' he says. 'Have they sacked you or something?'

* * *

Jory arrives in Glastonbury twenty minutes later, shortly after Edward has sent Blythe affably on his way with an invitation to dinner that evening. He finds Malory waiting for him in the shop's back room.

'We've got to move the Grail,' she tells him without preamble.

'What? Why?' asks Jory. 'It's good to see you.' He tries to move in for a kiss hello, but she's pacing agitatedly up and down instead.

'I just got off the phone with Rev,' she says. 'He thinks the Circle want it so they can cure Paul Parsons. Which seems pretty bloody likely, actually, because Julian Blythe was here about ten minutes ago, angling for an invitation to dinner.'

'Really? Blythe was here?' Jory says. 'Well, just don't give it to them; we've got an agreement. You mean cure Paul's *hand*?'

Malory sighs impatiently. 'Yes, Julian was here. He was trying to go undercover, though he claims he's just here on holiday. I can't really imagine the Circle are going to take no for an answer. And no, of course not Paul's hand, he's got the same kind of dementia Dad had, apparently. I'm going by what Rev said Squig told Laney there, though, so don't take that bit as gospel.'

'Squig told Laney…' Jory tries to work this out. 'My God, if Paul's gone mad then Laney must be –'

289

'His Elaine of Corbenic, yes. We've all worked that out already, sweetheart.' As if reminded that she loves him, Merry steps over to him for a moment and kisses his ear. 'It's good to see you too, but I need to think about this. Healing Paul's mind would be a legitimate use of the device, and we'd probably be up for it, given appropriate guarantees, but somehow I don't think the Circle will be happy to leave it there. Again, this is through the grapevine, but apparently Sir Charles is blaming me for what's happened to Paul. If he can't make me be Morgan le Fay, I have to be Dame Brisen, apparently. In point of fact I haven't left the shop all day, but he'll say I talked Laney through the procedure over the phone or something.'

Again, Jory catches a hint of something evasive when Malory mentions cursing people. He's no doubt she has been here in Glastonbury all the time – Edward would surely have noticed if she hadn't been – but the way she dismisses the Seneschal's suspicions seems just slightly glib.

She carries on talking, though, preventing him from dwelling on such murky thoughts. 'Besides, Julian wasn't here as a messenger – the daft sod's planning to steal it, I'm pretty sure. So we can take it that the Circle want custody of the Grail. Rev's idea was to take it up to Thetford – he's actually sent Finn down by coach to pick it up.'

'Finn?' Jory's surprised. 'He trusts an adolescent girl with that?'

Malory smiles. 'Sorry, I forgot you've been out of the loop today. Finn's a good choice partly because she's unobtrusive and unlikely to be on the Circle's radar, but mostly because she's the new ally of Much the Miller's son. Which is interesting timing, to say the least, because Squig's apparently just been adopted as Sir Charles' squire.'

'Sir Charles? What happened to Stephen?' Jory's barely making sense of any of this. It's at times like this – well, all the time in fact, but at times like this especially – that he's grateful for Malory's apparently limitless parallel-processing capability.

'I don't know yet,' Merry admits. 'I'm looking into that. The thing is, we can't let the Chapel have the Grail either.'

'Well, not according to the accord,' Jory admits. 'But if the Circle are breaking their side of that –'

Malory interrupts him. 'No, not because of the accord. Rev says all this was David's idea. He realised that the Circle would be looking for it, apparently.'

'Well, I guess he knows more about Arthurian myth than anyone else at the camp,' says Jory, joining in the popular trend of ignoring my existence. 'I don't see –'

'That, dear heart, is because you won't shut the sodding bollocks up and *listen* while I'm explaining,' Merry patiently points out. 'Yes, both sides supposedly want the Grail because of Paul. But I don't think that's what's really going on here. You remember Blaze's prophecy?'

'How could I forg…?' Jory says, then, catching the look in Malory's eye, shuts the sodding bollocks up.

'Assume for the moment,' she suggests calmly, 'that all my questions are rhetorical ones. Blaze said that the pierced Grail's functioning as the sword-in-the-stone device. Whoever pulls the arrow from the cup will be the true bearer of the Pendragon.' Her look dares him to object. When he doesn't, she continues: 'I doubt more than a couple of people realise it yet, but none of this is about Paul at all. It's about strategic positioning for a war nobody could have predicted just a week ago.

'Squig's gone in just a year from kitchen-boy to the Seneschal's squire. *Sir Kay's* squire, don't forget. Who does that remind you of? Rhetorically, I mean,' she adds as Jory opens his mouth again. 'It reminds you, obviously, because you're used to be a Knight and an English literature graduate to boot, of the young Arthur in *The Once and Future King*, which virtually every Knight in the Circle will have read as a boy. In fact, Squig's claim to that identity's stronger even than the Knights know – White actually has the boy Arthur spend time in the woods with "Robin Wood" and the Merry Men, anachronistic though that is.

'On the other hand, in the Chapel camp we have David Stafford – a man who despises the current leadership of the Circle, and who we strongly suspect of being allied to Richard the Lionheart, a king who returns from his crusade to purge the abuses of his wicked regent brother, and proclaim his own rightful kingship. *Now* can you think of any other reason why both sides would suddenly be wanting to get their hands on an object with the properties Blaze ascribed to the pierced Grail?

'That one wasn't rhetorical,' she adds, seeing Jory's conflicted expression. 'It was Socratic.'

Jory shakes his head violently, in the hope that this will help to sort the thoughts lying in a jumbled heap at the bottom of it. 'You're saying…,' he speculates, '…that both sides are going to want the Grail so they can … legitimate a claimant… to the Pendragon device. But that most of them don't know it yet – just David and someone on the Circle side, we don't know who. Am I warm?'

'Got it in one,' Malory says, and kisses him on the forehead. 'I think someone's trying to direct things so that the Pendragon comes back. Again. And just to make things interesting, they've set up two possible candidates for the position. Now help me get that poor relic out of here before everyone comes grabbing for it.'

* * *

Malory sends Jory outside to check for signs of Circle surveillance. Edward has described Julian's disguise to him, between bouts of chuckling, and Jory can't see him anywhere up or down the street. Nor are there any of the anonymous-logoed vans the Circle uses for surveillance work, not that there's anywhere they could park unobtrusively on this narrow High Street. For now they're assuming that Blythe's here solo, but if the Seneschal has any sense, he'll be sending down reinforcements. They need to get the Grail gone quickly.

There's some discussion about logistics. 'We'll need to keep the shop open,' Merry says. 'There's no reason we should actually be here when Julian shows up due for dinner at seven, but if he sees us closed before five he's going to realise something's up. This is a small town, he could walk past several times before then even if he isn't actively watching us.'

'Fair enough,' says Jory, 'Besides, someone's going to need to meet Finn and get her away from any Circle interest.'

'Quite,' says Merry. 'And her coach is due in at six-thirty. That doesn't give you much of a margin to get her out of here before Julian twigs, I'm afraid.'

'The coach stops at Wells,' says Jory, who's done the journey that way once or twice. 'I'll head her off there and get her back to Thetford by midnight.'

'Good plan,' Malory agrees. 'We won't see you there, obviously.'

'Where will you go?' Jory asks. He'll miss this place desperately, he realises, this home they've used for a while, temporary and contingent though all such refuges are.

'Might be best if you don't know,' Malory says. 'For now, at least. Just in case. I'll be in touch.'

His heart wrenches, but he can see the sense in this. He nods mutely.

Merry's car is in a residents' parking space nearby, but after consultation they agree that Blythe may be watching it – may even, if he came well-equipped, have planted a tracking device – so she should take Jory's. Solemnly, they swap keys.

'Dad's coming with me, of course,' Malory adds. 'Are you OK keeping the shop open by yourself?'

'I'm sure I'll manage,' Jory says. The business is just a front, after all. He could give the last customer of the day the keys to the place and it wouldn't much matter.

While Edward keeps a watch out for inconvenient customers, Malory unlocks the display counter holding the pierced Grail, lifts it carefully and packs it up in her trusty holdall, wrapped up in an old denim jacket to protect it from damage (and prevent the point of the arrow from breaking through the canvas). Then she thrusts a breadknife through a large orange, arranges it in the top of a coffee-mug, and drapes a Goddess Wisdom tea-towel over the lot to look roughly as if the Grail's been covered up for the night.

Jory does another sweep for Julian just as the taxi they've ordered arrives. Again there's no sign of him. Malory gives Jory a fond kiss, though not a lingering one, and breathes, 'Let's have more fun next time.' Then father and daughter clamber hastily aboard and strap themselves in for the forty-second ride around the corner to where Jory's car's parked.

Jory spends the afternoon apologising to a succession of perfectly pleasant people for his rudimentary knowledge of dowsing, divination and runecasting, and his comprehensive ignorance of Edward's esoteric and arcane pricing principles. He fields a call from Rev Cantrell checking that everything's OK, but contrives to be interrupted by a customer before he has to actually lie to him. At five sharp he turns the shop's sign to closed, checks the street carefully for the still absent Blythe and leaves, locking up behind him. Fortunately, his overnight bag is small enough that he can carry it unobtrusively; anything else that's still at the Wendimans' has to be considered lost to the Circle.

He drives to Wells, stopping off on the way at a pub for a leisurely half and to use his laptop: a trawl of their old dead-letter-drop sites brings up a message from Malory telling him that she and Edward are at a motel and will proceed to their actual destination in the morning.

By 6:10 he's waiting at Wells bus station for the coach from London, which arrives ten minutes late, at 6:25. Finn's not been answering her mobile, which is perfectly reasonable for a thirteen-year-old girl who doesn't know Edward's landline number, and though he's left a message, Jory isn't particularly expecting her to get off here.

After he explains to the driver and climbs aboard, though, Jory quickly sees that none of the kids on board is her.

'Didn't she get on at Victoria?' he asks the driver. 'She's thirteen, white, tallish for her age, quite thin. Wears glasses. Probably ones she's mended with duct tape.'

'Oh, *her*,' says the driver. 'Tap-tap-tap on the laptop all the way to Shepton Mallet, yes? Yeah mate, I remember her. She had a push-bike in the luggage, said she was going to ride the rest of the way. Didn't say where to. She'll be along soon, I should think. Mate?'

He has to shout the last bit, though, because Jory's already haring back to the car park.

* * *

Julian Blythe turns up early for dinner. Having already failed spectacularly in his instructions to 'uninvolve' the Wendimans, he reckons he might as well take advantage of Edward's dinner invitation for the opportunities it may afford. Certainly, with the shop open till fiveish and the residents preparing for a dinner guest, he's been unlikely to find any before then. Since his earlier visit he's phoned Theo Harte and updated him as noncommittally as he could, meaning that he now at least knows why the Grail is needed so urgently. Harte's promised a detachment of men-at-arms first thing in the morning, but Blythe's still hoping he can obtain the item without fuss tonight.

Not wanting to alert the Wendimans more than he has already, he's kept his holiday garb and ridiculous hair extensions. His armour and weapons are back at the B&B, but he hardly has a choice about that. If the Seneschal's right and Malory's hostile, he'll have to defend himself with what comes to hand. He's willing to bet that one of those earthenware figurines can pack a pretty decent punch if necessary.

The first thing he notices as he walks up to the Tree in the Well is that the lights are off. That's not abnormal for a shop out of opening hours, of course, especially in an ecologically conscious town like Glastonbury, but it's an overcast evening, and since Edward told him to come to the shop door it seems unusual that they wouldn't have left the lights on for him.

Of course he is early… but then he realises he can't see any light from elsewhere in the building either.

It's at this point that he notices that the door's slightly ajar.

You may have gathered, what with one thing and another – the fiasco at the museum, the long trek round the Borders failing to locate the Sons of Gore, the foot-in-mouth incident at the Fastness, the fundamental inability to go undercover without looking like an utter tit – that Julian isn't the sharpest sword in the armoury. Gaheris is a pretty unremarkable Knight, too. He hangs around with Gawain and the other Orkney brothers, Agravaine, Gareth and little Mordred, but generally – apart from a fleeting incident of matricide, which we can overlook because it happened just the once – he seems to be there just to make up the numbers.

Nonetheless, Julian Blythe is a Knight of the Circle, and the Circle isn't in the habit of employing fools. (Sir Charles has his limitations, but he's no fool. Wigsby's… a special case.) There might be a number of innocent explanations for a shop's lights being off and its doors ajar, but you'd need to be an idiot not to spot that something sinister might be going on, especially if your own reason for being there is also to do something sinister.

Blythe hangs back and peers through the window, though his view's slightly obstructed by the bicycle someone's leaned against the shop-front. Inside, he can see someone in the shadows – not too tall, quite slight, wearing a bulky backpack – crouching and peering into the display case.

He considers his options. A stealthy approach is out of the question – as soon as he pushes the door open, the shop-bell will announce his presence. His only choices are to charge the thief, whoever it is (some minor faction like the SS or the Adam Bell gang, he assumes – he'll worry about that bit later), or to wait outside for him to emerge with the Grail.

But no – the thief might decide to leave by the back way, or some accomplices might turn up to assist him. This way Blythe at least has the advantage of surprise. Done considering his options, he takes a few steps back into the road and rushes at the door, hurling it open with a jingle

296

and a resounding crash. The thief turns, a look of pleased surprise giving way to alarm. The momentum of Blythe's powerful and muscular body carries him slamming into what he's realised, during the brief time available to him, is a girl, and quite a young one at that.

She hurtles backwards, caught mid-turn, and smashes into the glass counter. A moment later, his charge still unstoppable, the impact of Julian's greater bulk shatters it. The girl collapses with the countertop, fragments showering everywhere. Desperately she grabs at his beaded extensions to save herself, but they're hopelessly ill-rooted in Julian's own short hair and snap away immediately.

The child's head crunches horribly against the counter's inner steel base. Beneath her, what Blythe assumed to be the Grail breaks with a squelch and clatter.

Aghast, Julian clambers away from the counter and this bloody, hideously sharded mess he's created. The girl's not moving, and blood is pooling around her head. He takes an appalled step backwards, and his foot crushes more glass.

He looks down and sees a pair of plastic-rimmed glasses, thick-lensed, cracked in pieces. At some point in the past, they've been broken and repaired with duct tape.

17. CHARLES RAYMOND, THE BUTCHER AND THE SHERIFF

One day – twenty years, perhaps, after the events I've been describing – a green plaque will be erected on the outside wall of the shop premises on Glastonbury High Street, by then a purveyor of waders, bait and fishing tackle called Salmon of Knowledge, which once housed the Tree in the Well.

It will read: 'FIONA "FINN" QUINN, ALLY OF MUCH THE MILLER'S SON, DIED HERE,' with her dates of birth and death. Then: 'THE FIRST FATALITY OF THE WAR OF THE DEVICES.'

To my mind, there've been others who might deserve that title. Liss Dashwood, to pick the obvious one; but also Frazer Daughtery, the Knight who died at Nutwood; Shafiq Rashid, the previous bearer of the Robin Hood ally; even Shaun Hobson, Shaf's predecessor, though that'd be delving further back into the history of the thing. The War of the Devices – or the UK Civil War as it'll be less evocatively known, to distinguish it from earlier English or British ones – has been a long time brewing.

There's no doubt, though, that young Finn's death at the bungling hands of Julian Blythe is the spark that will finally ignite the barrel of gunpowder and blow the unity of the nation to kingdom come.

The Circle's reach is long and its muscle mighty, but at a time when it's already under its most intense media scrutiny, even the country's most ancient order of lawkeepers can't cover up the death of a young girl at the hands of one of its agents. There were witnesses to Blythe's precipitate entry to the shop, some of whom rushed almost immediately to investigate the violent noises which emerged. The Avon and Somerset Constabulary aren't far behind them, nor are the journalists, citizen and professional.

A lid could still be kept on the worst repercussions if, say, Blythe had the sense at this point to let himself be arrested under an assumed name: the Circle would have to cut him loose and let him do time for the greater good, but he's a loyal soldier and would surely take a hit for the team. If only someone slightly brighter were around to suggest that to him.

As it is, he keeps shouting to everyone who'll listen that he's a Knight of the Circle and that this crime scene's under Circle jurisdiction, in full view of several mobile phones and with Finn's blood literally on his hands. At present, of course, a Knight of the Circle is the last thing he looks like, which makes the footage all the more eye-catching. By the time Theo Harte gets wind of the situation and contacts the police officer in charge to confirm that Blythe is indeed operating under a Circle mandate, it's gone viral across the internet, and nothing's going to excise it, short of a major asteroid strike.

Nobody mentions the Nestine-Gull Grail, of course, and it's only when he's finally able to talk to Julian over a police phone that the Seneschal discovers that, far from having saved the relic at a terrible price, Blythe's actually lost the damn thing entirely.

Meanwhile, the Chapel camp's as tense as a suspension-bridge hawser as we follow the unfolding story. The early reports of a woman murdered at the Tree in the Well were confused, and we didn't know whether to be more afraid for Finn or Merry: the confirmation that the victim was a juvenile naturally comes as no comfort to anyone. Though Finn isn't named, there's no-one who believes it wasn't her – except for her ma, Marlene Quinn, who goes into instant and heartbreaking denial. Scar and Zara have to restrain her – sympathetically, of course, but still with a certain amount of physical firmness – from rushing down to Glastonbury and trying to find her daughter, a move which would unquestionably end with her in Circle custody.

The news makes no mention of anyone else at the address, and given the obvious shambles that's been going on there, we're all hoping that Jory, Edward and Merry got away – perhaps with the Grail – though in that case how Finn got caught is baffling all of us. They aren't answering their phones, though.

Someone who does answer his phone is David, but the rest of us are in such a state of agitation, grief and fury that nobody pays any attention even when he slips away from the camp in the direction of the forest's nearest car park. We only notice that he's gone a couple of hours later, when he pops up on Rev's laptop, taking part in a discussion on a late-night news programme of the current controversies surrounding the Circle.

'Isn't that that David guy?' Laney points out, and we all crowd around to watch.

'...in the studio tonight,' the extremely well-known presenter's saying, 'are Sir Charles Raymond, the Seneschal of the Circle; David Stafford, a former Knight of the Circle and one of its most outspoken critics; and Bretwalda Ward, the leader of the far-right Saxon Shield organisation, who was arrested by Circle forces on Monday and released on a technicality this morning.'

I whistle. A number of people are booing mindlessly, but most of us realise that this is a showdown we'll definitely be wanting to watch.

'Sir Charles, if I may,' the presenter asks. 'How can you possibly justify this – what looks like a judicial murder? The Circle's out of control, surely, isn't it?'

'What happened this evening was tragic, Austen,' the Seneschal replies, painstakingly remembering the man's household name. 'A member of a terrorist organisation was killed resisting arrest. It happens, I'm afraid. Of course when it's a young person it's very upsetting for all involved. The Knight in question is absolutely devastated.'

He's obviously been carefully coached by his PR people. For the Seneschal himself to appear on national television isn't unprecedented, but it shows just how seriously they're taking this at the Fastness.

'He didn't look devastated on the video footage,' Austen Morten points out sardonically. 'He looked like a teacher had caught him beating up one of the smaller kids.' To my surprise, I realise he's actually out for the old man's blood. Finn's senseless death has evidently struck a nerve with the public.

Sir Charles is realising this too. 'Well, the man was in shock,' he extemporises. 'As are we all. It's tragic; absolutely, erm... tragic.'

'This "terrorist organisation",' the journalist drawls. 'Would it by any chance have been the Green Chapel?' I wonder whether they've found that out from David, or whether it's just a lucky guess. Everyone at the camp is quiet now, staring at the handful of laptop screens, or at smartphones, where the programme's playing out in miniature.

'Well,' the Seneschal says heavily. 'Our investigations are continuing, and –'

'You said she was a terrorist, Seneschal,' Austen reminds him. 'Was she or wasn't she?'

Raymond clears his throat. 'Our assumption at present is that she was involved with the so-called Green Chapel, yes. I'll remind you that they've been responsible for a number of outrages – the raid on the British Museum, the arson attack at Wellbrook Leisure Centre, the illegal occupation of the Lindenvale nuclear power station...'

'And yet you collaborated with them as recently as Monday, in a raid on the Saxon Shield headquarters in Canterbury,' Austen suggests.

'Our representatives have already denied that,' Sir Charles states hotly, but with careful precision. Lying directly may offend the Circle's code of honour, but paying professionals to lie for them is a loophole they've exploited on several occasions.

The interviewer brings Ward in. 'Bretwalda Ward, how do you feel about the Circle abetting terrorists?'

'Well, first of all, Austen, I'd take issue with the way you introduced me,' she simpers, more odious than ever now she's in her element. 'One, it's wrong to say my discharge was down to a mere technicality, and two, the issues we campaign peacefully on go beyond the meaningless distinctions of left and right. We just want a fair deal for the indigenous Saxon people of this country, just like our Native American and Indigenous Australian brothers and sisters do in their own countries.

'To answer your question, though,' she continues smoothly over the interviewer's splutters of disbelief, 'it does seem ridiculous that the Circle's gone within a week from enlisting these left-wing anarchists to help in their ongoing campaign of persecution against the Saxon Shield, to killing a thirteen-year-old English girl just for being one of them. It looks awfully as if the Seneschal picks and chooses his friends based on who's the most useful to him. The fact is, though, Austen –'

'That is the most outrageous –' blusters Sir Charles, but Ward's a pro and doesn't even let him disrupt her flow.

She goes on, '– that this isn't even a new thing for the Circle. As David pointed out just this week, the Circle actually *funded* the Saxon Shield up until two years ago, before they decided to attack us in our offices at Thankaster. One day we were on their friends list, you might say, the next they'd unfriended us – but when the Circle unfriends you, it means an assault with swords and guns. So no, Austen – I'm shocked, but not surprised by this at all. It's beginning to look like a habit.'

'David Stafford,' Austen suggests, 'you actually led that raid on Ms Ward's organisation two years ago, didn't you? Do you have any views on the Circle's arrangements with the Saxon Shield?'

'I think you know I have, Austen,' David replies quietly. 'The Circle's recklessness in getting involved with the Shield – which, I'm sorry to say, *is* a far-right organisation, and a vile one at that – got my life-partner Trevor Macnamara killed. And what I'd very much like to hear from the Seneschal is an explanation of *why* the Circle, which is supposedly dedicated to upholding the law in this country, saw fit to bankroll a gang of racist, fascist, homophobic terrorists who tortured one of his own men to death.'

'I'm sorry, I won't sit here and be called...' Bretwalda Ward begins, before realising that nobody's interested in her right now, and wisely shutting up.

'Well, Sir Charles?' the interviewer very nearly sneers. 'Why was the Circle so keen on subsidising fascism?'

'We weren't –' Raymond's very visibly rattled. 'That was an operational matter, which I can't discuss –'

'Whatever it was, Sir Charles,' David objects, 'it was important enough to get one of your men killed. Alfred Noake and Colin Hill were planning a paramilitary uprising using Circle money. Is that what you wanted, Sir Charles? A fascist coup in this country?'

'That's a ridiculous idea,' Raymond protests, with little conviction.

'Answer the question, Seneschal!' Austen insists. 'Was the Circle bankrolling a right-wing coup d'état?'

'Of course not – well, that is –' Sir Charles's innate honesty's causing him real difficulties here.

'Would *they* have let you kill civilians whenever you wanted, without any comeback?' the interviewer insists. 'Is that the sort of Government you want? A fascist junta?'

'No! Of course not, we –' The old man sounds actually distressed now.

'Then why, Sir Charles?' That's David, and he's sounding upset too. 'You may not feel you owe me anything, that's between you and your conscience, but Trevor was loyal to you right up to his death. Don't you owe *him* the truth? What were you hoping to achieve?'

'We didn't *want* those horrid little sewer-rats in office!' the Seneschal barks suddenly, goaded beyond endurance. 'We wanted what would happen afterwards – and so should you, Stafford, if you were ever really one of us! It would have been the time of Britain's greatest need! The whole idea was to bring –'

He trails off, apparently realising where he is and what he's said.

Austen's completely baffled, so David steps in. 'To bring the Head back. Was that it, Sir Charles?'

Sir Charles bows his own head. 'It was,' he admits gruffly.

At Thetford, Rev's trying Merry's phone again, but she's still not answering.

'Which Head? I don't understand,' protests Austen Morten.

'He means P-Pendragon, Austen,' David explains. 'The Head is King Arthur. The Circle has an article of faith, you see. Their vendetta against groups like the Green Chapel isn't primarily an issue of politics or morality, but of mythology.'

'You're referring to the Circle's largely Christian ethos,' the presenter guesses wildly. 'But surely that's shared by other –'

'No, Austen, forgive me, but I'm not,' says David quietly, and the journalist, who's shouted down politicians and diplomats and once forced a senior civil servant at the Treasury to resign in tears on live TV, shuts up in the face of his device's authority. 'The Circle believe that, in all their actions, they're being directed by the spirits – *devices* is the word they use – of the Knights of the Round Table.'

'*Really?*' Austen boggles.

'I think we've heard enough of this.' Sir Charles is attempting to rally, but like Ward he finds that the conversation's moved on from anything he might have to say.

'Oh, yes,' says David. 'They believe that their enemies are King Arthur's enemies. And whatever you or I may think of that, it's a powerful motivator.

'The myth of the Round Table has shaped so many of the ways we think about being British,' he says. 'The awe we hold our monarch in, as if she'd been appointed by God himself. The way we defer to the royal family, the bishops, the lords, even so-called captains of industry, as if they were the heroic figures Arthur surrounded himself with. The way we as a nation trust to authority, prefer not to stick our necks out, refuse to rock the boat. Even our national anthem isn't about the p-people, but about the person reigning over us. And that makes a kind of sense if your King was once a paragon among men, and might be again one day. But the Circle aren't paragons. Men is all they are.'

'But – this is pretty startling, isn't it, Sir Charles?' Austen's rallying somewhat. 'Is it really true that the Knights of the Circle believe there are *spirits* guiding them?'

Sir Charles is silent, having nothing he can reasonably say. (At the Fastness, we'll learn later, Theo Harte is desperately trying to put a call through to the Director-General of the BBC.) The Circle's normal practice, on the rare occasions when someone accidentally spills the beans about the devices to an unauthorised party, is to wait and see whether they publish anything and then suppress it. That doesn't work so well when you're on live TV in front of eight hundred thousand people.

'Forgive me, Austen,' David says again, 'but that isn't the question you should be asking. Yes, they believe that, but whether they're right or wrong, the question is why any Knight of the Round Table would think it fitting to gatecrash a small boy's birthday party, or to k-kill a young girl. That *is* the question, isn't it?'

'I suppose it would be, yes.' The interviewer knows when to go with the flow.

In the studio, David says, 'The fact is, Fiona Quinn *was* a member of the Green Chapel. And the Chapel also take their inspiration from myth – but not the myth of King Arthur. They, or I should say *we*, follow the second great legend of Britain: the one which continues to inspire our radical tradition.'

At the camp, we can see where this is going – and while the revelation of the Circle's most fundamental secrets has been the cause of rather subdued cheers and ribald commentary from the assembled company, none of us want David to tar the Chapel with the same brush. In desperation, Rev tries David's own mobile, hoping at least to put him off his flow, but unsurprisingly it goes straight to answerphone.

He continues, 'That legend prompts us to stand up in defiance of authority, to question and criticise and when necessary to *fight* it, when we know that that authority is in the wrong. It's the legend of an outlaw, branded a criminal by the royals and bishops and barons of his own time, who lived on the margins of society, punishing the powerful and supporting the poor.

'I'm talking about Robin Hood, Austen,' he adds, seeing the man's complete bamboozlement and correctly guessing that it will be mirrored in many of the nation's households. 'A man who felt that wealth, respect and power had been earned not by the strong but by the weak. A lot of people in this country – and I'm guessing it's even more after tonight – believe like Robin Hood that the Circle have no right to their supposed authority, that they've utterly betrayed the trust the people have put in them. Those of us who feel that way need to make our voices heard – and our strength felt. If people want to remember Fiona Quinn, there's a banner ready for them to rally to, Austen, and that b-banner is lincoln green.'

It's at this point, as David reveals that he's been studying the Chapel's traditions in more depth than any of us realised, that the screen goes blank and is replaced by a BBC logo and a reassuring voice apologising for the technical difficulties.

To be fair, I gather the Director-General put up quite a fight.

* * *

And in a motel room at a service station near Birmingham, Malory shrugs and says to her dad, 'Well, David just declared war. What do we do now?'

* * *

By two in the morning, there's only a handful of us still awake at Thetford. When the Green Chapel are at camp, parties into the night are, if not exactly the norm, certainly not exceptional, but nobody feels like living it up tonight. In time we'll have a wake for Finn, but for the moment no one's in the mood. Marlene's weeping in her tent with a couple of close friends. Everyone else is asleep except Rev, Scar, Zara and me, and Big Jack Bennett.

Jack's been in his hometown of Derby for the last week on Chapel business – distributing some of our hard-thieved cash to his network of needy families there – and has missed the drama of David's arrival and departure. He hurried down to join us, though, as soon as he heard about Finn. We've welcomed him back with a quiet dram or two, and now we're sitting in a ring on the edge of the campsite, keeping up with the all-night news on the radio, TV and internet, where the reaction to David's sensational revelations is being played out.

We've heard no more direct from David, or from Jory and Merry.

David's interview and its implications are getting a lot of airtime, though, at first strictly on the non-BBC news sources, but after a while, as someone obviously realises there's no hope of containing the story now, creeping back onto the BBC as well. The government response is muted, a junior Home Office minister dragged out of bed (or more likely some late-night Westminster drinking session) to pooh-pooh the allegations as the paranoid ravings of a disgruntled ex-employee.

From the wary interest of the non-government pundits, though, the website comments and the views expressed by phone-in callers, it's clear that the revelation that present-day Britain is constantly grappling with the influence of long-dead figures from a reactionary mythology has made sense of a number of things for quite a lot of people. What's more interesting, from our point of view, is the number of voices who, now it's been made publicly clear what exactly we stand for and what we're against, are expressing cautious support for the Green Chapel.

Given their continuing absence from the news, we assume that Jory, Merry and her dad are together in a safe house somewhere – until we hear a rustling in the trees nearby, a bobbing torch-beam emerges, and Jory's voice calls out a subdued 'Hello!'

'Dan!' Rev's hurrying to greet him straight away. 'What's happened, big fellow? Is Merry OK?'

Jory nods. 'She's fine. Edward, too. But Rev, Finn…' He sounds utterly defeated.

'I know,' Cantrell says. 'We've all seen, buddy. It's been all over the news.'

'What the hell's happened, Dan?' Big Jack's scowling. 'You knew she were coming. Rev says he told Merry. What was she doing on her own at that shop?'

'I couldn't,' Jory says. As he comes closer to our lanterns, I can see he's been crying. 'I couldn't save her, Jack. I couldn't get there in time.'

When he first came to stay at the camp, two years ago now, Jory made himself useful in various ways, and one was helping out with the kids. He's known Finn since she was eleven, a studious kid with knack for getting up awkward trees and a love of daft 'knock knock' jokes. I wouldn't say they had a special bond or anything, but she's still a kid he knew. Her death has got to hurt, if not as badly as it's hurt us.

'So where the fuck were you?' Zara asks.

'Sit down, Dan,' Rev says soothingly. 'Tell us all about it.'

Jory looks round. 'Is David here?'

'You really haven't been watching the news, have you?'
I say.

So Jory sits and tells us what happened. How he and
Merry decided we and the Circle were both after the Grail,
that both sides had a hidden agenda we might not even be
aware of, how someone might be manipulating all of us.
How he and Merry took it upon themselves to make it their
priority to get it clear of Glastonbury so that neither of us
could have it, either to heal Paul Parsons or to bargain for
our lives. How in the process they left our girl Finn to the
dubious mercies of a Knight of the Circle, who promptly
killed her.

'I swear, that wasn't part of the plan,' Jory protests
huskily. 'I tried to meet the coach at Wells, but she'd already
got off. I think she must have thought she was covering her
tracks or something. Playing at spies... She cycled from
Shepton Mallet to Glastonbury and went straight to the shop.
When she found no-one there, she must have broken in...
and that's when Julian Blythe found her.'

'Found her and slaughtered her,' I say.

'I don't think he meant to,' Jory mumbles wretchedly. 'He
must have thought she was stealing the Grail. He thought he
was coming round for dinner...'

'For Christ's sake, you *invited* him there?' Big Jack
explodes. 'With a defenceless kid coming, you asked that
murderous wanker to drop round for drinks and nibbles?
God's shite, man!'

'Ease up, Jack,' Rev says. 'Finn was young, sure, but she
had an ally. She wasn't defenceless.' With difficulty, Bennett
controls himself. 'So where's the Grail now?' Cantrell asks.
'I told Merry what we need it for.'

'With Merry and Edward,' Jory replies. 'I don't know
where they are now, and I'm afraid I couldn't tell you if I did.
Not with David part of the Chapel now. We can't trust him,
Rev.'

'We can't trust *him*?' I burst out indignantly. 'We thought
we could trust *you* not to get one of us killed. *Finn* trusted
you, Dan, did you think of that?'
309

Jory holds his head in his hands. 'I'm sorry,' he says. 'It was a fuck-up. An awful one. I'll never... but it was just an accident. It was nobody's fault, not really. Not mine, not Finn's, not even Blythe's, I think –'

It's the wrong thing to have said. Scar's on her feet immediately. 'You're gonna *defend* that prick?' she yells. 'Oh yes, your pals the King's men, they canny do no wrong, can they? So fucking well-intentioned and *polite*. And now a girl's lying dead 'cause you left her with one of those shites, and you've the nerve to stand here and tell us it's nobody's fucking *fault?*'

Zara puts a hand on her arm, and she subsides. Then, slowly and deliberately so that he doesn't think she's similarly enraged, Zara turns to Jory and says flatly, 'You bastard, Dan. You think we forget who you really are? You killed Shaun Hobson. You got Shafiq arrested and killed. And now Finn is dead too because of you.'

Jory looks at us all. In that moment I see quite how badly the poor sod's suffering, but I keep my face stony. He realises he'll get no succour from me. 'Rev,' he says, 'please...,' but Cantrell's shaking his head.

'No, Dan,' he says. 'Trust is what keeps the Chapel together. If you can't trust us, and like Dale says, we can't trust *you*... We can't have you here, big fellow. God will forgive you for what you did to Finn – no, Scar, he will,' he adds as she snorts with contempt, 'but we can't. Not while things stand the way they do between us. Bring us the Grail, and we'll talk amends.'

Jory stays silent for a long moment, then he shakes his head. 'I can't do that, Rev,' he says. 'I'm sorry.'

Rev spreads his hands. 'Then don't come looking for us here, big fellow. 'Cause we'll be long gone.'

Jory swallows, nods, picks up his torch and leaves.

'You always were a rubbish Robin Hood!' Jack yells after him.

* * *

There's quite a crowd outside Kelliwick House the next morning, as Hutchings drives Sir Charles in for work. Most of them are outside the main doors to reception, but they're spread out far enough around the building that some of them spot the Seneschal's Rolls-Royce as it approaches the car park entrance, and soon the vehicle's surrounded.

There are angry, shouting men and women; young and old; a few children being kept back by their parents at the periphery: all ages, all ethnicities, and dressed like any cross-section of the capital's populace, united by nothing more than indignation at the way the Circle's been treating ordinary people all their lives. Many wave banners with Finn's face on, or with slogans: 'JUSTICE FOR FINN,' 'CLOSE THE CIRCLE' and 'KING ARTHUR DIDN'T KILL KIDS' are all prominent (although as the Children of the May would point out, the last is lamentably inaccurate, according to the *Morte D'Arthur*). To Raymond's consternation, a couple of them have taken David's final words on last nights' telly to heart, and are waving flags in varying shades of green.

Among them are journalists, cameras and microphones fighting their way through the crush to lean in and bellow questions at the Rolls' closed windows. 'Is the Circle out of control, Seneschal?' 'Will you be apologising personally to Fiona Quinn's family?' 'Do you believe King Arthur's coming back?' Within minutes, Sir Charles' grim face, staring directly at the car park gates and making no acknowledgement of those surrounding him, graces the homepage of every UK news website, generally with a caption along the lines of 'BAD KNIGHT, SENESCHAL?'

Theo Harte, who's briefing Raymond over the phone as the Rolls grinds slowly through the crowd, edging the more demonstrative demonstrators roughly aside, would agree that it's been a very bad night indeed. 'Stafford's given three interviews already this morning, as the Green Chapel's spokesman,' he tells his boss. 'He's been positioning the Chapel pretty effectively as an anti-Circle protest group, while also reminding people of the, er, positive messages of the Robin Hood legend.'

'Spare me,' the Seneschal barks. 'What are the important people saying?'

'Well, sir, the government's been less than fulsome since the Quinn incident. Privately the Home Secretary's briefing that an independent enquiry's inevitable. The PM hasn't said a word about us since the Addis affair. I've been trying to get the Palace to make a statement, but they're not returning my calls. Sir, I'm new to this stuff, but I had a girlfriend who used to like watching *The West Wing*. I'd say we're being frozen out, sir.'

'West *what?* Sir Charles is on his shortest fuse this morning. 'What the blazes are you yammering on about, man?'

'Nothing, sir. Just a TV programme, sir. Sorry, sir.' Theo hasn't slept since Peterborough, and not well then. His ability to handle the Seneschal is at a low ebb.

'Don't talk to me about the damn TV, Harte,' Sir Charles snaps, as an adolescent boy leans over the car bonnet in front of him. 'I've had enough of it to last me a lifetime. Hey! You little – Hutchings, did you see that?' But the youth's already skittering away as fast as he can through the crowd, the stainless-steel figurine from the nose of the Rolls clutched in his hand. 'Get a bloody move on, for God's sake, or they'll have the wipers next! Run over a few toes, man. They'll soon get out of our way.'

Hutchings amps up his slow crawl to a determined shove, and sure enough the demonstrators and journos begin to melt away in front of the Rolls's bonnet.

'Get the police down here, can't you Harte? Clear these thieving yobboes out of the way. Can't imagine why they're not here already,' Sir Charles complains.

'They're stonewalling us too, sir,' Theo replies. 'I mean, I'm trying sir, honestly, but after Mukherjee dropped Kinsey in the soup, they haven't wanted anything to do with us. The Met's had bad press as far as police brutality goes, sir; I think they'd rather we dealt with this ourselves.'

'Then deal with it, Harte! Do I have to tell you every damned thing?' The Seneschal gives a groan of relief as the car-park portcullis opens and the Range Rover finally makes its way inside. Men-at-arms press forward from the interior, holding the crowd back until the grille sinks to the ground again.

Hutchings swings round to the bottom of the stairwell, and Sir Charles climbs out, still listening to Harte on his headset. 'It's not just London, though, sir,' Theo goes on. 'There've been anti-Circle demos in Edinburgh, Cardiff, Belfast, a dozen English cities. Some people dressed as Robin Hood's Merry Men have taken over Nottingham city centre – not the hoodies, fancy-dress costumes, we think. We're checking it out, sir, but we think it's copycats rather than the Green Chapel themselves. In a couple of places the police *have* cracked down, and it's turned into a full-scale riot. The whole thing's gathering momentum, sir.'

'And that's before –' Harte's voice quavers slightly at having to break this to the Seneschal, but he presses on: 'Word's going round that there's going to be a big rally this afternoon, sir, here in London. No info on the venue as yet. It's illegal without advanced warning and a permit and so forth, but, um, it doesn't look as if that's going to stop them. They're expecting speakers from the actual Green Chapel, the works. Then a march – ending up here, of course.'

The Seneschal simmers for a moment as he strides across the courtyard. A platoon forming up nearby salutes him. 'How many men-at-arms have we got in the building?' he asks.

'Two hundred and four, sir,' Harte replies at once.

'Then send them out,' insists Sir Charles. 'Clear that rabble off the streets. Send a damn message.'

'Sir, I'm not really convinced –' Theo begins.

Raymond roars, 'It's not your job to be *convinced*, Harte! Damn it, man, you're my aide! If I give you an order, I shouldn't need to bloody well *convince* you!'

'No, sir. Sorry, sir,' says Harte again.

* * *

By eleven o'clock, the city of Nottingham has declared its support for the Green Chapel.

'It's done *what?*' Sir Charles splutters in utter apoplectic disbelief.

Theo tries to explain. It seems that Nottingham's Lord Mayor and City Council have issued a statement saying that the city appreciates the British people's love for its most famous son, Robin Hood; that it considers the Green Chapel to be a legitimate vehicle of civil protest inspired by his legacy, and not the criminal organisation that the Circle has unfairly branded it as; and that the Knights' jurisdiction will be deemed to stop at the city limits until such time as the Circle submits to and agrees to abide by the recommendations of a public judicial investigation.

'But that's outrageous!' Sir Charles is incandescent. 'They don't get to *decide our position!* It's enshrined in law and the constitution! The Chapel has a criminal record as long as the M1! How do they think they can get away with that?'

He, Harte and a dozen other Knights including Felton, Frith and Posnett have spent the morning in the boardroom, strenuously and diligently panicking. Blaze leans back on a chair at the other side of the room, his feet on the great circular table, ostentatiously at ease.

Harte swallows. 'Constitutionally, sir, they can't. But… a poll this morning showed that sixty-two per cent of Nottingham voters favoured the Chapel, and barely eight per cent supported us. I don't think they're thinking beyond the next council elections.'

'That won't do them much good if they're *all in prison!*' the Seneschal rages.

'They don't think it's gonna come to that,' Blaze points out reasonably. He arrived at the Fastness mid-morning, just as the crowd dispersed by the men-at-arms began reassembling. Though it's never had a reputation as a racist organisation, the Circle's public standing is at such a low ebb that none of those picketing reception could actually believe he worked there, and he just strolled in. 'The way they see it, the Circle's gone toxic. They think the law'll be embarrassed to prosecute.'

'But that's...' Raymond realises he's run out of synonyms for 'preposterous'. 'Has this ever happened before? A local government defying Crown authority in this way?'

'Not... recently, sir, I shouldn't think, no,' says Theo Harte. In the Circle's terms, 'recently' can cover a period of several hundred years. 'Unfortunately, they're not alone. They're the only local government to defy us so f– I mean, *obviously* they're the only local government to defy us, but there've been MPs, lawyers, bishops – even a junior army general, off the record, of course – saying that the government shouldn't give the Circle its support. A good many of them have mentioned the Chapel favourably too, sir. Sir, this is absolutely unprecedented.'

'How is this happening, Blaze?' Sir Charles demands peremptorily.

The black man swings his legs down and leans forward. 'Devices,' he says simply.

'Well, thank you for that, Sherlock bloody –,' Raymond begins, but Blaze holds up a hand.

'You've always known they shape our culture,' he says. 'Those sneaky archetypal fuckers dictate how people in this country think, one generation to the next. It's just we haven't seen them do it so *fast* before.'

It's impossible to keep the Seneschal quiet while someone else is answering his questions. 'So why –'

'TV,' says Blaze, again going for the pithiest possible explanation. 'Up till now, how many people at a time knew about the devices? Few hundred Knights and squires, maybe fifty Chapel, all of them villains and rogues and renegades and strays... can't ever have been more than around a thousand.

'Last night, you and that bloke Stafford told nearly a *million* people, all at once – and that interview's been all over TV and radio and the papers and the internet since. Must be five, six million have seen it now. Millions of ordinary Brits who kind of remembered the names "King Arthur" and "Robin Hood" as being the good guys, but didn't have any idea that that was all it took to keep us and the Chapel in business. Now those people know what their belief does, they can start to choose which side they give it to.

'That's what we're seeing happening here, Seneschal,' says Blaze. 'This is where the ordinary people of Britain pick which set of devices to support.'

* * *

'For more than a thousand years,' Rev Cantrell's telling us Chapel people, taking up an entire carriage on the train down from Ely to King's Cross, 'the Circle have had it their own way. This kingdom of Britain, with all its glory and power, has been theirs – because the myth of King Arthur is a *myth* of power. Power granted by God, true, power wielded by a brave and noble man for the good of his fellow-men, sure – but power no less, for all of that. Even though Arthur was finally defeated, the story says, he's going to come again in glory for one final triumph.'

'Our myth, though... our myth's been one of *powerlessness*. Our heroes are the outlaws, the dispossessed, the disenfranchised. They stick it to the authorities whenever and wherever they can, but in the end the authorities hold all the cards.' When he was proper clergy, Rev was high-church Episcopalian, but he's getting a good old Southern Baptist head of steam up now. 'When Robin dies, are there any prophecies about *him* coming back? Are there hell. When the state crushes a rebel, that rebel's gone for good. Just as it's Arthur's nature to be king, it's Robin's nature to be outcast. Maybe there's a lesson there for all us scapegoats.

'But that's just how it is: Camelot rules, Sherwood suffers. A King's man lashes out, and our sister Finn dies. Because that's what people remember. Because that's what people *believe.*'

He lifts his hands high as the train hurtles through the outskirts of Welwyn Garden City. 'Now the British people have figured they can *change* what they believe. What happens now is down to them.'

Agnostic though I am, it's all I can do not to raise my own arms and yell back 'Hallelujah!'

* * *

'It's not quite as simple as that, of course,' Merry explains to a disconsolate Jory over the phone, as she navigates the green Mini between Shrewsbury and Oswestry. 'These are the same issues we've always faced, with the Chapel and the Circle pushing one another apart. We did our best to mend the rift at Nutwood using the power of symbolism, but realistically it was always a long shot. Perhaps if the Chapel and the Circle hadn't come into conflict over the one thing that was supposed to be uniting them... but no,' she adds, 'a symbol like the Grail was always going to attract this kind of attention. We were being very naive there.

'I'm afraid whoever's doing this has a huge amount of historical momentum behind them. We know when the process of polarisation started, and we know of times it's expressed itself violently before. Arthur's reign, of course, and the lifetime of the original Robin Hood, such as they both may have been. The last Civil War was another, although it's been less comprehensively mythologised. Get out of my blind spot, you bastard,' she adds, leaning on the horn.

'Yes, my love,' she sighs, 'I said "the last Civil War". Meaning *most recent*, not *final*. I'm not holding out much hope there, I'm afraid.'

She shrugs, invisibly to Jory. 'It seems our generation's just another flashpoint. We've done our best to fend this off, but ultimately we're just a couple of people born in the last third of a century. This war's been brewing since the Neolithic.'

317

* * *

The rally takes place at two o'clock in Trafalgar Square. The Metropolitan Police are expecting it and have deployed a fleet of vans containing riot police, but they're taken aback by the sheer volume of people who arrive. There are ten thousand people in the square by noon, and more turning up by the minute. By the time the event has been advertised as starting, the number's something like fifty thousand and rising, and it's fast becoming clear that they simply don't have the manpower to police it.

Eventually, after some argument amongst themselves, the officers in charge agree – as if they had a choice – that the illegal rally may take place. There's never been much love lost between the Circle and the Met: the former's habit of swanning in and taking over crime scenes wholesale whenever there's a whiff of a device involved has seen to that. Indeed, given the Knights' recent record, a fair number of coppers, even these mid-ranking ones, are probably wishing they could be the other side of the riot shields. The constabulary withdraw to the nearby side-streets (traffic having long been diverted to join creeping queues elsewhere), but maintain a watchful awareness. The crowd cheer and wave their placards.

These people have come here today from all over London and from every part of the country, and before that from every halfway populous nation in the world. A careful demographic survey – which in fact a small team of postgrads from UCL are doing their best to carry out at this very moment – would reveal little homogeneity in their origins. Those joining in at home can see, within a few feet of where one harried TV reporter's standing, a Glaswegian in a Celtic shirt seen sharing his bevvy with an off-duty receptionist from Canada House; two elderly Asian ladies cooing over a baby in a sling, whose father is dismally failing to sell them copies of the *Socialist Worker*; and a lanky Somali kid chatting with a couple of daring teenage radicals in matching Westminster School scarves.

Even so, aside from the youngest kids and those unfortunate tourists who've got caught up in the whole thing, there are few here who speak poor English; few (apart from Americans and Aussies and other ex-colonials) who've lived in the country less than a few months; none at all who, if you'd asked them this time yesterday, would have drawn a blank at the names of Robin Hood and King Arthur. These people are all participants, marginal perhaps but with a broad working knowledge nonetheless, in British culture.

The statements they're making are equally diverse. 'JUSTICE FOR FINN' is still a popular one, as are 'KNIGHTS BELONG IN THE DARK AGES' and the stark 'KEEP AWAY FROM OUR CHILDREN'. A few have striven to be creative with their anti-Circle slogans, resulting in 'CIRCLE FIND YOUR MORAL COMPASS', 'NO MORE KNIGHT TERRORS' and – inevitably – 'STRANGE WOMEN LYING IN PONDS DISTRIBUTING SWORDS IS NO BASIS FOR A SYSTEM OF GOVERNMENT'.

Just as many, though, carry pro-Chapel, or at least pro-Robin-Hood, sentiments – rather rudimentary ones, but most of these people don't have our familiarity with the Chapel's history. 'MAKE ENGLAND MERRY AGAIN' is one, slightly parochial, one; then there are 'DEFENDING THE PEOPLE'S RIGHTS' (a quote from *Robin Hood: Men in Tights*, I note) and the obvious 'ROB FROM THE RICH, GIVE TO THE POOR'. One placard reads 'DOWN WITH THE SHERRIFF OF NOTTINGHAM', which is not only misspelled but highly unfair given today's developments. (In fact, the current Sheriff – the holder of what's these days a mere ceremonial post – was the one who announced this morning's momentous decision. By now Doncaster, Lincoln and Carlisle have also declared themselves for the Chapel: far more significantly, since it suggests that this isn't the automatic default assumption any more, Winchester and Colchester have declared for the Circle. The Welsh Assembly's debating its position even now.)

Photos of Finn are still in evidence in the crowd, as are a few of Boston Addis crying at his birthday party, but they're supplemented by other familiar faces: Jonas Armstrong's, Kevin Costner's, Michael Praed's, Errol Flynn's. (OK, there are a couple of Russell Crowes too, but I've been confiscating any of those I get near.) More than half the people here have come wearing green, many of them in the hoodies the Chapel are known to sport. Some wear jerkins and carry bows and quivers (most of them fake, but apparently not all). An enterprising clan of street traders have spent the night acquiring all the little green hats with feathers on in Greater London, and are making the kind of killing Jack the Ripper would envy.

There are green flags everywhere, making it looking as if we've been invaded by Gadaffi-era Libya. The song's being sung, as well: it wouldn't surprise me if some of the people here were those who joined in our chorus in the Village Tavern at Nutwood.

Soon after we arrive, a teenage boy saunters up to Rev and immediately starts chatting him up. I recognise the type – we're just round the corner from Piccadilly, after all – but despite the wide range of vices he assiduously practices, Cantrell's no chickenhawk.

To my surprise, though, a few minutes later Rev's bringing the kid over to the rest of us, beaming, with an arm around his shoulder. 'This,' he tells us, 'is Ron. He's got something to show us, haven't you, Ron?'

With pride, the lad holds up a stainless steel 'Spirit of Ecstasy', the bonnet figurine from a Rolls-Royce. 'Neat trophy, innit?' he grins. 'I liberated it off of the Sensual's Rolls this morning.'

'Tell the good people what you told me, Ron,' Rev says, still smiling.

'Well, I had this visitation, didn't I?' Ron grins. 'I'm keeping myself entertained watching telly round a gentleman friend's residence, I'm watching the news about that poor girl got herself offed, then I look up and there's this other lad

on the couch with me. Scruffy-looking kid about my age –
seventeen, eighteen – got up all in green like a leprechaun or
some twat.' Despite the assurance he affects, Ron doesn't
look a day over fifteen to me. 'He says to me, "Get yourself
down to that big office block down London Bridge way,
Kellywag House or whatever, and get yourself a token of
esteem off that Sensual bloke off of the telly. Then take it
to my people up Traf Square." Of course, he wasn't really
there, was he? 'Cause my, ah, business contact couldn't see
him. He thought I'd been taking some kind of nefarious
narcotic substance, and chucked me out on my arse.' He
grins his cocky grin again.

Scar gives him a weary scowl. 'You know we're gonna
need to test him, Rev. He could be a plant.'

Cantrell smiles. 'I don't see him as Circle material,
somehow. But yeah, sure we'll test him. For now let's just
say we may well have another new Much.'

* * *

At quarter past two, Big Jack Bennett clambers up onto
the Fourth Plinth (currently occupied by a gigantic sculpture
of a toothbrush in a mug), to open the proceedings. We of
the longer-term Chapel contingent – 'longer-term' because,
mindboggling though it is to consider, most of the seventy
thousand or so people here are declaring some kind of
allegiance to the Green Chapel – have gathered ourselves
along the balustrade next to the plinth, looking out across
the great greenish mass of people, our backs (and those of
a couple of thousand other people) to the National Gallery.

David is with us, wearing a plain black hoodie, and if
some of us wish he'd thought to consult us before declaring
a popular uprising in our name, none of us really feels this is
the time to bring it up.

'Brothers and sisters!' Big Jack bellows. Maxx and some
friends, veterans of many an illegal rave, have set up a string
of stomach-vibratingly powerful portable speakers around

the Square. 'Brothers and sisters,' he repeats a few times until everyone goes quiet enough that they can listen.

'You don't know me,' he says. 'My name's Jack Bennett. If you know the stories of Robin Hood, you'll have likely heard of his friend Little John: well, in the Green Chapel they call me Big Jack. Just like the Circle don't have a King Arthur, we Chapel people don't have a Robin Hood just now, and I reckon that means it falls to me to talk to you all.

'I bet some of you'll be wondering, "Who is this ponce, telling us he's some big bloke with a quarterstaff from a story, who must have died hundreds of years ago, if he were ever real at all?" The thing is, though – that stuff, the quarterstaffs, the bows and arrows, all that Robin Hood business, it doesn't matter very much. It inspires us, aye, and we try to be like those original Merry Men, but it's not what being Green Chapel is about.

'What do you need to know about us?' Big Jack asks. 'Well, I'll tell you. We think some people in this country of ours have grown rich and fat off the labour of others. We think the people in power, in Parliament and in that palace up the street, are out for whatever they can get for themselves, not for the people they're supposed to serve. We think this island of ours, its land and wildlife as well as its people, has been wrung dry for centuries, by generation after generation of selfish, rich, old white men.

'We think the ordinary people of this country have been pushed out and trodden down and broken apart until they can hardly lift their eyes to see the world those other people live in.

'We think that everyone – the poor, the unemployed, the workers, the immigrants, the disabled, the Muslims, the black, the old, the gay – *all* deserve the same respect and dignity the people in charge get given. And we propose to give it to them, and hang the laws made by those self-interested bastards.'

There's been intermittent cheering punctuating everything he's said so far, but this gets a lengthy ovation.

'And *that*, brothers and sisters, is what the Green Chapel's about,' Jack declares. ' Everything else – the talk of Normans and Saxons, barons and outlaws, sheriffs and friars – all that's just window-dressing. Everything we stand for can be summed up in eight words you all know already: *rob from the rich, give to the poor.* In this country, *all* the wealth, *all* the power, *all* the privilege and respect and dignity is in the hands of a few rich bastards. You don't,' says Jack, 'have to believe in people out of stories to know that *that needs to change.*'

There are more cheers, a lot of them.

'There's some, though,' he goes on, 'who don't think that way. Some who think their myths and legends are enough to justify the way things are. Who think that kings and barons and knights should be in charge, because of a king once who – they say – was better than all the rest. Some people can't let go of those old stories and see things how they are – and that affects us all. We live in a country where a man calling himself a Knight can kill a young girl and walk away scot free, because of who he thinks he is. That privilege has got to be taken away.

'Some legends help us grow as a people; some hold us back. Some legends show us better ways to be human, and to be British; others do nowt but tell us that the old ways are the best. Some legends tell us to take a stand against the oppressors, whatever the cost; some tell us that God's on the oppressors' side and we might as well give in to them.

'Well, what I say is – give me the legends that are on the side of real people, not of money and wealth and power and inheritance, because those others aren't fit for me to wipe my arse with!'

...You get the idea. Jack used to be a union agitator at a Derby car factory, and he's always had a way with words; but Little John's a leader among men, with an outlaw band of his own before he joins forces with Robin, and always Robin's only serious rival for leadership. Together – and boosted by the attention of so many people here in one place, concentrating on the man and his ally – their oratory's pretty bloody impressive, but I'm not going to repeat it all to you, because while he's talking, Scar comes back to us from a lengthy circuit of the square, her scarlet hoodie blood-bright against the field of green, and hisses, 'Those SS pricks are here.'

'Really?' I say. I realise I shouldn't be shocked – this is probably the most significant mythopolitical event in our lifetimes. It makes sense it would attract scum like the Saxon Shield. If Merry were here, she'd probably say something about every ecosystem needing scavengers.

'Not just them,' Scar adds. 'I saw Dogheads, and Gormund Boys. There'll be others too.'

'The SS won't like that,' I muse. The Gormund Boys are a black urban gang who identify with a really *very* mythical 'King of the Africans' who once, according to the always exaggeration-prone Geoffrey of Monmouth, tried to invade Britain and Ireland. 'They're not standing near each other, are they?'

'That's no the point,' says Scar. 'They're all waiting for the Circle to turn up. They're no interested in justice for Finn, they're just here for a scrap.'

'Bollocks,' I say. Despite Jack's rhetoric about seizing all the rich and powerful's stuff, the ostensible plan for today's one of non-violent protest. 'This could turn into a bloodbath.'

'But you don't need to listen to me,' says Big Jack at this point. 'We've got a man here who knows more about the Circle than anyone else. You've seen him on the telly, I expect, sticking it to those bastards. I'm pleased and proud to hand over now to Dave Stafford.'

As David climbs up onto the plinth next to Jack, to rapturous applause, I see movement – large movement – over in Duncannon Street, beyond St Martin-in-the-Fields. Like I say, the traffic's been vacated for hours now, and anyway this doesn't look mechanical. I clamber up discreetly onto the plinth, on the other side of the toothbrush facing away from most of the crowd, and peer over in that direction.

'Bollocks,' I repeat with feeling.

* * *

History won't be forgiving to Charles Raymond over what happens today, but it's worth considering his position, and his options.

The Circle's work is a sacred trust. It protects the nation, and its people, from real dangers – just in the past few years, they've come up against serial killers, spree killers, escaped prisoners, gangsters, terrorists, neo-Nazis, professional hitmen, a suicide bomber and, on one occasion that neither Jory, David or Stephen was involved with, a lone nutter with access to fissile material. That these people were all inspired by myths wouldn't have made the damage they were planning any less devastating.

It's supremely important, Raymond knows, that the Circle should continue its work unimpeded. Anything less could be disastrous. If entire cities become no-go areas for his Knights, all kinds of horrors could be allowed to fester there unsuppressed; and if the pressure of public opinion results in the Circle being defanged and neutered across the entire realm, that realm itself could crumble.

For the first time in centuries, this has to be considered a real threat. It's happened during Raymond's watch as Seneschal, and it's all because of the Green Chapel. Thanks to Stafford's indiscretion, the fringe organisation's support base, and its public profile, stand higher than at any previous point in history; and the fact that the Circle is also in people's minds as never before only means that the traditional foes stand equal. For the Chapel to win this fight for the nation's loyalties would, the Seneschal judges, be disastrous.

We're way past the point where containment would be any use, however – Ron's lightning recruitment shows that pretty clearly, although of course Sir Charles doesn't know about that yet. While at this moment Raymond could in theory take out the Chapel's core membership in a single drone strike – excluding Taylor and Wendiman but with collateral damage to a public artwork which has been irritating him –

325

the allies Little John, Will Scarlet, Friar Tuck, the Saracen, Much, Alan a'Dale – yes, and even Gilbert Whitehand, Will Stuteley, Arthur a'Bland and David of Doncaster – would arise again in moments, buoyed up on the nation's sudden unprecedented absorption in the Robin Hood myth.

Instead, Raymond has somehow to crush the Chapel's newfound popularity. And while there might be subtle ways of doing that – with propaganda, blackmail, false flag quests and the like – Sir Charles has never been a subtle man. If Mr Lister was still advising him; or if the Prince John device – or the Sheriff of Nottingham, whichever Sir Charles actually represents within the Robin Hood schema – were more in the ascendant; or even if Sir Kay (who in some stories is capable of a certain base cunning) had had a different bondsman in this generation, things might still have turned out differently.

As it is, though, the Seneschal only knows how to tackle enemy ideas in one way. Which is why he's recalled every Knight, squire, page and man-at-arms on the Circle's roster to London today, as well as calling in favours from the secular army. Over the protests of the Ministry of Defence, he's sent out Knights to every barracks in the Greater London area to swear in something like twelve thousand soldiers as temporary Circle men-at-arms.

While the Trafalgar Square rally's been kicking off, they've been amassing in Jubilee Gardens, in the shadow of the London Eye, before crossing Waterloo and Westminster Bridges at a march. Now they're proceeding down the Strand, up Whitehall and along Pall Mall, approaching the Square from eight different directions (nine if you count a small force under Harold Lenton, sent up the Northern Line to secure Charing Cross Tube station).

No, there's no subtlety here, no clever strategic thinking. This is a show of force, nothing more: an intimidating first salvo in what the Knights can already see is going to be a long, bloody conflict. Only when the enemy – the people who've thrown their weight so precipitately behind Robin

Hood and the Green Chapel – are utterly demoralised and disillusioned, all their hopes of a better world quashed...

...only then can the Circle get on with its real work of protecting them.

* * *

A thunderous murmur of hooves, an orchestra of screams, and the Knights of the Circle enter the Square at a gallop. The greater force of cavalry – a hundred at least – have been sent in through Duncannon Street, to target the core body of Green Chapel agitators. Elsewhere, squires, pages, men-at-arms and the co-optees from the secular army, under the command of at most four or five Knights, are pouring in through the other exits.

The Circle's code of honour is... not relaxed, exactly, but applied rather differently in times of war. Killing unarmed civilians is absolutely beyond the pale, of course, but in an actual battle, if a group of enemy combatants is between a Knight and an enemy who's considered to be of equivalent class, the laws of chivalry certainly don't preclude him hacking a path through them from the comfort of his horse.

The trouble is, like most complicated systems of law, the Circle's moral code is susceptible to certain broad adjustments in semantics. For instance, the Circle is, by virtue of the very fact that this attack is happening, at war with the Green Chapel. If a very large number of common people is surrounding a small knot of Green Chapel who are known to bear devices, cheering them on, it's surely more reasonable to define said rabble as Green Chapel combatants by virtue of their obvious enthusiasm – and thus fair game for being injured en passant by a phalanx of charging Knights – than as an inviolable civilian human shield.

If they didn't want to be attacked by the Circle, the Knights might argue if they weren't so busy attacking them, they shouldn't be so visibly siding with the Circle's enemies – in the placards which fly as they panic and scatter, the printed slogans splattered by the blood which arcs from the Knights' swords, the slogans they were shouting before they gave vent instead to horrified screams.

Behind the horsemen, in through Pall Mall and Charing Cross, march the footsoldiers, whacking and smashing with their batons at skulls and ribs and limbs. Old Admiral Nelson on his pedestal looks down approvingly as they trample and traumatise, maul and manhandle this unruly rabble. Men, women and children fall before the onslaught, heads cracking, arms bending and splintering, blood and other fluids spreading and staining the august York-sandstone pavement.

The protestors fight back, of course. Some have come prepared to do just that. From trees, from the plinths which bear the Napier, Havelock and George IV statues, and even from the fountains in the centre of the Square, the archers begin shooting.

Most are amateurs. Some only bought their weapons this morning. The vast majority of their arrows miss or impact painlessly, but a few – lucky or genuinely skilled – do real damage. Some men-at-arms and ordinary soldiers fall: a couple even die. And another honourable prohibition in the Circle's code – the one against being the first to use projectile weapons – is overcome.

Circle-issue and regular SIG P226s shout out, a well-placed shot here and there, and the archers fall. The fountains, as if revelling in the cliché, begin to run red.

As Scar observed, there are others who came here for exactly this. The Gormund Boys, the Dogheads and Red Ravagers, even a small knot of British Beasts who've escaped Stephen's arrests – though not Mark Addis – are piling towards the infantry, indiscriminately knifing both the enemy and anyone who gets in their way. And then – from the plinth of Nelson's Column itself, from which they've shoved anyone who's climbed up to escape the melee, the surviving Saxon Shield open fire. They yell 'Out! Out! Out!', the battle-cry of the doomed defenders at Hastings, as their Heckler & Koch MP5 submachine-guns scythe through the

Circle forces. The judder of the guns is brutally loud. The Shield are ridiculously outnumbered, of course, and they've made themselves a target – but this is their moment of self-aggrandising glory. The army return fire at once with MP5s of their own, and in a minute or so there isn't a Shieldsman or -woman left standing.

This is roughly when the battle becomes a rout. The Circle's troops and their supporters are better armed and better disciplined, and came here expecting a fight, whereas most of the Green Chapel supporters wanted a peaceful protest. Barely directed by David's cries – still relayed over the pirate sound-system – the greater number of our people stampede for the entrance to Pall Mall, where the Circle troops are least numerous and where they can force their way clear through sheer force of numbers.

None of us with allies in the Chapel have any illusions about what's happening here, either. With those hundred horsemen slashing their way towards us, heraldic patterns gleaming like brightly-coloured jewels against their drab street armour, we know we can't stand against this onslaught and win.

Even Big Jack understands that, I think, as he strides forward into the scattering crowd, his bulk keeping him upright against their buffets, and yells at the advancing horsemen, 'Come on then, you shitehawks! Come here and see what the Green Chapel are made of!' He's carrying the quarterstaff he cut from Thetford oak that morning, advancing towards the mounted, armoured men with absolute fearlessness.

The rest of us watch in horror as Jack reaches the horses, roaring wildly. His first blow knocks the bondsman of Sir Tristan from his saddle, and gets Sir Geraint's bearer, Harry Plaice, on the backswing. Their shields, a gold lion and three red serpents' heads, fall clattering to the paving-slabs. Tristan's man stays down, but Plaice manages to grab the neck of his horse as he falls. He keeps one leg hooked over her back while Big Jack swipes at him, but the horse can hardly be expected to put up with this. She rears, with Plaice hanging desperately on, and knocks Bennett over with her hooves, then lunges down at him as he rolls urgently out of the way.

Big Jack leaps to his feet, staff at the ready, but a Knight with a red lynx on a gold shield has reached him now, and slashes down at him with his sword.

Over his hoodie Jack's wearing his donkey-jacket, which he told me once belonged to his grandfather, a coal-miner who fought the Germans at Boulogne and was evacuated from Dunkirk. It's a tough old garment, with leather panels over the shoulders and back, but it hardly counts as armour, and Sir Lucan's device-bearer has struck him with great force. He bellows more in anger than in pain as his left arm comes away just below the shoulder, and blood cascades from the wound.

He swings his quarterstaff one-handed, knocking Lucan's man from his horse. He thrusts it head-on into another Knight who's charging at him – Doug Felton, as it happens, carrying the stars-and-stripes of Sir Lionel – and catapults him over his mount's rump. But Harry Plaice has regained his seat now, and he's circling in for the kill. Jack glares and raises his quarterstaff as the other Knights draw back, leaving the field to Plaice.

Scar and Zara have produced guns of their own and are firing at the Knights, but the shields and armour are doing their work and no bullet's found flesh so far. Besides, Jack's a tall man and they're having to aim high to miss him. Plaice quickly has grazes to his armour, but no injuries to his person. Jack raises his quarterstaff again, parrying blow after blow from the Knight, but he's weakening now from his injury, and in the end a sharp rap to his wrist sends it flying from his grip.

Jack reaches up and grabs Harry Plaice by the shield-arm, tugging at him with all his weight.

As he falls, Plaice brings up his sword and plunges it into Big Jack Bennett's eye. The big man finally collapses into the crowd.

The rest of us have been watching this performance in amazement, but now we grab Scar and Zara and drag them off towards the Pall Mall exit. It's clear to the rest of us that the only sensible course is to live to fight another day. Behind us, the Knights begin to canter in our direction once more, as Plaice climbs yet again onto his horse.

Our people burst through the Circle lines – some of our many thousand falling to the troops as they fall back, but most of us breaking through by the weight of our warm bodies, smashing as well through the ranks of riot police the Met have lined up further back. We charge away up Pall Mall and the Haymarket, dispersing out into St James' and Mayfair and Fitzrovia, making for safety or regrouping for further mayhem.

There are pitched battles, running clashes, skirmishes. Some stuff gets set on fire, because frankly it's not as if any of us live round here. We set up temporary boltholes in shops, pubs and cafes. Some enterprising souls – who've probably seen *Les Misérables* just round the corner in Shaftesbury Avenue – begin to shift cars, tear down trees and break up furniture to build barricades.

By midnight, the looting and arson have spread throughout London, a score or more cities across the nation are rioting in sympathy, and the Prime Minister's declared a state of emergency.

18. THE BLACK KNIGHT AND THE KITCHEN SQUIRE

It's a week before we regroup, the cut-down core of the Green Chapel, having cadged lifts or hitched rides or chanced our luck on late-night trains.

Nottingham, like the other cities which declared for us, has escaped the civil disturbance, although there've been peaceful demos in our support. Some of the pro-Circle urban areas have also escaped, mostly by clamping down on anything that looks even vaguely like a protest before it gets going, but the biggest, most diverse conurbations – Birmingham, Bradford, Leicester – have been battlegrounds. We've done our best to help with tactical advice, scattered as we are, but in effect the new Green Chapel contingents in those places are on their own.

Parliament's been useless, not that they were ever good for much. Even the government's split: some ministers are sticking staunchly to old loyalties while others, outraged by Sir Charles' poaching their soldiers for a bloodbath, have denounced the Circle as a rogue organisation. A few, thinking they recognise the early hallmarks of a genuine popular revolution, have even tried to curry favour with the Chapel. Their disunity and fence-sitting has made them look irrelevant to people who suddenly have much more pressing issues on their minds.

Meanwhile, smaller authorities are declaring affiliations all the time. Hull, Liverpool and Manchester are for the Chapel, along with some of the northern English counties; Oxford, Cambridge and most of the south-east are for the Circle – as is Cornwall, always marginalised but with a huge historical loyalty to Arthur. Wales is for the Circle, but there's a lot of anger about it in the industrial south. Northern Ireland, unsurprisingly, is split.

Holyrood is professing strict neutrality, though the views of ordinary Scots are said to be acrimoniously divided. A Celt Arthur may have been (or not, of course), but if so he was a southern Celt: Scotland was one of the lands he invaded. Nor is Scotland ready yet to go it alone in the devicial arena – the hopefuls who've popped up proclaiming themselves the new Rob Roy, William Wallace or Bonnie Prince Charlie have been met with robust Scottish scepticism and slunk away discouraged.

England is fissuring along faultlines of poverty and privilege: a rough boundary's already detectable, running diagonally from the Bristol Channel to the Wash. There's plenty of dissent on either side, though. Bristol is for the Chapel, but Bath's for the Circle. York is Circle; Leeds is Chapel. There are reports of fighting along the Brighton-Hove border.

Across the country, Chapel-inspired movements have been mobilising – not just in demonstration against the status quo, but in direct action too: besieging major banks and corporate headquarters; sabotaging power stations and fracking centres; setting up camp on the sites of proposed roads and runways. The 'Chapelist rebels' (as the media's started dubbing us) are forming our own militias, motley companies of veteran picketers and demonstrators, homeless ex-squaddies and opportunist thugs whom the original Merry Men might perhaps find eerily familiar. Meanwhile, the Circle's diverting every man it can from the regular army, using its (now extremely notional) Crown sponsorship as a pretext.

In the biggest English cities and south Wales, the army's trying to keep the peace between the factions, but there simply aren't enough of them to put down what amounts to two simultaneous armed insurrections. Besides, the power of the devices is such that troops sent in to quell Chapel-Circle conflicts tend to discover new loyalties very quickly.

* * *

We meet at one of our oldest haunts, in every sense – a venerable pub in Nottingham called Ye Olde Trip to Jerusalem.

The name sounds twee, but it's earned it. The building's a mere three hundred years old (which still makes it noticeably older than, say, the United States of America), but there's been a tavern on the site since 1189 AD – the era of the Third Crusade which its name commemorates, during the supposed lifetime of the original Robin Hood. It's built directly onto the outcrop known as Castle Rock, and the pub's backrooms and cellars extend into a system of caverns which underlie Nottingham Castle itself. It may or may not be, as the legend painted on its streetside wall proclaims, 'The Oldest Inn in England', but there's no doubt of its antiquity.

We're in one of those backrooms now, where a leather-upholstered wooden settle hugs the walls, and one of the pub's fine old polished-wood bars sells a selection of real ales. Even at midday, the cavern's lit solely by artificial light, and the low sandstone ceiling gives the place a claustrophobic feel.

'I remember this place before the smoking ban,' I say. 'It was eye-watering.'

'You mean people really lit up in pubs?' Ron the rent boy marvels. 'When blokes told me that, I always thought they were taking the proverbial.'

Rev Cantrell smiles gleefully, and pulls out a packet and a lighter. 'There are advantages to outlawry, kid.'

We've had no chance to mourn Big Jack and Maxx – who also died at Trafalgar Square, cut down by a Circle sword, then crushed underhoof by a Knight bearing the device of Sir Anwas the Winged – but for the moment, we've more urgent priorities.

David of Doncaster has adopted a new ally, but she's up in Doncaster itself, helping people there prepare for the forthcoming struggle, and doesn't seem inclined to come down and join us. There's no word of a new Little John. Nobody's seen Brian since the battle either, though no new Will Stuteley's made contact with us yet, and the Circle certainly took prisoners that day. About a dozen undeviced Chapel people – old-school Chapel, that is, not our uncountable new supporters – are missing or known to be dead.

As well as Rev, Ron and me, Scar and Zara have made it to the Old Trip, and Lee and Ahmed. Of the unallied, there's Twink, Vicks, Laney – unless she really is Elaine of Corbenic – and a couple of others.

And then, of course, there's David.

David's been a trouper since Trafalgar Square – speaking up for us in the media, addressing rallies in Northampton, Leicester and Derby, embodying our values publicly while privately making strategic and tactical suggestions far too sensible to be dismissed. Everywhere he's gone, he's worn that ink-black hoodie (though sometimes with a bulletproof vest underneath), until some people are wondering why the Green Chapel don't live up to their name and wear green.

It's an odd thing about the Chapel, really. *Obviously* we're outlaws, free men and women who reject all authority and pledge our fealty to no-one. Those values David is out there preaching are ones of independence, collectivism, liberty… but still, it's kind of useful to have someone to champion them for us.

For anarchists, we do rather like our leaders. Goes with the territory, I guess.

By virtue of its foundation myth, the Green Chapel has accreted around the Green Knight – aka Robin Hood

– and so his human allies have tended to be the focus of our community. Certainly Shaun and Shafiq commanded our unswerving loyalty, except when they were being dickheads. Jory's relationship with the Chapel has been spikier, but once most of us had come to accept him as Robin's latest avatar, he could count on us – even Jack – to carry out his plans with minimal argument, in ways which wouldn't have worked with the rest of us.

And Merry... well, the respect, esteem and, frankly, love which the rest of us have for her can look at times, I have to admit, a little bit culty.

Now Merry's in hiding, and Jory's been told he's not welcome any more, we're increasingly looking to another exile from the Circle for direction. A Knight who wears black and is looking around at this twelfth-century watering-hole with interest and a certain puzzlement.

'I rather liked it,' I admit to Ron, meaning the pre-ban smoking. 'Gave the places atmosphere, even if was the sort of atmosphere you'd find on Venus.' Rev takes a deep drag on his cigarette and offers the packet round. These days we have faster ways of killing ourselves than the one last decade's government tried to ban.

David's been staring at the Crusader swords mounted on the wall. 'I'd thought...,' he muses. 'But no, of course it doesn't work like that. And he may never have come here, in actual fact.'

'What are you on about?' I ask him.

'I'm talking about my device,' he says. 'My ally. I think it's time I came clean to you all.'

* * *

Nobody in the Chapel's been paying much attention to the response to the situation from outside the UK – we have our hands full with the domestic stuff. In fact, the international reaction mostly consists of horrified astonishment that a first-world country, a member of NATO, the EU and the

UN Security Council, can fall apart apparently overnight. Close daily attention to the foreign media coverage reveals a progressive downgrading of the UK's status from 'has-been world power with some okay pop music' towards an inevitable endpoint of 'tinpot banana dictatorship'.

The mythopolitical aspect is mostly being downplayed, although a few smaller nations are proudly announcing that they, too, have homegrown organisations equivalent to the Circle. Sadly, Sri Lanka's Ten Giant Warriors and Ukraine's Bohatyri Muromtsya aren't impressing anybody very much. The major global players like the Founding Frontiersmen and the Pilgrims of Xuanzang are keeping their existences quiet for now, adding to the impression that this is a quaint local phenomenon.

They're also keeping their distance, as if afraid of contamination. Only the UK's closest neighbours, who have little choice but to pay attention, have sent actual representatives of their own devicial orders to assess the situation.

Sir Charles has assigned the disgraced Stephen Mukherjee as liaison to these observers, on the basis that he doesn't want to waste a reliable Knight on babysitting duties. From what Stephen can gather, the emissaries are lucky it's not Wigsby giving them a tour of London's contested boroughs.

Stephen was at Trafalgar Square, of course, like every other Knight within striking distance of the capital, but he didn't acquit himself well – certainly not sufficiently to make up for the Boston Addis fiasco. Like all the other Knights, he remembers forcing his horse to trample her way through the thick-pressed crowds, ducking the arrows and stray bullets, slicing and hacking a path towards the Chapel people at the plinth. Unlike the rest of them (at least as far as he knows), he spent the battle hoping desperately not to do too much damage, praying he wouldn't be responsible for any deaths that day.

He was too far away to come to the aid of the Knights attacking Jack Bennett, but the man's stature was such that the fight was difficult to miss.

Like all of them, Stephen was following the Seneschal's orders. Not that he'd seek to excuse himself that way: he understood them too, appreciated the moral case for them. The trouble is, he simply doesn't believe it any more.

It's as if the lens that's been focussing his attention on the hunt for Adze and the Beasts for the past year has shattered, opening his vision up to the wider picture. The world has spread out into three dimensions, become holistic, hologrammatic, a panorama without filters. He sees – or at least guesses at – the consequences of every action, its ramifications and side-effects, and it's enough to paralyse him. In every face he passes, he sees the small boy whose birthday he ruined, the parents whose home he invaded, the protestors he sliced aside at in the pursuance of his chivalric duties.

All he can do now to redeem himself – in his own eyes as well as Sir Charles' – is to persuade Dermot Healey and Marie-Odile Laclos of the justice of the Circle's position, in the hope that they'll convince the Children of Oisín and the Paladins de la Republique to weigh in on the Circle's side and bring this conflict to a swifter end.

* * *

'Really Jory, none of this is your fault,' Merry insists yet again. 'But *please* carry on explaining to me how you personally killed Finn and Jack and destabilised the entire United Kingdom, because that's exactly where we need to focus our attention just at the moment.'

'But…,' Jory complains, hearing and hating the whine in his voice. 'If I'd just been there for Finn…'

He knows she's right, though. He didn't ask Finn to come to Glastonbury – indeed, he did his best to avert it. Far from abandoning her, he was trying to protect her. The fact that that didn't work out as planned, and the horrific way the aftermath has escalated, has been entirely outside his control.

Malory tempers her obvious impatience. 'Finn's death was a tragedy, sweetheart, but it's all but irrelevant now. The Grail was the catalyst, as it was always going to be. I know it hurts that Rev and the others blame you for what happened, but I doubt any of them except Marlene are even thinking of Finn now.' (Which is true, I'm ashamed to say.) 'Everyone has bigger and more urgent things to tackle, you and me included.'

They're walking on the beach, near the bungalow Merry and Edward have rented in Prestatyn. Although they're right on the Welsh-English border, about twenty miles from Liverpool as the crow files, there's little here to show that the realm has turned upon itself in internecine struggle. In fact, it's rather pleasant. The early-September day is warm, with a drizzle so fine it's fading into mist, and the sun is gleaming white behind the clouds like an infrared image of itself.

The very public death of Big Jack Bennett's shaken Jory all over again, though. Over the past few years, the gigantic man's become like a brother to him, albeit a brother whose wedding he missed because he didn't like his fiancée and who yells at him about it every time they see each other. Now he's gone, and it's as if his bulk was anchoring history. It's rising now like a hot-air balloon, its ascent out of Malory's or anyone's control.

Prestatyn was a last-minute decision, as Merry told Jory when he arrived. ('We were all set to hide out in Llangollen, of all places,' she explained. 'Dad's got friends there, old friends from his university days, and it just seemed like the place to go. Well, we were flustered at first, and then terribly upset about Finn. We got as far as Oswestry before I realised what was nagging at me – Llangollen's right by an Iron Age hillfort called Castell Dinas Brân, which is one of the possible locations for the castle of Corbenic. Can you imagine – an old man and his daughter, trying to hide the Nestine-Gull Grail right on the doorstep of the Grail-Keeper's castle? We'd have lit up the mythosphere like a beacon. The story-blindness can creep up on any of us; we need to remember that. So, we carried on to Prestatyn.')

Now the old man guards his treasure in a well-appointed holiday chalet, while his daughter restlessly roams the sea strands, gazing out across the Irish Sea towards the Isle of Man, the abode of the sea-god Manannán mac Lir who figures in the earliest myths of both Fionn mac Cumhail and King Arthur, and occasionally buying herself an ice cream.

Jory shakes his head violently, as if to shed his guilty malaise like shower-water. It doesn't work of course, but perhaps if he concentrates on following Malory's plan, it will begin to weigh less heavily on his scalp. 'So what do we need to do?' he asks.

'Well, firstly we need to keep the Grail safe,' Merry says. 'Although, I doubt they're going to be looking too hard for it. In theory, one of the claimants to the High Kingship –'

'Who, just to go back a bit, are Squig and David?' Jory interrupts. 'I'm still finding that hard to believe, Mal. They're both people I know. Lovely blokes – at least, they used to be – but neither of them's remotely majestic.'

Malory shrugs. 'Nor was Arthur, before his acclamation. A lot of his early reign's spent persuading everyone he's a worthy ruler. And that was *after* he pulled the sword from the stone. Like I say, in theory, that – or rather, pulling the arrow from the Nestine-Gull Grail – will be the first step for either of our aspiring Pendragons to legitimize himself.'

'In theory,' Jory repeats. 'In practice, though…?'

'Well,' Merry says again. 'To be honest, I doubt either of them's in much of a hurry, now they've had time to think about it. Neither of them would want the other getting hold of it, obviously, but as long as it's kept hidden out of everyone's way, it's not a priority. Because what are their claims, exactly? Squig worked in a kitchen, and now he's squire to Sir Kay's device-bearer. David probably holds the device of a *different* king, albeit one who's generally remembered as heroic. Take away the device-fuelled hype and hysteria, and they're both pretty damn tenuous.'

'But,' says Jory, 'surely the hype's the point? You told me the devices have whatever power we imbue them with. If David or Squig manage to persuade enough people that they're the Pendragon, won't they... well, become the Pendragon?'

Malory nods enthusiastically. 'That's the theory. And with belief on this scale, it would probably work. I can only theorise about how the Pendragon device would manifest, because as far as anyone knows it hasn't since Arthur himself, but it hardly seems likely it would arise spontaneously out of nothing. The mutation of a different device would be a plausible mechanism, and there's a lot of that going around at the moment.

'But,' she goes on, 'consider how things must look to Squig and David themselves. They can't *both* be carrying the Pendragon device, after all. And of course Arthur himself never imagined he might be king before it was thrust upon him – he had no idea of his parentage – so even if one of them *is* carrying it, he's probably in denial about the fact. Both of them must think they have to fool people into seeing them as the Pendragon.'

Jory moodily kicks a stone into the ruffled sea. It vanishes without a sign. 'So you think they'd rather avoid testing themselves, in case the Grail doesn't recognise them? That... kind of makes sense, actually.'

Malory flashes him a grin that makes his knees tremble suddenly, as if remembering happier times. 'Of course it does. This is what I'm good at, remember?'

'Well, that and some other things,' Jory suggests.

She hits his arm playfully. 'Try to focus for a moment longer, love. Of course, at the Fastness it's Blaze calling the shots, not Squig – but I've a suspicion he's got private reservations as well. He's not been Merlin for long, and making someone into the Pendragon isn't something any Merlin's achieved since the first one. As long as we have the Grail and the Circle and Chapel don't, the status quo suits everyone.'

'But won't they both want to get it so the other doesn't?' Jory's just going through the motions now, as so often in their conversations. It's not as if Malory won't have thought this through.

'But then what reason would they give for not using it immediately? No, if they take the Grail, they have to go through with the test of kingship, and I don't think either of them's ready for that just yet. Perhaps later, when we've all seen what war can do to a country...' Malory shivers. 'But no, not yet.'

'So that's all there is to it? Just keep the Grail safe?'

Merry shakes her head decisively. 'Of course not. Dad and I can manage that on our own. We need you to flush out whoever's been stirring this whole thing up. And hopefully do a bit of good in the meantime.'

* * *

'Well,' says Rev Cantrell slowly, leaning back against the settle and stretching his arms out along the shoulders of Twink and Scar, 'this is a twist.' His cigarette hangs louchely from his lips, half-smoked.

David nods sympathetically. 'It didn't feel fair to keep you all in the dark.'

Scar scowls at her pint and chaser. 'Too fucking right,' she mutters.

Above the gloomy backroom of the Trip to Jerusalem, oppressively heavy, rise the walls of the castle which King Richard I besieged in 1194, using the collection of siege engines he'd brought back from the Crusades, after his brother John's supporters had occupied the place. Local legend has it that Richard, or at least his men, had rested here five years earlier on their way out, giving the pub its name.

There's obviously a certain fittingness to the fact that we're sharing it with his human ally now. Since one of Prince John's men was very likely the Sheriff himself, this is the very locus where the legends of Robin Hood and Richard the Lionheart intersect.

'This isn't right,' agrees Zara. 'It's not personal about you, David, but this is not right. We're not King's men and women, we are the Green Chapel. We don't serve Elizabeth II, we don't serve the Circle's Head and we will not serve Richard bloody the Lionheart either. We are our own men and women, not yours.'

'That's totally a given,' David says. 'There's no question of anyone serving anyone. And I know Richard's stock with people of your faith isn't exactly high.'

Rev nods slowly. 'You know, I don't think we should be too hasty about this.'

Scar snaps at him at once. 'So you're saying what?' He jerks his arm away from her shoulder. 'We sell out now, aye, just when the whole country's coming over to our side? The fuck away with that, man.'

Cantrell nods placidly. 'Like you say, the fuck with that. But like Dave says, joining forces doesn't mean *serving* anyone. What he's putting on the table here is an alliance, right, big fellow?'

'Absolutely,' David replies. 'My aim is to claim the Headship of the Circle, and sack that buffoon Raymond. Once that's done, I'm sure there's a lot we'll have to offer each other. But to get there, I'm going to need your help. For the moment, our goals clearly coincide.'

'Let's focus on that, shall we?' says Rev. 'Because honestly, we'll be assuming you're out to screw us in the long run. No offence, big fellow – because you I like – but I wouldn't trust the Lionheart ally as far as I could throw it. Which isn't far, with it being insubstantial and all.'

'I don't get it,' Ron says. 'If you don't trust this Lionarse bloke, why make him boss of the Circle? Don't seem all that astute to me.'

'Yeah, I'm not sure about that.' I'm frowning, trying to work this out. 'He'd be better than Charles Raymond, at least. Plus, whether we trust him or not, once he's there he owes us a favour. Don't you, David?'

'I will indeed,' David agrees. 'I can guarantee you a *permanent* truce between the Circle and the Chapel, after I'm installed as Head.'

Lee shakes his head. 'Sorry mate, but we've heard that one before.'

'I'm going to reform the Circle from the centre outwards,' David promises. 'Get rid of all the bitterness and bigotry and cynicism this Seneschal's sowed there. The Circle's meant to be a force for good – it shouldn't be wasting its time persecuting people who are only trying to help others. On my watch, it won't. The Head's an authority none of the Knights would dare to defy, not even Raymond.'

'Yes?' Zara still sounds sceptical. 'So you will not be the boss of us, just of the Knights?'

'Bollocks, Za!' snaps Scar. 'Like you said, his ally's a fucking *king*. We don't trust his sort round here.'

'Oh, come on, Scar!' Laney offers unexpectedly. 'This is David we're talking about. Don't we trust him? I've picked up from watching all of you that it's the person who counts, not the ally. The Knights may reckon their devices control them, like poor Paul did, but we know better, don't we? If David's in the driving seat, can't we trust *him* not to betray us?'

Even Zara's nodding slowly now. 'I think Laney's right. So long as an alliance is all it is. We won't give – foalty?'

'Fealty,' I correct her quietly.

'We don't give our fealty to anyone,' Zara repeats fiercely.

'We won't be King's men,' Ahmed agrees. 'There has to be no question of that.'

'No question whatsoever,' David smiles. 'As Head, I'll have all the men I want, believe me.'

Rev snorts.

'And to get yourself made Head…,' Scar says, '…you'd need to get the Grail, right? That cup with the arrow through it, that Merry's got and isn't giving us?'

'Well,' David says, 'if we can persuade her to give it up, that would be splendid. If not, we'll just have to manage as best we can.'

'Hnh,' grunts Scar, and says no more for the rest of the conversation.

* * *

Though it doesn't occur to Stephen to consider the matter, Malory would very probably say that the French Paladins and the Children of Oisín are evidence of evolution among the devices, of the memetic archetypes' surpassing ability to adapt themselves to changes in the human cultures that constitute their environment.

The legends of Fionn mac Cumhail and his war-band the Fianna, and of Roland and his Twelve Paladins, date from the feudal eras of Ireland and France. Both heroes were as much the subjects of monarchs as Lancelot and Gawain – though like Arthur, the Emperor Charlemagne and the High King Cormac mac Airt have been notably absent from their nations' rosters of recurring devices. However, unlike the Circle in their Anglican monarchist enclave, the devices of France and Ireland have been forced to adjust their survival strategies to states which are, notionally at least, secular republics.

The Oisínians' route has been the more complex one – between the Act of Union in 1800 and the founding of the Free State in 1922, they were effectively a local franchise of the Circle, under the authority of the Seneschals – but there's no doubt that the metamorphosis required of the Paladins du Roi, as they were known before 1789, was the more catastrophic. These days, the bondsmen and -women of these warriors of old are pledged in service to their sovereign peoples, and on the whole their devices haven't had a problem with that (though heaven knows what Charlemagne and Cormac might say if they did return).

Stephen's brought Healey and Laclos to see the Bermondsey barricades, the nearest outpost of Chapel sympathisers to the Fastness. Here, an entire network of sidestreets surrounding a housing estate has been walled off, mostly with cars in varying states of intactness, supplemented by heavy street furniture, the wreckage of fridges and washing-machines, piles of collapsed masonry, barriers thieved from police road blocks and, proudly cutting off access to one whole avenue, the burnt-out carcass of a double-decker bus. The air is sour with the residue of the smoke.

'Such damage as this,' Laclos observes, 'will cost a lot of money to repair. Whoever wins,' she adds neutrally. The bondswoman of the chevalier Huon of Bordeaux is a slim Parisienne with a bob-cut that Stephen thinks – accurately as it happens, although he believes he's being uncharitable – makes her look like a lesbian. Perhaps in a display of her uninvolvement, she's elected to visit the front lines wearing an elegant charcoal-grey skirt suit and silk scarf.

'Don't worry, we won't ask you fellows to host Eurovision for the next few years,' Healey deadpans. The grizzled Irishman bears the device of Conán mac Morna. From Stephen's rather minimal reading-up on the internet this morning, Conán is considered the joker of the Fianna, though he's a more serious figure than Sir Dagonet at Arthur's court. Like Laclos, he's come in civvies, in his case a rumpled blue suit and two days' stubble.

At this time of the day, it's quiet at the barricades. A small squad of secular army stand nearby, uneasily hoping not to be called upon to keep the peace, but other than the occasional shout of defiance and the odd thrown bottle, there's little going on behind the barriers. The sounds of a dozen different music systems drift from the street and the neighbouring houses. The only tune that Stephen recognises is 'Anarchy in the UK' by the Sex Pistols, which is being played round the clock on certain radio stations, often alternating with 'London Calling' by The Clash.

Stephen attempts a smile at Healey's witticism, but he really hasn't the heart left in his body.

Instead, he presses on with his own argument. 'You see our problem, though, of course. These people are determined. They've dug right down in their own turf. If we tackled them head-on, of course we could bulldoze the barricades and arrest the ringleaders in just a few hours, but then we'd be pressing on to the Old Kent Road, Elephant and Castle, Rotherhithe… Just taking London back could take us weeks, and that's assuming the areas we pacify stay pacified. And meanwhile whole swathes of the provinces are in open rebellion.'

'"Rebellion",' muses Laclos. 'This is the word for a revolution that fails, yes?'

Stephen weighs this up. 'I think it's a fair word to use until it succeeds,' he says. 'Which this one can't possibly.'

'You've satisfied yourself the Circle's going to win, then,' Healey says.

Again Stephen chooses his words carefully. 'It's going to take time,' he says, 'and as you say it will cost a bally fortune. But in the long run, yes. We need to reassert the normal order. The Head's authority has stood unquestioned – well, not unquestioned, of course, we believe in freedom of speech and all that – but unchallenged, for one thousand, five hundred years. This Green Chapel shower have no experience of running things at all. If they're allowed to take control it'll be a bloody shambles. These ordinary people have no idea of what the Circle do for them; they couldn't possibly manage without us. It's for their own sake. Harsh, but there you have it.'

The Fiann and the Paladin exchange a look, and Stephen realises he may have overstated his case. It's an easy mistake when you're dubious about the position you're arguing, as he remembers from the debating society at school.

The thing is: yes, the Children and the Paladins were loyal to their kings once, but that was a long time ago. A few of the oldest Fianna when Healey first joined, perhaps, might have had some residual allegiance to the British crown, but neither Healey nor his boss in Dublin, the mac Cumhail, has ever served a state that wasn't a republic. And the Paladins' purges were more than two centuries ago.

'So these people, these citizens of yours,' asks Healey sombrely. 'They're wanting to be free to rule themselves without your Circle interfering? That's what you're saying, son, is it?'

'Free from the domination of kings and aristocrats,' Laclos observes lightly, and Stephen realises he's radically misunderstood these foreign devices.

The Circle can't expect any help from the Children or the Paladins. From the point of view of their post-revolutionary mindsets, this is a long-overdue adjustment in Britain's affairs. Unless the devices of one of the other remaining monarchies decide it's in their interests to intervene, the Knights are on their own.

* * *

'So what makes you so sure someone's been stirring things up?' Jory asks Merry, as they share a neopolitan sundae at a down-at-heel but cheery beachfront café. 'Why can't the Chapel and the Circle be pushing against each naturally, like opposite poles of a magnet?'

Malory gives him a tiny frown. 'Opposite magnetic poles attract, love. This is more like, um… when a photon hits an atomic nucleus, I suppose, and creates a particle and an antiparticle whose momentum forces them apart. Although I'm not sure physics analogies are necessarily helpful.'

Jory sighs. 'OK.' He takes a spoonful of strawberry ice cream.

She pushes her glasses up her nose. 'In general terms, yes – unless we'd actually succeeded in reunifying the Chapel and the Circle, this war was probably going to be inevitable. But that didn't mean it had to happen *now*. The legends of Camelot and Sherwood have coexisted for hundreds of years. It's not hopelessly egotistical to think we might have calmed the storm for another decade, perhaps even another generation – *if* David hadn't goaded Sir Charles into spilling the beans about the devices all over the mass media.' She takes another scoop of vanilla.

'So David stirred things up,' Jory suggests.

Merry waggles her spoon at him. 'Not alone, no. And I've a feeling Blaze didn't come up with *his* plans entirely independently, either. I think someone's manipulating both of them, playing both sides against one another. We can only hope the same person isn't manipulating us too.'

'So who?' asks Jory. 'I mean, all due respect, Mal, but this is sounding a tiny bit paranoid.'

Malory smiles. 'Remember how you're not the psychologist in this relationship? These aren't vague oppressive forces I'm talking about; it's a definite person or group of people. We just don't know who yet. Whoever it is made contact with David through Ibrahim Al-Khuzaie, paid for his travel home and put him in touch with the *Squaring the Circle* production people. The same person has been embezzling from the Circle and donating most of the proceeds to Bretwalda Ward to revive the Saxon Shield – the Shield who, let's not forget, were the cause of David's grudge against the Circle in the first place. Put all of that together, and this begins to look an awful lot like *grooming.*'

'Good grief,' says Jory, who hasn't fitted all this together properly before. 'And Blaze?'

'What I gather,' says Merry, 'from the scraps of gossip that still reach me from the Circle, is that Squig – or Jason, as he calls himself now – got the gig as Sir Charles' squire because he found Paul Parsons after his breakdown. Raymond will have been influenced by Blaze in that decision, obviously, but Blaze couldn't have arranged for Jason to find Paul in the first place unless he had information about where he was. Which suggests that somebody hexed Paul, left him in the woods, then tipped Blaze off.'

'Unless Burn put Paul out of action himself,' Jory suggests dubiously. 'Perhaps Paul found out he was ex-Chapel?'

Malory nods, conceding the point. 'It's possible. Although he does legitimately hold the Merlin device, so I don't think a revelation like that could seriously affect his standing. And sabotaging the Lancelot device would be fairly out of character for Merlin. We can't rule it out, but if we believe someone's been working covertly to manufacture one potential Pendragon, it's not much of a stretch to assume the same people are at work here.'

Jory nods. 'OK,' he says again. 'And what we do about this is...?'

Malory grins. 'We try to expose them, of course. Whoever's doing this, they *wanted* this war. I thought they wanted the Pendragon back, but they could have had that by now. By setting up opposing contenders, they've delayed that outcome, not hastened it. They must have wanted to break the accord, to pit the Circle against the Chapel again. Whether they expected it to succeed on this scale, I don't know, but now it has, they'll want to prolong it, at least until whatever end they had in mind is achieved. And what would be the worst possible thing, from the point of view of prolonging the war?'

'Well,' Jory says, 'for Squig or David to be confirmed as the real Pendragon, I suppose. For one of them to pull the arrow out of the Grail. Once that happens, it's a foregone conclusion, and the whole thing peters out.'

'That's the one,' Merry agrees. 'The thing is, if I'm right, our mysterious conspirators will be the *only* party who actually want the Grail – purely to keep it out of David and Squig's hands. So what we're going to do is this. You're going to go public, just like David did.'

'*I* am?' asks Jory. 'Why would anyone let me on the TV?'

Merry looks exasperated. 'Because you're the only Knight of the Circle apart from David to have defected to the Green Chapel. Because you did it first, and because you actually led the Chapel for two years. Because you're the missing Robin

350

Hood the Chapel carefully aren't talking about. Because you, unlike anyone else who's currently speaking for the devices, actually want peace between the factions. And because you want to recruit people, deviced and undeviced, to help you keep that peace. Are those enough reasons?'

'Well, I suppose so,' Jory concedes. 'Am I really going to do all that?'

Malory looks at him with deadly seriousness. 'My love, of course you are. Because somebody needs to. Go to Jade Kinsey first – she's the only person in the country with manpower, expertise and no horse of her own in the race. See who you can subvert from the Chapel and the Circle – they all know you, and some of them must be unhappy with the way things are running away from them. Talk to your pal Janene, too, and be open to approaches from other rogue devices – the not-too-evil ones, anyway. You're going to need any help you can get.

'And then at some point,' she adds, 'someone's going to make contact with you and start dropping hints about the Grail. And that person, or whoever they're representing, is going to be the one responsible for this.'

* * *

Jason is finding the attention the Knights are paying to him baffling, and not a little creepy. They stare at him covertly when he walks nearby. They fall silent whenever he comes into a room. Sometimes it seems as if they want to touch him, but then draw back at the last moment, as if he might be contagious.

('Enjoy it, dude,' has been Blaze's advice. 'It's nothing to the respect you're gonna get when everyone knows you're the Pendragon.'

'Am I the Pendragon, though?' Jason asked him the last time he said this. 'I don't reckon I'm Much any more. The voice I get's changed. It's older and posher, and more... like Welsh or Scottish or whatever. I reckon, anyway. It's difficult to tell accents when they're in your head. But that don't mean I'm King Arthur, Burn.'

'Don't matter, does it?' Blaze explained, exasperated. 'You haven't got to *be* the Pendragon, you've just got to act like him.'

'But if I'm not…' Jason protested. 'Well, it's not quite right, is it? It's not honest. It's not…' – he tries out the word, which he's not sure he's ever used seriously before – '…not *honourable.*'

Blaze shook his head. 'Fucking hell, bruv, sounds to me like you're well on the way.')

The Knights are standing oddly around him now, as they gaze up at the widescreen TV in the boardroom. All the other squires stand further back in the room, deferentially behind their Knights, but when Jason tried that the Knights parted in front of him, leaving a space which sort of pulled him into it. Now he's standing at the Seneschal's side, with William Posnett to his right, while on Sir Charles' left, Theo Harte fiddles about with the wi-fi on his laptop, trying to get the sound to come through from YouTube.

Jason watches this for a while before eventually, unable to cope any longer with the ineptness of Harte's faffing-about, he blurts out, 'I think the sound's muted on the TV, Mr Harte.' Harte finds the remote control and unmutes it. Jason cringes inwardly at the faint susurration of awe which passes among the assembled Knights.

'– in Cornwall and Brittany,' David Stafford is saying onscreen, 'once believed that Arthur had been turned into a raven after the battle of Camlann: indeed, some say his name comes from the Celtic words *arr dhu*, meaning "very black". ' To address the Circle he's dressed for once in his full Knightly regalia, though muted to a uniform heraldic sable. 'When I take my place among you, I will take up my own device, but until then I've promised I'll wear, and bear, only black.

'When I was last in Britain,' David says, 'I fought the Saxons, who inflicted on me a hurt so grave I thought I'd never recover. I boarded a boat and was taken away, to heal my wound in a distant land. You knew me as the bondsman of Sir Galahad, but that's changed. Now I've returned, a raven King come to take up my place in the Circle, as Galahad took his at the Round Table; but my place at that Circle is in its centre, and the arms I take up won't be a red cross, but a golden dragon.

'I'm the Pendragon,' he declares, 'and you owe me your fealty. Already the men and women of the Green Chapel have abandoned their Green Knight and flocked to my cause. You're the bondsmen of Arthur's own Knights: can you do less than they have?

'I'm the Pendragon, and I have come in Britain's hour of greatest need, a civil war in which the devices themselves direct the sides. Accept me as your head, and Britain can once more have peace.

'I am the Pendragon: Arthur, King of the Britons – the once and *present* King. The Circle will bow to me.'

The video finishes, and the YouTube panel offers a scattershot collection of videos the Knights might like to watch next. Jason spends a few seconds reading the captions and being amused that one of them's billed as 'a roundtable discussion', before he becomes aware that everybody in the room is looking expectantly at him.

'Oh. Right,' he says. He clears his throat. There's a rapt hush, as keen attention invades the face of every Knight and squire in the room.

Jason clears his throat again. 'Right,' he repeats. 'Well, that's a load of bollocks, for a start.'

* * *

It's only fair to say that, behind the scenes, both David and Blaze – and Jason, of course, but his control of events is strictly limited – are feeling terrible about this whole thing.

Jason feels like a traitor as forces under the Circle's command, all of them looking to him for inspiration if not actual leadership, stamp down on Chapel people and on ordinary men and women across the country. He's considered ordering them to just stop fighting, but Burn has told him in no uncertain terms – and he believes it – that if he does this he'll be chucked in the Benwick Institute before you can say 'Seize the impostor!' For now, he just has to trust that Blaze knows what he's doing, and that David, who he sincerely believes to be an evil influence on the Chapel, can be stopped.

Blaze and David are acting under the influence of devices with strong strategic planning skills. Still, neither of them foresaw the outcomes of their scheming thus far. Burn had no suspicion that events were going to escalate so quickly, leaving Squig exposed in a position of symbolic (if not practical) power; whereas David, though he's been trying to inflame popular dissent against the Circle, never expected it to reach such pandemic levels. Both of them are frankly appalled at the scale of their achievements so far, and terrified of the consequences should their schemes not work out... but both are too committed now to withdraw.

David has challenged the Circle – openly, now, across a thousand news outlets. The very best he can hope for if he fails is a lifetime in Benwick: unless he avoids fighting, which neither his character nor his device will accept as an option, his death in battle seems by far the more likely outcome.

Blaze, too, has taken on the Knights, but in a different way: what he's attempting is a huge con trick, aimed at giving himself – the Merlin device, that is, because at present he's buggered if he can see who else is up to the job – control of the Circle via a puppet King. As Merlin, he too has the downer of knowing that, in the long run, some form of imprisonment is basically inevitable.

In short, Malory's surmise that the claimants and their advisors are not wholly in control of events is a justified one. Privately, every one of them is winging, and it's probably accurate to add bricking, it.

* * *

Over the next week, Jory parleys his status as an ex-Knight of the Circle and former leader of the Green Chapel – confirmed for the record, with visible reluctance, by Chief Inspector Kinsey – into a slot on the primetime TV news programmes.

He uses it to plead for a cessation of hostilities between the devicial factions and to announce the forming of a new body, the Shantih Foundation, to campaign for peace and to direct aid to those non-combatants whom the fighting will cost their homes, their livelihoods or their breadwinners. (The first name he considered was 'the Wounded Land Foundation', but that's too tied to Arthurian myth, so instead he picked out the final word of Eliot's *The Waste Land*, which according to the poet means a kind of serene, divine peace. It's Sanskrit, anyway, so helpfully neutral as far as ancient British conflicts are concerned.)

The speech Jory gives on TV is accordingly peppered with *Waste Land* references, all setting lands in order and shoring fragments against ruins. It's impassioned, sympathetic and humane, and has no effect on the national situation whatsoever. It does, however, start to bring some of his fellow peacemongers out of the woodwork.

The deal he struck with Chief Inspector Kinsey, who hates his guts on general principles but is even more vehemently opposed to the Chapel and the Circle tearing the country apart between them, is not an amicable one, but allows him to call on her resources when she agrees it's necessary. He's freely pooled all his intelligence with her – saving only the location of the Grail, which she has no interest in whatsoever – and after some magisterial swearing she seems to have taken most of it on board. In return she's given him access to her own intelligence network, which is stretched to its utmost but still bringing in some useful information about the activities of the Circle and Chapel command structures.

Jory hoped Janene Long would be with them, but despite the neutrality she professed earlier, reports from Carlisle suggest the Adam Bell gang's weighing in on the Chapel side. She's not returning Jory's calls, in any case. The first actual defector to the Shantih Foundation is Brian, the avatar of Will Stuteley, who's been in hiding since the battle at the Square, wanting nothing to do with either the perpetrators of the massacre or its victims. He's been living rough in central London, saw the whole interview on telly huddled in a pub, and is waiting outside the studio when Jory leaves.

Over the next day or so there follow a trickle of Green Chapel hangers-on, a few of the Circle's less indoctrinated pages, and more and more of the general public who are sufficiently uninspired by both the Circle and the Chapel that they're willing to fight against them.

'My little girl's signed up with them Green Chapel people,' says one, a careworn man of middle age with a soft Devon accent. 'She always loved stories about Robin Hood, ever since she was a little 'un. She's only seventeen now. Never took any interest in politics before, but now she says she's off to fight for justice and freedom and all that nonsense. Terrible row we had about it. They get in your head, these people do, twist your ideas round so you don't know what you think no more – and that Circle ain't no better neither. She'd die for Robin Hood, my girl told me. I haven't heard from her since, Mr Taylor. I want a stop to this.'

'They took away my home,' another, an impatient elderly woman, vigorously protests. 'Two very rough-looking men came to my door and told me they needed to use my guest bedroom. They said my house was in an important strategic position. Well, it is on a hill overlooking a motorway – *was*, I should say, because it's not there any more. I complained when they built it, the motorway I mean, but naturally nobody listened. The men were very polite about it, but they wouldn't take no for an answer. Well, what could I do? I left them to it and went to stay with my niece in Scarborough, and a few days later we saw my house on the news – or what was left of it. One side or the other had blown it up, evidently. I'd lived in that house for thirty years. Now I don't even care to live in a country where that sort of thing happens.'

'He's in a coma still,' a third sobs, a tearful black woman whose husband sits silent and rigid holding her hand. 'They thought he was carrying a gun. It was a hockey stick. He'd been to practice earlier. He was wearing a hoodie he's had for years. It's not even green. But he was out after the curfew. Just with friends, we think. He's a good boy, a kind boy, but he never sticks to the rules. We've always been good people, we've never had any trouble-makers in our family. We've always thought he'd settle down. But when the men shouted at him, he was scared and he ran away. He didn't realise she was running towards another of them. And when the man hit him he fell, and hit his head, and... Now they say he may never wake up...'

By the afternoon of the second day, Jory's worn out from listening to the stories of legitimate grievance and immense personal tragedy. That's when Scar arrives.

'You told us that bastard was trouble,' she tells Jory, the moment she's shown into the Portakabin outside New Scotland Yard that Kinsey's requisitioned as his temporary office. 'You said we couldn't trust him. Like a stupid fucker, I wouldn't listen.'

'You mean David,' Jory says. The Black Knight's latest video's notched up millions of hits already.

''Course bloody David,' Scar confirms. 'High fucking King, my arse. Says he doesn't want us to be King's men, but now Big Jack's dead, he's telling the world he wants fealty from *everyone*. He's out of control, and those daft sods at the Chapel won't listen. Even Za won't have any of it. Well, fuck her. Fuck the lot of them, and fuck him most of all. Put me to work, Dan. I want to end this mess.'

Unfortunately, Jory's ideas for going about this aren't exactly precise. His brief has to be preventing bloodshed as far as possible, but with battle lines opening up across the country, and so far barely a hundred people signed up to the Shantih Foundation, he has to choose his battles carefully. He puts Scar in charge of a fast-response unit for central London, turning up at flashpoints where protestors and the men-at-arms are about to get physical, and getting between them as a human shield. It's visceral, tough, unpopular work: Scar's in her element.

The third confrontation she polices this way, between Chapelists and a party of Knights at the Bermondsey barricade, brings in Stephen Mukherjee. 'I've had it, Taylor,' he confides. 'I'm going errant. I can't be a Knight of the Circle any more – I've lost my purpose, but worse than that, I think the Circle's lost its own. We can't protect the people by attacking them – if the Circle turns its hand to *that*, we're more dangerous than any rogue device. I'm here to serve the people, and anyone who thinks they're a King can go hang.'

This gets him a modest round of applause from the handful of Foundation people in the room at the time, and a manly hug from Jory. 'I know there are others who are unhappy, too,' Stephen adds. 'If you like, I can make a few calls.'

And so, as troops led by Knights of the Circle (the squires, the pages, the men-at-arms co-opted from the secular army regiments) begin, in a score or more cities and a hundred strategic locations across the nation, to vie with Chapel forces (our ad hoc militia, our rank-and-file protestors, the army and police units coming over to our side)… Jory's own small army starts, slowly at first but with increasing momentum, to assemble itself.

So far, though, nobody's asked any questions about the Grail.

19. THE FALL OF NOTTINGHAM CASTLE

A month later, we're readying the Old Trip for a siege.

The Circle have been taking the initiative. They've split their main force in two, and turned them inwards and outwards. One half is at work in London, quashing resistance throughout the capital, securing it as the fortress of the establishment Brutus built it to be: a process every bit as messy and inconclusive as Stephen predicted. Londoners are faced with the stark choice of leaving the capital (which to most of them is simply unthinkable and would only cause more strain and tension everywhere else), and living in something even more like an Orwell novel than they're used to.

The other half of the Circle's army has been sent to Nottingham, to retake the Chapel's symbolic heartland.

This was pretty much what we expected, of course, and we've made preparations. As I've said, the last time Richard the Lionheart returned from the Middle East and fought the wicked regent who'd taken over the place while he was away, it was him besieging Prince John's forces in the castle here… but what goes around comes around.

Whatever its instinctive loyalty to the legends of Robin Hood, Nottingham is full of civilians – although a bunch of them have already left, mostly heading north – and a drawn-out, bloody battle would serve no one. Our best chance of prevailing in this war is not to become attached to any particular base of operations, but to melt into the countryside and run a guerrilla campaign in the style of those original outlaws of Sherwood.

Rev's already established that Merry's 'Sherwood distributed devicial emanation', strengthened by the conscious belief of so many minds, now extends to large groups of our new supporters as well as our established ones. He and David, already becoming a strategic partnership, anticipate ambushing supply convoys, infiltrating the Circle forces, assembling flashmob armies in urban centres to fulfil specific goals before dissipating again.

('Have to say this would all look a hell of a lot easier with the Robin Hood ally, though,' he told us all when reporting this. 'Dave's guy's not known for that kind of trickery. Well, us Merry Men can be tricksters, too. We'll just have to work with what we've got.')

All of which means that, after putting up the necessary show of token resistance to stop the Circle thinking they're winning an easy victory, we're letting them have Nottingham. The Knights' forces have been met with scrappy fighting on the main approaches to the city, and a couple of more serious running battles in the suburbs, before facing our militia – augmented by the Nottinghamshire Police Force serving at the command of the city council, and even some military deserters from the local barracks – in Old Market Square. Now our people, commanded there by David and Zara, are to delay them while those of us at Ye Olde Trip to Jerusalem get things ready – then to disperse and mingle with the non-combatant population, most of whom are carrying on their normal daily routines as best they can.

The rest of us – David, Zara and Ahmed included, of course – will be making our stand here.

* * *

Rev Cantrell's phone rings as he's lugging a crate across one of the pub's back rooms. He puts the box down with care, impatiently tugs the phone from the pocket of his cargo pants and answers it. 'Yes?'

'Rev, it's me,' Jory says. 'Dan.'

'I know,' sighs Rev, 'I recognised the number. What do you want, *Jory?*'

He can almost hear Jory wince at the other end of the line. 'I've been on the phone to the Circle,' the ex-Knight says. 'Trying to get them to sit down with you and negotiate.' Over the past month, Jory's been doing his best to position himself and his small body of defectors and concerned citizens as a neutral arbitrator between the devices – a role that's had much more affirmation from the undeviced, and largely terrified, public than from the Circle or the Chapel, who are barely tolerating them for appearances' sake. When he learned about the Circle's advance on Nottingham, Jory sent several hundred Shantih Foundation members to form a human shield across the roads into the city, but the Circle arrested them before they got there, and released them far enough away that they couldn't intervene.

Quite how this activity ties in with Jory's own ally – and indeed whether that's still Robin Hood, or whether Jory's supple subconscious persona has mutated again into something altogether different – is something Rev hasn't figured out yet. If there's a story where Robin turns against his own people in his way, he's yet to find it.

'Well, that's mighty thoughtful of you.' Cantrell sits down on the crate for a moment, absent-mindedly, then carefully stands up again. 'Except we didn't ask you to do any such thing.' Around him, other Chapel people continue to shift the heavy boxes into the room.

'Don't be so stubborn, Rev,' Jory replies. 'The Circle have thousands of men in Nottingham, including forty Knights. You know you can't win this one.'

'Maybe we can, maybe we can't,' Cantrell replies. 'Maybe there's more than one way to win.' Gingerly he tries to push the crate along the floor with his foot, but it's too heavy. 'Look Jory, we're kind of busy here right now, so I'm going to have to –'

'They want David,' Jory butts in. 'He's their price for leaving you alone. Julian Blythe says, if you hand him over, they'll withdraw from Nottingham and give you twenty-four hours' grace to evacuate.'

'That so?' Rev sighs. 'And what would you expect us to do about that, big fellow?'

There's a longish pause. Then, 'Just consider it, Rev. They know about the Trip – they've been surveilling you with drones. They know exactly where your HQ is, and they're coming just as soon as they've broken the back of your resistance.'

'I never expected anything less,' Cantrell says. We know about the quadcopter camera drones – indeed, we know that it's reluctance to provoke international reprisals that's kept the Circle from using larger combat UAVs on us British citizens, rather than mere surveillance models. That reluctance is unlikely to last the duration. 'Are we done now?'

There's a long pause. Then Jory says, 'Good luck, Rev,' and hangs up.

Cantrell sighs and shakes his head. 'He's a good kid, really,' he confides to the bar at large – then hefts the crate and staggers over to place it on a pile that's been built up behind the bar.

* * *

Ron's gawping at a tablet-screen BBC news feed over the shoulder of a lad called Eric, a robotics postgrad who knows Vicks from the university.

'I'm on the ground floor of Debenhams in Nottingham's Old Market Square,' the veteran war reporter confides to the viewers. 'Through the windows we can see the fighting between the newly-arrived Circle troops and the Green Chapel forces controlling the square.' The state broadcaster's walked a tightrope of neutrality since the fallout over Austen Morten's defenestration of Sir Charles, and tries to avoid emotionally-charged words like 'assault', 'occupy', 'attack' and 'defend'.

She elaborates: 'Huddled around me are ordinary shoppers who braved the warnings of possible conflicts today to clothe their families, and who are now trapped here with us until the fighting moves on. Every few minutes a group of shoppers tries to flee the square, hands in the air or waving white clothing above their heads. With me are a father and his young children, whose mother was in a nearby Starbucks when the Circle troops arrived. Three minutes ago, that café was hit by a stray grenade: it looks as if...'

Her voice goes hoarse suddenly, and the polished, clipped anecdote gives way suddenly to something aghast and shellshocked. 'I'm sorry,' she says, 'I can't... This is... This isn't Syria or Ukraine. I grew up near here...' She looks near tears.

Eric mutes the woman's voice and minimises the window. 'Oi!' Ron grumbles. 'I was proper engrossed in that.'

'Sorry,' Eric mumbles, not sounding it. 'Got to check the footage.'

Eric can't fight – he has terrible asthma, although frankly if his reason was sheer physical cowardice, I'd respect that, too – but he's been helping out in the ways he can. A week or so ago he worked out how to tap into the visual feed from the Circle's BAE Systems reconnaissance drones. So far he can't hack them sufficiently to control their flight or change the image (which would have distinct possibilities), but the intelligence they've been accidentally giving us has been invaluable.

The screen fills up with an aerial view of the square, currently filled with smoke and struggling people and horses, as well as those scurrying members of the public trying to flee the fray.

* * *

'You're clear on the plan?' I ask Vicks and Laney.

'I helped make the plan,' Vicks replies, irritated.

'Yeah, I know,' I sigh. 'We just need to be sure we're on the same page.'

Vicks shrugs. 'Lee and Ahmed hold the outdoor drinking area with Zara and David when they get here. It's going to be ally-on-ally combat, so the Knights have to order their ordinary soldiers to keep back, and tackle our guys themselves.'

'It's the honourable thing to do, isn't it?' mutters Laney.

'The Knights will be using swords,' I say. 'So David will too. The others have their bows.' Theoretically, under the Circle rules, that could get them shot by the men-at-arms – and if they were packing guns, it certainly would. We're hoping the bows will count as borderline enough that the Knights are happy to tackle the defenders themselves. It's a horrendous risk, but we're short on combat-ready allies. Ron's too green to be trusted with this, Rev's needed to shepherd everyone else to safety, and I – well, you know what I'm like.

Besides, though Lee keeps it quiet, in the ballads Gilbert Whitehand's as good a shot with the bow as Robin himself.

Ron strolls over to join us at that point. 'And how long's that stage of affairs going to persevere for?' he wants to know.

'Doesn't have to be long,' I say. 'Probably only a minute or so before they fall back and defend the main door. We've got the other doors and windows bricked up, so they'll be able to hold that for rather longer.'

'Like Horatius on the bridge,' Laney observes, surprisingly. It's not a story I tell often, the siege of Rome in the sixth century BCE having little to do with the motherlode of English folklore, but after all she had a classical education.

'Kind of,' I say. 'They'll make as good a showing as they can, fighting off those bastards. They've got allies, sure, but they're massively outnumbered. Only a few Knights can attack them at once, but they'll be coming in fresh every time.' And, if the men-at-arms *are* given the order to fire, the four at the door will be easy targets. 'Once that line of defence fails, they'll duck inside and barricade the door. Then they'll follow us the hell out of here.'

I've said that the Old Trip has caverns and cellars which extend beneath the castle walls and into Castle Rock. For a long time, there were rumours that the pub had a secret passage connecting it to the Castle itself, but that was filled in when the Castle was rebuilt as a ducal mansion in the seventeenth century.

The mansion was never built to be defensible, so despite its strategic position on high ground, we've not made use of it in this fight – indeed, with the assistance of the staff at the University Hospitals, we've set it up as a field hospital where the wounded from both sides can be evacuated. This means, of course, that the Circle forces will respect it as neutral ground, and not try, say, dropping breezeblocks off the castle walls onto the pub roof.

It also means that there'll be a lot of traffic up and down the road to Castle Rock: ambulances, and the vans and minibuses belonging to local businesses which the hospitals have requisitioned to fulfil the same function. And this, in turn, will make it pretty easy for the dozen or so Chapel people who've been occupying the pub in our capacity as bait to make our way out of the castle, after we climb the tunnel into the mansion's cellars that Vicks, with her explosives knowledge, has spent the last month painstakingly reopening.

* * *

'That bastard Blythe's in charge?' Lee repeats, when Rev tells him and Ahmed what Jory said. 'We owe that bastard for Finn.'

He's not a man of many words, Lee, and he chooses them carefully.

'It's a shame Plaice is not here too,' opines Ahmed. 'We could make it for Jack as well.'

'Oh sure guys, make it personal,' Rev says. 'Great way to stick to the script. You both know what you need to do.

Give them everything you've got, sure, but after that, you get out, along with the rest of us.'

Ahmed nods. Lee grunts sceptically.

'They're coming!' Eric shouts. On his screen, the drone has detected two figures, one hooded in green and one wearing black armour, leaving the square at a run. The flying camera swoops to follow them south down the road called Wheeler Gate. At the bottom of the screen, we can see that some of the mounted figures are giving chase.

Cantrell claps Lee and Ahmed on the back. 'That's your cue, guys. Get out there, give them hell – and then come back to us, OK? Oh, and tell Dave I said hi.' He rounds Eric, Ron and the other stragglers up like a mother chicken and ushers them all towards the stairs down to the cellar.

* * *

Ahmed and Lee step out and take up their positions, bows at the ready.

The Old Trip's in a mews called Brewhouse Yard, which runs under the castle walls. It's set back a little way from Castle Road, a side-road that's largely industrial and whose businesses back onto an A-road called Maid Marian Way. Old Market Square, where the fighting's going down, is the other side of that. The Circle troops might approach us from the north, down Friar Lane, or from the south end of Castle Street itself, or from the other end of Brewhouse Yard. If they've got any sense, they'll come at us from all three directions.

Now, weaving through the car park of the FE college opposite, pursued by four Knights on horseback, come Zara and David, dashing to join the others. David's back in his matte-black armour now, with his Knight's sword and shield. Zara looks bruised but exhilarated from the scuffle at Old Market Square. Her bow's slung across her shoulders, and a fresh bucket of arrows is standing waiting among the durable outdoor furniture. Behind them thunders a knot of four Knights.

Almost as soon as the Knights appear, Lee fells one of the approaching men with an arrow – an expert shot at the weak point under the helmet, which has the Knight, bearing the device of Sir Tor, falling, bleeding, onto the tarmac. Ahmed is less ambitious, laming the horse carrying the device-bearer of Sir Eliwlod and forcing him to dismount. Joining them, Zara turns her aim to the third Knight, but Sir Ulfius's device-bearer is too quick, the red wolf on his gold riot-shield deflecting several sure shots. The fourth man, whose vertical gold serpent marks him out as the device-bearer of Sir Colgrevance, is nearly upon them.

David has climbed onto a table, which gives him the Knights' advantage of height, though none of their additional mobility and stability. Colgrevance's bondsman charges at him, but his horse, spooked by the flying arrows, veers at the last moment, and he and David slash each other with their blades. David, who's not having to control a horse, is better able to counter with his shield, and though the impact throws him off the table, his blade has injured the Knight's sword-arm. From the ground, he stabs sideways at the horse, but his point glances off its armour.

Shouts from the direction of Friar's Lane suggest that more Knights are galloping to join the fray. Meanwhile, Lee and the others are keeping up a hail of arrows which has panicked Sir Ulfius's bondsman's horse into throwing him. It hurtles past the archers, off down Brewhouse Yard, towards the Museum of Nottingham Life.

By now, Sir Eliwlod's man has climbed onto the horse deserted by the bleeding servant of Sir Tor, only to be felled by a better-placed arrow from Lee. Sir Ulfius' representative staggers to his feet and is knocked over again by the second unguided horse, whereupon he has a little rest for a while.

Zara offers a hand to haul David upright, and together they turn to face Sir Colgrevance's avatar as he reasserts control over his mount, wheels round and charges back towards them. He has a deep cut where his articulated gauntlet meets his ceramic-polyamide vambrace, and when

Zara sends an arrow bouncing off his faceplate, he nearly drops his sword.

Behind them, Lee and Ahmed await the noisy riders now approaching down Castle Road. Colgrevance's man seems to baulk at facing Zara's killer aim, but he's committed to his charge. He ducks an arrow, and impales himself on David's strategically-placed sword. The point pierces his armour at the neck, between gorget and helmet.

He falls, gurgling horribly and bleeding like a burst water-balloon, and David has to use a foot to tug his blade free of his throat.

By now, Lee and Ahmed are shooting at a party of some twenty Knights as they come into view around the side of Castle Rock. David sees the white-on-black cross of Sir Arphasar go down, and the garish multicolours of Sir Aglavale. At their head rides a Knight bearing the golden double-headed eagle on a purple background, within a wavy red border: the arms of Sir Gaheris, over which Julian Blythe crouches. Lee continues methodically aiming, drawing and releasing.

'Let Blythe through!' orders David, and the archers obey, stepping aside smartly as Blythe charges through, swinging his sword. Meanwhile David's upended one of the pub tables into his steed's path, and slashes viciously at Blythe as the horse swerves to avoid it.

The blow doesn't connect, but ducking it is enough to unseat Blythe from his careering mount. He hauls himself to his feet with his shield, parrying another blow from David as he does so, then the two Knights are laying into one another with their swords, the plain black and purple-golden-red shields ringing with the sound of their strikes.

'David, there's no time!' cries Zara urgently. The rest of the mounted column's nearly on them, and their remaining arrows are dangerously few. She and the other archers fall back to the pub door, where the second phase of their defence was always supposed to happen, just as Blythe swings his sword in a wide, low curve which connects with the joint in David's armour at the knee.

Blood splashes, vivid carmine red on the pavement. David goes down and Julian Blythe raises his sword – just as his horse comes hurtling past, spooked by the arrival of further Knights at the bottom of Brewhouse Yard, and knocks him flying. Lee continues to shoot at the approaching horsemen while Zara and Ahmed rush out, grab David by the armpits and drag him back to the doorway.

If anyone had the leisure to take in the symbolism, they'd see a Crusader supported by two Muslims, but everyone here has other matters on their mind.

* * *

The tunnel out of the Old Trip's cellars leads up at a sharp angle through the grainy sandstone of Castle Rock. We've been preparing for this for a couple of weeks, so there's a string of electric lights along one wall (we tried it along the ceiling, but our backs kept bumping against it – we have to go bent double most of the way), iron pitons banged into the rock to hang on to, and a string of wi-fi relays so we can keep an eye on the fighting outside, and whether there's any Circle activity in the Castle up above.

I'm bringing up the rear, with young Eric just in front of me. We're only a minute from the top when he stops, staring at his tablet, and says, 'Shit.'

'What is it?' I ask, very much hoping it isn't going to detain him here for long.

'Shit shit shit,' he says again. 'David's down.' He fumbles for his inhaler.

'David?' I say. 'Oh no. Oh Christ.'

'He's not –' he says, then stops to puff his Salbutamol. 'He's not dead, just hurt. But Dale, it's going to take them longer…' He puffs again.

'Yeah,' I say. Then, agreeing with him, 'Shit.'

Our plan involves the defenders being able to barricade the door, then follow us quickly once they're inside. They need to get a good couple of minutes' headstart on the

Knights, or the whole plan goes tits-up. With an armoured man to carry, it's going to take them longer than they can afford – and losing four experienced allies in one go isn't something we can countenance.

'Oh Christ,' I say again. 'They're going to need help.'

Eric peers guiltily at me over his inhaler.

* * *

At the door, Zara stands flanked between Ahmed and Lee: now that it's down to hand-to-hand combat, she's incomparably the best of them and is holding off the Knights with David's sword. The others have machetes, which are hardly going to cut much mustard against the armoured Knights, even if they have sportingly dismounted.

It's not an optimal defensive scenario, is what I'm getting at, and Zara's labouring hard by the time I get there.

David's lying behind them in the doorway, struggling to get up. I fiddle desperately with his sable armour, unfastening the confusing clasps which clamp the bits together. He's muttering something, but if it's the instructions, I can't make it out over the sound of the battle a few feet away from us.

At length I drag him to the cellar, trailing blood and shaped chunks of beetle-black ceramic as we go, then rush back to the door, where Zara's panting as she fends off a Knight carrying a red-and-ermine striped shield – Sir Bors, I vaguely remember.

'Get inside, you stupid sods!' I shout, and start to heave one of the tables upright.

Zara glances back, sees what's up and smiles gratefully – a rare occurrence, I can tell you. Lee ducks back, pulling Ahmed with him, and the three of us quickly get the table ready to haul into position.

'Zara, now!' I yell, and smoothly she makes one last swipe in Nick Frith's face, steps backward and slams the door shut. In a moment, the other two and I have the table in place, and with her help we back it up with a couple more, before running like the clappers.

By the time we get to the tunnel, David's leaning up against the wall, and half-pushing, half-dragging him between us, we scurry up the rocky chimney like ferrets up a cardboard tube.

I end up going last again.

* * *

A minute or so later the doors cave in at last, to a rousing cheer from the Circle troops. The men-at-arms who've been swinging one of the outdoor tables as a battering ram go in to lift the indoor ones out of the way, then step aside and let the Knights through.

Julian Blythe's the first to walk into the abandoned front bar, flanked by Nick Frith and young Seb Dunmoor, the bondsman of Sir Lucan who hacked off Jack Bennett's arm back at Trafalgar Square. The three of them were the main Knights harrying David and the others at the door, so they've earned this. Dunmoor, who's only been a Knight a couple of months and still has unrealistic expectations, is feeling disappointed that he hasn't managed to dismember anyone else today.

'It looks deserted,' Frith says. 'They must be hiding in the cellar.' Behind them, other Knights shoulder their way in.

'That's not going to get them very far,' Blythe observes. 'Pretty crowded, too, I should think.' He details two Knights to check this room thoroughly, then presses on into the interior.

A black trail of discarded Circle armour leads from the front bar to the cellar door, looking like somebody's peeled a London cab. Dunmoor picks up David's abandoned breastplate. 'Why would they dump all this, though?' he asks.

Blythe gazes at the pile of beetle-skin pieces for a moment, then shrugs. 'No, not a clue.' He wanders through to the back room.

The cellar door is locked, so Dunmoor and the bondsman of Sir Loholt start beating at it with their sword-hilts while

Frith follows Julian into the cavernous space. 'What are all those crates doing piled up there?' Blythe wonders aloud, pointing at the giant stack behind the bar, and the other huge pile against the far wall. 'That's no way to store beer.'

'This is weird,' mutters Frith. 'Blythe, there's something going on here I don't like.'

'I say, what's this?' Blythe says, and bends down to look at the cheap palmtop that's been propped up next to the lowest crate. The screen is black, but it seems to be wired up to something hidden behind the pile. 'Oh, fu –' he begins.

…I'm speculating, of course. By now I'm in the cellars of the ducal mansion, shoving the manhole cover back on top of the tunnel and helping the others heave a pile of sandbags on for good measure, with Rev attending to the injured David, Eric gasping and wheezing, Vicks tapping grimly at her smartphone. There's no-one in the Trip who I'll be able to interview later. Some Knightly devices give their bearers a certain facility with lucky escapes, but there are limits.

So really, when I tell you now that Julian Blythe is looking at that palmtop when it lights up suddenly, triggered by the chain of wi-fi repeaters, and that he has the time to understand exactly what's going to happen in the next microsecond, it's basically wishful thinking.

He was never particularly bright.

* * *

The walls of Nottingham Castle are nine hundred and fifty years old. Castle Rock, of course, is far older, consisting of compressed fluvial deposits first laid down in the Triassic Era, so a couple of tons of gelignite's not going to bring the whole lot down. (We should bloody well hope not, anyway, given that we and a bunch of wounded people are in the field hospital up top. Luckily the mansion's over the other side of the outcrop, and we've asked particularly that the grounds be declared out of bounds to staff and patients.)

Still, the blast's enough to shake us like a rollercoaster in an earthquake.

The three-hundred-year-old pub building at its foot is destroyed at once, naturally, its whitewashed masonry and attractive stone tiling bursting apart to scythe through the men-at-arms and secular troops who stand outside awaiting the Knights' orders. The caves and cellars which form the core of the eight-hundred-year-old tavern fare no better, collapsing instantly under the pressure of the explosion. A fireball races up our escape tunnel, incinerating half the wi-fi relays and baking the others into instant uselessness before stopping at the sandbags.

And, shaken literally to their foundations, the ancient castle walls topple and crumble, the cliffs beneath them billowing out into airborne debris, a cloud of rocks which becomes a landslide, rolling down and crushing hundreds of Circle troops beneath its rubble, just as their Knightly commanders are buried underneath the wreckage of the pub, in the tomb we made out of the oldest inn in England.

20. JORY TAYLOR AND THE SPY

Now, I know what some of you may be thinking.

What's happened, you may ask, to my much-vaunted bardic impartiality? I've talked before now – at least, I expect I have, knowing me – about the need for a storyteller to stay aloof from events, keeping on the fringes, remaining uninvolved: approving the heroes' actions, naturally (or disapproving them, as need be), but retaining that impersonal distance that gives his or her stories the hallmark of objectivity.

What am I doing now, you may well ask, cheering on the grisly death of Julian Blythe, another human being whose main crime's having been a bit thick in the wrong place at the wrong time – and, for that matter, in those of hundreds of his followers, who were to blame only because they chose the one I like less out of two self-evidently good causes?

…Well. I'm sorry to break it to you, but all of that stuff I said – it's bollocks, and self-serving bollocks at that.

Some of the best and most enduring stories are told by those intimately involved in them. I mean, haven't you people read *Moby-Dick*? *Great Expectations*? *Bridget Jones's Diary*? I'd say all those narrators were involved in the action myself, and they're all pretty damn partial too.

The fact is, it's an excuse, and a pretty transparent one at that. I *prefer* to stay uninvolved. I'm fond of all these people, of course I am, but they live dangerous lives. If something terrible happens to them – like it did to Jack and Finn and Liss and Shaf and Shaun... well, I don't want to be carrying that around with me. I want to be looking at it to see how it fits with other pieces of their lives, with the shapes other people's lives make, seeing how to transform it into something that makes some fucking *sense*.

A story, in other words. Because the key thing about stories is, they're not true.

If I don't do that... well, it goes without saying, doesn't it? The one person I *really* don't want to see hurt, the person who I really care about, is me. And if I started setting enough store in these people or their causes that I was prepared to put myself in harm's way for them, fight for them even...

...then it might be me lying bloody on the York sandstone paving-slabs, or the shop-floor lino, or the patio or the patch of waste ground or the service-station car park. And I really can't stress enough how much I *don't want that*.

That's who I am. Like everyone, though, I'd like to think better of myself than that. So naturally I try to persuade myself – along with anyone else who'll listen – that that's what a storyteller is.

It's a vocation, you see. A calling, and a noble one. It means making sacrifices. In many ways, you know, it's almost a curse...

Well, bollocks to that. There comes a time – not for everyone, and if it never does for you I'm genuinely glad of it, but some of us don't have that luxury – when if we want to keep any respect at all for the human being we wake up as every morning, we have to do better than that.

Sometimes you have to admit whose side you're on, and bloody *do* something about it.

* * *

Jory reads about the demolition of the Old Trip, and the massacre and subsequent disarray of the Circle troops, with a peculiar mix of horror and relief. So many have died, a lot of them known to him: he used to go to the pub with Julian, knew Dunmoor when he was a newly-minted page, enjoyed occasional games of chess with Sir Loholt's bondsman Geoff Maclaren... It turns out, too, that the avatar of Sir Colgrevance was Ned Ballard, Paul's former squire, acclaimed as a Knight a mere week ago. On a human level, it's horrifying.

And yet, as it becomes clear that the Chapel people who made it into the ancient pub somehow escaped – our video claiming victory, narrated by yours truly and stating that only Circle troops died at the Old Trip, clears that one up – he's filled with a guilty gratitude that it's not worse. The Chapel's ties have always felt more sentimental, more personal to him, than the professional attachments of the Circle.

It's not just the violent deaths which instil him with unease, though. The ruthlessness which we, his surviving friends, showed in planning, baiting and executing a trap which took so many lives, horrifies him. Our trick was an ingenious one, worthy of Robin Hood himself; but Robin's traps usually leave their victims with an out, some way to escape with their lives and limbs – if never their pride – intact. This... this was wholesale slaughter. And worse... no, not worse of course, not worse at all, yet somehow more chilling... we were prepared to sacrifice Ye Olde Trip to Jerusalem, a place of huge importance in our heritage, to achieve it.

His goal of reconciling the opposing devices has become more vital than ever, even as it's become huger. Jory's no visionary, but he can see what this country's becoming. So far, the high ideals at the hearts of both sides have meant that it's been mostly combatants who've been hurt: civilians, even those who haven't fled the combat zones, have often been allowed to go about their business unmolested, meaning that some semblance of the nation's civic, cultural and economic life has continued in lockdown mode. That's never going to last. As the Chapel increasingly resort to this kind of trickery, a natural caution is going to mean the Circle start to treat everyone in Chapelist areas – and eventually, perhaps, every civilian – as a potential enemy.

Jory's already moved the Shantih Foundation to a new headquarters, outside the greater Fastness the Circle's trying to build London into. This office building is in neutral territory, and belongs a Swedish firm which hastily decided a month ago that for the time being they wouldn't be expanding their operations into the UK. Their touching eagerness to help out has made Jory wonder whether more international intervention is Britain's only hope now. He's considered flying to New York and petitioning the UN to send a peacekeeping force, but what holds him back – apart from a parochial feeling of embarrassment, as if he'd be inviting people round to dinner in the midst of a domestic row – is the fear that the devicial order of some superpower might use the UN's presence as an excuse to assert control.

So far the War of the Devices has been confined to the British mainland. If it went global... No, Jory isn't even going to go there.

The Shantih Foundation may have begun as a manoeuvre in what he sometimes grumpily thinks of as Malory's endless game of chess against the world, but over the past month it's become a quest, a direct action, of Jory's own, as urgent and vital as any he undertook for the Circle or Chapel.

Shaking his head, Jory leaves the aerial images of the giant pile of rubble beneath which so many Knights are buried, and skims the rest of the news. There've been more clashes in Lewisham and Brixton: there's footage of burning buildings and broken roadways, hooded figures capering around a tank that's been set alight, Circle troops descending en masse with riot-shields and truncheons to quell the dissent in the capital. A Knight has been killed by 'rebels' in St Albans. A knot of suspected Chapel conspirators have been arrested in Portsmouth – following a heavy beating, by the look of them – and will soon face trial.

Absorbed in miserable study, it's only on the third clearing of a female throat that Jory realises someone's at his office door. For a delighted moment he imagines it might be Malory, but that isn't to be his luck today.

'Laney,' he says, and hurries over to shake her hand. 'It's good to see you.' She's wearing a kind of hybrid of the crustie style she shared with Liss, and the trophy-girlfriend look she sported with Paul: long blonde hair in braids, not dreadlocks; multiple piercings marked out with studs, not rings; a brown canvas dress; surprisingly practical-looking walking boots.

'Dan,' she says, acknowledging him graciously.

Jory hurries over to the corner of his office, where he's set up a coffee machine and a kettle, and busies himself with making them tea while he thinks through the implications of her arrival. It's all but impossible to keep tabs on individuals in all this turmoil, but Jory's best sources last placed the eighteen-year-old in Nottingham, probably with the party at the Old Trip. In one way she's a natural for the Shantih Foundation, having been affiliated with both Circle and Chapel, but Jory had assumed her original loyalties had reasserted themselves.

He shouldn't jump to conclusions, though. She might just be here with a message. 'So,' he asks, as he hands her her tea (black, two sugars), 'what brings you here, Laney? It's been a long time.'

'I'm not here to defect, if that's what you're thinking,' she says at once.

Jory nods soothingly. 'Of course.'

'Not because I'm loyal to the Chapel, or any shit like that,' she adds in her cut-glass accent. He hadn't realised how much she sounded like Liss these days. 'I mean, they're my mates and all, but... well, after what happened at Nottingham... I mean, if things had been different, one of those Knights could have been Paul.'

Jory nods again.

'This whole war...,' Laney says, '...I've decided I don't want any part of it.'

'Me too,' says Jory gently. 'That's why I'm doing what I'm doing. That's what the Shantih Foundation's all about.'

'Well, OK.' Laney says, looking away suddenly. 'What I mean is, I don't *want* to defect. I mean, I'll do it if that's what it takes. If you insist on it.'

Jory frowns. 'Of course I don't. You're a free agent, Laney.' Then an inkling of what this conversation might be about comes into his head. '"If that's what it takes" for what, though?'

'To...' She stops and tries to light a cigarette. She fumbles it and drops the packet, which Jory gallantly picks up. 'Sorry,' she says. 'I've been shaking like a jackhammer the last couple of days. Don't know if it's the explosion, or...' She takes a long, deep drag. 'God, that's better.'

'Like I said, Dan,' she goes on, 'I want out. I want to leave the country. Go somewhere else. Somewhere there isn't a... fucking war on. Somewhere they don't have devices, if there is anywhere. Are there devices in, I don't know, Barbados?'

'I've never really looked into it,' Jory admits. 'What do you need, Laney? Money?' He's already guessed that this isn't it.

'No,' she says alarmed. 'Shit. Not that. My parents are loaded, you know that. They want me safe as much as I do. No.' She takes another shuddering breath of her fag. 'I don't want to go on my own, Dan. I want Paul.'

'OK,' says Jory thoughtfully. 'As far as we know, they've moved him to Tud House for further tests. That's well inside Circle territory, though, and they've amped up security since —'

'It's OK, I know some people,' Laney says quickly. 'Some of the Knights reckon the Circle owes me and Paul. They'd help me get him out of there. That's not the point. The thing is, there's no point taking him with me the way he is. He'd be better off in a hospital. I need him there to keep me safe. I need him as my boyfriend, not a basket case. I need him... whole.'

'I see,' says Jory sympathetically, finally ticking a box in his mental checklist that's been empty for the past month. 'You're telling me you need the Nestine-Gull Grail.'

* * *

He makes a few phone calls, packs a couple of bags, then takes her to Prestatyn. He's still driving the green Mini, which is too ordinary to alarm anyone unaffiliated with the combatant parties, but which those who know him will leave well enough alone. They skirt south round Birmingham, a nexus of Chapel-born dissent which the Circle is still struggling to control, and pass through leafy country roads – albeit with the occasional looted farm or burnt-out cottage – past Stratford, Worcester and Malvern before entering Wales near Radnor.

The border's patrolled by Dyfed-Powys police, who check their papers at the 'Croeso i Gymru' sign. (The West Mercia police have a man on the other side of the road, for appearance's sake, but Wales is still precariously at peace, and for the moment, the Welsh are far stricter about letting English troublemakers in than vice versa. Bone fide refugees are being channelled to the south, across the Severn Bridge.) Jory's recognised as the head of the Shantih Foundation, and is reasonably assured of safe passage, but since the Welsh Assembly's loyal to the Arthurian cause he's arranged for fake ID for Laney, on the offchance that the Circle's looking for her.

They drive north for hours, along mountain roads that Jory instinctively thinks of as treacherous but which the local drivers who constantly roar past them in annoyance clearly consider routine. There are a couple of times when he's aware of another car, a red Vauxhall Astra in the distance behind them which is coincidentally following the same route they are, but he doesn't notice any reaction from Laney. She's tense and shivery, chain-smoking through the window and insisting on stopping at a tiny village along the route to replenish her cigarette supply. She speaks very little, although she does give Jory a vivid account of how things went down in Nottingham.

They set out at lunchtime, and it's nearly sunset by the time they pull up outside the Wendimans' holiday chalet with its sea view. Merry hurries out to welcome them, gives Jory a perfunctory kiss, then puts her arm round Laney and ushers her inside. 'I was so sorry to hear about Paul,' she says, and Jory remembers, in slight surprise, that they can't have seen each other since that frantic week in July when everything changed.

'Dad's playing golf,' she explains minutes later, as she supplies them both with more tea. 'Well, since the light's going, I suppose he'll be in the bar by now. He's been making friends there – he's got a cover story he maintains. I think he tells them I'm his live-in help, but he's always vague about the details so half of them probably think I'm sleeping with him.'

She bustles about, making them supper: Jory insists on helping, but then so does Laney, and the tiny kitchen becomes so crowded she orders them to go and sit down again. Jory roots in Edward's drinks cabinet for sherry and pours them all a generous aperitif.

Edward turns up just as Malory's dishing up the spaghetti with pesto and olives – vegan pesto, she explains, because she wasn't sure what Laney ate these days. 'Pretty much anything, to be honest,' is Laney's reaction, and she certainly wolfs down the pasta dish.

Edward is, as Malory predicted, somewhat tipsy and characteristically jovial. He tells a complicated story about some faux pas for which someone at the club is being ostracised, which entails explaining some of the more esoteric rules of golf, an imposition which Laney bears with patience. After dinner she lights a cigarette, and seems surprised and mildly bewildered when Malory asks her to take it outside.

When she comes back in, she's all business. 'So, can I see it then? The Grail?'

Jory painstakingly doesn't glance over at the old tea-chest that's being used as a picturesque maritime coffee-table. The Wendimans also keep their gazes carefully level. 'That's up to Malory and Edward,' he says.

'Not tonight, I think,' Merry says. 'I'm knackered. We'll talk about it in the morning, if that's OK. There'll be a lot of logistics to sort out if you're going to get it and Paul together, a lot of safeguards. I can't deal with that tonight. Is that OK?'

Laney nods. 'Sure,' she says.

'We've only got the two bedrooms, I'm afraid,' says Edward. 'These two get the double bed, of course, but you're welcome to mine. The sofa in here's good and long.'

'Oh no, Dr Wendiman, I couldn't turn you out of your room,' Laney insists, looking keenly around the room. 'I'll sleep in here. Like you say, it's a huge sofa.'

'Well,' Edward says reluctantly. They bicker about it for a bit, but in the end Laney insists that she wouldn't sleep knowing that she'd deprived an old man of his bed, and that she'd far rather sleep in the living room, with the TV and the comfortable sofa and the tea-chest to use as a bedside table.

And so the matter's decided.

* * *

When they get up, horrifically early the next morning, to insistent knocking on the door, to nobody's surprise at all, Laney has vanished, and the tea-chest's empty.

'She scarpered ten minutes ago, at oh-five-thirty,' Stephen Mukherjee informs them breezily. 'Took your Mini, Taylor, I'm afraid.'

Scar leans out of the window of the red Vauxhall Astra that's waiting outside. 'Kinsey's following the wee robbing bastard. If we hurry we can catch them up.'

('They're all in position,' Edward reported after dinner last night, as soon as Laney and her cigarette were out of earshot. 'Chief Inspector Kinsey asked me to let you know that if you've brought her here chasing fairies she'll pull your scrotum off and feed your testicles to the seagulls. That woman has quite a way with imagery.'

'I'll have to take the risk,' Jory sighed.)

Jory dashes back into the chalet and unzips the golf bag he brought in from the car last night. Inside are his Knight's sword and the bow he used at Nutwood, along with a new box of fibreglass hunting arrows. He dithers for a moment about which to take. If he's facing an enemy from the Arthurian cycle, a sword might be de rigueur, but he's out of practice these days. He'd trust himself more with the bow, but it's useless close-up and... *Sod it. Defer the decision.*

Putting both weapons back in the bag, he zips it up and dumps it in the Astra's boot.

'Kinsey's keeping us abreast,' Stephen tells him as he clambers into the back seat next to Malory. 'They're on the coast road, heading west for some reason. Bit of a poser who she could be meeting that way. Unless she takes the Holyhead ferry to Dublin.'

'She won't take the Grail out of Britain,' Merry declares, punctiliously securing her seatbelt. 'Unless I've drastically underestimated the Children of Oisín's dislike of us, whoever's stirring up this war will have a homegrown device.'

'Why this way, then?' Scar asks. 'Why no back into England, where the action is?'

'She's meeting her employer,' Jory reminds her. 'Presumably they want her to hand the Grail over somewhere out of the way.'

'Or maybe wherever it is has some significance,' Malory muses. 'There are plenty of Arthurian sites between here and Anglesey.'

Laney dumps the Mini outside Llanfairfechan, where she hitches a lift. 'Blue Toyota hatchback, Irish plates,' Kinsey reports over the phone. 'Looked like a random pickup. Man and woman, white, early twenties, baby in the back. I'm guessing they're heading for the ferry, at least.'

Laney jumps ship at Bangor services. She has breakfast at the Little Chef, where Kinsey watches her carefully, even following her into the ladies to make sure she doesn't leave the Grail there to be collected. Even in plain clothes it's tricky for the Chief Inspector to stay inconspicuous at such an early time in the morning, with the place all but deserted, and Laney will know her now if she sees her again. She doesn't seem particularly suspicious, but she's clearly nervous, glancing continually at the car park and smoking like a chimney. Since she knows everyone in the Astra by sight, they park up round the back of the petrol station and buy breakfast at the Travelodge while Kinsey updates them by text.

After breakfast, Laney hangs around in the car park, casually chatting to anyone who looks young and approachable, until she's cadged a lift with a couple of Swedish tourists from the motel. Wales is still untouched by the war, and despite the warnings of their embassies a lot of tourists here are still finishing holidays before heading home.

The Swedes, like Laney, are wearing stout walking boots. They have to shift their heavy rucksacks so she can sit in the back.

Kinsey gives them five minutes' headstart, and Jory's party give Kinsey another five. The last thing they want is to catch up with Laney and tip her off.

As they drive, Malory's scrolling through screen after screen of notes on her laptop. 'Mount Snowdon,' she mutters. 'AKA Eryri, Yr Wuddfa Fawr, Mount Arvaius or Aravia, Mount Erith. Let's see... Arthur defeated a lake monster there, the Llyn Barfog afanc. There's an Arthur's Cliff and an Arthur's Lake, although the names are in Welsh, of course. The prophecies of Merlin talk about an eagle nesting there, but as that comes right after a bit about lion-cubs turning into saltwater fish we'll probably be wanting to discount that. Some sources say Vortigern built a tower here, probably meaning the hill-fort on the southern slopes called Dinas Emrys. Some local legends say that Arthur died on the mountain, but local legends always say that sort of thing...

Oh,' she says, sounding dismayed suddenly. 'Of course. It was also where an old friend of yours lived, Jory – Retho of Arvaius.'

The car's warm with four people in it and the heating turned up against the morning chill, but Jory shivers even so. 'Retho?' he says.

Retho of Arvaius was the rogue device borne by James Ribbens the Beard Collector. A ferocious giant who got his kicks from killing kings and stitching a cloak out of their beards, Retho was killed by Arthur after demanding that the High King hand over his facial hair. Jory beheaded the serial killer more than two years ago in a suburban back garden – but that, of course, means that the device has had two years of freedom in which to find another host.

'Really?' he says. 'Could Retho have provoked a national civil war? It's hardly his modus operandi.'

Malory considers. 'It all depends which iteration of the device we're dealing with,' she says. 'In later legend, Retho became King Ryons of Norgales, and *he* was involved in a lengthy war against King Leondegrance, Guinevere's father. I have to admit this seems a bit subtle for him, though.'

It's soon clear that the Swedes are heading for Llanberis, the foot of the easiest ascent up the mountain, and also of the lower terminus of the Snowdon Mountain Railway. The first train leaves at nine, half an hour's time, and Laney seems happy to wait, despite being pressed in hearty Scandinavian accents to join in an ascent of the mountain by foot.

Scar parks the Astra in the car park provided for climbers, thankfully out of view of the train station, and they confer – Kinsey, who's still keeping an eye on their quarry, joining in by phone.

'It's simple as fuck,' Kinsey insists. 'I make contact, tell her she'll do time for burglary if she doesn't co-operate, then send her up the hill to meet whoever's there – only we go on the train with her. We get to the top, she makes the meet – whether that's at the summit or somewhere else on the mountain – then we swoop in and apprehend the fuck out of both of them.'

'Too risky,' Malory insists. 'She might find a way to warn whoever it is. We can't risk ending up with just Laney – we need her contact, even if that isn't her boss.'

'What's your alternative, then?' Kinsey asks. 'Those trains have a single carriage. They get pushed up this thing by Thomas the fucking Tank Engine. We can't get on without her recognising us. She knows you all, and after the Little Chef she'll get spooked if she sees even me.'

Jory leans forward. 'Kinsey, you say the engine *pushes* the carriages up? Can you describe it?'

'Yeah.' Kinsey sounds puzzled. 'May not actually be steam, I can't see a funnel. But it's old, so same design. Long bit with all the wheels and workings, cabin at the back with room for – oh fuck, yes. I see what you mean.'

Jory gives an enormous, boyish grin. 'You know what? I always wanted to ride with the driver in one of those.'

* * *

There isn't room for all of them, of course. After a somewhat heated argument – because Stephen, inevitably, was also a vintage train enthusiast as a kid – they agree that Kinsey will have a word with the railway company, and commandeer space in the driver's cab for her, Jory, Malory, and Jory's golf bag. Stephen will stay here and keep watch, while Scar takes the Astra round to the base of the second most popular path down from the summit, in case Laney somehow gives them all the slip and heads down that way.

Jory, Kinsey and Malory wait until Laney and a sparse few tourists are safely ensconced in the carriage, then pile into the cab. This engine's a diesel in fact, though apparently there's a steam train that also runs on the line, so rather to Jory's disappointment it can be driven by just the one man. The Welshman's seethingly furious at having his cab invaded by the English, and doesn't say a word to them all journey, though he comes close to physical violence when Jory keeps asking him what all the dials and levers do.

At the upper terminus, the three of them get out the other side from the tourists, and watch carefully as Laney disembarks. The train runs very nearly to the summit itself, stopping just before it reaches the visitors' centre, which is built into a little hollow just behind the arrowhead of the peak. It's a sunny September day, the morning light glinting on the crystal-blue lakes, and although there's a keen wind up here, the mountains surrounding them are heartstoppingly beautiful.

Laney looks around herself carefully, failing to spot her three observers skulking now between the engine and the carriage, pats the canvas shoulder-bag in which – they all heartily hope – she's still carrying the Nestine-Gull Grail, then sets off along the ridge away from the lake beneath.

A figure's waiting there for her, at the head of a path that veers off steeply to the left and down a lower ridge. He's small, and nattily dressed in pricey-looking mountain gear including climbing-boots, calf-length socks and a stout rucksack. He's wearing tinted glasses, which he takes off, breathes on daintily and wipes on a handkerchief before replacing on his nose.

'Oh shit,' says Jory. He nips back to the cab where he left his bag.

'He must have hiked up from Dinas Emrys,' Malory tells Kinsey, peering at an ordnance survey map purloined from tourist information in Llanberis. 'I think that's down that way.'

'Which one was Dinas Emrys?' the Chief Inspector asks.

'Where King Vortigern built his tower,' says Malory. 'The site turned out to have a dragon problem. He had to get Merlin in to help him with it.'

'Okay,' snaps Kinsey as Jory returns with his sword. 'So what am I bloody missing?'

'That man used to work for the Circle,' Jory tells her. 'His name's Mr Lister. I don't think I ever knew his first name.'

387

'It's Lester, actually,' says Malory. 'I don't think he likes using it much.'

* * *

They watch while Laney and Mr Lister confer quietly, Laney with some very expressive gestures. Jory guesses she's asking him why the hell, of all the places on the British mainland, they had to meet up here. Lister's own body language is as precise and controlled as ever.

He must have wanted revenge, Jory supposes. Revenge on the Circle for sacking him, revenge on Burn for making it happen, revenge on Merlin for being the good wizard when he as Maugantius' bondsman is stuck being the wicked one. He's certainly found an extreme way to exact it, but that's the devices for you. Assuming that the war claims many of the present crop of device-bearers, Jory supposes Lister's banking on becoming a mentor to whatever blighted post-war generation is left rebuilding the ruins – once this era's Merlin is conveniently imprisoned (whatever form that takes this time) and out of the way.

'How long do we wait?' he mutters, already knowing the answer. They have to be certain Lister's here in order to receive the Grail.

Eventually, the little man reaches behind him and unstraps his rucksack. Laney reciprocates, unshouldering her canvas bag and unzipping it.

As she does so, Lister takes a careful look around – a leisurely sweep of the mountaintop, taking in the view, nothing shifty or nervous about it.

He's obviously more observant than Laney, though, or perhaps just less befuddled by nicotine, because as his eyes rake past the train a tiny frown blemishes his brow.

He looks again, his eyes widening.

'Shit!' Kinsey says. 'He's made us!' And she's clambering over the coupling between the engine and the carriage, charging in Lister's direction and hollering 'Police! Nobody move!'

Jory's after her instantly, sword in hand. Malory follows them a moment later.

Lister shoves Laney over with his left hand as he bends to scoop up the canvas bag with his right. He pulls the zip shut as he turns away, and shoulders it as he runs like hell.

Kinsey elbows her way past a couple of indignant climbers, bellowing 'Police! Clear the way!' Jory's on her heels, and soon overtakes her – Kinsey's tenacious, but she's a short woman and doesn't have his length of stride. Malory leaves them to it for the moment and helps the dazed Laney to her feet, enlisting the climbers' help to restrain her.

Lister isn't a tall man either, but he's trim, and obviously keeps himself more active than you might expect. His lightness is a useful quality in a pursuit like this, giving him some fleetness of foot. What's more, he came prepared: his climbing-boots are a lot surer on the ridge than Jory's Doc Martens.

Still, moving at speed on a mountaintop is best attempted, if it must be at all, by fellrunners and similar insane people who do this kind of dangerous thing routinely for the challenge – and even then there must be a pretty high casualty rate. (I'm guessing, anyway. I don't have the figures or anything.)

What's more, Mr Lister has chosen to flee the way he came – and the Watkin Path, which leads from Llyn Dinas up to the summit, is strictly ascent-only. The higher reaches, in particular, are infested with sharp rocks and scree, and idiotically steep slopes. Lister's only gone a few paces before he realises this, but by then Jory's on his heels and they're both committed. The ex-advisor leaps and clambers and slides lithely along, using his smaller weight, his grip and his familiarity with the path to his advantage. As he runs, Jory feels like a rhino trying to follow a mountain-goat, and knows this can't end well.

Then Lister cries out and stumbles, a dark shaft protruding from his thigh.

Instinctively Jory glances back, to see Malory nocking a second arrow into the bow he brought. When he looks back again, Lister has disappeared from view.

Jory races ahead to where the disgraced advisor was, then peers down. He's slid on some scree, ten metres or so down the mountainside towards the lake beneath them.

(Its name's Llyn Du'r Arddu, incidentally, which either means 'Black Bear Lake' or 'Arthur's Lake', depending on who you ask.)

Jory hurtles to an unsteady halt and stares down as Lister staggers to his feet again. He tries to pull the arrow out of his thigh, then yelps with pain. He takes a couple of stumbling steps along the level, but his leg gives away beneath him and once again he tumbles. This time, his momentum takes him to a cliff edge.

Lister grabs at the ground as he slides to a stop, but it's disintegrating into scree beneath his hands.

Jory begins to clamber down to him, but he's clearly never going to get there in time.

Lister gives a high-pitched scream as his situation asserts its impossibility. He falls much further this time, and this time he doesn't get up.

* * *

It takes a while for the mountain rescue team to reach the crippled climber, and much longer for them to get him safely onto a stretcher back up to the visitors' centre. A helicopter's been called for a medevac, but Mr Lister's neck was broken in the fall, and no-one's holding out much hope for his survival. That he's currently alive at all, let alone conscious, is nothing short of a miracle, though not an inexplicable one if you're aware of the devices and their capabilities.

Malory's relieved to see the rescuers have also retrieved Laney's canvas bag, which she quickly confirms contains the Grail. By insisting that he's a material witness in a case involving hundreds of deaths so far, Kinsey succeeds in getting the three of them a few minutes with Lister as he awaits his own.

One of the rescuers is muttering darkly about jurisdiction, even so. There's a lot of pro-independence feeling among the Welsh these days, and it's a fair bet that the North Wales Police are going to take a keen interest in that arrow-wound.

'You bastard,' Kinsey tells Lister by way of greeting. 'If you weren't about to croak, you'd be so fucking nicked.'

'That's not helpful, Jade,' Malory tells her gently, and to Jory's surprise the terrier of the law backs off a little. He realises she must be terrified of all of this – of death, of the devices, of this suspect who her unofficial colleagues insist is some kind of evil wizard. At this point in her career she has a clearer idea than most of the undeviced public about what the allies can accomplish, but she must still wonder what their limits are. Could this man heal himself? Come back from the dead? Pull off some kind of telefantasy mind-swap and walk away in Kinsey's body, leaving her inhabiting the wreckage on the stretcher?

Jory is confident that Lister can do none of these things. The man's mortally hurt, and even for someone with a device as powerful as his, that means he's going to die.

Laney's already confessed – if confession is really the word for her outraged defiance – that Lister recruited her at her parents' house, a few days after he was sacked. He promised her revenge for her best friend's murder, through ruining the man who killed her – Paul Parsons, who she's spent the past year getting close to, deceiving him into loving her so she could prepare him more thoroughly for Lister's curse of insanity. Later, she acted as his eyes and ears within the Chapel, supporting David's position there even as Lister, using the identity of one of the women at the Modron Dobunna Centre, fed Blaze the information he needed to set up Jason as the opposing contender.

'Are you in a lot of pain?' Jory asks Lister. He doesn't know what he wants the answer to be.

Lister smiles, an echo of his prissy smirk of old. His voice is weak, but supercilious as ever, as he croaks, 'I can't feel anything beneath my chin, as it happens. Although I will admit to a dreadful headache.'

'What did you think you were doing?' Jory asks, as gently as he can manage. 'Corrupting that poor girl, making her complicit in so many deaths...'

'Corrupting?' Lister wheezes, but his lungs can't manage a laugh. 'Oh, she was *quite* the eager beaver, Taylor. Positively zealous, in fact.'

'And the deaths you've caused?' Jory insists. 'You've started a war, Lister. People are dying, right now. I only hope they stop the killing when we tell them how they've been manipulated.'

'Oh no, I don't think that's very likely.' Lister wants to crow, Jory can tell, but his voice won't manage more than a whisper. 'I'm afraid it's far too late for that now. It's been a very *efficient* plan, if I do say so myself. It would have worked perfectly, if only my device had been less... vainglorious. All I needed to do was to survive...'

His eyelids are beginning to flutter now. He hasn't got long left, Jory can tell. Then they snap open again, and he says, in a stronger voice, 'I suppose you realise this is only the beginning of your troubles, Taylor? Your young friend Blaze isn't the only one who can make extrapolatory prophecies, you know. If you think I've caused you trouble, just wait... until Morgan le Fay... makes herself known...'

Jory forces himself to be brutal. 'Just tell me one thing, Lister, before you – go. The Circle only sacked you because they got a new Merlin to replace the old one – but you'd coexisted happily with the old one, for a while at least. You cursed Paul Parsons to keep Laney sweet – and to hurt the Circle, of course, but that was after they'd already sacked you. What I still don't understand is – why did you curse Edward Wendiman?'

And this time, despite everything, Lister does laugh – a horrid, barking cough that brings blood with it. 'You think *I*... did that?' he splutters. 'No, Taylor, no. You'll have to... look a little... *closer to home*... for that one... I'm... afraid.'

And with a final, blood-bespattered chuckle, Mr Lister breathes his last.

III
THE ADDER'S BITE

21. 'LONG LIVE ROBIN HOOD!'

And so at length, after the Battle of Trafalgar and the Siege of Jerusalem, we come to the Stonehenge Summit.

The rival armies of the claimants are camped in fields to the north and south of the Stonehenge Visitor Centre. The stone circle itself lies a fair way off to the east, guarded by a carefully vetted private security company who report directly to English Heritage.

To the south, beyond the closed A303, Circle flags – because, averse though the Knights are to corporate logos, it turns out you just can't fight a proper civil war without a flag – flap from a dozen flagpoles, interspersed with banners bearing the arms of individual Knights. The emblem's a simple gold ring on a blue background: the colours of the Pendragon's own banner, awaiting the form his device will impose once it's confirmed. (Despite what some Chapel supporters claim, it doesn't look very much like the Eye of Sauron.)

Beneath the flags stand British army bivouac tents, mobile command centres, field hospitals, tanks, armoured vehicles and artillery platforms. In fields beyond the camp, troop-carrying helicopters stand uneasy, still, awaiting the slightest excuse to whirl their rotors into action.

Just as far to the north – and you can bet the distances have been precisely measured – stands the Green Chapel camp, a motlier affair, though its bright colours lack gaiety on this wintry, grey morning. Lincoln-green banners flutter in the early wind, above a chaos of tents, marquees, pavilions, yurts, tepees, caravans and mobile homes, surrounded by a looser cloud of cars, vans and minibuses.

Here, too, are armoured vehicles, but where the Circle's units are standardised, these have an eclectic, scavenged, sometimes homemade feel: captured tanks and armoured cars in varying states of repair sit next to flatbed trucks and trailers with machine guns welded to them, jury-rigged rocket launchers, even a ragged battery of working cannon liberated from castles and museums across the country.

At the prearranged time, a flare goes up from the Visitor Centre, and the armies approach.

The Knights lead the Circle forces: rank upon rank of them now, mounted on their armoured horses, their own outfits gleaming dully in the early-morning light. Their swords are, for the moment, sheathed. Their shields are every colour of the heraldic palette: sun gold, grass green, sky blue, night black, bone white, blood red, exposed-muscle purple. Their numbers have been inflated beyond all precedent by every device the Fastness has been able to invoke: names like Sir Petipase, Sir Servause le Breuse, Sir Ozanna le Cure Hardy, even the unlucky Sirs Balin and Balan, all pressed into service for the first time in centuries.

Somewhere in their ranks, too, are a new Bors, a new Gaheris, a new Colgrevance; even a cross-speckled purple riot-shield denoting a new Sir Percival. (Despite their best efforts, though, the Circle's been short a Sir Gareth since that British Boar crushed Frazer Daughtery at Nutwood.) Conspicuous by their absence are Palamedes' chequerboard, Lancelot's triple red bar, Galahad's red cross and Gawain's golden pentacle: the devices of the three deserters and of poor, mad Paul Parsons remain tantalisingly beyond use.

Behind them, squires follow, and pages, and men-at-arms numbering in their thousands now, their combat fatigues the colour of their tents, their guns holstered, their faces grim and wan.

At the head of the Knights rides Sir Charles Raymond himself, the keys on his shield boasting of a solution to this mess that the Circle really doesn't have. Flanking him on their own horses are Jason Smith, the rumoured Pendragon-in-waiting – still a squire for now, his unmarked shield a grey absence among his followers' bright emblems – and Bernard 'Blaze' Maddox, riding awkwardly in a loose-fitting purple suit, unarmed but for his steel staff and his dragon-sigil ring. To their left and right are the shields of Sir Ector and Sir Lionel, still carried by Theo Harte and Doug Felton.

Advancing from the north, the Chapel armies come not in regimented ranks but in loose columns: the marching of militant protestors, not of career military. At our heads march the allies not yet stolen from us.

Our lineup's changed since the start of the war. On the right, Rev and Ron are joined by Shell, the new ally of David of Doncaster, and by daughter of Carlisle Janene Long, whose quickness in picking a side is explained by her Adam Bell fixation rapidly transferring itself to Little John after Big Jack Bennett's death. They're followed by their respective gangs of supporters: the Friars, the Millers, the Donnies and the Quarterstaffs. On the left come the Saracens, the White Hands, the Blands and the Bards, led by Zara, Lee, Ahmed and – much though I'm less than euphoric about the fact – me.

At our flanks come less familiar comrades-in-arms, with their own followers: Janene's mate Keith, who's taken over Adam Bell's mantle from her, and a quiet but well-read Green Chapel stalwart called Kim, who's unexpectedly been picked as an ally by Right-Hitting Brand, a Merry Man so obscure none of the rest of us had even heard of him.

It's a respectable team formation. Still, if ever we could have done with Will Scarlet, Maid Marian and, above all, Robin Hood to stand with us, it would have been today.

For the most part we have no uniform beyond a shared preference for green, and carry as many types of armament and armour as our troops have the resources and imagination to assemble or create. In the middle, though, ride our best weapons against the Circle: the Black Knights. David Stafford, the Lionheart, still bearing his own black shield, leads a whole phalanx of cavalry, decked out in armour freed from a Circle weapons depot and painted an oily black. They ride coal-black horses (and where they're not completely black, they've been touched them up with shoe polish, the psychological effect being what's important here).

These men and women form the Chapel's own, very new chivalric order. Many of them were Chapel people who knew horses well enough to be trained to ride and fight at the same time, but others – and since all the riders carry the same sable shield, it's impossible to tell which – bear the devices of the various sinister Black Knights from Arthurian legend, the time for their revenge come round at last. (I'm told that even Jory's old adversary the Black Knight of the Black Lands rides with us, having absconded single-footed from the Benwick Institute and kitted himself out with a prosthetic leg.)

The opposing armies – we – halt two hundred metres either side of the Visitor Centre, gazing at one another past that weirdly primitive structure. Though built from steel, zinc and glass, and the size of an out-of-town supermarket, it looks more like a skin canopy held up by sticks than anything constructed in the twenty-first century. Beneath this roof, two boxy structures stand, while between them a passageway guarded by a ticket office grants access to the stones.

Beneath that giant metal woodlouse, the welcoming party awaits us.

There's the politician who I guess must still be the Home Secretary, surrounded by scared-looking advisors and protection officers, doing her level best to look important even though she has no part to play here. A small deployment of UN peacekeepers is in attendance, a stern reminder of what might be imposed on us if a truce continues to elude us today. Accompanying them is a knot of observers from foreign devicial orders, including the Founding Frontiersmen as well as various European fraternities. English Heritage have sent their chief exec, backed up by a handful of the private security force. A detachment of infantry represent the loyalist remnant of the British Army, who still maintain a token presence on Salisbury Plain. A squad of Scots Guards are here on behalf of still-neutral Scotland, while a troupe of Household Cavalry represents the Crown, whose ancient ties with the Circle were severed months ago.

And then there's the Shantih Foundation, our hosts here. Kinsey and some of her police, tarted up in their rarely-seen dress uniforms. And various deserters from the Chapel and the Circle.

(All in all, a targeted nuclear strike at this point could pretty much wipe out the organised devicial structures of Great Britain, leaving us open to any order of foreign devices that felt like wandering in and taking over the place. We have to hope nobody's thought of this, or in a decade, our kids could be serving the avatars of Baba Yaga and Koschei the Deathless.)

A tannoy system's been set up, and Jory Taylor's voice booms out, 'On behalf of the Shantih Foundation, I'd like to welcome you all to Stonehenge. We're very grateful to you for coming. Let's hope we can achieve something today.' He sounds tired. 'Please send your representatives forward, as agreed.'

The leaders approach on foot, each accompanied by four lieutenants.

David, Rev, Zara, Lee and Janene are met by Stephen Mukherjee, dressed in his armour and the shield he's still entitled to as Sir Palamedes' device-bearer – the only one of the three Circle runaways who still wears it. 'Stafford, old man,' he says informally, shaking David's hand. 'Glad you could make it.'

'Stephen,' David nods back. 'It's good to see you. I wish the circumstances were better.' He still limps a little from the wound he got at Nottingham.

'Don't we all,' Stephen agrees with feeling.

Marianne 'Scar' Millar, who wears her scarlet hoodie, greets Sir Charles, Jason, Blaze, Harte and Felton. She doesn't acknowledge either of the Chapel turncoats. 'Seneschal,' she says instead, with small effort to disguise her contempt for the title. 'Thanks for being here.'

'Let's just get on with it, shall we?' Raymond replies, tight-lipped. Jory spent some time pondering whether the old man would be more antagonised to be welcomed by Scar (once upon a time a prisoner of the Circle, before she humiliated them by escaping) or the deserter Mukherjee, before concluding that under the circumstances Sir Charles would probably take offence at being met by the Pope.

'Come this way, then,' Scar replies shortly, and conveys them into exhibition hall of the Visitor Centre, just as Stephen brings in the Chapel party.

Jory Taylor's waiting for them in the plain circular antechamber whose screens, if this attraction were open, would be displaying a continuous loop of the evolution of the monument. Behind him in the main museum area stands a circle of chairs. His sombre pinstripe suit is augmented by a green tie with a gold pentacle tie-pin, and a radio-mike.

The Chair of the Shantih Foundation clears his throat echoingly, then realises the mike's still on and switches it off.

'I expect,' he says more quietly, 'you're all wondering why I called you here.'

* * *

It may seem strange given their patchwork histories, but the Salisbury Plain summit is the first time the claimants – or 'pretenders', as each is often disparagingly called by the other side – from the Chapel and the Circle have actually met.

It's taken a long time for Jory's people to arrange it. With Mr Lister unavailable to testify following his timely demise, proving conclusively that the War of the Devices has been a callous scam on a previously unprecedented scale hasn't been easy. Kinsey's report of the ex-advisor's confession bore weight with the secular authorities, but not with the combatants, and both sides have cause to mistrust Laney's word. Diligent digging by the police has, however, turned up evidence of some of Lister's most significant activities – his embezzlement from the Circle, his relationship with the Saxon Shield, his arrangement with Ibrahim Al-Khuzaie and the identity theft he perpetrated on one of the Nine Witches of Gloucester.

The shape of the narrative is clear enough and ties with Jory's account of how both sides have been duped... but even so, as Lister himself predicted, the war's so far advanced and has become so acrimonious that the simple revelation of his intervention wasn't enough to bring everybody to their senses. To many of us, it no longer matters how it started.

I'll not go into all the history – time enough for that in the decades to come, when entire libraries of data and paper will be devoted to it. The Battle of New Malden, the Harrying of the North, Operation Domesday – every one of them has left its scar on the psyche of the nation, and in extreme cases its geography as well. (Certainly the Cerne Abbas Giant isn't looking so pleased with himself these days.) The Chapel's campaign of lightning assaults and subsequent disappearances, of assassinations and highly-targeted asset damage, has served them well, but the Circle's logistical superiority has been taking its toll. Symbolic and historic buildings from Winchester Great Hall to the London Guildhall have exploded or gone up in flames, but as often as not there's been retribution, in the form of violent raids against dissidents in the Circle heartlands and resistance fighters in their occupied cities.

People – many people, most of whom know very little of the internecine interplay between Britain's deep-seated mythic archetypes, and couldn't care less about which side is responsible – have been killed in the crossfire, maimed or wounded by the bombs or shelling, seen their partners or children die or lost them in the bustle of the border checkpoints where the refugee columns enter Scotland, been burned out of their homes or starved out of their towns and cities, died from infection or collapsing buildings or the malevolence of opportunist gangs. In war, it's never the heroes who suffer the worst, whatever they may invite you to think.

The propaganda war's been subtler, with both sides attributing war crimes to each other. Atrocities have happened, it's true – more often than not at the hands of the gangs or ill-chosen allies rather than the principals, but both our libraries of stories have their bloodier aspects, and there've been atavistic reversions by individual device-bearers to the kinds of legend where Sir Balin thinks nothing of decapitating a woman who's harmed his family, or Much of beheading a pageboy to make sure he doesn't inform on them.

There's a lot more severing of heads in Britain these days than we've been used to, it has to be said.

Perhaps sensing a trend her French relatives might have found familiar, even the Queen's abandoned the capital – reluctantly I should imagine, given that the Blitz couldn't shift her father, but wisely enough, given her age. Rumour places her in seclusion in Balmoral, with plans to evacuate to Gibraltar if Scotland, like Wales, succumbs to the fighting.

Where can Britain go from here? It's probably not much of a surprise that the one constant among the country's shifting borders and allegiances over the past months has been an increasing groundswell of support for the Shantih Foundation, the one homegrown body who are beginning to look like they might conceivably put an end to the carnage.

Which is – as everyone knows, despite Jory's awkward joke – why we're here today. The Stonehenge Summit's meant to thrash our differences out once and for all, under the watchful eyes of all our dedicated followers. I know that Rev's been pressing David for weeks to accept whatever terms Jory has in mind: despite his fire and fury, Cantrell's an empathic bloke at heart, and his stomach for bloodshed has long since turned. David, though, is eager to press further and harder against the Circle, and believes that the Black Knights are the final weapon we need to achieve that.

I suspect – rightly, it'll turn out – that a similar debate's been going on at the Circle. Blaze can't help but feel for his old comrades in the Chapel, but Sir Charles is an old warhorse, and stubborn like a mule. The harder they try to persuade him to consider Jory's terms, the harder he'll set his heart against it. He thinks, like David, that this whole thing is a waste of time, but like David he has to go along with it for show.

Frankly, we wouldn't be here at all if it wasn't for the Grail.

* * *

The Visitor Centre is a ten-minute walk from the stones themselves, and it's not until the final approach that the delegates can see the pair of mismatched figures standing in the centre of the old stone circle.

Stonehenge is unquestionably a well-chosen location. Older by far than either legend, it nonetheless has associations with both Robin and Arthur: Merlin's rumoured to have raised the stones, and one of the many Neolithic earthworks littering the neighbourhood is called Robin Hood's Ball. It's Britain's most ancient and one of its most potent symbols – and of course, as many of us in the inner echelons of the Circle and Chapel know, it was the impact point of the prehistoric blow whose aftershock's now shattering the country like a stained-glass map.

It's an ancient place of worship, and a fortress: a ring of stones on the green plain. A circle that's also a chapel.

Tall and massively immobile, the sarsens with their bluestone lintels stand guard around the inner horseshoe of megaliths and trilithons, an oppressive weight embodying the inertia against which today's efforts can barely strain. On either side of the central so-called Altar Stone (actually a megalith which fell over at some point during the past few

404

thousand years) stand Malory and Edward Wendiman, the keepers of the Grail. Edward – who before his illness was, in his spare time, the high priest of some eccentric neopagan cult – is wearing white druidic robes. Malory's in jeans and a T-shirt, with a baggy cardie. Their tents flap in the wind a little way to the east, respectfully outside the henge's bank-and-ditch enclosure.

Between them, on the Altar Stone, an object stands. It's covered by a green-and-white-checked tablecloth, but is clearly the size and shape of the transfixed Grail.

In the distance behind them, beyond the tumuli and plantations which litter the plain, the assembled armies can be seen, dark masses hugging the ground like poisonous fog. (The plan isn't for them to stand to attention for the entire duration of the peace talks, of course. At a point when due ceremony's felt to have been observed, they'll be sent back to wait at the camps.)

Jory approaches, flanked by three delegates from each side. (It should have been one, but Sir Charles insisted that he and Blaze had to accompany Jason, so David's brought Rev and Janene along for parity.) It will be interesting, Jory thinks, to see how each of them responds when that tablecloth's whipped away. The object underneath – or more precisely, the symbolism it's generally agreed to be imbued with – still has power to strike awe into the hearts of those with devices of their own.

For his part, Jory learned to live with the Grail long ago. The internal voice which sang to him from the vessel was always Malory's, and he's closed his ears to that voice now.

No device, Jory knows, has ever made its host do the impossible. They don't bring supernatural or sci-fi powers; they can only help us make more of our natural abilities. He can't see any reason to believe that what Malory calls semi-autonomous culturally-inflected archetypal memeplexes are autonomous at all: on the contrary, there's plenty of evidence that they only exist in people's heads.

And… well, there's a word for that.

The devices, Jory would tell us now if any of us felt like asking, are nothing more than a vast shared delusion. Malory told him years ago now that from a Jungian psychoanalytical point of view, alliance with a device counts as a neurosis. During the past months, Jory – who over the years has identified with archetypes corresponding to Jung's Solar Hero, Shadow and Trickster – has come to believe fervently in that analysis.

We – the Circle and the Chapel and the British Beasts; the Gormund Boys and Sons of Gore and Paladins and Frontiersmen; all our equivalents in every culture and all our predecessors back through the millennia, since, perhaps, the dawn of human consciousness – are suffering, he'd say, from a massive and pandemic mental illness. We've convinced first ourselves and one another, then our children and descendants, and now at last our entire civilisation, that the voices we hear in our heads are those of the heroes of old, when in fact they're just that: voices in our heads.

For much of Jory's life, he's invested his identity in different kinds of faith: in God, the Circle, the Chapel, the devices, latterly in Malory. Like many Anglicans, he's found his Christianity sorely tested lately by the actions of the Circle and the Chapel. Likewise, he now believes that the devices are a delusion, with all the destructive characteristics Dawkins' disciples ascribe to religion.

And Malory…

* * *

'What did you do?' he asked her, all those months ago in that other Visitors' Centre, the one atop Mount Snowdon, as he turned away from Lester Lister's broken corpse. A chill had come upon him, creeping in from his extremities and up his back, leaving a numbness behind it. 'What did you do?' he repeated.

She'd heard everything Lister said, of course, as had Jade Kinsey: their whole exchange. The question he'd asked, and the answer Lister had offered. Kinsey looked pissed off with the world in general, as usual, but also faintly bothered. Malory looked as pale as a Victorian consumptive.

'Jory, I –' she said.

'You heard what Lister said,' Jory stated for the record. 'He was dying. There was no reason for him to lie. He didn't curse your dad, he said. Someone else did that. Someone closer to home.'

Malory was silent.

'He meant you, Mal,' Jory insisted brutally. 'You're the only person he could have meant.'

Kinsey was out of her depth, but she knew what people were supposed to say in this sort of situation. 'Drop it, Taylor,' she told him. 'He was fucking with your head, that's all. Stirring shit up –'

'He wasn't,' Malory whispered, and Kinsey went abruptly quiet.

Jory knew he should have been aflame with righteous anger, but instead he felt a cool and logical sense of vindication, a pleased awareness that all those times when he'd fretted about betrayal, a fear which seemed so absurd and paranoid at the time, he'd actually been perfectly rational and correct.

'Is that why you shot Lister?' he asked. 'Were you afraid of what he'd tell me?'

'Of course not,' Malory said quickly. 'I wanted to stop him running. If you'd chased him down that path, you could have been killed. I just wanted to stop him – I didn't know he'd fall so far.'

'She shot his leg, Taylor,' Kinsey reminded him firmly. 'She could have aimed for something a fuck of a lot more vital.'

Except of course, Jory seethed coldly, *that if she shot to kill I could hardly have missed it. This way she can claim she never meant for him to fall.*

'And Edward?' he asked. 'Did you cripple your father's mind just to protect me?'

Malory took a deep, deep breath, then raised her eyes to his and kept them there. 'I did, actually. To protect us both, in fact.

'When I visited you at the Green Chapel camp,' she said, 'when Shaf was holding you prisoner there – my cover story was that I was attending a conference in Newcastle. When you were reported missing, Dad tried to contact me at the university, to check I was OK, and when they told him they hadn't seen me, he got worried. I spun him a tale later about staying with a friend nearby, instead of on campus – but he knows me well, and he's not an easy man to fool.

'When the Circle rescued you,' she went on, 'and found the remains of the Chapel camp at Kielder forest, he put two and two together. He dug into things a bit more, and... well, you know how clever he is. And at the time he was *Merlin*.'

'He found out about you, and you silenced him,' Jory said harshly. 'It sounds like that's becoming a habit.'

Malory flinched. 'It was the single worst thing I've ever done, Jory. If Dad had told the Circle about me – and he'd have had to, he knew where his duty lay – it would have ruined him as well as me. And yes, you too, because they would have had to assume you were compromised. Even so, I didn't mean for what happened to happen. I panicked, I had a moment of blind confusion, and in that moment my device... followed its story. Remember when you beheaded Shaun Hobson, Jory, because that's what Sir Gawain does to the Green Knight? Well, the Lady of the Lake imprisons Merlin. It's one of her plot functions.'

Jory nodded slowly. 'And then, after the Circle knew all about you, he was no danger to you any more. So you kidnapped him and reversed it.'

Malory's throat made something between a gasp and a sob. 'Jory, I was *desperate* to reverse it. Can you imagine how it felt, seeing Dad in that state and knowing it was all my fault?'

'And *all that time*,' snapped Jory savagely, 'you lied to me. Every time we talked about it, you were lying. You told me it was Lister who cursed him.'

408

She seemed older now, her shoulders stooped. 'I *knew* —' she began. She took a breath. 'I'd made a mistake. I was putting it right. Dad knew what I'd done, but I'm his daughter. I knew he'd forgive me. But you…'

'*Me?*' Jory wasn't sure what she was accusing him of, but he was damn sure he wasn't going to let it pass. 'What did I do?'

'Jory,' she told him, 'you're a good person. An altruistic person. Not someone who can tolerate wickedness. So I knew damn well you'd react like this. I knew you'd judge me. And… I couldn't bear that.'

'Too right I'd judge you,' Jory replied, clamping down viciously on everything inside him that urged him not to do that, that he of all people – thief, traitor, deserter, serial decapitator – had no right to judge anyone. 'Your father may forgive you,' he said, feeling the dull inevitability of the cliché even as it passed his lips, 'but I can't.'

Malory bit her lip, shook her head, gave a quick sigh. 'I know.' Her eyes were wet in the bright morning sunlight.

She turned and walked quickly to the door.

'Malory,' Jory called as she reached it. 'Malory!' he said again, sharply.

She stopped but didn't turn.

'Are *you* Morgan le Fay?' he asked her.

She kept her back to him. 'Fuck you, Jory,' she said, and left.

* * *

The last time I was happy, he thinks now, as Malory looks up at him and the approaching combatants with sombre eyes, *was when I was riding that damn train.*

* * *

Back in the exhibition hall, the rest of the delegates are hanging awkwardly around, waiting for the sightseeing group to come back. This is supposed to be just a quick glance at the Grail, a viewing in situ to demonstrate that Jory's made good on his promise to bring it here, so it can be available – assuming all the necessary preliminaries can be talked through, arrangements agreed and conditions set – for the two candidates for the Headship to, in the fullness of time, test themselves against it.

If we ever reach that point, we're looking at three possibilities.

One: David turns out to be, through a miracle of devicial mutation, the Pendragon. If that happens, there's a realistic chance that most of the Circle will feel constrained, in view of Blaze's prophecy, to accept that judgement and submit to him – thus ending the war, for now at least.

Two: Jason passes the test instead. This would seriously compromise David's credibility, with a knock-on effect on his standing in the Chapel forces, possibly (though not definitely) weakening us, and making us perhaps more amenable to proper peace talks.

Three: neither candidate will be able to withdraw the arrow from the Grail, in which case Shantih's rather optimistic hope would seem to be that everyone will give up fighting and go home to wait for the real Pendragon. Whether that would actually happen is profoundly dubious, of course.

It's pretty uncertain all round, but the principle – that a mutual test, assuming both parties can be persuaded to agree to such a thing, stands a good chance of reducing the nation's overall suffering – is probably logically sound.

Meanwhile, though, we wait.

Harte and Felton are huddled by themselves in the museum area, peering forlornly at display cases of flint tools and midden-bones. Scar's tried to make small talk with them, but it's not really part of her core skill set, focussed as that tends to be on hitting stuff. Instead she's over with Stephen, Zara and Lee, comparing war stories. (Behind them there's a wall of quotes about Stonehenge from such luminaries as Hardy, Pepys and Siegfried Sassoon. Sir Lionel Nestine-

Gull's view that 'This circle of Stonehenge was Merlin's master-work, through the which he hath shaped the minds and memories of England's yeomanry,' sits next to a quote from *This Is Spinal Tap*.)

Lee's telling them all about the Battle of Skegness, and the escape to the boats across the mined beach, when old Brian, Will Stuteley's ally, steps inside and beckons earnestly to Stephen. After a moment's conferring the renegade Knight looks alarmed and says 'I say, are you sure? Where?'

He hurries back over and says, 'Scar, old girl, I'm frightfully sorry, but you'd best take it from here. Something rather urgent's come up.'

He leaves abruptly, heading for the Circle lines.

Lee's about to go on with his story when he realises he's been left alone with Zara and Scar, between whom there's been something of an atmosphere since their arrival here. Lee's a sensitive chap – with, apparently, a previously unsuspected interest in Neolithic archaeology – so wanders off to look at the displays.

A long, awkward pause between the women ensues.

Eventually Scar says, 'How've you been?'

Zara is immediately scornful. 'There is a war on, Scar. How do you think I've been?'

'Well, you're no dead,' Scar observes. 'All your bits are still attached. Puts you ahead of some I could mention.'

'I could too,' says Zara shortly. 'Even some who are still fighting.'

There's a pause. Then Scar says quietly, 'I'm still fighting, Za.'

'Not for us,' her ex replies contemptuously.

'Aye for you,' snaps Scar. 'For every fucker, no just one side or the other. We're trying to stop you reckless wankers killing each other and everyone else.'

'Oh.' Zara's flat voice is laden with sarcasm. 'So you betrayed us all just to protect me? I didn't realise. I am touched, Scar, really.'

'You daft cow.' Scar's voice is as tender as it ever gets.

411

"Course I did. You already lived through one war, you poor sod — why the fuck'd you want to go through all of that again? No bastard should have to do that. I'm trying to end this stupid thing for *you*.'

'Oh, so you are trying to end it,' Zara snaps. 'You and those men. Jordan Taylor, who has betrayed both sides. That old fool Brian. That Knight who has forgotten even how to be foreign here.'

Scar sighs. 'There's women too. Kinsey and Merry. Aye, Zara, Merry, remember her? You would've walked barefoot on glass for her, back before all this.'

'That was then,' says Zara. 'Merry betrayed us too.' She cocks her head suddenly, then turns to Scar, eyes narrowing. 'Scar, did you hear that?'

Scar's face is grim. 'Aye,' she says. 'Some prick's shooting a bloody gun.'

* * *

A few minutes ago, when the group with Jory had nearly reached the Altar Stone, Malory stepped forward.

'Welcome,' she said. 'It's good to see you all.' Avoiding Jory's eye, she smiled at both parties equally. 'How have you all been?'

There was some shuffling, and a muttered 'Get on with it' from the Seneschal. Only Janene Long saw fit to answer properly.

'Doing well, thanks. Yourself?' she said, a faint undercurrent of mockery in her tone. The newly allied members of the Chapel don't have the same respect for Merry we all had in the old days, and there's always been that bit of chemistry between Janene and Jory.

'Forgive the theatrics,' Jory said, taking charge. 'We felt a bit of ceremony was called for under the circumstances. Not too much, obviously.' He toyed for a moment with a joke about pagan rituals, perhaps about how in wartime everyone has to make sacrifices, but rejected it as potentially offensive

412

to both the Christians and neo-pagans present. 'Malory,' he asked stiffly, 'would you do the honours?'

Merry stepped forward and lifted the cloth up reverently, allowing everyone present to see that the relic was indeed the Nestine-Gull Grail transfixed by Shafiq's arrow, and not an orange in a coffee-mug with a breadknife stuck through it.

Jory could feel the others, Knights and ex-Knights especially, suppressing the urge to kneel and revere the relic. Jory himself had had plenty of practice by now, and the Merlin device grants Blaze a certain coolness around sacred artefacts, but Raymond was rusty, and quivered slightly as he inclined his head in respect.

Out of the corner of his eye, Jory saw David flinch at the sight of the cup and visibly steel himself. He supposed it was possible his fellow errant had never seen the Grail before – the Circle used to keep it locked away in a museum, after all, and David was in Iraq when it was used at Nutwood – but it suggested a stronger reaction than he'd been expecting.

Rev looked respectful, of course, but not terrifically impressed. Janene said, 'That thing again?' but subsided when nudged.

Intriguingly, to the other side of Jory, Jason was making much the same effort as David, only with slightly less success.

'You're satisfied,' asked Jory, 'that this is indeed the Nestine-Gull Grail, pierced by the arrow I fired, and that the prophecy Blaze made at Nutwood, which he's repeated quite a lot of times since then, relates to it? Hang on,' he adds now, holding up a hand as Sir Charles starts to speak. 'Be quiet a sec, Seneschal. Sorry, but... do the rest of you hear that?'

They all turn to stare west, towards the massed ranks of the Circle troops.

* * *

Five minutes ago Stephen was hurrying across the Visitor Centre car park, towards the Circle lines. 'Are you sure?' he asked Brian again.

Brian, who'd collected an iPad from another of the Shantih Foundation people at the door, showed him the photo on the screen. 'That him?' he asked.

'Damnation,' Stephen groaned. 'Thank you, Brian, yes, that's the bugger. Where is he now?'

Brian gestured helplessly towards the tens of thousands of men standing ahead of them in formal ranks.

Stephen snatched the tablet and looked again. It was a still from a video by a Shantih volunteer of the Circle's advance, recorded for posterity and general publicity purposes. (There's an absolute bar on media here today, domestic or international.) Another had been taken simultaneously of the approaching Green Chapel forces, of course, as agreed beforehand: nobody was doing anything here which hadn't been laid out in minute detail in the prior arrangements.

…Well, except for running the video through Scotland Yard's facial-recognition software, to identify known members of any rogue devicial groups who might have wanted to disrupt the proceedings. That had been Jory's idea, and it wasn't something either of the combatant factions would have been terribly happy about.

It had been a jolly good thought though, Stephen now realised. The men-at-arms were wearing the visors up on their British army GS Mk7 helmets, so the visible face looked exactly as it had in the photos Stephen had spent so many hours staring at.

Only the snake's head on the crash helmet was missing.

Reaching the Circle ranks, Stephen had a quick word with Ross Cornish, the new bondsman of Sir Percival, who'd been left in command in the absence of the five summit delegates – then plunged through, beyond the Knights and squires, into the rows of men-at-arms. Being visibly a Knight, he found the rank and file parting before him in habitual deference, although his device (and indeed his face) were well known as that of an errant.

As he hurried deeper into the body of the Circle army, Stephen consulted the video again. Based on where and when it had been taken, and Mark Addis' position in the marching column, he could pinpoint roughly where the man should have ended up. He shoved his way through closely-packed bodies, elbowing them aside now with rough impatience.

Enlisting with the men-at-arms would have presented Addis with very few barriers – plenty of men were doing it, and the Fastness needed all the warm bodies it could get. Adze had been a soldier before he was a convict. Under the circumstances, a lax sergeant-at-arms might well gloss over a criminal record if it meant gaining an experienced man.

If Adze was here, though, it wasn't to fight loyally for the Circle. Nor, despite his association with the late Jack Bennett, did Stephen think he was here as a fifth columnist for the Chapel. Mark Addis got his kicks from chaos, violence and vandalism. He'd dropped entirely off Stephen's radar these past months, but this war would have seen him in his element. Stephen's best guess now was that he was here to see that it continued.

An army relies on co-ordinated discipline, especially when required to stand about the place and do nothing while its leaders sit and chat. One man defying that discipline, breaking rank and causing deliberate confusion among his own side, could create untold disruption. Such a man might start a war – or prolong one.

Stephen thought he must be nearing the position now where Adze would be standing. It occurred to him suddenly that the disruption to the army's order that he himself represented might well be tipping the biker off that he was approaching.

As he ploughed through that solid mass of armoured humanity, a hand caught his arm. Stephen tried angrily to shrug it off and press ahead, but then a soft voice hissed in his ear, 'Yeah, you'll do. My little boy has nightmares about you, you Paki shit.'

Stephen heard the sound of a standard-issue SIG P226 being discharged close to his face, but by then he was diving for the floor, and the shot merely glanced the side of his headgear. In his confusion the glimpse he'd had of Adze's face was overlaid by the adder he remembered from the biker's crash helmet.

Desperately Stephen rolled, crushing the iPad, and struggled to bring his shield out from under him. The men around Adze were reacting, but too slowly to prevent the man from firing again, hitting Stephen in the shoulder, then the neck. The third bullet found the vulnerable point between helmet and gorget, and pain tore through the muscle tissue there. Urgently Stephen tried to raise his hand to staunch the bleeding, but he couldn't feel his limbs any more and had no idea whether he'd succeeded.

* * *

Now Adze struggles between a dozen other squaddies, his gun dropped, his arms raised. The Circle's rules of combat will not allow them to kill him now he's surrendered, although they'll give him a bloody good kicking.

Others are kneeling at Stephen's side. 'Medic!' one of them shouts. 'We've got a Knight down!'

The shock of this announcement, following on from the gunshots, spreads through the ranks.

'Fuck the Circle!' Adze yells. 'I'd've killed the bloody lot of you if I'd had the chance! You'll never have peace so long as the Green Chapel's still going! Up with the Merry Men! Go Sherwood! Long live Robin Hood!'

22. 'HAIL THE HIGH KING!'

The sound of the gunshot and the cry of alarm quickly reach the nearest division of Knights, and particularly the field commander in charge of this battalion of troops.

And this is where... well, put it this way. There's no hierarchy as such among the Knights – that was the entire point of the Round Table, after all. It's actually a paradoxically egalitarian organisation, provided your idea of equality is to exempt your top echelon of officers from the pecking-order everyone else is subject to. Unfortunately, it means there's no clear way to reward merit, either.

Of course the most prominent, best-known devices – Lancelot, Gawain, Percival, Galahad, Bors, Kay, even Mordred when he's around and still on the Circle's side – tend to get entrusted with the more difficult missions. But those particular devices are, you may have noticed, in short supply at this point in the War – that's why the young and relatively untried Ross Cornish has been left commanding an army. After that, positions of trust tend to be allocated by seniority – which means the oldest Knights get them, regardless of ability. And nobody, of course, expected a decision made by this one field commander among many to turn out to be the crucial one.

So it's actually to the Circle's credit... in a sense... that the nearest commander to the place where Stephen happens to be shot is Desmond Wigsby, bondsman of Sir Dagonet the jester, and the Knight with the single worst judgement of any human being in the Circle (and probably about half the horses).

True to form, the Knight whom Wigsby sends galloping to investigate is his most inexperienced colleague, Chris Timms, the new young bondsman of Sir Aglavale. Eighteen years old and a page when the War began, Timms has risen quickly in the Circle's wartime structure, and was invested as Aglavale's new device-bearer a slightly indecent five days after his predecessor's death at Newbury. Today's his first encounter with the enemy as a Knight, and he's opted for gung-ho as the only feasible alternative to shit-scared.

Timms charges back into the ranks of men-at-arms, confirms perfunctorily that there's a Knight down, shot by a filthy traitor shouting Green Chapel slogans, and gallops away as the field medics arrive. Stephen's black-and-white riot-shield fell face-down when he collapsed, and Timms (who should, perhaps, avoid a peacetime career as crime scene investigator) doesn't think to ask who the fallen Knight is or what he was doing so far back in the ranks.

'Betrayed, by God!' Wigsby shouts when he imparts the news, then looks reproachful when Timms doesn't reply, 'No, by the Green Chapel!' Wigsby's voice is as plummy as the brandy he's been sampling from his hip-flask while they wait here. 'Well, we won't stand for that, will we lads?'

Several of his fellow Knights chorus an obedient 'No!' Others look dubious. One who's nearer his own age says, 'Look, Desmond, we should get on to Cornish about this…,' but Wigsby shouts him down.

'Nonsense! He'll follow our lead quickly enough once he sees what's what. Here Timbo, you ride and give him the news,' he tells Timms. Like all the other commanders, Wigsby has a field radio, but in the excitement of the moment he forgets the fact. 'Tell him we must act – quickly!'

Timms stares at him, then gallops off down the lines towards Ross Cornish.

Wigsby beams expectantly at his fellow Knights. 'I said, we must act – quickly!' They stare blankly at him. 'Oh, really, aren't any of you going to say, "Yes, we must go over the top!"?'

There are frowns and clearings of throats from the mounted men.

'Honestly,' Wigsby expostulates at last, as his field radio begins to squeal, 'I'm surrounded by amateurs.' Then, with a mighty yell of 'Charge!' he draws his sword, and does.

A moment later, the stunned Knights under his command gallop after him, with a dozen squires and thousand or so squires and men-at-arms scrambling to follow.

* * *

There's chaos at the stones.

'They're attacking!' Sir Charles cries as the distant roar goes up from the Circle forces. 'What do those idiots think they're doing?'

'You conniving old bastard!' Janene's shouting. 'You've been bloody planning this!' She grabs the old man by his lapels, but he punches her hard in the stomach and they go down fighting. The Seneschal's kept himself in trim physically in a way he's never managed mentally, and the two are better matched than anybody would have suspected.

David is already pelting back towards the Visitor Centre, with Jason at his heels.

'Well, this is fucked,' says Blaze bitterly. Far away, the Chapel forces are reacting to the oncoming mass of Circle troops with panic and increasing quantities of gunfire. The rest of the Circle forces are organising themselves for a more disciplined assault.

Rev groans. 'This was our last chance, guys. Somebody's blown it.'

'It's the twilight scenario,' says Edward. 'We told you it was a risk, Jory.' Janene and the Seneschal have rolled between two fallen bluestone pillars and are expressing their understandable frustrations with the situation through the medium of personal violence.

But Jory's staring at the Grail. He remembers a time when it sang in his mind, enjoining him to pledge his faith to God, Arthur and the Circle – and how he struggled with that faith when disobeying its commands.

'The only thing that keeps that arrow in there's our belief in the devices,' he says, thoughtfully reaching for the checked tablecloth. 'You told me so yourself, Malory.'

These days the cup is silent to him, inert and lifeless.

Rev's looking at him with a wild speculation. So, after the moment it takes him to cotton on, is Blaze.

Jory says, 'Could someone who didn't believe in them pull it out, then?'

'Jory, I hardly think –' Malory begins.

But Blaze and Rev are, for once, ahead of her. 'Sure,' one says, and 'I reckon so,' replies the other.

Jory gathers up the relic in the tablecloth as Malory insists, 'The last thing we need's a *third* Pendragon claimant.' Ignoring her, he sets off at a run towards the Visitor Centre. Cantrell and Blaze size one another up for a moment, then go haring in his wake.

'That's never going to work,' says Malory. 'Is it?'

Edward puts an arm around her shoulders. 'I don't think we get a vote, my dear. Come on, let's separate Sir Charles and Miss Long before they start getting romantic.'

* * *

Stephen's bullet-wound isn't life-threatening, as it turns out, but the annoyance he's causing the field medic who's trying to dress it for him may be.

'I thought he was the Questing Beast,' he explains to the man, as another orderly pulls off Stephen's gauntlet to give him a morphine shot. 'It was the spotted flanks and the yellow haunches. You can't really paint hooves on a motorcycle.'

'Try not to talk, sir,' the medic admonishes him. Around them, feet are rushing off in the direction of the Chapel lines, while away in the further distance, hoofbeats and bloodcurdling yells can be heard.

'But that was just the bike, you see,' says Stephen. 'Take that away, and all you have left is the helmet.'

'This really would be a lot easier if you kept quiet,' the medic repeats, his deference to Stephen's rank beginning to wear thin now.

The morphine roils into Stephen's bloodstream, and he subsides with a murmur of 'It's the adder. He was the adder all along...'

'Yes, sir. Sure you're right, sir,' replies the medic wearily.

* * *

But Stephen is, in fact, right. Just by dismounting from his Norton, Adze has stepped from one page of the Arthurian bestiary onto another.

Camlann was Arthur's final battle. There, the two sides facing one another were the knights still loyal to the High King – the ones who remained after the feud with Lancelot over Guinevere – and the rebels led by his bastard son, the usurper Mordred. But Arthur – and according to Sir Thomas Malory, he was advised on this point by the ghost of none other than our old chum Sir Gawain – decided that it might be politic to reach some kind of accommodation instead of everybody killing each other quite so much. And so the leaders of the armies sat down to talk.

You might think, perhaps, that Mordred would never have gone for it – and maybe you're right. Perhaps he'd not have stuck to any bargain that was struck that day. But after a while, by all accounts the negotiations were going swimmingly, with Mordred agreeing to rule Cornwall and Kent as king in his own right while Arthur ruled the rest of the British lands, and nobody demanding custody of the Isle of Wight.

While they were parleying, though, one of the knights in their armies – and it doesn't even matter which side he was on – got bitten by a snake.

TH White, latecomer to the party that he is, makes it a harmless grass-snake which the knight only *thinks* means to bite him, which adds some extra irony. But in nearly every reputable version of the Camlann story, it's the other snake that's native to Britain. You know, the mildly venomous one.

You can guess the rest, I'm sure, even if you don't already know it by heart. The knight draws his sword to kill the adder, someone spots the glinting blade and shouts 'Treachery!' and alarums and excursions ensue. Battle is joined, nearly everyone's killed, including Mordred, and – barring alleged supernatural intervention – Arthur, and Britain's plunged back into the Dark Ages. It's 'For want of a nail, the kingdom was lost,' with the kingdom being the entire stable social order, and the nail a modicum of basic common sense.

It's Stephen's dimming view, as the world recedes from him, that the field medic doesn't fully appreciate the relevance of this.

* * *

The Chapel understand battle tactics better these days than ever before. You can't hold out for long against an armoured cavalry charge unless you have an unlimited supply of armour-piercing ammunition, which isn't exactly easy to come by. Ron's company of Millers, who lie directly ahead of Wigsby's charging troupe, melt away before them as they approach, the individuals rushing for safer ground, mostly into the columns of Friars and Staffs to left and right.

This leaves the Knights exposed to what's already approaching from their right flank – Stafford's Black Knights, responding admirably to the situation in the absence of their commander. Neochivalric they may be, but the Black Knights have developed their own code of honour rather than borrowing the Circle's antiquated notions – and the submachine-guns they carry *are* loaded with AP rounds. Ahead of them, the Knights and their mounts start collapsing bloodily as the projectiles burst through their carapaces. Desmond Wigsby executes a particularly amusing pratfall, with his legs in the air, before being trampled horrifically to death by the panicked steeds of the Knights following him.

The Black Knights can't be everywhere at once, though, and within minutes other companies of Knights on horseback are approaching the Chapel lines, the Chapel people doing their best to defend themselves with conventional bullets and our patent burning or exploding arrows. At the Visitor Centre – now looking very much like a focal point in the chaos – the combat-trained security guards and soldiers are forming a defensive cordon round the exhibition centre, the regular army, UN, Scots and Crown loyalists quickly overcoming their differences in viewpoint in the face of the immediate threat.

Inside, Harte, Felton, Lee, Zara and – rather to everyone's surprise – Scar are all clamouring to be let out to join in the battle, but Kinsey's people have them restrained. The Home Secretary's shouting indignantly, but whether she's demanding a helicopter out of here or an escort to the loo, nobody has the leisure to find out.

It's beginning to look like this will be the final battle – in a war whose victor, if there even is one, won't be left with much of Britain to enjoy.

* * *

As the running figures on the plain come into view, riders head out to meet them. The two claimants are heading, sensibly enough, for their own respective sides, so shortly a Black Knight's surrendering his horse to David, while Jason's being hoisted up behind the young bondsman of Sir Kainus the Strange, and the two are riding back towards their own forces.

Behind them come Rev Cantrell, Blaze and Jory, who's hoping the jostling doesn't shake the arrow out of the Grail before they get there. Ahead of them, the battle surges back and forth, but so far it hasn't spread this side of the Visitor Centre. A lone Knight of the Circle does reach them and offers Blaze a ride back to their lines, but Blaze commandeers his horse and sends him running back to their armies.

Jory mounts the horse and gallops for the Centre, clutching the Grail to his chest, while the wise man and the holy man follow at their own pace.

Seeing him approach and recognising the Chair of the Shantih Foundation, the Scots Guard part to let him through. Their own horses skitter in consternation as he continues his charge past the small cluster of replica Neolithic houses, through the central passage and out the other side to face the focus of the mêlèe, rather to the surprise of the Household Cavalry waiting there.

Still mounted on the horse, in front of the Visitor Centre between the café's outside seating and the cash machines, Jory holds the Grail aloft and bellows, 'Stop fighting, you absolute and total cretins!'

Nobody hears him, of course, but then he turns the radio mike on and repeats it, without the 'cretins' part. Meanwhile, the Grail's having its usual effect.

The fighting dies down in a growing semicircle, spreading out from Jory's position on the forecourt. Nobody lowers their guard, but the focus of their attention shifts and, as they warily realise that their opponents are watching too, they allow their current life-or-death struggle to pause for a moment.

I won't say that nobody on our side – who are generally less susceptible to the Grail, not to mention less prone to take their cue from their leaders – slips a surreptitious knife in while the Circle forces are distracted. You can't really stop that sort of thing. But it's quickly apparent to all of us that something bigger's going on. So intense is the anticipation, in fact, that even the unallied – who are by far the majority of everybody on the Plain – begin to feel the holy terror that the Grail's always so spuriously induced in the Knights of the Circle.

Jory waves the Grail around, the checked tablecloth draped incongruously over his left shoulder, and yells, *'This ends today!'*

This causes terrible distortion on the tannoy, but the reaction it gets seems for the moment to bear Jory out. Swords and guns and bows are lowered, horses shushed, eyes wide. A feeling of whispered suspense radiates across the Plain, much further than his actual words can carry.

More quietly, Jory declares, '"Whoever pulls out this arrow from this cup is the rightful High King of Britain!" Isn't that the prophecy? And since it seems we can't be trusted to govern ourselves sensibly without one, perhaps it's about bloody time we had one again! Perhaps this, finally today, is the time of Britain's greatest need!'

Behind him, Blaze and Rev Cantrell have arrived, let through in their turn by the Scots, and now come panting to stand on either side of his mount. Jory glances at them for a moment, then unclips his mike and passes it down to Cantrell.

'But who's it gonna be, huh?' the scrawny man asks the crowd in general as Jory climbs down from his horse, then pats and whispers to it gratefully. 'You know we Green Chapel folk aren't ever going to accept a Circle squire as our head guy.'

'Yeah, and the Knights might put up with David Stafford at first,' says Blaze, taking the mike in turn, 'but they wouldn't like it. Chapelist, errant *and* gay? That's worse than having a black Merlin.'

'Before long he'd have a rebellion on his hands,' Rev agrees. 'Just like Jason Smith would from our side.'

'But it ain't our decision,' Blaze says. 'It's the Grail that decides.' He cuts the mike.

A susurrus of awed whispers begins to spread, in Chapel as well as Circle mouths, as Jory grasps the cup firmly in one hand, the silver arrow in the other. The bondsman of Merlin puts a hand on his left shoulder, the ally of Friar Tuck does the same on his right, and Jory mutters, 'I'm going to look a right prat now if this doesn't happen.' Then he pulls.

The silver arrow slips cleanly out of its woody socket, as smoothly as sliding a book from a shelf.

* * *

We all experience it – Circle and Green Chapel, deviced and unallied alike. It's like being pounced upon and wrestled to the ground by lightning. Like being mugged by a tsunami.

Before our eyes, Jordan Taylor's appearance has changed... well, not in the least actually, but far more radically, the *meaning* of it has. Where previously we looked at this well-built, square-jawed blond man in his early thirties and saw a well-known public figure, the Chair of the Shantih Foundation, an ex-Knight of the Circle and one-time Green Chapel activist standing beneath the zinc and steel canopy; now the same man in the same well-tailored pinstripe suit is...

...our High King. Our liege lord. The Head of the Circle, the King of the Britons, the once and future King. The lord of Camelot, the hunter of Twrch Trwyth, the victor of Caerleon and Badon and Saussy. Son to King Uther, husband to Queen Guinevere, friend to Sir Lancelot du Lac, uncle to Prince Gawain of Orkney, brother to Morgan le Fay, father to Sir Mordred; and – according to TH White, if no-one else – the one-time comrade of 'Robin Wood', Maid Marian and Little John.

He's become, not to put to fine a point on it, King Arthur bloody Pendragon. The greatest hero of the nation of Britain, and by orders of magnitude its most powerful device. If we thought Merlin was the bees' knees before, it was only because we'd never met his protégé.

It's more than that, though, if we look closely. Like a dress whose colour accentuates a woman's eyes – or a man's,

I'm not prejudiced – the figure's King Arthurness somehow highlights something that was there already, but which we'd come to overlook: his Robin Hoodness. You'd expect the Pendragon to drown out any other devices, but Robin's still there, flickering in the quirk of his mouth, the laughter in his eyes: the champion of the poor, the righter of injustices, the man who humbles tyrannical lords. *This* monarch can be all of that, as well.

The High King lifts up the Holy Grail in his left hand, the Silver Arrow in his right. The Knights who are still seated dismount, and across the plains of Salisbury, fifty thousand men and women kneel together as if we'd rehearsed it. On the forecourt, Rev Cantrell and Blaze do likewise.

I see Kinsey bending the knee too, and Scar and Zara, and Lee. The thought of rebelling against *this* King – the thought that he, like anyone else claiming authority over us, might be political anathema – doesn't enter our heads for a moment. The Green Chapel, like the Circle, are literally enthralled.

'It is my will,' the High King declaims in a voice which – though, yes, exactly the same as it was before – is redolent of the authority conferred upon Arthur long ago by God, 'that there be peace among my people.' At some point, he's reacquired the radio mike, but Blaze's sleight of hand was smooth enough that not a person present noticed it happening.

Shame creeps through the crowded masses like a blush: dismay and misery that we've let down our ruler – and our people, our country – in such a terrible way.

'Where,' asks the Pendragon, 'is Jason Smith? And where is David Stafford?'

In their position, I'd have been sorely tempted to ride south as fast as my horse could carry me and get the first available ferry to Cherbourg, but instead both walk forward, heads bowed, and stand silently before their King.

He gazes severely at the men who so recently aspired to his status, and says, 'They say that Richard the Lionheart refused to bow before the Holy Roman Emperor, claiming that he was born to a rank which recognised no superior but God. Will you refuse to bow before me, David?'

'No, my lord,' David replies, and kneels.

'Then, old friend,' the High King says, 'you shall bear the device of the Lionheart no more, but once again shall be my faithful Knight, Sir Galahad.'

The change which comes over David then is minuscule compared with what we saw in Jory a moment before, but everyone's attention is on him and it's clear enough to all of us that what the Pendragon has decreed is now true. There's a collective gasp.

The King confers with a Household Cavalryman for a moment, and is handed the man's ceremonial sabre.

'And Jason,' says the High King, and at once Squig falls to his knees. 'You came to the Circle a kitchen-boy and have risen to the rank of squire, the squire to Sir Kay's device-bearer. Do you still believe that this entitles you to a position of kingship?' He hefts the sword.

Squig's visibly trembling. He squeaks, 'No-my-lord.'

'Then,' the Pendragon tells Jason, gently touching the blade to each of his shoulders in turn, 'I name you for what you are: Sir Gareth, also known as Beaumains, the kitchen-boy, who came to Camelot incognito so that he would not benefit from his brother Gawain's renown, and who became a knight on his merits alone. Will you accept this name, Jason?'

Jason gulps and nods gratefully. This time there's no change as such. It's as if this is what he's always been, and the High King's words have merely revealed a truth that was already there.

The King returns the sabre as the new Knight stands, then dismisses the pretenders. He calls over his shoulder, 'Janene Long, ally of Little John; Charles Raymond, bondsman of Sir Kay – you may approach too.'

Dishevelled and bloody, Janene and the Seneschal come through the Visitor Centre passage to where the Pendragon stands, then turn to face him.

'Charles,' the High King says, 'I know how you've longed for this day.' And indeed, there are tears pouring down the old man's cheeks as he kneels – tears of relief, and guilt, and most of all a nakedly adoring love for the figure standing glorious before him. 'Your longing has driven you to do terrible things.'

Raymond clears his throat, but still his voice is a croak as he replies, 'I accept my responsibility for them all, my lord.'

There is a long pause, then the Pendragon says, 'I forgive you for what you have done, Charles.' Raymond rises, and the King embraces him. 'You will no longer serve as Seneschal of the Circle, but you leave with no disgrace, no blot on your name, and anyone who states otherwise will answer to me. I wish you a peaceful and contented retirement.'

The ex-Seneschal nods, whispers, 'Thank you, my lord,' and steps back to join the crowd.

'Janene,' says the High King. 'The Green Chapel, like the Lionheart, believed themselves answerable to none but God. In that you were sincere and idealistic, and I will not blame you. You have not seen my new device before today, but you – like your late predecessor, Jack Bennett – know that I am also the ally of Robin Hood.' We all see the look that's exchanged between Janene and Rev.

'Five thousand years ago,' says the Pendragon, 'the primal device of the Undying King was split, on these very plains. The Wounded King, who would one day become the High King Arthur, went one way, and the Green Man, who would become the outlaw Robin Hood, went the other. This nation has suffered terribly from their sundering. In me, today, the two are once again united. Will you embrace me, Janene – as your Green Knight, and as your High King?'

There's a hush – for this, surely, is the crucial question. Whatever Rev Cantrell may think about the matter, it's Janene, as Little John's ally, who speaks for the Merry Men here – just as John once spoke for his own band when Robin offered them the opportunity to join their forces.

Janene says, 'Aye then, let's get it done with,' and hurls her arms round him, giving him a big, full kiss on the lips.

There's riotous laughter, more because of the tension breaking than because anyone finds this particularly funny. In truth, I think we're all relieved to hear anyone say something other than 'Yes, my lord,' or 'No, my lord.' Enchanted we may be, but it's clear we still have free will. We haven't been turned into a nation of zombies.

The High King laughs heartily, though there's something furtive in his expression for a moment. Most people aren't in a position to see it, but where I'm standing, I can see the Wendimans, Merry and Edward, waiting at the other end of the passage through the Visitor Centre.

When the Pendragon's laughter subsides, he tells us all, 'We are at peace, then. Go back to your camps. Shortly we will summon the media here, and I will address the nation. There will be a great deal to discuss, and roles for many of you. For now, I need to prepare. Go all of you, my people, with my blessing.'

A beat, and then someone shouts, 'Hail the High King!'

And the crowd respond with 'Hail the High King! Hail the High King! Hail the High King!' in unison.

He turns, and walks inside the building, still carrying the grail and arrow.

* * *

The only people not kneeling during all of this have been the UN delegation. They can sense this new device's power – nobody present could fail to – but they aren't British, and the serene authority of this new figure doesn't cover them. Politeness and respect are called for, certainly, but actual obeisance will have to wait until the High King's status as head of state is confirmed.

'Holy shit,' declares Agent Frank Mallucci, the Founding Frontiersman who's specifically the agent of the legendary pioneer Daniel Boone. 'That was one hell of a show. These

Brits sure like their deference, huh?' The observer from the Nibelungentreue nods shortly.

'It's a turn-up, right enough,' Dermot Healey observes more quietly to Marie-Odile Laclos. Whereas Mallucci's in a double-breasted suit of the kind associated with US government agencies, as a show of respect for the day's solemnity both Fiann and Paladin are wearing the ceremonial armour of their respective orders.

'Not just for the British,' Laclos says, nodding grimly.

'He'll be an interesting neighbour, that's for sure,' Healey agrees.

'He may want to be more than that,' says Laclos. 'King Arthur was not just the ruler of Great Britain, you know? The kings of Ireland and Brittany were also his subjects.'

Healey takes that in. 'Feck,' he says. 'We'll be needing to talk to our presidents, then.'

* * *

Inside the Visitor Centre gift shop, Jory Taylor sags and leans against a counter. 'Jesus Christ,' he whispers, having made very carefully sure the mike's off this time. 'Jesus christing Christ.'

'We'd have been forgiven for getting that impression, yes,' says Malory Wendiman from the doorway. '*Needlessly messianic* doesn't even begin to cover it. You know what you've done, don't you?'

Jory nods, his exhaustion painfully visible. 'That was just the start. I have to keep this up now.'

'For the rest of your life, if this is going to work,' Malory says. 'And heaven only knows what happens after that. If we're lucky, you'll act as a kind of reboot for the nation's psyche, and we can go back to normal once you're dead. If not… well, you've delayed the Dark Ages for a while, I suppose. How long, though? How long do you think you can live under the pressure to perform like *that* all the time?'

Jory sweeps away a display of 'Stonehenge Rocks' T-shirts, and sits down heavily. 'I won't need to. The devices act more intensely at first, isn't that the theory? I can dial it back a bit over the next couple of months.'

'Even so, Jory,' she says. 'You'll be the head of state. There's a reason why the Queen – or do I mean the ex-Queen now? – reigns but doesn't rule, you know. There's a reason why prime ministers and presidents serve fixed terms.'

'I'll make arrangements,' Jory says. 'I'll work out how to keep things together after I die.'

'Best make it a priority,' says Malory. 'You could be assassinated tomorrow.'

There's a pause, as they both remember how much that prospect would once have meant to her.

'Honestly, Jory,' she bursts out, 'what were you *thinking?* What is this to you, a gigantic con trick? You don't even believe in the devices any more, do you?'

Jory shakes his head slowly. 'Honestly, no. I mean... the whole idea's just ludicrous, isn't it? I mean, when you think about it. Honestly, it doesn't stand up to common sense.'

Malory shouts, 'That is the most –,' then holds her head tightly for a moment. 'People say that,' she resumes, her voice measured and controlled, 'about evolution and climate change. *Stupid* people, Jory. Just because you can't understand all the details of a scientific theory, that doesn't mean it's nonsense.'

'I know the *idea* of the devices affects reality,' Jory protests, 'but only because it affects *people*. Did it matter to Paul whether Laney was "carrying the device" of Elaine of Corbenic, or whether she was just acting like her? I mean... the stories are useful. Genuinely inspiring. Posing as the king... that's the sort of thing Robin Hood might have tried to get away with. But still...'

Malory snaps, 'None of this is really about the devices, though, is it? You know everything you did about them before – why change your mind? No, this is all because of you and me. You've rejected me, so now you feel you have to reject my work as well. That's incredibly childish, Jory.'

He sighs. 'Don't psychoanalyse me now, Mal. I'm done with all of that. I'm going to need your help with other stuff now. You and Edward, as well as Blaze and Rev and Kinsey and the others. Together, we're going to need to run this country, and that includes managing this daft pseudo-science of yours.'

'Gracefully put,' pouts Malory. 'And the answer's no. Dad and I are going, I'm afraid. The course you've chosen is too risky. We can't be a part of it. Someone needs to be left to pick up the pieces when it fails.'

She turns to go but pauses at the threshold.

'Malory,' says Jory slowly. 'If I'm King Arthur... well, I'll need a queen. And, given everything... it had really better be someone I can trust.'

She stands still for a long while as she digests that. Then she wipes her hand briefly over her eyes and says briskly, 'No Jory, I don't think so. I don't think you'll see us again.'

With that, she leaves the Centre.

* * *

Ten minutes after Malory Wendiman's departure, the High King emerges once more.

'David,' he commands, 'I'm appointing you my Seneschal. In that capacity, could you get me a telephone and the Circle's priority codes? I need to place a call to Balmoral.'

David hurries off, and the Pendragon turns to Scar. 'Marianne –' he tries, then seeing her expression, '– Scar. There are a lot of wounded people here today. Stephen among them, I'm told. Get on to all the local hospitals, let them know it's safe to send ambulances and paramedics. We need to save everyone we can.'

'Aye...,' Scar says – adding, as if the words have been extracted unwillingly from her by some uncomfortable surgical procedure, '...my lord.'

'Oh,' he adds as she goes to do his bidding. 'Take Zara with you, too.'

She looks mutinous for a moment, then nods and beckons her ex to join her. The two women leave together.

'Theo,' the Pendragon says to Harte. 'I believe Paul Parsons is still at Tud House?'

'Um, yes,' says Theo, surprised. 'I mean, yes, my lord.'

'Take this to him,' says the king, pulling the Nestine-Gull Grail out of the side-pocket of his jacket, where it's made an unsightly bulge. 'He's suffered enough. His belief in the devices was strong enough to cripple his mind, so this will free him. Where's Chief Inspector Kinsey?' he asks as Harte scurries away.

'Here, sir,' she replies at once. He inclines his head in approval at the title she's given him.

'Jade,' he says. 'I imagine there are reporters on the other side of your roadblocks, clamouring to be allowed to join us here. Would you arrange for them to be escorted to me, please?'

She goes too, and the High King turns to the Home Secretary. 'Now,' he says. 'I believe we need to discuss the transfer of sovereignty...'

* * *

It'll be smoothly done, of course – no need for resignations or abdications. Plenty of kings served under Arthur, after all – that was what 'High King' meant. Provided supreme authority rests with the person of Jordan Taylor, monarchs and Prime Minsters – and Home Secretaries too – can be permitted to come and go in the usual fashion.

That stuff will take days to sort out, though. There's a more immediate future to attend to. The High King's intervention came too late to save that poor berk Wigsby and hundreds of others, including Right-Hitting Brand's short-lived ally Kim. Many more are injured: not just Stephen, but

Ahmed and Ron and Twink and Lenton and Cornish and Obote, and any number of others. The Black Knight of the Black Lands has lost his other leg.

There'll be funerals, with military honours for the Knights of the Circle and riotous piss-ups for the Chapel people. There'll be a trial, finally, for Mark Addis – who the Circle will hand over to Kinsey as soon as Jory learns about his presence here – and endless hospital visits. And then, at some point...

Well, we haven't crowned a High King in Britain for fifteen hundred years, and we're going to have to work out what the proper form is. (Presumably someone has to dig out a crown from somewhere, for a start.) I shouldn't be surprised, though, if that involves a great big party, too – and answering shindigs across the country, from Lowestoft in Suffolk to Belleek in County Fermanagh, from St Agnes in the Scilly Isles to Skaw in Shetland, as a nation that's been cowering in its Anderson shelter emerges to celebrate VE Day.

And through all the affairs of state, and all the personal meetings too, I know the Pendragon will have a use for me. The days to come will lay the foundations of history as surely as the Acts of Union or Magna Carta. There'll be diplomatic meetings, speeches to Parliament, TV interviews and walkabouts, all needing to be recorded for posterity. The High King will be only too pleased to have a friendly bard on hand who he can make his royal chronicler.

Enough of Alan a'Dale – I'll be Taliesin again.

There'll always be more work to be done. This isn't all about one man. There's sure to be some who reject the Pendragon's rule – because that's part of the legend as well. There'll be rogue warlords to suppress, foreign powers to confound, outlaws to banish. You can't build a utopia without breaking heads – and that has to be our goal, if the promise of Arthur's return becoming fact at last is to mean anything.

It'll take us a while, but in the end we'll get there.

Because – while none of this, now more than ever, is about me – I know the truth of it all.

You think this is a happy ending? It's neither.

I was there, you see. Right up until the end.

To be concluded in *Trojans*

ACKNOWLEDGEMENTS

The Nestine-Gull Grail in the *Devices* trilogy is partly inspired by the Nanteos Cup, a late medieval wych-elm bowl which some historians – not reputable ones – have identified with the Holy Grail. Even so, the opening of *The Locksley Exploit* was completed nearly a year before the relic was stolen from a private home in Hertfordshire in July 2014. At the time of writing, it has not been recovered.

Life is less likely to imitate art in terms of the political status quo which my characters encounters in Iraq and the Middle East. I've assumed that little will change in the interim between the book's writing and its publication, which is perhaps the least probable outcome of all. By the time of publication, these passages may be best viewed as alternative history.

I've mentioned many of my sources for the King Arthur and Robin Hood legends, in the text of this novel, in *The Pendragon Protocol* and on my website at www.devicestrilogy. wordpress.com. Like its predecessor, *The Locksley Exploit* borrows eclectically from multiple versions of both, from the Medieval Welsh *Triads* to the BBC's *Merlin*, as seems to suit the story best – although I also admit to taking liberties with the conventional narratives when the need emerges. (Most egregiously: according to Geoffrey of Monmouth, Maugantius is Vortigern's consulting demonologist, and isn't explicitly – although he could perhaps be – one of the unnamed magicians who recommend sacrificing Merlin.) The stories of Saints Brelin and Bellen, of Gor and Madog and of the unnamed Neolithic chieftain (like those of Sir Pelles and Sir Bertilacus, and of Prince John's visit to Huntingdon) are more or less completely made up.

'The Red Flag' was written in 1889 by the Irish labour rights activist Jim Connell, who I hope wouldn't be too offended by my frivolous adaptation of it in Chapter 10. It's usually sung to the old German folk-tune we associate with the Christmas song 'O Tannenbaum' ('O Christmas Tree' in English). For advice on more recent genres of music – as well as the animal designs on the heraldic images at my website, and general encouragement – I'm indebted to Blair Bidmead.

Though it's quite a different kind of event, the description of the Nutwood Festival owes much to my twenty-five-year on-and-off experience of the Greenbelt arts festival (http://www.greenbelt.org.uk/).

Once again Helen Angove, Rachel Churcher, Finn Clark and Dale Smith contributed sane and helpful comments on my first draft, and once again I'm grateful to Emma Barnes and everyone else at Snowbooks for all their work.

My most profound thanks, though, must again go to my family, especially my loving son and my critically astute and extraordinarily generous wife.